W9-CBL-273

"The purest techno-thriller I've seen in years. This book may define the genre."
Stephen Coonts on *Ultimatum*

"Taut...gets off to a bang-up start....A fast-paced thriller that cuts to the chase often."
Kirkus Reviews

EXPOSURE

"*Exposure,* Pineiro's fifth book, is suspenseful and exciting."
                                  —*The Baton Rouge Morning Advocate*

"Grisham fans will enjoy this well-written version of *The Pelican Brief* meets *The Net.*"
                                  —*Austin American Statesmen*

Praise for Other Works by R. J. Pineiro

"A story as frighteningly real as tomorrow's headlines."
                                  —Richard Henrick, bestselling author of
                                  Crimson Tide on *Retribution*

"Pineiro has a superb command of the shadowy world of nuclear proliferation and the forces of Islamic extremism that could lead to a nuclear attack on the West. *Retribution* is a blueprint for nuclear terrorism in the twenty-first century."
                                  —Dick Couch, author of *Pressure Point* and *Silent Descent*

"A tightly plotted, fast-paced thriller that reads like future history . . . Pineiro's vision of what might be evokes visceral fear."
                                  —Mark Berent, *New York Times* bestselling author of
                                  Storm Flight on *Retribution*

"The action has a dramatic, urgent flair that has entertained readers and audiences since the days of Errol Flynn. All in all, if you like books that you almost can't put down and that keep you on the edge of your seat, you won't regret reading *Ultimatum.*"
                                  —*Austin Chronicle*

"*Ultimatum* is the purest techno-thriller I've seen in years. This book may define the genre."
                                  —Stephen Coonts, *New York Times* bestselling author of
                                  Flight of the Intruder

R. J. Pineiro

EXPOSURE

TOR®

A TOM DOHERTY ASSOCIATES BOOK
NEW YORK

NOTE: If you purchased this book without a cover you should be aware that this book is stolen property. It was reported as "unsold and destroyed" to the publisher, and neither the author nor the publisher has received any payment for this "stripped book."

This is a work of fiction. All the characters and events portrayed in this book are either products of the author's imagination or are used fictitiously.

EXPOSURE

Copyright © 1996 by Rogelio J. Pineiro

All rights reserved, including the right to reproduce this book, or portions thereof, in any form.

Cover art © 1996 by PhotoDisc, Inc.

A Tor Book
Published by Tom Doherty Associates, Inc.
175 Fifth Avenue
New York, NY 10010

Tor Books on the World Wide Web:
http://www.tor.com

Tor® is a registered trademark of Tom Doherty Associates, Inc.

ISBN: 0-812-54389-0
Library of Congress Card Catalog Number: 96-21301

First edition: September 1996
First mass market edition: February 1998

Printed in the United States of America

0 9 8 7 6 5 4 3 2 1

For my twin sisters, Irene del Carmen and Dora Maria. Our separate lives in distant places will never erase the wonderful memories of our youth;

and

for St. Jude, Saint of the Impossible, for making this and other projects possible

Acknowledgments

I am greatly indebted to the following individuals for their help and support throughout the process. All errors that remain, of course, are my own.

My best friend and beautiful wife, Lory Anne, for her unflagging faith, love, patience, and encouragement during the many, *many* nights and weekends that I spent writing and rewriting this story. *Muchas gracias* for the past fifteen years. I'm looking forward to the next fifteen.

My beloved son, Cameron, age eight, for his curiosity, innocence, imagination, and endless appetite for tales of all kinds. It is always my pleasure and privilege to tell you a story.

My good friend Dave, who gives of himself so generously, for doing his best at keeping me technically honest, and for his keen attention to detail while proofreading the manuscript.

Gary Robert Muschla, for his feedback on several sections of the story.

Andy Zack, the finest editor in the business, for his brilliant suggestions and top-notch editorial work on this and all of my previous novels. All authors should be so lucky.

Matt Bialer, my astute and loyal agent at William Morris, for taking a chance with me back in 1990, and for sticking by my side ever since. Special thanks also go to Matt's superb assistant, Bonnie Obernauer, for looking after my interests.

Tom Doherty and the entire staff at Tor/Forge, for treating me like one of the family, and also for publishing the best-looking books in the industry. Special thanks go to Stephen de las Heras and Kevin Seabrooke for their terrific support during the production process.

My parents, Rogelio and Dora, for instilling in me the values, the discipline, and the courage that have taken me this far.

Mike and Linda Wiltz, wonderful in-laws, for their love and thoughtfulness, and for a terrific time during Mardi Gras '96.

Michael Wiltz, my highly responsible and studious teenage brother-in-law, for making us all proud with those school grades and awesome SAT scores.

Kevin Moser, a kid with a great imagination, for sharing my son's passion for reptiles and insects of all shapes and sizes.

Bobby Moser, the most generous, good-hearted, and hardworking teenager I know. He also happens to be my brother-in-law. Hang in there, kid. The best is yet to come.

R. J. Pineiro
Austin, Texas, 1996

Our scientific power has outrun our spiritual power. We have guided missiles and misguided men.
—Martin Luther King, Jr.

To err is human, but to really foul things up requires a computer.
—Anonymous

Prologue

PALO VERDE NUCLEAR PLANT, SOUTHERN ARIZONA
Sunday, August 2

Why in God's name did this have to happen on my watch? thought the middle-aged plant manager sitting behind a computer terminal as he began to sweat. His trembling fingers hammered the oversize keyboard while lights flashed and alarms blared in the windowless control room. But he couldn't afford to let the ear-piercing noise distract him from his last-ditch effort to prevent a disaster.

Behind him stood a dozen operators, all wearing the wide-eyed look of a deer caught in the headlights of a semi as they focused on the letters, numbers, and diagrams flashing on the multicolor screen.

For reasons no one understood, twenty minutes before, at 1:40 A.M., the plant's automatic control system had shut off three of the five feedwater pumps channeling water into the reactor's cooling system. Backup pumps had automatically come on-line to force more water into the cooling system, but two days earlier, workmen had accidentally left the valves between the backup pumps and the pipes closed. The lack of coolant caused the primary cooling system to over-heat, resulting in more steam, which increased the pressure inside the primary cooling system. To alleviate the building pressure, a venting valve had opened to release a puff of radioactive steam into a holding tank. But the valve had malfunctioned—it stuck open. Instead of just blowing a small cloud of steam, it began to leak coolant from the re-actor, filling the floor of the holding tank with radioactive water. The moment the control system detected the over-heated reactor, control rods dropped in among the uranium fuel rods, shutting down the chain reaction. But the normal radioactive decay of the reactor generated large amounts of heat. With the primary cooling system quickly drying out, temperatures inside the reactor's core rocketed.

Lights had flashed inside the control room, but the infor-mation on the monitors had confused the lead operator. The control system had shown no open valves in the primary cooling system, even though one venting valve was stuck open. It had also shown the auxiliary pumps already on, even though no additional water was getting to the reactor. Thinking that the system had too much water, the lead op-erator had shut off the remaining two feedwater pumps. The reactor core had begun to boil dry.

A few minutes later, realizing his mistake, the lead op-erator had then turned on all available feedwater pumps, but the shock of cool water flooding a dry, hot system caused multiple ruptures in the pipes. The water never reached the sizzling reactor.

By the time the plant manager stormed inside the control room, the zirconium cladding covering the uranium fuel rods was already melting. By now the stuck valve had closed, but over two million gallons of hot, radioactive wa-ter had escaped the system, overflowing the holding tank, and spilling into the containment building—a large structure surrounding the reactor with thick walls of steel and concrete.

"Fuel rods are sagging!" an operator screamed from the other side of the room, monitoring another screen. The fuel rods, long hollow tubes of zirconium housing thousands of uranium pellets, and arranged in a square grid at the center of the reactor, were bending due to the soaring temperature.

"Call out the core temperature!" the manager shouted as his fingers continued to pound the keyboard and his eyes took in the mounds of data peppering the display.

"Sixteen hundred degrees!"

"Pressure's building up in the core!" another operator screamed from his station. "We gotta vent or it's gonna blow!"

The manager silently cursed his predicament. If he didn't reopen the venting valve to alleviate the rising steam pressure inside the reactor, the resulting explosion could crack the containment building, exposing the naked reactor to the environment. Reopening the valve, however, meant more coolant escaping the reactor.

"Damn!" he shouted as he typed a set of commands that forced the venting valve open, releasing a large cloud of steam into the already overflowed holding tank. More coolant followed the initial superheated steam. Because of the burst water pipes, radioactive water and steam leaked into an equipment warehouse adjacent to the containment building. The warehouse, lacking the steel-and-concrete walls of the containment building, could not withstand the steam's rising pressure. Thirty seconds later, an explosion preceded a river of radioactive water flowing out of a torn door, cascading down the warehouse's access steps and toward the gravel parking lot, where terrorized personnel already ran for their vehicles. Small clouds of heavily radioactive steam also escaped into the atmosphere from the warehouse's shattered windows.

The distinctive rattle of radiation bells now replaced all other alarms. Panic filled the control room. The manager could feel it in his gut. It was as real as the radiation was invisible.

"Masks, everyone! Masks!" screamed the manager without leaving his keyboard.

Two operators opened an emergency cabinet and began to pass black respirator masks to everyone in the room.

The plant manager grabbed the phone, dialed in the code for the PA system, and declared a site emergency. All personnel outside the thick walls of the control room had to leave the area immediately, except for the emergency team. Equipped with radiation-proof suits, the team was ordered to head into the warehouse to contain the flood. Only half of the emergency team obeyed. The rest followed the dozens of graveyard-shift workers racing out of the plant.

The manager called the offices of the Nuclear Regulatory Commission in Phoenix. Normally Palo Verde had two resident NRC officials. But the graveyard shift had only one, and he had gone home sick two hours ago. The other had left on a two-week vacation the day before and his replacement wasn't due in until tomorrow.

It was now three in the morning. The manager got a recording.

"Son of a bitch!" He slammed the phone, dialed the NRC crisis center in Bethesda, Maryland, and explained the situation. The NRC official at the other end promised him a team of experts from Phoenix within the hour.

The team didn't arrive until five. By that time the thermometers inside the reactor had long stopped working. A column of XXXXXX scrolled across a monitoring screen. The last recorded value had been 2,200 degrees centigrade.

Palo Verde was experiencing a core meltdown.

Control rods had liquefied and dropped to the floor of the dome, already filled with mounds of molten zirconium and uranium pellets. The extremely hot metals threatened to melt through the steel-and-concrete bottom of the containment building and into the layers of soil and rock beneath the plant.

Members of the NRC team began contradicting one another and calling the crisis center for advice. No one knew exactly what to do. Although the plant's skeleton emergency crew had managed to prevent any more radioactive water from leaving the warehouse, a hydrogen bubble had formed at the top of the reactor dome, threatening an even larger release of radiation if the pressure climbed above the sixty-pounds-per-square-inch rating of the containment building surrounding the reactor. Digital readouts showed a vessel pressure of 45 psi and rising, and oxygen content slowly inching up to 9 percent. At 11 percent, there would be enough oxygen inside the containment building to ignite the volatile hydrogen.

NRC officials reached the governor's mansion. The NRC requested the immediate evacuation of all the towns in a twenty-mile radius from the plant, particularly the fifteen thousand residents living in nearby Palo Verde. The governor readily agreed, but the moment the Emergency Broadcasting System reached thousands of radios and television sets in the vicinity, the general public panicked. Within a matter of minutes dozens of collisions resulted in blocked roads, which only added to the growing hysteria of nearly twenty thousand people trying to evacuate the area.

The time was now nine o'clock in the morning.

With the help of additional NRC officials, plus dozens of volunteers wearing radiation-proof suits and working three-minute shifts in the extremely "hot" environment, enough connections were made to restore water into the reactor.

But it was too late. The oxygen content reached 11 percent.

"Mother of God! *No!*" screamed a technician sitting next to the plant manager.

The pressurized hydrogen inside the containment building ignited. The resulting shock wave cracked the containment vessel as the pressure peaked to 230 psi for three seconds, before dropping back down to 54 psi. But the damage had been done. An enormous bluish column of highly radioactive vapor escaped through the cracked containment building and rose in the clear skies of southern Arizona. The winds carried it east, toward Phoenix, a mere twenty-five miles away. The drifting cloud left a one-mile track of deadly contaminants along its path.

Millions of gallons of cold water, heavily doped with boron to absorb neutrons, finally reached the blistering radioactive mass collected at the bottom of the pressure dome. But not before the equivalent radiation of a fifty-kiloton nuclear bomb escaped the containment building.

In nearby Palo Verde, citizens stuck in traffic watched in horror as the radioactive cloud, guided by the winds, swept over their city. Many ran out of their vehicles. Others rolled up the windows and turned off their air conditioners. Some hid inside buildings as the smoglike cloud, like a chastisement from the heavens, indiscriminately descended over men, women, and children, over pasturing cows, dogs, cats, roosters, and insects. Birds fell from the sky, dying of radiation poisoning. Next went all pets. Dogs and cats began to drop, their heaving chests breathing the isotopes that consumed their living cells at a staggering rate.

A man ran away from his pickup truck as the cloud enveloped him. For just two minutes he breathed the radioactive air, exposing himself to the equivalent of four million chest X rays. By the time he reached the next block, he was already dead, only he did not know it. He felt light-headed, disoriented. Bending over, he vomited. Dropping to his knees on the sidewalk, the man regurgitated blood and bile, and felt urine flowing down his legs. A minute later the convulsions began and he collapsed on the concrete, shaking, twitching, vomiting, his pants soiled with urine and blood. His dying eyes watched the street, saw the people running, falling, getting up and falling again, staggering, crawling. He heard them screaming, crying.

A horrified woman held her convulsing infant as she began to tremble inside the thick radioactive cloud. The screams of those around her mixed with her own, and with the heart-wrenching wailing of her baby boy, whose blue eyes rolled to the back of his head, his tiny arms wrapped around her wrist. The air filling her lungs ate her from the inside, like an invisible shark, quickly, suddenly, without remorse. Her son died as she fell to her knees, weeping, uncontrollably crying. Then the vomiting began. To her horror, her arms let go of the infant as a paralyzing spasm took control of her body, of her whole self, sending her crashing headfirst against the sidewalk, next to her dead child. She died, mouth fully open, contorted eyes looking at her son, black vomit covering her face and neck.

The cloud of death swept through the city of Palo Verde in less than twenty minutes. By the time it began to disperse in the stretch of desert between Palo Verde and Phoenix, all fifteen thousand residents had already perished, or were going to die within the next twenty-four hours, from severe radiation poisoning.

News of the disaster and the incoming cloud arrived in Phoenix and Tempe, where the people also turned all exit roads and highways into traffic jams. Luckily, the radioactivity level that reached the large metropolis three hours later was but a minute fraction of the thick cloud that had extinguished all life in Palo Verde, except for the rats and the insects.

A thirty-square-mile area surrounding the plant and the small city were sealed by the Nuclear Regulatory Commission. Only authorized personnel wearing radiation-proof suits were allowed to enter it.

NRC officials who reached the town of Palo Verde the day after the disaster found it a breeding ground for disease. Rats and insects fed on the dead. It took one full week for a contingent of six hundred soldiers from the army, the National Guard, and technicians from the NRC, wearing radiation-proof suits and working in two-hour shifts, to remove all the decaying bodies, many of them already half-eaten by the scavengers. Most had to be cremated outside of town by selected units of the U.S. Army Corps of Engineers to prevent the spread of radioactivity and disease.

In the weeks that followed the disaster, the Department

of Energy and the NRC ran a full investigation on the accident.

The closed valves that had prevented the auxiliary pumps from providing backup coolant at that critical moment were the result of human error. Technicians servicing the valves had left instructions to the personnel of the following shift to reopen the valves. Somehow the paperwork got lost.

The stuck-open valve was old and had already been scheduled for replacement by the maintenance department. But the new valve, a German brand, had been delayed by U.S. Customs in Miami.

The multiple tests and diagnostics run on the reactor control system's electronics showed nothing abnormal.

Nothing.

All computer systems responded as programmed. Engineers and technicians from twenty different computer equipment vendors ran their own independent tests on their particular subsystems and also concluded that their software and hardware were operating as designed. No one could explain why three feedwater pumps had been shut down at exactly 1:37 A.M., kicking off the chain of events that led to the worst peacetime nuclear accident in the world.

Fifteen thousand people died as a direct result of the accident. The official NRC report, issued two months after the accident, showed that among the survivors, over four hundred thousand were exposed to 150 rems, or the equivalent of 150,000 X rays, of radiation, and approximately seventy thousand more received a dose of 50 rems or below before the cloud of vapor fully dispersed in the atmosphere.

Palo Verde came under heavy fire from an enraged American public. While lawsuits rocketed and thousands of Arizona residents worried about the strong possibility of cancer in their future, the Department of Energy and the NRC began the long and dangerous cleanup effort, a job experts estimated might take ten years to complete at a cost of three billion dollars. A ten-foot-high chain-link fence was erected around the perimeter of the hot zone, posted radioactive fallout signs warning the public against entering.

It would take close to seventy years before radiation dropped to a safe level. Until then the area was off-limits to anyone but the personnel directly involved in the cleanup effort.

No one was ever able to explain why the computer system had issued a command to close the main feedwater pumps.

1 Algorithms

Man is still the most extraordinary computer of all.
—*John F. Kennedy*

BATON ROUGE, LOUISIANA
Tuesday, November 10

The crimson Louisiana sun burned through the light fog hovering above the LSU campus, exposing stately oaks, clear lakes, manicured lawns, and a large array of granite-and-glass structures. A flag post in the center of a huge round clearing marked the heart of the university, overlooked to the west by the tall Memorial Tower, to the east by the opulent School of Law, to the north by the modern School of Music, and to the south by the largest student union building in the South. Four stories high and built of the same traditional granite as the rest of the buildings on campus, the union housed restaurants, theaters, bowling alleys, conference halls, the school's main post office, and the university co-op.

Farther to the west, toward the Mississippi River, two modern structures broke the traditional architecture of the

LSU campus. The coliseum-like Tiger Stadium, home of the LSU Tigers football team and also dormitory for three thousand freshmen, and the costly Assembly Center, a multi-event, air-conditioned arena hosting everything from home basketball games to the best concerts in the state.

At the south end of the campus, another structure stood out among older, traditional buildings. It was the Center for Engineering and Business Administration (CEBA), a modern, three-story, square structure. A large open courtyard in the center of the building provided engineering and business students with a relaxed place to study, away from the stressful classroom environment and crowded libraries and cafeterias.

The large parking lot surrounding CEBA usually filled up by eight o'clock in the morning. Pamela Sasser, associate professor of computer engineering, felt quite lucky at 8:50 A.M., when she pulled up in her six-year-old blue Honda Accord just as a white truck was backing out of a front-row spot.

A dark Corvette slowly drove down in the opposite direction, while Pamela waited with her blinker on for the white truck to finish backing up. Her blue-green eyes narrowed at the Corvette's driver, who accelerated and began to turn the wheel toward the vacating spot. Pamela stepped on the gas the instant the truck got out of the way, beating the Vette by a fraction of a second.

A blow of the horn and a middle finger stuck against the side window, the Corvette's driver admitted defeat before resuming his morning hunt.

Pamela turned off the engine and pulled on the parking-brake handle, silently celebrating victory with a smile as she watched the Corvette disappear from her rearview mirror.

The Honda's door swung open and a pair of penny loafers at the end of long legs in tight faded jeans stepped onto the damp pavement as Pamela sat sideways while making sure that the inch-thick computer printout on her lap was the one that had kept her awake until one o'clock in the morning. Computer results from other projects piled up on the front

passenger seat. Taking just the one printout and her purse
and keys, Pamela closed and locked her door.

Hugging the purse and the results of three hours of execution time on one of her department's Hewlett-Packard
workstations, Pamela joined a mixed mob of students and
faculty heading for nine o'clock classes.

After ten years studying and teaching at LSU, Pamela
could navigate the campus in her sleep. She glided through
a turbulent river of students going in and out of classrooms
without difficulty. Her long black hair fell in lustrous waves'
over her shoulders, slightly bouncing with every step. Unusual, almost Asian eyes crowned the high cheekbones on
her triangular face.

Barely aware of several male students hungrily watching
her walk by, Pamela reached the stairs at the end of the hall.
Her small office was on the second floor, but she continued
up to the third floor, where the crowd thinned to just a few
dozen students, and the noise level dropped by several de-
cibels. Reaching an office halfway down the corridor, she
stopped and knocked once.

"It's open! Come on in!" called a rheumy voice from
behind the large metallic door.

Pamela turned the knob and leaned her right shoulder
against the door to push it open while embracing the purse
and printout. Inside, a man in his late sixties, dressed in a
tweed jacket and dark trousers, with a yellow bow tie adorn-
ing his white shirt, gave Pamela Sasser an easy-knowing
grin. His sunken blue eyes, still alert and intelligent in spite
of his age, studied Pamela from behind a pair of spectacles
perched on the end of his nose. His gaze dropped from Pamela's face to the printout she hugged.

"Good morning, Professor."

Motioning her to close the door and have a seat, Dr. Eugene LaBlanche, senior professor of nuclear engineering,
said, "Morning, Pam. How did it go?" His bushy white
brows rose every time he finished a sentence.

Setting the printout on LaBlanche's generous-size desk as
she sat on a vinyl chair across from LaBlanche, Pamela Sas-

ser said, "Doesn't look good, sir." She opened the printout to a section heavily scribbled with red ink. "There's nothing wrong with the algorithm. It runs just fine on the Hewlett-Packard workstation."

"And on the Cray and the SUN systems as well," added the veteran college professor, his face wrinkled and flecked with age. "But *not* on the Microtel system."

Pamela tapped a red fingernail on a section of the computer printout. "The Microtel workstation gets lost right here, but not every time. I timed the error yesterday and it only comes up about every tenth time."

"Very bizarre," he said.

"And somewhat nondeterministic," Pamela added, using a technical term to describe an event with no predictable output.

LaBlanche nodded, leaned back on his high-backed chair, and interlocked his hands right below his chin, a frown flashing across his pale face. He briefly turned his attention to the off-white Microtel SC-200 workstation monopolizing the left side of his desk before removing the silver-framed spectacles and rubbing the bridge of his nose. "Strange and unpredictable," LaBlanche mumbled, putting the glasses back on, turning around on his swivel chair, and facing the windows behind his desk, overlooking CEBA's sun-filled courtyard.

Pamela remained quiet, her eyes gravitating to the clear skies over LSU. Six months ago Dr. Eugene LaBlanche had approached Pamela with a request to write sections of a control systems algorithm that would revolutionize the safety mechanisms in nuclear plants. Working nights and weekends at the Microtel SC-200 workstation in Dr. LaBlanche's office, Pamela had hammered the code. To expedite her work she had also remotely linked into her department's Cray, located in CEBA's basement.

Two days ago, she had come across an alarming discovery while running the algorithm to perform a computer simulation of the control system of a nuclear plant: About every tenth time the Microtel SC-200 had given her a different

result than the Cray. She had reported this odd discovery to
Dr. LaBlanche, who repeated the runs and confirmed her
initial findings. Using identical inputs, when the algorithm
was run on the Microtel system, it generated a different set
of outputs than when run on the Cray, but only about every
tenth time. Otherwise the results from the two systems were
identical. The professor had then asked Pamela to perform
a correlation exercise by running the algorithm on a SUN
workstation. The SUN matched the Cray *every* time. As a
final check, LaBlanche had asked Pamela to run the algorithm on a Hewlett-Packard workstation. Pamela had yesterday evening, taking the results home to review them. The
HP also matched the Cray and the SUN every time, meaning
there was a nondeterministic behavior in the logic of the
SC-200 system, which was driven by the Perseus microprocessor, one of Microtel's flagship computer chips.

"Did you do a backup this week?" asked LaBlanche,
turning back around after a few minutes of silence.

"Yes, sir," she responded. "I backed up the algorithm
on a new diskette and destroyed the backup from the previous week. I've got the floppy locked up in my office."
Per LaBlanche's instructions, Pamela backed up the algorithm to a diskette once a week, destroying the prior week's
backup.

"This is not good, Pam," LaBlanche said, setting both
hands on his desk, fingers lightly drumming the wooden
surface. "The folks at Microtel are not going to like hearing
about this one, especially since it could be related to Palo
Verde."

Pamela Sasser breathed deeply while briefly recalling the
gruesome images from CNN. Linking Palo Verde to Microtel would spell disaster for the high-tech consortium. "Do
you know for certain that the Perseus was driving the control
systems at Palo Verde?"

LaBlanche slowly shook his head. "I know they've
shipped millions of Perseus chips into the commercial market," he said, patting the side of the off-white workstation.
"But I'm not sure how wide their industrial market is. I'm

quite certain, however, that any application where the Perseus is used to run control systems software is at risk.''

''But aren't the SC-200s shipped into the commercial market also at risk?'' asked Pamela.

''To some degree, but think about it, Pam. Under normal operating conditions, this bug might not surface for years. What would you do if once every five years your SC-200 momentarily glitched before going back to normal?''

''Probably nothing,'' she responded. ''Our Cray goes down more often than that, and we just reboot and keep going.''

''My point exactly,'' said the professor, his bushy brows lifting over his blue eyes as he spoke. ''But in a control system, the bug might surface much more often than that, possibly with far more significant consequences than just having to reboot a machine.''

''What are you going to do?''

''I met the chief technical officer of Microtel last year, during the unveiling of CEBA West,'' LaBlanche said, referring to a large addition to the building for extra research and development lab space, courtesy of a series of grants from Microtel.

Opening a drawer and producing a shiny black-and-gold business card, LaBlanche continued. ''James R. Kaiser, CTO. Smart fellow with good sense. I'll contact him first and explain the situation and potential danger.''

Pamela uncrossed her legs. ''How do you think Microtel's going to react?''

LaBlanche frowned and slightly shook his head. ''Hard to tell with these corporations. I hope Microtel handles it better than Intel's handling of the Pentium bug back in ninety-four.''

Fiddling with the collar of her shirt, Pamela said, ''What if the Perseus was used at Palo Verde? What do you think's going to happen then?''

LaBlanche frowned, his shiny blue eyes locked with hers. ''It could be a mess of incredible proportions, starting with a massive recall of costly microprocessors. But the real trouble would start when the lawsuits begin to flow out of Arizona. About fifteen thousand people died and hundreds of thousands more were contaminated because of the accident. I'll venture to say that the mighty Microtel will cease to exist, its assets probably sold to its competitors. But that's a worst-case scenario, Pam. It might not get to that. I'll try to reach Microtel today. I'll let you know how it goes. How's your schedule for the rest of the week?"

"Pretty tight, as usual." Aside from her doctoral thesis work, which in itself consumed a significant portion of her time, Pamela had teaching responsibilities for five classes each semester, two of them large introductory courses for freshmen.

"How about lunch on Friday at the Plantation Room? In three days I should have contacted Microtel and gotten a response."

"The *Plantation Room*, Professor?" she asked, quite surprised that LaBlanche had invited her to the highly exclusive restaurant on the top floor of the LSU Union.

"My way of saying thanks for helping me write the algorithm."

Pamela smiled. "All right. Sounds good, sir."

"Great," he said, clasping his hands. "Noon?"

"Sure. I'll be there." She checked her watch. "I have to run now. Got to prepare a class. Would you like me to drop off the diskette with the final backup later on? I think my part on this project is basically over."

LaBlanche put a finger against his bottom lip and stared in the distance for a moment before responding. "No. Not just yet. I have the original in my workstation. It's always safer to keep a backup in a different place."

"No problem. See you Friday." Pamela grabbed her purse, stood, and turned around to leave.

"Pam?"

Pamela Sasser stopped by the doorway and glanced back at the professor. "Yes, sir?"

"I just wanted to say thanks again for all the help on this one."

Pamela smiled. "It's the least I can do," she responded. Dr. LaBlanche had been Pamela's teacher and counselor during her undergraduate work in nuclear engineering and postgraduate work in computer engineering. Dr. La-Blanche had supported and sponsored Pamela to earn her associate professor status with the computer engineering department.

"I just wanted you to know that I really appreciate what you did," LaBlanche said, standing up, walking around his desk, and patting Pamela on the shoulder. "Now, I know you have a very busy schedule. You have a class to teach, and I have a very important phone call to make."

BATON ROUGE, LOUISIANA

Thursday, November 12

Carrying a stack of examination forms, Pamela Sasser walked into her office at 8:15 A.M., forty-five minutes before she had to give an exam to a group of freshmen. She briefly glanced at the interior of her office, four walls of peeling off-white paint, a plain metal desk, a vinyl swivel chair, and a single filing cabinet under the glow of overhead fluorescents. She didn't have a computer in her office. She wasn't important enough yet.

Dumping the heavy stack on her small desk, she headed downstairs, toward the computer center, a large white room filled with rows of terminals. At this time of the morning only a dozen kids sat behind the amber screens, pounding the off-white keyboards.

Pamela sat behind one of the Hewlett-Packard worksta-tions in the rear of the room. She typed in her standard log-in ID and password to gain access to the LSU computer system. She then did a remote log-in into a group account in the Department of Computer Engineering. This account had a special privilege that enabled its user to dial into host accounts at any major corporation providing LSU with grants. The link had been established to provide LSU and its major technical investors with a fast avenue to transmit requests for experiments, status reports on current projects, and final reports on completed projects.

Pamela typed a group ID and password. The large screen changed to:

Welcome to
SUPERUSER
Please enter corporation:

Pamela hesitated for a moment before typing in Microtel. Since her conversation with Dr. LaBlanche on Tuesday, she had wondered about the possible connection between the Perseus flaw and the disaster at Palo Verde. She wanted to do a little mainframe digging to satisfy her mounting curiosity.

The screen changed to:

Dialing. Please wait . . .

About thirty seconds later, she read:

WELCOME TO MICROTEL, Inc.

Selections: A.   Engineering
              B.   Marketing
              C.   Sales
              D.   Production **CONFIDENTIAL**
              E.   Finance **CONFIDENTIAL**
              F.   Legal **CONFIDENTIAL**

Pamela had been this deep in the system before and she understood why a corporation wouldn't want anyone looking into their production, finance, or legal matters. Their engineering database was accessible for certain projects. Their sales numbers and marketing plans were usually no secret for previous years since they were even reported in annual stockholder's brochures. She thought about looking into the marketing database, but decided against it. More interested in getting a list of previous customers, she selected Sales. The system responded with another menu.

MICROTEL SALES DIVISION

Selections: A. 1980-1997 Sales
               B. 1998 Sales **CONFIDENTIAL**
               C. Organization **CONFIDENTIAL**
               D. Sales Offices
               E. 1998 Customer Base
                   CONFIDENTIAL
               F. North America—1985-1997
               G. Europe—1991-1997
               H. Asian Pacific—1992-1997
               I. Mexico and South America—
                   1993-1997

She looked at the available choices, selected F, and followed it with 1992, figuring she would start her search in that year. Another menu came up, giving her a choice between the industrial and military sectors. The military sector was listed as confidential, so she selected the industrial sector.

The screen went blank for a few seconds. Pamela checked her watch. It was now 8:45 A.M.

The new screen displayed:

MICROTEL SALES—1992

Industrial Customers—North America
               A. Aerospace
               B. Chemical
               C. Oil & Gas
               D. Nuclear
               E. Automotive
               F. Telecommunications

She went straight for the nuclear industry option, going down the relatively short list. It only had five entries listed in alphabetical order:

1. DIABLO CANYON 2. PACIFIC GAS & ELECTRIC, CA
2. NINE MILE POINT. NIAGARA MOHAWK POWER, NY
3. PALO VERDE. ARIZONA PUBLIC SERVICE, AZ
4. PEACH BOTTOM 3. PHILADELPHIA GAS & ELECTRIC, PA
5. SOUTH TEXAS 1. HOUSTON LIGHTING & POWER, TX

Her eyes stared at the third entry.

Palo Verde.

All that really meant was that Microtel had sold equipment to Palo Verde. Nothing else. She now needed to see what *type* of equipment was sold.

Pamela looked at her watch again: 8:52 A.M.

Rats!

Logging out of the system, she ran up to her office, grabbed a two-inch-thick stack of exams from her desk, and hurried back down to a first-floor classroom, where over one hundred freshmen took their seats.

Pamela walked straight to the small desk at the front of the room. Everyone quieted down as Pamela began to pass the forms to the students in the first row while saying out loud, "Keep the examination forms facedown until I tell you to start. This is the last test before the final in four weeks. This test consists of four parts, each worth twenty-five points for a total of one hundred points. You'll have exactly *fifty* minutes to complete all four sections, so I suggest you don't spend more than *twelve* minutes on each section, or you won't finish in time. I will need to see *all* of the work and the assumptions you used to solve each problem to give you full credit for each correct answer."

It took her another minute to distribute the four-page examination forms before she checked her watch.

"Don't forget to write your name at the top of *each* sheet. Good luck. You may start . . . *now.*"

The sound of paper shuffling filled the room as everyone turned the exams over almost in unison and began scribbling.

Pamela walked back to the desk and leaned against it while keeping a watchful eye on the kids. She had never caught anyone cheating, and she wasn't sure how she would react if she ever did. This group seemed harmless enough, so her mind kicked back to Palo Verde. Before logging back into the Microtel network, she had to go to the library and do a little research on the accident. She might even stop at the nuclear engineering department. Pamela remembered having heard some professor say something about a trade journal publishing an in-depth technical article on the accident.

The fifty minutes seemed to drag as Pamela impatiently waited to satisfy her mounting curiosity. For the undergraduates in the room, nervously writing, erasing, pounding calculators, and shaking their heads, however, those fifty minutes had probably felt like fifty seconds. Pamela heard the typical moaning and groaning as she said, "Time's up. Please turn your examination forms over and pass them down to the right."

Ten minutes later she had unloaded the forms on her desk and cruised through the heavy student traffic in CEBA corridors, reaching the small reading room of the technical library of the Department of Nuclear Engineering.

Pamela walked up to the librarian, a foreign student-worker wearing a green turban and a body odor she noticed the moment she pushed the glass door open. He sat behind the counter, which separated a dozen rows of shelves packed with books from the reading area, which consisted of three desks and two sofas.

"May I help you, pretty lady?" he asked in a heavy Middle Eastern accent while grinning, showing Pamela a gold-capped front tooth while his right hand straightened the headdress. His brown eyes dropped to her waist and back to her face.

"Yes," she said, flashing her faculty ID card. "I'm a professor in the Department of Computer Engineering and am looking for old issues of some of your trade journals."

The grin slowly faded as he reddened while looking at her quizzically. "Which magazine, ma'am?"

Pamela shrugged. "I'm not quite sure. It was the one that

ran a special technical report on the Palo Verde accident.''

"Most of them did. Just a moment." He walked back and disappeared in between two rows of shelves, reappearing a minute later with a half dozen magazines.

"You might want to go through these first," he said.

"May I check them out?"

The Arab kid grinned once more. "Sure. ID number?"

Pamela gave it to him.

"I need them back in three days."

"No problem."

After making a stop at the rest room, Pamela reached her office in another minute, closed and locked the door, shoved the examination forms to the side to make room, sat back on her vinyl chair, and put her feet up.

The first magazine, *Nuclear Engineering Quarterly*, had a fifteen-page article, including photos of the melted reactor taken by a motorized probe a month after the blast. After scanning the dozen color photos, she browsed through the verbiage, searching for key words.

Halfway through the fifth page she found what she was looking for. The Nuclear Regulatory Commission could not explain the reason why the control system monitoring the temperature in the reactor's cooling system had inadvertently shut off three feedwater pumps when the recorded temperature inside the reactor had been slightly higher than normal. If anything, the control system should have either issued a command to increase the water flow or ordered the slight introduction of control rods among the fuel rods to reduce the fission process enough to decrease the temperature of the reactor.

So this was a problem with the control system software and hardware—a problem which apparently the NRC and officials at Palo Verde were never able to reproduce again at any other nuclear plant in the months following the accident. Although she didn't have anything to do with the control system algorithms running at Palo Verde, she knew that the software would be quite similar in concept to the one she had developed for Dr. LaBlanche. All control systems softwares were based on the same principle: A number of inputs are processed many times over using selected mathematical operations. The result is the controlling output, which, in the case of Palo Verde, had apparently not been the correct one. The control system software at Palo Verde would have selectively executed mathematical operations based on many variables—the pressure inside the cooling system, the temperature of the cooling water, the amount of heat generated by the reactor, and many more. The variables never stopped changing from the moment the reactor went on-line, and were analyzed and weighed against one another through the use of mathematical operations to keep the core temperature within safety limits. A combination of those variables could have caused the Perseus to malfunction, just as it did with Dr. LaBlanche's algorithm.

That's if the Perseus is part of the system.

Spending the following hour going through the other magazines, Pamela familiarized herself with the initial problem and the sequence of poor decisions and bad luck that had resulted in the worst nuclear accident in the world. Now she had to find out the type of Microtel hardware in use at the plant—in particular the hardware that made up the control system of the main feedwater pumps. Did it share electronic components with the SC-200 system? And more specifically, did it include any Perseus microprocessors?

She needed to do another search in the Microtel system, particularly in the type of equipment sold to Palo Verde during the late eighties and early nineties.

But it was almost eleven o'clock in the morning, time to teach a long freshman class. Pamela grabbed her teaching materials and headed back downstairs, lectured for ninety minutes, returned to her office, finished reading the last magazine, and finally cut loose at almost one o'clock in the afternoon.

Her stomach growled.

Lunch was going to have to wait.

Instead of going back to the computer room downstairs, which by now would probably be packed with students, Pamela went to the main LSU library, where faculty members had access to private research rooms on the second floor.

Pamela walked in one of the private rooms and locked the door. The carpeted place reminded her of her own office, small, windowless, with a plain desk, a vinyl chair, and old paint on the walls. But unlike her office, it had a Hewlett-Packard workstation.

Sitting behind the keyboard, Pamela dialed back into Microtel, gaining access in under a minute. She worked her way down the nonconfidential menus to the hardware sold to Palo Verde during 1992, but before she could retrieve the information the screen abruptly changed to:

```
XXXXXX ACCESS DENIED XXX ACCESS DENIED XXXXXX
           SECURITY VIOLATION ER7000
        ILLEGAL REQUEST LOGGED AT 13:45:00
XXXXXX ACCESS DENIED XXX ACCESS DENIED XXXXXX
```

The system kicked her out, leaving Pamela staring at the LSU Superuser selection menu.

Pamela wasn't worried about anyone being able to trace this request to her personal account for two reasons. First, even though most security systems reported every violation, most companies didn't act on every violation report, just the ones that involved accessing files that were clearly marked as confidential. The one Pamela had tried to access wasn't tagged like that. Second, in the event that Microtel did try to get to the bottom of this violation, the illegal entry would lead them to the LSU Superuser account, which just about every faculty member and over fifty authorized graduate students could access.

She typed System Status, and the display provided Pamela with a screenful of statistics on this particular account, including the number of users currently logged into Superuser: thirty-eight. Pamela smiled. She had figured that being the middle of the day, there would be a lot of users working in this account.

The fact that the information was not tagged as confidential but was protected from being accessed did trouble her. She decided to take another chance and dialed back into Microtel, working herself down the menus. This time, however, she chose Diablo Canyon Nuclear Plant instead of Palo Verde.

Pamela leaned back as the screen displayed all the hardware Microtel had sold to Diablo Canyon in 1992.

She rubbed moist palms together while reading the information on the screen, which indicated that a lot of control system hardware had been sold to the California nuclear facility, hardware which shared many of the components also included in the SC-200 workstation.

Including the Perseus microprocessor.

Perseus-driven systems controlled many aspects of the nuclear plant, including full automatic control of the reactor feedwater system.

She leaned back, an index finger pressed against her lips. If the Perseus drove part of the control system at Diablo Canyon, it probably also did at Palo Verde.

She went up the menu and chose Nine Mile Point in New York. Once again, she was able to obtain the requested information, which was almost identical to the hardware sold to Diablo Canyon. She tried the two remaining nuclear plants and found them both using Perseus-based control systems.

So there is a connection.

Logging out, Pamela left the library and returned to CEBA, where she tried finding Dr. LaBlanche, but the professor was out. Pamela tried calling him at home but got his answering machine instead. She hung up without leaving a message, opting simply to wait until lunch tomorrow to disclose her finding.

Pamela headed for an afternoon packed with classes. At seven o'clock in the evening, she decided to call it quits for the day, and she headed for her small apartment in Tiger Town, a student village of apartment complexes, bars, and shops just north of the campus. She parked in front of her first-floor unit, got out, unlocked the door, and pushed it open.

Her place was quite small: a living-breakfast area in the front, a short hallway connecting to the single bedroom in back, a narrow kitchen halfway down the hall on the right, and a bathroom opposite the kitchen.

After closing and bolting the door, Pamela dropped her purse and keys on the breakfast table and began to unbutton her shirt on her way to the bedroom. Next went the jeans, which she kicked off before walking in her underwear to the stereo next to the bed and putting in a CD.

With soft jazz filling her apartment, Pamela finished undressing and jumped in the shower, figuring the hot water would help clear her head. But Microtel kept popping in her mind. She felt a growing concern about Palo Verde, and the other nuclear plants, using Perseus-based systems.

Steam began to build inside the small bathroom. Pamela closed her eyes and let the water caress her neck and upper back.

After showering, Pamela Sasser dried her long hair, using the towel to wrap it all up in a bun over her head. Using another towel, she dried the rest of her body, grimacing at the slight sag of her once uptilted breasts. It was actually a very slight sag, but in her mind it represented another sign of her approaching middle age, just like the fine wrinkles she had noticed around her eyes a year ago.

Standing naked in front of the mirror above the sink, Pamela applied a small amount of wrinkle cream right above her cheekbones and next to her eyes, and softly rubbed it in with her fingertips.

"You're beginning to show the mileage, honey," she whispered at her own reflection.

In spite of the few wrinkles and the slight sag of her breasts, she considered herself quite marketable for her age. She still weighed the same as she did ten years ago—although that 125-pound line kept getting harder and harder to hold. Her fine neck and arms kept the smoothness of her teenage years thanks to the body lotion she began to rub after putting away the wrinkle cream. And her legs still had the firmness of her track-team days during her undergraduate years. She actually blamed part of the breast sag to the thousands of miles she had run for LSU during her early twenties.

After spending fifteen minutes blow-drying her hair, she slipped into one of several extralarge LSU football jerseys, which she regularly used as nightgowns. Pamela shoved a pack of butterless popcorn in the microwave and grabbed a can of diet Coke from the refrigerator. Sitting up in bed and turning off the stereo, she reached for the remote and tuned in to CNN.

The screen was filled with the smiling face of Preston Sinclaire, Microtel's president and CEO, during a rally in New Orleans last weekend. The former West Point graduate and Vietnam hero, now a billionaire, was using his sterling reputation and his fortune to make a bid for the White House next November. Standing next to the governor of Louisiana and the mayor of New Orleans, Sinclaire waved at a crowd of thousands gathered at City Park, where Microtel had sponsored a huge crawfish boil.

Pamela shook her head. She had already seen the first commercials on TV a month ago. Even with the elections still a year away, Preston Sinclaire had already begun to set himself up to run as an independent candidate, using his military career to vouch for his courage and integrity, and using his well-managed and highly profitable corporation as an example of how to run the country.

Pamela Sasser turned off the television set and the overheads, wondering how Microtel would react to the Perseus flaw and to the fact that Palo Verde used Perseus systems.

One thing she knew for certain: Microtel's reaction would be quite negative.

BATON ROUGE, LOUISIANA

Friday, November 13
The low humming sound of lunch conversation hung in the air at the elegant Plantation Room, on the secluded

fourth floor of the LSU Union, accessed by a private elevator. Only members could dine at the five-star restaurant. From the cream of the LSU faculty and staff to local and state government officials, the century-old club recreated the atmosphere of the Old South: fine china, polished silverware, opulent chandeliers, antique furniture on hand-waxed hardwood floors, waiters dressed in white uniforms and white gloves standing in pairs next to each table, ready to fill a glass of tea or light up a cigar. It was not until the late sixties that women were allowed inside the Plantation Room, and even then it was discreetly discouraged.

As she sat opposite Dr. Eugene LaBlanche at a corner table with a phenomenal view of the east side of the LSU campus, Pamela Sasser counted fewer than a dozen women in the place. Most, like herself, probably had to be invited by a lifelong male member.

"This is really nice, Professor. You really didn't have to do—"

"Nonsense, my dear. This is my way of saying thanks for your help on the algorithm," interrupted LaBlanche, who wore the same tweed jacket with a pair of light gray slacks, a white shirt, and a red bow tie.

Pamela, who felt out of place wearing her usual jeans, starched long-sleeve shirt, and penny loafers, touched the collar of her shirt while discreetly studying a restaurant she had only heard of since arriving at the LSU campus a decade ago.

A waiter handed LaBlanche a menu at the exact moment that a second waiter handed Pamela hers.

"Besides," continued LaBlanche, putting on his spectacles and pushing them down to the tip of his nose. "Sharing a table with a beautiful woman makes some of my colleagues green with envy." The professor pointed with the edge of his menu to a table of six men in their sixties dressed in business suits. All of them quickly turned their heads back to their plates the moment Pamela glanced in their direction.

"Ha! You old farts! Caught you looking," added La-Blanche under his breath. "Try to match *this.*"

Pamela lightly kicked LaBlanche under the table. "*Professor,* you behave yourself," she mumbled between her teeth while leaning over the menu.

LaBlanche gave Pamela a warm smile, his sunken blue eyes glittering in the candlelight. "You've always reminded me of the daughter I never had, Pam. Thank you for being friends with this grumpy old man."

Pamela sank back in her chair. The comment had caught her off guard. In all the years she had known the old professor, he'd seldom displayed that kind of affection. She didn't know what to say. Such expressions of affection were almost completely alien to her. While the professor saw her as the daughter he never had, he was *nothing* like the father she had had. Her father, a corrupt cop in Beaumont, Texas, beat her mother every time he got drunk, which was almost daily, and more than once tried to get into his teenage daughter's bed. Pamela had refused, and her father had beaten her too. Pamela had once tried to call the police, and the situation worsened. She learned the hard way that cops look after their own, even after the drunk, abusive ones. The beatings intensified, until the day Pamela ran away at eighteen, right after her high school graduation. She had used every penny she could get her hands on and had left home, crossed the state line to get out of her father's jurisdiction, and reached Baton Rouge, where she immediately got a waitress job, enrolling in LSU two years later. That was over a decade ago.

"I—well, thank you, sir," she managed to say, her mind blocking past memories. "I've always had a great deal of respect and admiration for you and your work."

His eyes dropping to the menu, LaBlanche sighed. "Well, Pam, this time my work—or I should say *our* work—is apparently giving Microtel a gigantic headache."

Pamela set her menu on the table and leaned forward again. "How did it go? I tried calling you yesterday to tell you that—"

"Why don't we order first?" said LaBlanche, checking his watch before waving over one of their waiters. Both of them came. "This place is great but too slow."

"May I answer any questions, Dr. LaBlanche?" the elder of the two asked, a man as old as the professor.

Readjusting the spectacles, LaBlanche asked, "Are your eggplants fresh?"

"Always, Professor," responded the waiter in an overly polite tone while giving LaBlanche a single nod.

"You should try the stuffed eggplants, Pam," said LaBlanche. "They stuff them with crabmeat and shrimp sautéed in butter, onions, scallions, celery, garlic, parsley, and eggplant meat." LaBlanche looked up to the waiter. "How did I do?"

"Perfect, Professor," grinned the waiter while Pamela shook her head and smiled.

"I'll try them," she said, closing her menu and handing it to her waiter as LaBlanche also closed his.

"I'll have the same and a glass of Chablis."

"Would the lady care for something to drink?" asked the same elderly waiter.

"Just water, thank you."

The younger waiter took off with both menus while the older one stepped back to a respectable distance.

"So," Pamela asked, deciding to hear LaBlanche's story first. *"What happened?"*

"The strangest thing," said LaBlanche. "After spending just five minutes with the chief technical officer, I got put on hold. Then the president of Microtel himself came on the line."

"What?"

"The eminent Preston Sinclaire wanted to have a word with me, Pam. That alone told me this was serious, *really* serious."

Setting her elbows on the table, Pamela asked, "What did he say?"

"That he immensely appreciated my contacting them as

discreetly as I did. He was quite grateful that I'd told no one about it yet. We spent some time discussing the basic elements of the algorithm: how I wrote it, where I wrote it, how I tested it, which instructions it exercised, how it worked. He kept me almost a full hour on the phone, pumping me for as many details as I could provide him. I chose to leave you out of this for now. I hope you don't mind. If the end result is just the recall of the chip and nothing more—like the Intel Pentium—then I'll mention the fact that I'd received a great deal of help from you. But if all hell breaks loose and Microtel comes under fire from the public and the government, you'll be glad I didn't get you involved.''

"That's fine, sir,'' said Pamela.

"Sinclaire invited me to visit Microtel's headquarters next week, and also asked for a copy of the algorithm, which I e-mailed to him on Wednesday,'' the professor continued as the younger waiter arrived with their salads and drinks. "Sinclaire wanted to run an independent study to confirm our findings.''

"Have they called back to let you know if they correlated with our results yet?''

"They were supposed to call yesterday. If they correlate— and you and I know they will—Sinclaire vowed to issue a press release before the end of the week.''

"But it's already the end of the week,'' commented Pamela.

LaBlanche's face became stern. "I know. I think I'm going to call Sinclaire after lunch to remind him of our agreement. I'm going to tell him that if Microtel doesn't issue a press release, I will. I'll remind him of what happened to Intel when its CEO ignored that college professor from Virginia. Word of a bug in the Pentium made it to the Internet. Intel got blasted with a wave of bad press. I think that'll get my point across.''

"What about the possible connection with Palo Verde?'' asked Pamela, already knowing the answer to the question.

"According to Sinclaire, Microtel did manufacture portions of the control system used at Palo Verde, but they used a different microprocessor."

Pamela shook her head. "I think he's lying, sir."

Almost choking on a mouthful of salad, LaBlanche quickly swallowed and said, "Excuse me?"

"That's why I tried to get ahold of you yesterday, sir. I did a little digging yesterday. . . . I, well . . . I used Superuser to dial into Microtel and snooped around their customer accounts. I know it's against university policy to use the—"

"And? What did you find?" he interrupted.

Pamela took just under a minute to explain her findings.

After a moment of silence, LaBlanche spoke in a low, controlled voice, waving a salad fork in front of him. "The nerve of that . . . that *bastard!* He not only *lied* to me, but he also said that his staff would start going through their sales files immediately, checking the use of the Perseus in the industrial market. I knew something was wrong the moment he got involved, but I never thought he would actually try to cover it up. Who does he think he's fooling? Doesn't he know that we can—"

LaBlanche suddenly stopped talking, his face wincing in pain.

"Professor?" Pamela said. "Dr. LaBlanche, are you all right?"

Although Dr. Eugene LaBlanche could still hear Pamela Sasser, he couldn't answer her. He had lost the ability to speak. He felt a burning sensation immediately below the sternum, almost like severe heartburn, but rapidly increasing in intensity and spreading to envelop his entire chest, making him feel as if someone had just driven a scorching knife into his rib cage.

And begun to twist it.

Slowly.

The salad fork in his trembling hand dropped over the china plate as the college professor reached for the collar of his shirt and jerked it down with all his might, totally oblivious to Pamela's scream and the commotion it created inside the Plantation Room. Buttons popped, cloth ripped, tight fists pounded against his wrinkled pectorals as a sizzling hot steel claw racked the inside of his chest.

Flames flaring across his nervous system, Eugene La-Blanche tried to fill his lungs with air but instead felt bile rising in his gorge.

Throwing up, feeling his bowels and bladder loosen, his trembling muscles no longer possessing the strength to hold him upright, LaBlanche collapsed over the white tablecloth, fine crystal, and china, lacerating his face and chest, gasping for air. As the professor lay there twitching, the stench from his soaked pants mixed with the coppery smell of his own blood and vomit, his tunneling vision watched blurred figures reaching for him, turning him over, shaking him, punching his chest. A face pressed against his own, lips tight over his mouth, forcing warm air into his dying lungs.

But a silent darkness had already engulfed the professor, his thoughts propelled to the periphery of his consciousness, leaving his core empty, alone, drained.

Pamela Sasser stood in shock behind the waiters trying to resuscitate LaBlanche. Her mind tried to absorb the event, struggling to come to terms with what she had witnessed. The entire restaurant took on a surreal look as paramedics arrived a few minutes later, shoving people aside, relieving the waiters in their reviving efforts, and working briefly on Dr. LaBlanche before taking him out in a stretcher to a waiting ambulance.

Its sirens echoing across the LSU campus, the ambulance left the LSU Union as suddenly as it had arrived, but as Pamela Sasser learned later that same day, the effort to save Dr. Eugene LaBlanche had been in vain. The LSU professor was pronounced dead on arrival at Our Lady of the Lake Hospital in east Baton Rouge.

BATON ROUGE, LA, Saturday, November 14 *(Morning Advocate)*—Dr. Eugene Raymond LaBlanche, 63, nuclear engineering professor at Louisiana State University, died Friday, November 13, after a massive cardiac arrest. He is remembered by the faculty and staff of the engineering department at LSU, where the professor worked for almost three decades. A memorial service will be held Sunday, November 15, at 3:00 P.M. at Christ the King Church in LSU. Arrangements by Carlton Funeral Home. All services donated by the engineering department of Louisiana State University.

2 Dangers

Wisdom consists in being able to distinguish among dangers and make a choice of the least harmful.
—*Machiavelli*

BATON ROUGE, LOUISIANA
Monday, November 16

Pamela Sasser drove up to CEBA's parking lot at exactly 6:45 A.M. She wanted to clean her desk before teaching her first class at eight o'clock. But Pamela was not in the mood for school this overcast morning in Baton Rouge. She was depressed. It wasn't until the funeral yesterday afternoon that LaBlanche's death finally sank in, as she'd walked up to the open casket. LaBlanche had been the closest thing she'd ever had to a father figure.

As she looked for a parking space, she noticed the flashing lights of two police cruisers parked in front of CEBA's main entrance.

Finding a spot in the rear of the lot, Pamela grabbed her purse and walked toward the entrance, where the usual crowd of students and teachers slowed down to take a peek at the patrol cars before heading inside the building for the infamous Monday-morning seven o'clock classes. Pamela did her share of rubbernecking. She saw no one inside the vehicles.

Wearing her standard outfit of stonewashed jeans and a starched, long-sleeve shirt, she left the patrol cars outside and was about to head for her office when she overheard two students talking about the robbery in Dr. LaBlanche's office.

The comment paralyzed her.

Robbery? Dr. LaBlanche's office? What's going on?

Pamela Sasser went straight for the professor's office and found the dean of engineering and a janitor talking with four Baton Rouge Police Department officers in the hallway. The BRPD foursome wore standard light brown uniforms and sported biceps larger than her thighs. She walked up to the small crowd surrounding the officers and noticed that LaBlanche's office had been stripped. The workstation was missing, and so were many of the professor's books and printouts.

What in the hell?

She listened to the questioning of the janitor, who had apparently opened LaBlanche's office at 6:00 A.M. to vacuum it and found it torn upside down.

Someone had stolen the Microtel workstation and his files.

Pamela Sasser took a step back, then another, before turning around and heading for her office, recalling what LaBlanche had said about Microtel issuing a press release by the end of last week if they confirmed the flaw in the Perseus.

She reached her office, her mind deciding that Microtel probably didn't issue the press release last week. Otherwise it would have been all over the papers by now. Preston Sinclaire had lied about the Perseus being used at Palo Verde. It didn't surprise her that he'd also lied about the press release.

Pamela thrust a hand into the small purse hanging off her right shoulder and produced a key, which she used to unlock her door. She switched on the overheads and stepped inside, deciding that Microtel was using Dr. LaBlanche's untimely death to its advantage.

Dropping her purse and keys on her cluttered desk, Pamela sat down and crossed her legs. Her long, thin fingers pulled out a 3.5-inch floppy from a center drawer. A blue label with CSA-BU26F handwritten across the middle indicated that this diskette was the control systems algorithm backup number twenty-six—the final backup diskette for the computer program.

Tapping a scarlet fingernail against the plastic cover of the diskette, Pamela gave the floppy a furtive glance while pushing out her lower lip. She held the only copy of the complex algorithm that existed outside Dr. LaBlanche's SC-200 system. To protect their work, LaBlanche had insisted on Pamela writing a security lock on the code such that it could not be copied from one diskette to another. Only LaBlanche's system could do a code installation in a diskette as part of their weekly backup.

Because Pamela and LaBlanche worked in different departments and were not supposed to be assisting each other in major research projects without the dean's approval—a blessing that usually took a few weeks to acquire—LaBlanche had decided to bypass this bureaucratic formality in the name of progress and had simply kept her assistance in the project a secret. She had been quite careful when reporting her progress to the professor. Most of it she did orally, although over the past six months she recalled writing a couple of status reports.

Leaning forward and running a hand through her long black hair, pushing it behind her shoulders, Pamela wondered who had robbed LaBlanche's office. One name quickly came to mind simply because it made the most sense. Microtel had much to gain by stealing LaBlanche's computer, where the algorithm resided. LaBlanche had told Sinclaire this fact and many more during the hour-long phone conversation they'd had last week.

If Microtel was responsible, what could she do about it? And what should she do about the diskette?

She had in her possession a copy of the algorithm that had started this mess. It was actually the only copy not in Microtel's hands—if they indeed had committed the crime.

But what would happen to her if she did go public with this information? What if she posted the bug on the Internet bulletin board, just like that professor from Lynchburg College had done with the Intel Pentium floating-point bug a few years back? Intel certainly didn't retaliate against the college professor.

The difference, however, was that the Pentium bug was not linked to a major disaster, like the Perseus could be. Microtel stood to lose much more than just revenue from a recall. Thousands had died at Palo Verde and hundreds of thousands more had been exposed to the radiation fallout that descended over Phoenix and Tempe.

This is a different ball game than the Pentium bug, Pam. This is serious shit.

Deciding against acting hastily, Pamela chose to wait until the end of the day before doing anything. She had to think this through quite carefully.

Pamela Sasser shoved the diskette in her purse and got ready for class, wondering as she did if the flaw in the Perseus could really trigger a disaster like Palo Verde.

DETROIT, MICHIGAN

Monday, November 16
The senior welder of the day shift at the Ford assembly line felt about as gray and angry as the early morning's stormy skies. Once again, he would miss his beloved *Monday Night Football* because his supervisor had just scheduled him to work a double shift for the second Monday in a row instead of alternating welders, like it stated in his contract.

He'd thought about starting trouble and going to his union representative, but he was in the process of getting promoted to assistant supervisor of this section of the assembly line and didn't want to do anything that might jeopardize an 8 percent pay increase. After his promotion he'd get to shaft others just as he was now being shafted. For now, however, he'd have to settle for a taped version of the game.

The senior welder walked down the busy assembly line, where the Ford Motor Company built the new Mustang.

A fine car, he thought. In fact, through the employee purchase plan, he'd bought a convertible model this past summer.

The senior welder walked up to the mammoth Arc-100, a menacing-looking array of robot arms capable of picking up large sections of the chassis of a Mustang with its two-foot-long claw grippers, and welding them together with the use of secondary arms fitted with arc welders. A control system program with a million lines of code directed the alienlike robot with its multiple arms moving in different directions at once to pick up a dozen sections of a Mustang and, within a minute, have the full chassis welded with an accuracy of a thousandth of an inch.

Standing behind the red safety stripes painted on the concrete floor, which kept all personnel safely away from the reach of those monstrous robot arms, the senior welder remembered when the system had been first installed two years before. Seven of his friends had gotten laid off by a machine that could produce 100 percent more output with ten times the accuracy of human welders.

But that was the price of progress. Ford either injected high tech into its assembly lines to crank up the quality of its products, or it risked losing business to the Japanese.

As the senior welder crossed the red line to take a shortcut toward the next station, lightning flashed outside the plant, clearly visible through the huge windows on each side of the long, rectangular building. A fraction of a second after the flash, he heard a strange noise coming from the Arc-100. It sounded like an electrical spike.

Inside the control system of the massive welding robot was a Perseus microprocessor, composed of ten million transistors, neuron-size devices that held data and performed logical computations. The Perseus executed hundreds of thousands of instructions each second to position the colossal arms into the precise location in space at the precise moment to perform the desired welding operation. The sudden voltage surge, already attenuated by the system's surge protector, created a minor glitch in several inputs of the Perseus, sending conflicting signals into the floating-point unit, the block of the Perseus that executed high-accuracy calculations. Normally, such a glitch would have created an internal exception, forcing the Perseus to execute a normal shutdown of the entire system. Instead, the glitch triggered a sequence of events that exercised a minor flaw in the circuitry of the FPU just as the Perseus was about to command a robot arm to pick up a side section of the aluminum frame from an adjacent conveyor belt. Instead, the Perseus ordered the arm to pivot 180 degrees and reach for the space in the opposite side of the conveyor belt, where the senior welder stood, two feet away from the red safety stripe.

As he turned around, terror overcame him. The robot arm, its massive claw gripper fully opened, grabbed him across the chest, picked him up, turned him horizontally, and crushed his rib cage before shoving him against another section of the chassis.

The senior welder didn't even get a chance to scream for help. He was already unconscious by the time the welding arm carbonized his torso, killing him, fusing him against the window frame of a Mustang chassis.

Alarms blared across the assembly line and the entire welding operation came to a grinding halt. Technicians and control-room operators rushed to the assembly line, only to freeze in silent horror at the macabre sight.

Diagnostic checks of the control system showed a fully functional welder. The Arc-100 was Ford Motor Company's star robot system, with a sterling track record since coming on-line. A total of sixty Arc-100 welders were currently on-line at various Ford plants across the country. Its control system, assembled by Ford itself from subsystems manufactured by a dozen American corporations, also drove many other robot models with an excellent reliability record.

After review of the security videotapes of the accident, the official report indicated that the tragic accident was the combination of a nonreproducible robot malfunction, triggered by an electrical glitch due to the storm, and the unfortunate carelessness of the senior welder for leaving the safety walkway.

3 Microtel

*Corporations cannot commit treason, nor be
outlawed, nor excommunicated, for they have no soul.*
                                                    —Edward Coke

BATON ROUGE, LOUISIANA
Monday, November 16

Dressed in a gray Armani suit, Preston W. Sinclaire stood
above the crowd as he walked elegantly, with a sportsman's
elasticity, down a long corridor, the fine fabric hanging
gracefully from his broad shoulders, a gray-and-maroon silk
tie barely swinging from a perfect knot. He was followed
by his bodyguards, one of whom carried his briefcase.

Sinclaire's black hair, shot with silver, fell right over his
brow line. His deep blue eyes scanned the moving crowd
without really looking at anyone, even though he knew
many eyes would be on him. His distinguished face, showing only the handsome damage of countless weekends spent
sailing and horseback riding, was well known not just within
the seven buildings that made up Microtel's headquarters,
but also across the entire state of Louisiana, and most recently, across the nation.

Sinclaire walked in silence, a concerned look painted on his otherwise poker face—the face that could change expressions for every occasion. The face that now hardened at the thought of losing everything he had worked for all his life. Much had happened in the past few days. Much had gone wrong and his people had *failed* to bring the situation under control.

Sinclaire didn't have much tolerance for those who failed, because he never had. A stellar career in the army had earned him the respect and admiration of the American public. The Purple Heart and the Congressional Medal of Honor had once been pinned to his uniform, along with a stack of ribbons that had impressed even the most liberal politicians. But it was his hidden ruthlessness and the malevolence with which he ran his affairs that had earned him the fear and obedience of those who knew his darker side, his secret agenda, his motivation for climbing the political ladder.

Sinclaire's group reached a security checkpoint. The guards, dressed in white uniforms and carrying side arms, instantly nodded when they recognized him.

"Morning, sir," one of them said.

"Morning," Sinclaire responded dryly.

Sinclaire's face was his security clearance, his ID card. No one in the state of Louisiana dared challenge him. He had once driven to the governor's mansion unannounced and was able to meet with the governor immediately.

That was power.

He took the briefcase from one of his bodyguards before leaving them behind, nodded to his secretaries, and went inside his office, where a man already waited for him. Sinclaire sat behind his desk and checked his watch. Seven o'clock sharp. Unless he went for an early-morning horseback ride, Sinclaire started his workday at seven, and he expected everyone on his staff to do likewise.

As founder and president of Microtel, Inc., Preston Sinclaire was one of the wealthiest men in the country. But Sinclaire was not born to wealth. In fact, the tall, handsome Cajun from Slidell—a town twenty miles northeast of New

Orleans—once was one of eight kids sharing a forty-foot trailer in a huge trailer city off a gravel road near the Mississippi Delta. His father had been an army officer, a hero in World War II, who lost his life in a car accident in 1957. His modest army pension forced his wife to go back to teaching at the local elementary school just to make ends meet. Preston Sinclaire, barely nine at the time, was raised by his older brothers and sisters, and he in turn helped raise the younger ones. Everyone pitched in at the Sinclaires'. Clothes and shoes were passed on down the line to the youngest one. Household chores were equally divided among the children. There was no other choice in order to survive.

But unlike his brothers and sisters, who went on to join the blue-collar workforce of southern Louisiana, Preston Sinclaire had an eye for opportunity. He had the gift of the keen businessman. He could see economic opportunity everywhere. At the age of nine, instead of delivering newspapers like his older brothers had done at his age, Preston Sinclaire divided the large trailer park into grids and organized a newspaper delivery scheme that distinguished itself by prompt service to every front door. As a benefit for those delivery boys who chose to join his organization, Sinclaire provided bicycle maintenance and repair, as well as monthly bonuses to those kids who delivered the most newspapers without a single customer complaint. At that young age, Sinclaire kept records on deliveries, routes, sales, expenses, profits, and bike maintenance. Soon he expanded to nearby trailer parks, promoting his value-added services over the competition and winning.

That was his trademark: Always win, no matter what it took.

He also succeeded in his academics. Straight A's all through middle school and high school plus a nearly perfect 1580 on his SAT provided him scholarships to several colleges. But Sinclaire had different plans. In addition to his business talent, he also loved the military. It was in his blood. He applied and was accepted to the U.S. Military Academy at West Point, where he spent four gruesome years getting a bachelor of science in technical business marketing and was commissioned a second lieutenant in the U.S. Army. Next came Vietnam, where the young officer spent five years, one mandatory and four voluntary. Sinclaire saw business opportunities in the long war. His heroism in battle got him promoted to first lieutenant and then to captain. In Vietnam his organizational and bookkeeping talents were eventually noticed by his superior officers. Captain Sinclaire became in charge of the supply warehouse at the American embassy in Saigon, where he once again took advantage of a business opportunity and set up a black market for all kinds of goods, from booze and cigarettes to sleeping bags and mosquito repellent. After Vietnam, he remained with the army for two more years at Fort Hood, Texas. At twenty-nine, the decorated army major, his foreign bank accounts fat with black-market proceeds, left the military and returned to southern Louisiana, just in time for the oil boom of the mid-seventies. Preston Sinclaire took full advantage of it. A wealthy and respected army hero, he used his contacts to raise venture capital to fund oil-drilling projects in south and central Louisiana and Texas. By the late seventies, smelling the fall of the Louisiana oil business long before his competitors did, Sinclaire sold all his assets in the oil business, surrounded himself with the best talent he could buy in the emerging high-tech industry, and founded Microtel in 1980.

Now Preston Sinclaire found himself at the reins of a thirty-billion-dollar corporation, designing and manufacturing everything from computer chips to missile systems. The prior year Microtel surpassed Pepsico, Boeing, and Procter & Gamble in annual sales, establishing itself as the fastest-growing, most profitable corporation in America today. Sinclaire also found himself at the front of a presidential race he fully expected to win next November.

Preston Sinclaire considered himself a winner, a survivor. But this morning, as he glanced at the somber face of his chief technical officer, the man who had been waiting for him in his office, Preston Sinclaire could see that he was not winning this particular game. Since receiving that fateful phone call from Professor Eugene LaBlanche last week, his CTO had run multiple tests on the copy of the algorithm LaBlanche had e-mailed Microtel. Preliminary confirmation had come twenty-four hours later: The Perseus, one of Microtel's most powerful computer chips, which not only drove the popular SC-200 workstation but also the control systems of nuclear plants, had a design flaw, a bug.

Following a weekend raid by Microtel's security chief, Microtel now had possession of LaBlanche's computer hardware and files, and last night Sinclaire's CTO had fully confirmed the problem. A "data dependency problem" he had explained to Sinclaire. A strange phenomenon in the floating-point unit of the Perseus, the place where high-precision arithmetic operations took place.

Preston Sinclaire looked into the eyes of his CTO.

"Jim, I know we've gone through this before, but I still can't believe that with all your degrees and experience you couldn't anticipate this kind of problem."

James Kaiser, a short man of sixty with a broad, veiny nose, sagging cheeks, and thinning white hair, slowly shifted his weight on the leather chair, fingers fidgeting with a yellow lead pencil. Clearing his throat, he said, "Preston, I'll tell you the same thing I've been telling you all along: Designing and manufacturing complex microprocessors is a risky endeavor. We hit the Perseus with multiple checks, trying to cover as many instructions and data types as we could, but the permutations are literally infinite. It's *impossible* to check every possible combination, not when we're dealing with millions of transistors. Look at what happened to Intel with their Pentium chip. After all the checks they ran, a small error slipped through in their floating-point unit. It cost them tens of millions in returns and their stock plunged."

"I *know* about Intel," said Sinclaire. "The difference is that the Pentium didn't cause a fucking nuclear disaster in Arizona. If it *had*, Intel wouldn't be around today. If the bug in the Perseus couldn't be linked to Palo Verde, then I wouldn't have any problem issuing a press release and going through a recall. But not when our mistake probably killed thousands of Americans and contaminated hundreds of thousands more. Now, exactly how *bad* is this bug?"

The old engineer slowly shook his head. "Again, very difficult to assess. The algorithm that Dr. LaBlanche has created pointed it out right away, although not every time."

Sinclaire leaned back. "LaBlanche said it was not easily repeatable. I guess you're telling me that you have confirmed his claim."

"Yes," said Kaiser.

"You still haven't told me how bad you think this bug really is."

"The problem lies at the heart of the floating-point unit, where the least significant bit in an extended-precision register, which is supposed to be static, loses its charge if not properly refreshed. Dr. LaBlanche's algorithm, *sometimes,* loads an extended-precision operand into this register. If the operand is not used within a certain amount of time, this particular bit bleeds its charge into the substrate, changing the value of the operand, which causes the Perseus to generate the wrong result. It's actually quite an interesting problem. Pretty easy to fix."

Interesting? Easy to fix?

Preston Sinclaire closed his eyes and fought the urge to grab his CTO by the throat and choke him. He couldn't stand the inflated egos of these damned engineers, who tended to forget that if not for businessmen like Preston Sinclaire, they wouldn't have the resources to create such "interesting" problems.

Yet, he had to indulge them because it was their ideas and designs that kept Microtel at the leading edge of the high-tech business.

"*Jim,*" Sinclaire said after almost a whole minute of silence, his voice carrying an edge. "I asked you how *bad* was this problem. I didn't ask how *interesting* it was, or for an explanation that requires a fucking Ph.D. to understand. Damn it, I don't give a shit about bits, registers, substrates, and fucking floating-point units! That's why I'm paying *you* a fucking fortune! Now, one more time. *How bad is this problem?*"

Reddening, Kaiser rubbed his chin. "According to my calculations, this one's quite rare. In the event that it *does* occur in a system, like it did in the control system algorithm in LaBlanche's workstation, it would generate an incorrect result only once in a very, *very* long while. We think that this 'rare' event is actually *extremely* rare under normal conditions. Given the infinite number of permutations of data and instructions that could be run on the Perseus, this one failing combination will occur only once in every fifty *trillion* executed instructions. Given the estimated number of instructions processed by a Perseus in one year, this problem has a fair probability of surfacing approximately once every ten years. That, of course, is just an estimate. It's entirely possible that someone with the right computer code, like LaBlanche, might hit the bug much sooner than that. On the average, though, I wouldn't expect this problem to surface very often."

Sinclaire leaned back, clasping his hands behind his neck. He could not let this one out. Exposure meant total disaster. This type of scandal would *sink* Microtel *and* Preston Sinclaire, whose presidential race would be tied to his credibility as leader of Microtel. If his corporation went down because of such a scandal, he would go down with it.

"How many other systems have Perseus chips?" asked Sinclaire, thinking of at least a half dozen applications controlled by the flawed microprocessor.

"Aside from the SC-200, about seven or eight, mostly in the industrial market, and all in fairly low volumes. We only had five Perseuses in the systems at Palo Verde. I'll venture to say that we have shipped maybe a total of five to six thousand Perseus chips into the industrial market. The workstation market is the big one for the Perseus design, with close to a half million systems shipped last year alone. One Perseus per system. I'll have actual shipments for you in less than a day."

"I want those Palo Verde files locked," Sinclaire said.

"We did that the day LaBlanche called, Preston. By noon today, all files related to our nuclear plant equipment sales, not just for this year but for every year, will also be kept tagged as confidential. We'll do the same for all other companies which have purchased Perseus or Perseus-based systems. We'll start treating industrial sales like we do military sales."

"Good."

"There is, however, an interesting set of computer access requests made from LSU last Thursday."

Sinclaire leaned forward. "Explain."

"Someone using the LSU Superuser account got into our system and began to browse through equipment sales to Palo Verde."

Sinclaire placed both palms on the table. *"What?"*

"Actually there were three break-ins. All happened last Thursday. One in the morning and two in the afternoon. Luckily, we had already locked the Palo Verde files. Failing to get info on Palo Verde, the hacker then requested information on equipment sales to Diablo Canyon, Nine Mile Point, Peach Bottom, and South Texas One. We didn't have tags on those accounts, so I assume that illegal user got a chance to see what we sold to those nuclear plants, namely, Perseus-based control systems."

Enraged, Preston Sinclaire slammed his fists on his desk before turning to the windows behind his desk, which gave him a clear view of the morning sky over downtown Baton Rouge.

"Damn it! I can't fucking believe that!" He turned back to face Kaiser. "And why did it take so long before we realized that someone broke into our system?"

"A screwup. I took care of it alre—"

Kaiser's words were interrupted by a knock on the door. Microtel's CEO closed his eyes while pressing his fingertips against his forehead.

"Yes?" Sinclaire said as one of the dark wood double

doors at the front of the office inched open. A light brown face under short, thick brown hair appeared in the doorway.

"Mr. Sinclaire?" A low voice with a trace of a Hispanic accent echoed across the dark paneled office. Maria Torres was one of his executive secretaries.

"What is it?"

"Sir, Mr. DeGeaux from security has asked me to give this to you. Something he found on some files he was investigating."

He waved her over. Sinclaire had instructed Nick De-Geaux, Microtel's chief of security, who had executed the robbery at CEBA in the predawn hours of Sunday morning, to sift through the paper files of the late Dr. LaBlanche in the hope of finding more information about the professor's algorithm.

Sinclaire took the wrinkled sheet of paper from the petite and attractive Maria. She then left the office, closing the door behind her.

Sinclaire pulled out a pair of reading glasses from his shirt pocket and adjusted them over his nose. The handwritten memo had no heading, only a date of April 17. Preston Sinclaire read it in silence, and then he leaned back and read it aloud.

April 17
Subj: CSA (Control Systems Algorithm) Ground Rules.
I have reserved 250 megabytes of disk space in the hard drive of the SC-200 station in my office for the encoding of the C-plus algorithm. The basic premise of my idea is to combine proportional, derivative, and integral control of a nuclear reactor by executing a circular analysis of a percentage of each input parameter from the reactor sensors before merging the data with additional circular analysis of the remaining percentages of each input. The concept here is to look at all the different stages of each input from the reactor all at once, and then add to the initial analysis. This circular approach—I believe—will provide a far greater system

reaction time to drastic changes in temperature inside the core and provide plant managers with a far more stable control of the whole process. The beauty of this algorithm is that it doesn't require a breakthrough in control system technology, like the current studies sponsored by Honeywell, Johnson Controls, and Siemens. Our simple and elegant algorithm will just change the way we process currently available operational data to present it to the user in a totally new and revolutionary way.

The goal is to complete the first revision by mid-September, and the final version by late October.

Follow two basic rules to ensure that the code remains safe:

1. Generate a weekly backup of the algorithm in a diskette (a two-megabyte 3.5-inch diskette to save just the actual C-plus source code).

2. Every week use a new diskette to back up the latest version of the algorithm. After verifying proper backup, destroy the diskette used for the previous week. Keep the backup diskette in your office. Install a copy-protection code in the diskette to prevent anyone from making copies of the stored data. The only way to generate a new diskette should be by installing it directly from the hard drive in my SC-200.

The president and CEO of Microtel slowly set the sheet of paper down on his desk, removed his glasses, shoved them back in his shirt pocket, and turned his attention to James Kaiser. "Jim, first there's a hacker from LSU sticking his nose into our network. Now it seems like LaBlanche has an assistant who has a backup of the algorithm? I thought you, DeGeaux, and the LSU chancellor had worked this one out. I thought we had *everything* related to this algorithm. What in the *hell* is going on?"

Kaiser slowly shook his head. "I'm not sure."

Preston Sinclaire rubbed his chin while regarding his subordinate with half-lidded eyes. "Jim, I'm going to tell you

this once and only once. I want *you* to get on the horn with
the LSU chancellor and *remind* him that this year alone I've
given his decaying school thirty-seven million dollars in
grants and equipment donations. That's thirty-seven *big
ones,* Jim. Also remind him of the condo I've set up for
him to fuck college girls without his wife knowing about it.
You remind him of his promise to us last Friday. He assured
us that everything we needed would be inside LaBlanche's
office. Now it turns out that somewhere in his fucking university there's a backup diskette of LaBlanche's work. Is
that some kind of cruel joke? I'm pissed, Jim. In that diskette there's an algorithm that exposes a bug in one of our
microprocessors. If that bug gets out and someone links it
to Palo Verde, we're history. You, me, our Washington colleagues, *everyone.* You with me so far?''

Kaiser nodded once.

''You find the hacker who broke into our system, Jim,''
Sinclaire continued, ''and I'll bet you anything you want
that you'll find the asshole who has the diskette.''

''I'm on it,'' Kaiser said, standing up and heading for the
door.

''Give me a name, Jim. That's *all* I need. A *fucking* name,
and I will take it from there.''

Without another word, Jim Kaiser left the room.

Rubbing his temples, Sinclaire forced his mind to relax.
Soon, he told himself. *Soon the situation will get under control.*

Thirty minutes later, Jim Kaiser searched through the files
of the LSU engineering department until he found the automatic Superuser log file. Looking at the log history, Kaiser
saw that, in clear violation of LSU rules, the user had not
entered the required user ID number following the automatically generated revision history. However, the date and
time of the three dial-ins had been automatically logged as
part of the revision history. The first dial-in had taken place
at 8:30 A.M., the second at 1:45 P.M., and the third attempt
at 1:48 P.M.

Jim Kaiser made a request to see the IDs of every user of Superuser logged in at 8:30 A.M. The system gave him fifteen ID numbers. Kaiser sent the short list to his laser printer. He repeated the process with the IDs logged in at the other two times.

Sitting behind his desk, Kaiser looked for the common IDs among the three lists. The list quickly shortened to one ID. Going back to his SC-200 system, Jim Kaiser reached the directories belonging to the Department of Admissions, where he made a query for the university records belonging to the ID.

Jim Kaiser then reached for the phone on his desk and called his superior.

Five minutes later, Preston Sinclaire dialed a secured long-distance number.

A long beep, similar to that of a fax machine, came through the receiver. Sinclairè punched in an eight-digit code òn the phone.

The line went silent for a few seconds before a voice said, "Preston?"

"Jackson, is the scrambler on?"

"Yes. It's safe to talk."

"Get our people ready. We have another problem," said Preston Sinclaire. For the next two minutes, he explained the situation to General Jackson Brasfield, Sinclaire's old West Point friend and Vietnam buddy, who had joined Sinclaire in his very profitable black-market business at the American embassy in Saigon, and then out of Fort Hood. After leaving the army, Sinclaire had left the military part of the business to Brasfield, who expanded it all the way to the Pentagon while Sinclaire diversified into oil and then high tech. Their clandestine operation now brought in over three billion dollars per year from military contracts, and not just between the Pentagon and Microtel, but also between the Pentagon and two dozen countries. From illegal arms sales to high-tech battlefield management software, Sinclaire and Brasfield could and did provide it, for the right price. Brasfield's position as deputy director of the Defense Intelligence Agency gave him access to covert operations intelligence data, which allowed Sinclaire's and Brasfield's black-market deals to always stay several steps ahead of any law enforcement organization, foreign or domestic. And as their network grew, so did their power and influence inside and outside the United States.

"Understood, Preston," Brasfield responded.

"Good. Call me when it's done," said Sinclaire before hanging up and checking his watch. He had another phone call to make. The bug in the Perseus would never become public knowledge, regardless of the consequences.

Just two miles away, at the Baton Rouge regional airport, a Federal Express jet landed after a ninety-minute flight from Dallas. The craft taxied to the ramp, where several Federal Express trucks pulled up to the loading ramp of the modified Boeing 727.

Just as he had done every morning for the past two years, the driver of the lead truck stopped several feet from the ramp, which had a built-in conveyor belt used by the 727's crew to unload the overnight mail. The driver got out and walked to the rear of the truck, where he opened the door and extended a metal roller track that latched to the end of the plane's conveyor belt.

"Howdy!" screamed one of the 727's crew members.

The driver waved as the first bag of mail came down the conveyor belt, glided over the rollers of the connecting track, and into the rear of the truck. Six more bags and several dozen packages left the cargo jet before the truck filled and the driver disconnected the track, closed the rear door, and drove straight to the main office near the airport, where several mail handlers untied the canvas bags labeled Baton Rouge and began to hand-sort small packages and envelopes.

It was at that moment that an error that had occurred ten hours before, at one of Federal Express's main sorting centers in Denver, Colorado, was discovered. Baton Rouge got the mail belonging to Pensacola, Florida, where at that very moment, mail handlers were also discovering the mix-up. The mistake, which was tracked to Denver, cost Federal Express over two million dollars. The automatic mail sorters blamed for the mistake, however, passed all diagnostics and tests.

THE PENTAGON. WASHINGTON, D.C.

Monday, November 16

At 9:00 A.M., Eduardo "Eddie" López pushed a supply cart down a long hall near the main offices of the Defense Intelligence Agency, the Department of Defense's agency chartered, among other things, with operating the military attaché system at every American embassy around the globe. With the prime directive of collecting intelligence data for the military establishment, the DIA was also used by the DOD to cross-check the intelligence gathered by its rival agency, the Central Intelligence Agency.

Eddie was thin, borderline skinny, but muscular. Round brown eyes, a fine nose, and a pair of full lips over a masculine chin made him a favorite of the muchachas at Güeros, a local Hispanic nightclub. But what made him even more popular was the fact that he also worked for the DIA. Nothing excited the chicas more than Eddie flashing his DIA credentials at them while making up covert-action stories. His coworkers had warned him that doing so could get him in trouble one day, but Eddie didn't care, considering the Latina girls he got in bed thanks to the DIA a fringe benefit. It was definitely worth the risk.

Eddie López had been a clerk at the DIA for only a year. Before that he had done errands for the navy and the air force.

He reached the office of the deputy director for intelligence of the DIA, General Jackson T. Brasfield, flashed his ID to the marines by the metal double doors, and went into the reception area, a large square room where both of Brasfield's secretaries sat behind their desks near the back win-

dows typing on their word processors. Brasfield's office was
to the right, behind a pair of bulletproof glass doors the DDI
seldom kept open. As he pushed the cart toward a set of
filing cabinets in between the secretaries' desks, Eddie noticed that Brasfield was holding a meeting inside his office.
On the left side of the room Eddie saw three smaller offices
and four cubicles; Brasfield's assistants and bodyguards sat
there, and two of them were on the phone.

"Hey, hermosa. Cómo estás?" he said to one of the secretaries, a gorgeous blonde.

"Hi, Eddie," she responded while shaking her head and
smiling. "Did you bring in the supplies I requested?"

Eddie slapped the side of the cart. "And I'll even store
'em away for you, hermosa."

The second secretary turned to Eddie. "We're also running low on tissues, toilet paper, and hand soap in the general's bathroom."

"Got it, Yolanda," Eddie said to the obese Hispanic secretary. "I'll bring them in later."

Both secretaries returned to their typing while Eddie
walked in front of the supply cabinet, positioning his body
such that the alpha beeper strapped to his belt faced the glass
doors of Brasfield's office. A sideways glance showed him
Brasfield pacing by the front of his personal conference table
while talking to three men, a bearded civilian and two clean-
cut army officers.

Eddie reached for the beeper and flipped a switch on the
side. A microscopic low-energy infrared laser beam shot out
of the unit, bounced off one of the glass doors, and returned
to the unit, where it was read by an inch-diameter dish antenna built into the side of the beeper. Slowly Eddie turned
a tiny knob on the beeper to sync up to the frequency of
the laser beam bouncing off the glass, which vibrated in
response to the sound waves from the conversation inside
the office. The microelectronics inside the eavesdropping
unit compared the frequency of the original laser beam with
that of the returning beam. The difference—Brasfield's
voice—was electronically modulated, enhanced, amplified,

and finally sent to a tiny, flesh-colored earpiece Eddie López wore in his right ear.

As he listened for the next fifteen minutes, Eddie slowly opened boxes of pens, notepads, envelopes, computer diskettes, rubber bands, paper clips, and two dozen other supply items used daily by the office of the DIA's deputy director for intelligence.

When he finished, Eddie checked his watch. It was 9:30 A.M. Having heard enough classified information to fill up a few pages' worth of notes, the Hispanic clerk returned to his tiny office just long enough to replace the eavesdropping gear with his DIA-issued beeper, and to use his cellular phone and make a five-minute call to a number in downtown Washington.

As he went back into the hall to finish his rounds, he noticed General Jackson Brasfield leaving his office and thought about calling the number preprogrammed in his phone again.

Never call more than once a day.

Eddie López remembered the rules imposed on him by his superiors, and kept on pushing the cart. He checked his watch again. He had two more hours of this before he could cut loose and do lunch.

4 Above the Law

These, having not the law, are a law unto themselves.
—Rom. 2:14

BATON ROUGE, LOUISIANA
Monday, November 16

At 9:45 A.M., Nick DeGeaux, head of security at Microtel, drove away from Microtel's large business park, comprising seven large buildings constructed on a six-acre site in north Baton Rouge, and headed for the LSU campus. On the way, he picked up his brother Tom, who worked in the shipping and receiving department.

Behind the wheel of his black Chevy truck with tinted windows, Nick took a long draw of the unfiltered Camel hanging off the corner of his mouth and placed a hand on the envelope filled with cash he'd picked up at Preston Sinclaire's office fifteen minutes ago.

Ten grand. Financial compensation over and above his regular salary for discreetly handling special jobs for the Microtel chairman.

A six-three ex-marine weighing a hefty 250 pounds of

well-placed muscle, and wearing a closely trimmed beard black and thick as his hair, Nick DeGeaux was in full command of the security operation at Microtel. His brother Tom, a high school dropout who had been arrested and convicted of armed robbery and aggravated assault eight years before and was paroled six months ago—thanks to the intervention of Preston Sinclaire during the parole hearing—just did as Nick ordered, like working for minimum wages at the receiving docks.

Tom DeGeaux did not share his older brother's height. At only five-nine and just below 150 pounds, blond with blue eyes, he had been the product of an affair his mother'd had with a bartender while their father fought in Vietnam.

Drinking from a can of Dixie beer, Tom belched, "What do we gotta do now?"

Nick regarded his brother through the wreathing cigarette smoke. The elder DeGeaux occasionally took his younger brother on special assignments to help along and also to check up on him, but questions like that one always made him regret his decision.

"I just told you twice, Tommy!" barked Nick. "Damn, you can be pretty fuckin' stupid sometimes!"

Tom DeGeaux gave his brother a crooked grin, showing two rows of tobacco-stained teeth. "If you're so damned smart, why is it that you're still kissin' Sinclaire's ass instead of startin' that security business you keep talkin' about?"

Nick's eyes returned to the road. "I'm trying to improve our cash position first, kid. We'll start the business soon enough and be in fat city in no time."

"Yeah, right. We ain't never been in no fat city, but there's a quick way to make it there though. You know, I been doin' some thinkin'. If you and I just hit a couple of banks, we could—"

Nick's tone was short and abrupt, and the index finger of his right hand stabbed the air in front of Tom's face. "Don't even say it, Tommy, 'cause I swear I'll stop the fuckin' truck and beat the shit outta you! Didn't those niggers in

Angola butt-fuck you enough for those years? It's a miracle you ain't got AIDS. Wanna get life this time? You just made parole, little asshole! You stick to me and my contacts and you'll do just fine.''

Tom DeGeaux sank into the seat and closed his eyes. ''All right.'' The thought of going back to the high-security prison in southern Louisiana always quenched any desire Tom DeGeaux had for returning to his old ways.

''Anyway,'' Nick said, both hands now on the steering wheel, ''this one should be a piece of cake. Just quietly break into an apartment and grab every single computer disk we can find.''

''I remember that part. What else?''

''We bring the disks to Mr. Sinclaire, and we go back and wait for her to show.''

''Then what?''

''Then we stay close to her. Watch what she does and report.''

''Like in the movies?''

Nick sighed. ''Yeah, yeah, like in the movies.''

''She cute, Nick?'' Again, a crooked grin of darkened teeth flashed at Nick DeGeaux.

The older DeGeaux shook his head. ''Don't know and don't give a shit. We do as we're told and we get another ten. Now shut up and let me think.''

They reached the apartment complex ten minutes later and verified that Pamela Sasser's Honda was already gone. Nick watched the parking lot while Tom broke into her apartment with amazing ease. In spite of his lack of brains and common sense, Tom DeGeaux was a master thief. He could break into and jump-start a car in under thirty seconds, and this apartment door he had done in less than twenty. Tom did all right as long as Nick was around to keep him from making dumb moves, like hitting a bank in plain daylight without a mask, and using his own car as the getaway vehicle.

Boneheaded judgment.

But that was Tom DeGeaux, and now he had his big brother to keep him out of Angola.

The DeGeaux brothers went inside the apartment and closed the door.

While Nick and Tom DeGeaux searched Pamela Sasser's apartment, Preston Sinclaire, followed by two armed bodyguards, walked into one of Microtel's research-and-development labs, located on the third floor of one of the modern buildings surrounded by man-made ponds and manicured grounds.

The lab consisted of many rows of tables covered with all sorts of computer hardware. Two dozen engineers and technicians dressed in white lab coats moved around the room, some holding notepads, others hauling an assortment of test and measuring equipment. A group of six scientists, their hands shoved into the sides of their lab coats, gathered around a table in the far corner of the gleamingly white room, under the bright fluorescent overheads.

The group crowded around Microtel's chief technical officer, Jim Kaiser, while he sat behind the keyboard of a brand-new Hewlett-Packard workstation.

After ordering his bodyguards to wait by the door, Preston Sinclaire donned one of the lab coats hanging off a rack next to the entrance, buttoned it up, and walked to the far end of the room while glancing at the millions of dollars he'd spent in state-of-the-art equipment. And this was just an R & D lab. The equipment in the fabrication building next door cost enough to buy a small country. And that didn't take into consideration the inflated salaries of Microtel employees. In order to lure top-notch technical people away from the more desirable high-tech spots around the country, like Sunnyvale, Austin, Phoenix, and Portland, Preston Sinclaire had to increase their pay by almost 50 percent. But in the end he came out ahead. Microtel consistently beat its competitors in the commercial, military, and industrial arenas.

Sinclaire walked in between two rows of tables and

looked at the different types of equipment. Sometimes he wondered how much of this stuff was really necessary to meet the goals detailed in Microtel's business plan, and how much of it was really purchased as "toys" for the techno-heads walking around the room. After so many years in the high-tech industry, Sinclaire still failed to come to terms with the excitement sometimes displayed by these nerds at the prospect of mere scientific advancement. Preston Sinclaire could care less about *scientific advancement*, unless it resulted in economic revenue. Nonprofit technical break-through was an impossibility in the world of business, better left for those academic types who lived detached from the real world. Once he reached the White House he planned to apply that same principle to the country, while making himself even richer in the process.

All of the engineers near Kaiser bailed the moment they caught sight of their CEO. Sinclaire had a reputation for publicly telling people to get busy when he caught them wandering around.

"Jim?" said Sinclaire as the engineers slowly went back to work on their projects. "Got a minute?"

Kaiser slowly nodded. "Yep. Just let me log off from this baby."

The two of them left the lab and headed out of the R & D building, walked across a cobblestone walkway bordering a pond, and went into the administration building, where they reached Sinclaire's office a minute later. The pair of bodyguards trailed them by a respectable distance. Maria Torres sat behind her desk working on her word processor.

"Maria, is Larry already in my office?" Sinclaire asked, referring to Lawrence Dolbear, Microtel's chief financial officer.

"Yes, sir. He just walked in."

"Great. Hold my calls, please."

"Yes, Mr. Sinclaire," she responded. "By the way, the video crew is setting up downstairs, in the lobby. They start shooting at eleven. They'll need you on the set by ten-thirty for makeup."

Sinclaire nodded and checked his watch. He still had plenty of time before starring in a new thirty-second ad, which would air next Monday across the country on all the major networks during *Monday Night Football*. Sinclaire's advertising budget for this quarter was over eighty million dollars, pocket change for the man whose picture appeared on the cover of last month's *Fortune*.

Inside the office they found Lawrence Dolbear, a short and thin man in his mid-fifties, impeccably dressed in a dark gray suit, sitting in one of the leather chairs in front of Sinclaire's huge rosewood desk. A great view of the Mississippi River could be seen through the oversize windows behind Sinclaire's desk. An HP-720 workstation covered a corner of the desk.

After closing and locking the door, Sinclaire said, "All right. Let's see what you two have to say."

Dolbear stood and adjusted the knot on his tie while looking at Kaiser, whose fingers fiddled with a mechanical pencil.

"I just confirmed my suspicions about the simplicity of fixing this bug, Preston. It only involves changing a few transistors," Kaiser began. "And I can make the change to our database as part of the new version of the Perseus that we're about to introduce."

For months Microtel had advertised to its customers that the Perseus was about to be upgraded as part of the normal life cycle of a microprocessor. The new version would be faster, cheaper to manufacture, and would include a new list of enhanced features requested by Microtel's customers during a nationwide survey conducted six months before. The new chip, the Perseus II, was just about to go into fabrication. But there was still time to make one small change to the design.

"How soon can it be done?" asked Sinclaire, leaning against the edge of his desk while inspecting the fingernails of his right hand.

"Right now. In less than five minutes I can log into the

system, make the change without anyone knowing about it, and log out. I'm the only one in this company with ROOT privilege. No one would ever know that the change was made."

"Fine," said Sinclaire. "Do it now. Use my workstation. How quickly before the new version comes out? And spare the sandbagging line that I keep hearing from the VP of marketing about four months before production ships. I know *damned* well it takes less time than that."

Kaiser sat behind Sinclaire's desk, reached for the HP's keyboard, and logged in. "We can start sampling prototypes of the new rev in four weeks. Initial production in two months. Full production in three months," he said while his fingers attacked the keyboard.

Sinclaire crossed his arms as he looked at the color graphics flashing on the nineteen-inch screen. *Two months for initial production.* In the meantime Microtel would be shipping microprocessors with a known bug.

"Do you have a list of industrial customers that are at risk?" asked Sinclaire.

Dolbear handed Sinclaire a computer printout.

XXXXXXXXXXXXXXX SALES FILE# 412-1019 XXXXXXXXXXXXXXX
XXXXXXXXX MICROTEL COMPANY CONFIDENTIAL XXXXXXXXX

Component:	Perseus
Description:	Advanced 64-bit Superscalar Microprocessor
Market:	Industrial

xxxxxxxxxxxxxxxxxxxxxxxxxxxxxxxxxxxxxxxxxxxxxxxxxxxxxxxxx

CUSTOMER	UNITS SHIPPED	APPLICATION
Raythenon	340	Medical X-ray System
Chrysler	980	Robotics Systems
Diablo Canyon	12	Control Systems
Dow Chemical	37	Control Systems
Boeing	240	Avionics
Ford	720	Robotics Systems
Nine Mile Point	12	Control Systems
Palo Verde	12	Control Systems

Peach Bottom	12	Control Systems
Federal Express	670	Mail Sorters
South Texas	12	Control Systems
Xerox	1480	Model GX7500 Copier
TOTAL SHIPMENTS	4527	xxxxxxxxxxxxxxxxxxxxxxxxx

xxxxxxxxxxxxxxxxxxxxxx END OF DATA xxxxxxxxxxxxxxxxxxxxx

Preston Sinclaire stared at the list for a few moments. One of the traits of a successful businessman was the ability to keep a problem from growing out of proportion, the ability to perform "damage control." Even if Microtel fixed the bug in the Perseus II, the fact still remained that many other installations could be at risk. And although many of those installations, like the control systems at chemical or nuclear plants, were supposed to have built-in safeguards to prevent a glitch in one part of the system from bringing the entire system down, Palo Verde stood as an example of when those safeguards had failed at the worst possible moment.

Turning to Lawrence Dolbear, Sinclaire said, "What's your plan, Larry?"

The seasoned financial analyst, whom Sinclaire had rescued from Wall Street after the market crash in October of 1987, grinned. "It's called 'selective recall.' The concept here's to replace Perseus computer chips only at the applications shown here." He pointed at the sheet in Sinclaire's hands. "These are the only applications where this type of error could result in an accident. None of the Perseus processors used in our huge commercial market would be replaced because an error there would go unnoticed by the millions of SC-200 workstation users in businesses and schools across the country. The Perseus II will continue to be marketed as an upgrade, only now it will also include this fix. We had already scheduled field upgrades as part of the monthly preventive maintenance work our field engineers conduct at all of our industrial applications."

His eyes on the color display while Kaiser brought up a screenful of schematics and rehooked a few transistors, Preston Sinclaire realized just how important it was at this point to recover the diskette and keep Pamela Sasser from talking. If his guns could do this, he just might be able to keep this whole thing from exploding in his face.

"So, let me get this straight," Sinclaire said while he watched his CTO perform high-tech surgery on the Perseus II schematic database. "What you're telling me is that we make this change and then we forget about it because the system's already in place to upgrade our industrial customer base, which is the only place in danger if the bug surfaces?"

"That just about wraps it up. And the financial impact will be none because we'd already planned to upgrade them."

"What about the commercial market?"

The former Wall Street analyst shrugged. "That's a different ball game. Approaching the wide-open commercial market with this would be the same as going public with the bug. It's one thing to go and replace a few thousand chips in the industrial market. No one would suspect anything, especially since we had always advertised to those customers that we would do free upgrades for the lifetime of their equipment. But we can't go and upgrade every single SC-200 workstation we've ever made. There's several million of them out there. The press would smell trouble, and all hell would break loose."

"But we *don't* have to upgrade the commercial market," said Jim Kaiser from behind the workstation, his eyes on the screen while he talked.

"That's exactly right," said Dolbear. "So what if an SC-200 work-station locks up once every few years, given the current odds of the bug appearing in such applications? Computer systems hang up *all* the time because of power glitches, Beta software, or what have you. As long as the user can reboot, and it doesn't happen again within a reasonable amount of time, I bet you we'll never hear a problem from the field. By the way, *do* remember that we've been *selling* to the commercial market for years and so far not one—*not a single one*—of our millions of customers has ever complained. They're not about to start now.''

"It seems too easy," Sinclaire said, a frown on his tanned face. "Nothing's ever that easy."

"It would seem that way," agreed Lawrence Dolbear, "but I've been going through the books and our current marketing plans and can't seem to find a hole in the strategy. Kaiser makes a quiet change to the Perseus II database, the chips are manufactured, get tested, and go to the field, where our field-applications engineers upgrade our industrial customer base—just as we've planned all along—and bring the bad chips to the factory, where they are destroyed. The industrial sector is safe, and the commercial market would never know the difference. Some commercial customers might choose to upgrade to the Perseus II to get a kick in performance and features, but that's just why we're doing the Perseus II in the first place: to increase our market share in the business and improve our profit margins. It just so happens that we're squeezing in a quiet little fix at the last minute to address this problem without anyone knowing about it. As long as Kaiser can guarantee that *nobody*—aside from us in this room—will know about the change he's making, then we just let business go on as usual. We let the new chips come out, we let our production people ship them to the field offices, and we let our field-applications engineers perform the upgrades, just as we've been planning to do it all along. It's bulletproof, Preston. *Fucking* bulletproof. Microtel goes on, and you can safely run for president without worrying about this.''

Preston raised a brow while nodding. "Guess you're right, Larry. Sometimes I just get too paranoid, especially with the upcoming election. You know the damned press is already scrutinizing my personal income tax returns for the past twenty years, plus investments, and even my personal life. Fucking hyenas like to dismember every presidential hopeful.''

Just then Kaiser turned around on the swivel chair and gave Sinclaire and Dolbear a smile. "Done. The chip goes to fabrication tomorrow and no one would ever know we made this change aside from us."

"Don't forget Pamela Sasser," Sinclaire said.

Kaiser and Dolbear exchanged glances but did not respond.

"Don't worry. I'm handling Pamela Sasser," Sinclaire added.

In addition to the work his own head of security was performing for him, Preston Sinclaire had also gotten word from General Jackson Brasfield that the assassin would be contacted in less than an hour. A lunch meeting in Washington had already been set up by Brasfield.

But Sinclaire didn't like the fact that it might take the assassin a few days to stage a death for Pamela. That would certainly give the associate professor of computer engineering enough time to expose the flaw in the Perseus. With LaBlanche it had been a different story. Sinclaire had tricked the old college professor into waiting until the end of the week, making him think that Microtel needed time to review the data and issue a press release. That had given the assassin the required time to complete the contract. But Pamela was a wild card. She could disclose what she knew at any time. But if DeGeaux recovered the disk in the meantime, there would be no evidence. . . .

"How about the risk of another accident?" asked Kaiser, interrupting Sinclaire's thoughts. "After all, it'll be several weeks before we do the field upgrades."

"Yes . . . there's still that issue . . . ," Preston Sinclaire said, letting his words trail off as he closed his eyes and exhaled heavily. A moment later he opened them. "How long have those Perseus chips been operating in the industrial market?"

"About five years," responded Dolbear.

"And just one accident so far?" asked Sinclaire.

"That we know of," responded Kaiser. "Keep in mind that Perseus chips in the field could have malfunctioned more often than that. It's just that most of the time the surrounding system has built-in mechanisms that prevent the error in the Perseus from bringing down the entire system. I bet you many times the operators of the equipment don't even notice a problem. The situation at Palo Verde worsened because regular built-in safeguards, like auxiliary pumps and connecting valves, failed to function as programmed. Instead, what was nothing but a minor loss-of-coolant accident—something nuclear plants experience more often than they're willing to admit—degenerated into a core meltdown. What are the odds of that happening again? I say basically negligible.''

"So we take the chance," concluded Sinclaire. "And I don't want to discuss this issue again, unless something comes up. Understood?"

"Yes, sir," both executives responded in unison.

"I'll handle the Pamela Sasser issue. Any questions?" Sinclaire checked his watch. It was 10:25 A.M. "Very well, gentlemen, I've got a promo ad to shoot."

As Sinclaire and his bodyguards headed downstairs, a clerk from the legal department headed upstairs. Sinclaire barely acknowledged her as he reached the double glass doors leading to the lobby and was instantly surrounded by the makeup and video crews.

The clerk was headed for the copy room. She had a legal document that required copying. Normally, the task of making fifty double-sided copies of the two-inch-thick document would have taken her at least two hours, but the new Xerox GX7500 copier, delivered to the copy room a week ago and already proven the fastest, cleanest copier in the entire building, would probably do it in less than an hour. Three additional GX7500s would replace older models later this week. The other buildings in the complex would get theirs before the end of the year.

The clerk frowned. Two people were ahead of her waiting to use the new system. She had the option of starting on one of the older models, but she chose against it. No other copier could handle the entire stack at once. In fact, she had yet to see anyone making copies from a document this big. Most people, like the two secretaries in front, either needed a few copies of an inch-thick document, or many copies of a smaller document. She was about to demand both from the large GX7500.

When her turn finally came, the clerk spent five minutes loading paper into the machine. Unlike older models, the new Xerox could take up to fifteen thousand sheets of white bond paper.

Setting the thick document into the autofeeder, she made the appropriate selections on the soft-touch control panel and pressed Start.

Since she had selected the double-sided setting, the machine began not to make copies but to count sheets. After it went through the stack, it began to suck them in once more at a very fast speed.

The clerk waited for the first copy to come out the back of the system a minute later. She picked it up, browsed through it, and, satisfied that the system would run on auto for at least the next fifty minutes, decided to head for the coffee room.

Inside the large Xerox GX7500 system, the unusually high number of document copies selected, combined with the double-sided selection, and the large number of copies per document, forced the Perseus microprocessor, already performing over fifty thousand tasks each second, to use its floating-point unit to keep track of the job. With every copy made, the inputs to the FPU changed. The FPU output, in addition to going outside the Perseus to issue a new set of commands to the copier's maze of high-speed motors, also fed back into the FPU, mixed with the data collected from a hundred different sensors spread out throughout the copier. Once every twenty-four million times, which occurred about every eight minutes in real time, the data would change in such a way that it would flow through the FPU's faulty circuit. The Perseus would issue a slightly different command to the Xerox system, resulting in single-sided copies for the next three copies, before the data feeding back into the Perseus changed such that the flawed circuit was not used.

By the time the job was finished fifty-three minutes later, six of the fifty copies made had three single-sided copies mixed with the double-sided ones. And because of the nature of the error, the affected pages varied within each document.

The clerk returned from her coffee break pushing an empty cart. She randomly checked three of the fifty copies. Satisfied that the GX7500 had once again performed flawlessly, she stacked the copies onto the cart and took them to the legal department.

5 Flashback

*All things are taken from us, and become the
portions and parcels of the dreadful past.*
                                    —*Alfred, Lord Tennyson*

WASHINGTON, D.C.
Monday, November 16

Harrison Beckett had killed before. But he seldom did it
with a firearm, at least not since his departure in 1981 from
the Defense Intelligence Agency. Far better ways existed to
rob people of their lives than pumping bullets in their heads,
and on this overcast and chilly afternoon in Washington,
D.C., Beckett headed for a meeting where he would learn
if he was to kill again.

Dry and cold air filled his lungs as Beckett reached the
corner of Euclid and Eleventh Street after a half hour of
walking around the city to shake any possible tails. There
had not been any.

His brown eyes scanned the large restaurant across four
lanes of congested lunch-hour traffic. Giovanni's, read the
large sign hanging high above the entrance to the two-story,
redbrick-and-glass building. Under soft yellow lights, people

had lunch behind large windows on both floors of the restaurant.

Harrison Beckett ran a hand through his short brown hair, singed with gray, falling right over his brow line. A tall, fair-skinned man dressed in a dark gray suit, Beckett gave the impression of someone who watched what he ate and worked out regularly. However, the lack of wrinkles or bags under his drooping eyes did not reflect his lifestyle. In his line of work, pressure and anxiety ruled the day, and twenty years of clandestine operations had indeed lined Beckett's once boyish face. But the reason for his current smooth skin and healthy appearance was something else: plastic surgery, which Beckett had undergone not out of vanity but out of self-preservation.

A queasy feeling ran through his stomach as he waited for the streetlight to turn, hands shoved into his pants pockets, the fingers of his right hand toying with a silver cigarette lighter. He hated public places and social gatherings, not only because he was exposed, out in the open, but because he had never felt comfortable surrounded by people he didn't know, or worse, people he knew little of, even if those people were willing to pay quite handsomely for his services.

Beckett was a loner. An only child raised in a small town in Kansas, he loved the open country and hated everything about large cities: elbowing crowds, jammed subways, buses, streets, malls, grocery stores, and restaurants.

The light finally turned and he began to cross the street, soft leather shoes splashing over wet asphalt. It had been snowing when he arrived at the nation's capital two hours ago, and that had suited Beckett just fine, spending most of the time at the airport's Admiral's Club taking a nap, conserving his energy. Rest and food were weapons experienced operatives valued highly. Sleep also kept him from thinking about the Marlboros he had struggled to give up for the past three months. The last reminder of his smoking days was a present from a woman who now only lived in the memory of the former DIA officer. The word *Layla* was etched across the front of the lighter.

A light breeze swirled his hair as he reached the opposite curb and approached the restaurant's entrance. He checked his watch. Twelve o'clock—right on time.

The hostess, a gorgeous blonde who had probably blown her entire salary on makeup and jewelry, came up to greet him.

"Good afternoon, sir."

"Hi. Jackson Brasfield's table, please," Beckett replied, eyes scanning the crowded foyer. Well-dressed men and women stood around the foyer waiting for their tables or walked across gray slate floors to the bar straight ahead. The smell of good Italian pasta fell on him, tempting even his uneasy stomach.

She immediately smiled, exposing glistening white teeth. "He's already here, sir. Right this way, please."

She turned around. Beckett followed the long blond hair gracefully bouncing through the crowd, the delicate clatter of silverware on china plates mixing with the hum of lunch conversation. The hostess stopped by a door leading to a private dining room in the rear of the first floor. Then she was gone.

Without knocking, Harrison Beckett turned the knob and went inside the candlelit room.

A short, stocky man in a U.S. Army uniform sat drinking red wine in the flickering yellowish light. Deep lines surrounded the coal black eyes of General Jackson T. Brasfield as he lifted his gaze to Beckett. A hairy hand brought a wineglass to a pair of full lips. Wrinkling his whole face in suspicion, the deputy director for intelligence of the DIA looked from behind a pair of horn-rimmed glasses, studying Beckett.

Beckett also noticed there was another person in the room, a shadowy figure sitting in the corner. He looked at Brasfield and then shifted his gaze to the stranger. "I didn't know we were having company."

"My assistant," the general said. "These kind of meetings could turn dangerous. I'm sure you understand.''

Beckett gave the faceless stranger in the dark corner of the room a furtive glance before turning his attention back to the DDI.

Pulling out a chair and taking a seat across the small table, Beckett regarded the officer with the big hooked nose and a breastful of ribbons and medals sitting beyond the cream tablecloth, sparkling silverware, and bottle of wine.

''We have a problem in Louisiana,'' Jackson Brasfield said.

Beckett dropped his gaze to the smooth tablecloth. His work in Baton Rouge had been clean. Of that he had no doubt. The binary chemicals he had used on Dr. Eugene LaBlanche had worked perfectly. Last Thursday he had introduced the first half of the poison into Dr. LaBlanche's drinking-water filter at his home. The chemical, which was absorbed by Dr. LaBlanche's tissues, was quite benign by itself. But it combined with the second part of the poison, another harmless chemical Beckett had sprayed on the Plantation Room's salad dressing on Friday, and the mixture temporarily became a powerful toxin that induced cardiac arrest, before turning itself into a mild chemical. Elegant work. Now Brasfield indicated that there was a problem.

A knock on the door.

''Avanti, Alfredo,'' said Brasfield.

The door opened, letting in enough light for Beckett to see just a glimpse of the face of Brasfield's ''assistant,'' who had been leaning forward and was partially caught by the light from the hall outside. He quickly leaned back, his face disappearing in the darkness. A feeling of déjà vu momentarily swept through Beckett's mind. The face had looked familiar.

A waiter with heavy black hair, a thick mustache, and an ear-to-ear grin walked into the room, closed the door, and approached their table.

''Ah, Generalissimo! È arrivato il suo amico speciale?''

''Sì, Alfredo.''

Beckett eyed the tall, skinny Italian as he turned to him.

"And what would the amico speciale of Generale Brasfield like to drink before the antipasto?"

"Scotch and water," responded Brasfield's special friend.

"Very well, signore." And he was gone.

Brasfield ran a finger up and down the stem of his wineglass until the waiter closed the door. "There is another target in Louisiana. A woman. She was involved with the professor."

Beckett gave him a slight nod. So this was a *new* problem, but related to his previous work, when the DIA had irrefutable proof that Dr. Eugene LaBlanche had been selling state-of-the-art computer algorithms to third world countries. In one instance, a DIA covert operative had tracked down one such algorithm to a Syrian black-market dealer of high-tech goods. In a separate case, a DIA officer in Sudan had reported that an American received twenty thousand dollars from a known Jordanian businessman for the delivery of two diskettes. The officer had photographed the American, and it had been Dr. LaBlanche. The DIA had done further checking and verified that Dr. LaBlanche had been vacationing in the Mediterranean during the time of the exchange. The professor was a traitor and had to be eliminated. Arresting and prosecuting him would have put too much burden on the DIA, because it would have meant disclosing classified information on overseas operations in order to generate the necessary proof to convict. Doing so would have jeopardized clandestine operations. So the Defense Intelligence Agency took the easy way out, and Beckett was just about the most qualified professional assassin in the business of discreet termination.

The waiter came back with Beckett's drink and a pair of menus. Beckett took a sip, letting the hard liquor warm his chest and settle his stomach. The combination of the drink, the crowded restaurant, and the uneasiness of meeting with the DDI made him crave a cigarette.

General Brasfield put the glasses back on and held up a hand, palm facing the waiter. "Vorrei il mio solito pasto, Alfredo."

"Molto buono, signore."

"Try the calzone alla Giovanni," said General Brasfield to Beckett in a casual tone before the waiter handed him a menu. "Best in town."

Wondering what was Brasfield's *solito pasto*—usual meal—Beckett nodded once at the waiter, who turned and left the room.

Sliding a thumb back and forth over two fingers, Beckett said, "My terms are the same as for the last job."

Brasfield smoothed the black tie of his uniform before reaching for the wineglass and taking another sip. "It's all arranged."

"Any preferences?" Beckett downed the scotch, set it down on the table, and leaned back. The alcohol relaxed him, but without impairing his senses; his sharp mind analyzed every facial movement of the army general, looking for a trace of deception.

Fingering his breast-pocket ribbons, Brasfield locked eyes with Beckett. "On my way here I drove past an accident on the road. Apparently a person had lost control of his vehicle and smashed it into a tree. A rescue crew was trying to pry the poor bastard's twisted body out of the wreck." He raised his glass to Beckett. "Guess if you gotta go, better go quick." He drank the last of his glass and poured himself some more.

"How soon?" Beckett asked.

"Forty-eight hours."

"*Impossible*. Can't be done cleanly that quickly, and you know it."

General Jackson Brasfield calmly drank, eyes boring through Beckett over the rim of the wineglass. "Perhaps I made a mistake. I'll have to find someone else."

Beckett didn't flinch. "You made *no* mistake, and you *won't* find anyone better because I'm the best there is. And I need a week."

"Four days. Half of the money will be handed to you tonight. The other half delivered as usual," Brasfield said, his eyes full of dark amusement, obviously enjoying pushing Beckett.

Beckett didn't like to be toyed with. He was a professional assassin. Perhaps after this job he should do the old general for free. He suddenly got the urge to walk out and never do another job for the DIA. But although he had other customers who were far less demanding, none of them had an annual budget as big as the DIA's, which, at $9 billion, dwarfed the $1.5 billion CIA annual budget. The CIA got the spotlight in the news, novels, and movies, but it was the DIA that got the real funding in Congress. The DIA, an agency which duplicated much of the military analysis conducted by the CIA, reported not to the director of Central Intelligence, but to the secretary of defense, who presented DIA reports and analysis to the National Security Council. A high degree of rivalry existed between the DIA and the CIA, particularly when it came to which agency had the best insight on a particular crisis. Both agencies still claimed they'd found the Soviet missiles in Cuba first, which resulted in the Cuban missile crisis in 1962.

Placing both hands on the arms of the chair, Beckett breathed deeply and looked at Brasfield. "I'm going to the men's room."

Brasfield silently raised his glass at him, and Beckett left the room, intercepting the blond hostess a moment later. "Rest rooms?"

A tilted head and a wide smile preceded her reply. "They're just to the right of the entrance, sir."

Beckett nodded and walked away.

Four days for a staged auto accident! Brasfield had either been drinking too much *vino,* or he was playing games. A week was comfortable. Four days was definitely pushing it, but it could be done. He had used four days for LaBlanche. Two running surveillance, planning the termination, and two more carrying it out.

Beckett relieved himself in a gleaming white urinal. He found the rest of the bathroom equally spotless. A huge gold-framed mirror ran the length of three blue sinks. A neat

stack of royal blue towels, each with a golden *G* embroi-
dered across the center, stood to his left. After washing,
Beckett snatched a towel and dried his hands while staring
at the marvels of cosmetic surgery, at the face an Italian
doctor had given him after his marginal escape from a termination team.

The termination team. In a flash, Beckett was back at the
train station in Cairo, Egypt. He heard the agonizing scream
that preceded his beloved Layla Shariff's collapse on the
ramp as bullets showered her, some ricocheting off the
smooth concrete surface. Beckett went into a roll, right hand
pulling the Beretta secured to a chest holster. He saw them:
four men in black holding Kalashnikov AK-47s. Beckett
fired back. Two of the gunmen dropped, their chests exploding from the hollow-point rounds of Beckett's automatic. Beckett fired his last rounds at the third gunman,
tearing his chest apart. The last one, a bearded man, tried
to bring his AK-47 around, but Beckett was already on top
of him, pinning him down against the concrete. The Kalashnikov skittered away from the struggling pair. Shouts.
More shouts. Sirens in the distance. The smell of gunfire
mixed with the fumes from diesel engines filled his lungs.
Pulling out a knife, Beckett slashed across his attacker's
face; the man turned, the glistening steel edge slicing off a
section of his right ear. Blood flowing down the side of his
attacker's face, Beckett slashed again, cutting deeply across
his chest and abdomen. The bearded man fell to his knees,
his face raised at Beckett. Emerald green eyes burning with
hatred, nostrils flaring, lips trembling, blood oozing out of
the corner of his mouth. The man collapsed on his side as
Beckett rushed to Layla's side, but her dead eyes, the contorted face, the trickle of blood running out of her nose and
over the small brown freckle above her lips told Beckett it
was too late. An explosion in his soul sent a trembling agony
of despair through his body. He had lost her. He had lost
her.

"Mister, are you all right?"

Both hands gripping the sink, Harrison Beckett snapped

back to the present. A man with a pink round face regarded him curiously.

Regaining his composure, Beckett commented casually, "It's the Alfredo sauce. Too rich."

The fat man relaxed and grinned. "Get those pains myself."

Beckett also grinned, splashing water on his face. The cool sensation relaxed him. Drying himself and adjusting the knot of his tie, Beckett momentarily froze, suddenly realizing that the shadowy face of the man accompanying Brasfield looked very similar to Layla's bearded assassin.

A coincidence? Beckett toyed with the possibility as he stared into his own brown eyes.

Then another voice shrieked at him.

Let it go, Harrison. Let it go. You don't need this job. You don't need the mess of dealing with the DIA. You have other customers, ones you can control.

Beckett returned to the room with the firm intention of turning the job down. He still had time to do so. General Brasfield had not yet revealed the details of the job. He could still walk away safely. In toying with him, Brasfield had given Beckett a way out of this. Beckett planned to turn down the job under the pretext that he had to have a week.

As Beckett sat down, Brasfield pulled out a pack of Camels and a lighter. He offered one to Beckett, who readily took it, pulling out his own lighter. With the cigarette between his lips, Beckett slid a thumb over the flame control of his lighter. Although he had already decided to turn Brasfield down, Beckett's curiosity wanted a second look at that face in the corner.

The moment Brasfield lit the flame of his lighter, Beckett did the same, catching a second glimpse of the bearded man. Beckett snapped a mental picture of the emerald green eyes and a pink scar traversing the stranger's right ear.

Dear God!

He felt as though a freight train had just struck him with all its force.

Impossible!

The man's nose was a bit thinner and the face was rounder than Beckett remembered, but it belonged to Layla's assassin.

But it cannot be! That man had died on that platform, his insides oozing out of his body from the twelve-inch-long track Beckett had carved across his chest and abdomen with the steel blade. Yet, here he was, sitting fifteen feet away from Beckett without the slightest trace of recognition. . . . *Harrison, you dumb shit! Of course he can't recognize you! You had plastic surgery!*

Could it be a mistake, maybe? Perhaps the world's most bizarre coincidence? But the scar on the right ear! The eyes!

Insanity! Madness! It simply can't—

"Well?" Brasfield asked. "What is your answer?"

Disciplined instincts taking over his external appearance, Beckett also pulled on the cigarette before saying matter-of-factly, "Four days it is," instantly regretting the words the moment they came out of his mouth.

Let it go, Harrison. Let it go.

Brasfield's face lightened. "I knew you could do it," he said, extracting a white envelope from a pocket inside the suit. "Your contact will meet you at one-thirty at the Lincoln Memorial. Here are the instructions, and also the airline tickets to Baton Rouge. You must get there tonight and start tailing the target."

Beckett took the envelope, spent a minute reading the instructions, and handed everything back to Brasfield as their waiter, Alfredo, came back with the food and another scotch for Beckett.

"Il pranzo, signori," Alfredo said, his mustache moving up as he grinned. "Fettucine al pesto for Generale Brasfield, and calzone alla Giovanni for his amico speciale. Buon appetito!"

"Grazie, Alfredo," Brasfield responded, the fingers of his right hand holding the white envelope.

"Prego."

After Alfredo left and Beckett began to dig into the cal-

82   R. J. P i n e i r o

zone, Brasfield waved the envelope. "What about transportation? Don't you want your tickets?"

"I'll arrange for my own transportation, thank you. I'll meet your man as instructed. In four days I'll collect the balance of the payment."

Brasfield raised an eyebrow and shoved the envelope back in his suit.

They ate in silence. Brasfield had been right on the money about this calzone. It was molto delizioso, but Beckett couldn't bring himself to enjoy it. His mind now explored the possibilities of the face he had seen, the emerald green eyes Beckett felt were staring at him from the corner of the room. Was it really just mere coincidence? Or was that man Layla's assassin?

After the meeting, Beckett walked near the Washington Monument in West Potomac Park, killing time before meeting his DIA contact, and also making sure nobody followed him. The question of the mysterious man was pushing him to the edge. The more he thought about it, the crazier it seemed. The similarity had been extreme. Beckett had not said much to Brasfield after their food arrived, and there wasn't anything else left to discuss. He had accepted the mission and that was that. Beckett not only hated being in crowds, but he also could never get a handle on small talk. So he'd just eaten his food and listened to Alfredo and Brasfield chew the fat for a few minutes toward the end of the meal. From the conversation, Beckett learned that Brasfield loved Italian food and dined there a few nights every week in the company of different female companions. Based on the familiarity shown by the waiter to Brasfield, Beckett wasn't at all surprised when he heard that.

But what about that man in the corner? Why was he there? Beckett grew quite concerned. In his business one remained alive by being paranoid, but there were extremes, of course. The trick rested in screening useless paranoia from lifesaving caution. During his years with the DIA, Beckett had seen many officers and agents go down because they had failed to separate the two. And that mistake had also resulted in the death of his beloved Layla Shariff.

In 1981, Harrison Beckett, a DIA officer working at the American embassy, learned that the DIA and the Egyptian military had leaked information to the Muslim Brotherhood on the security measures being taken to protect Egyptian president Anwar Sadat during an upcoming military parade. To this day Beckett clearly remembered the moment when his agent, Layla Shariff, an executive secretary to one of Sadat's aides, showed him irrefutable proof that extreme factions within the Egyptian military and the DIA had had a series of meeting with leaders of the Muslim Brotherhood, a group of Muslim fundamentalists who loathed Sadat for traveling to Israel and making peace with Menachem Begin, then the Israeli prime minister. Apparently, huge military contracts between the Pentagon and Egypt would be canceled if the peace process between Israel and Egypt got under way. A plan had been put in motion to assassinate Sadat during the October 6 military parade commemorating the eighth anniversary of the 1973 war between Egypt and Israel. Working for one of Sadat's aides, a general who was in on the plot to assassinate the president, Layla came across oral and written information that left little doubt in her mind about the plan, which would be carried out by members of the Muslim Brotherhood.

Beckett had been stunned when Layla, an agent Beckett had recruited the year before to spy on the Egyptian military for the DIA, presented him with undeniable proof of the conspiracy against Sadat. By that time, Beckett had long fallen in love with the beautiful Egyptian. At that meeting Layla had also told Beckett that, although she had no proof, she feared her boss suspected her. With the military parade only a week away, Beckett calmed her down and sent her back to work while he figured a way out of this mess. But within hours of the meeting with Layla, Beckett spotted a surveillance team tailing him. At that moment Beckett realized that he and Layla were in extreme danger. Trying to flee Cairo by train had been a dumb move on his part. A termination team had been waiting for them at the station.

Beckett cursed the DIA for the secrets it kept from its field operatives. His current profession allowed him to be in full control. Running the entire show gave Beckett a freedom of action that at times seemed quite intoxicating, particularly because for Harrison Beckett authority based on position, rank, or title had no force whatsoever. In his operative mind, only ideas that made sense should be implemented, regardless of who thought of them. This personality trait, considered a liability by his superiors during his DIA days, was his most important asset as a contract assassin, because it gave Beckett the ability to think on his own, conforming to rules that made sense while quickly discarding those that didn't. It provided Beckett with the gift of openness and objectivity to new ideas, new concepts, new possibilities.

Possibilities. Beckett's mind continued to speculate as he took in a deep breath of cold air. A light breeze swayed the branches of nearby trees by the Vietnam Veterans Memorial, where a few dozen people strolled up and down the marble wall. Had the shadowy figure sitting in the corner of the room been Layla's assassin? And worse than that, could it be possible that Brasfield suspected who Beckett really was and had used the meeting and the "assistant" as the stage to verify his suspicions? Did Brasfield cook up the story about a woman working with Dr. LaBlanche just to draw Beckett in, test him, and have him eliminated if he failed?

As he stared at the rippled image of the Washington Monument on the long reflecting pool that led to the Lincoln Memorial, Beckett began to wonder if the Defense Intelligence Agency had finally caught up with him after all these years, after the insane plan he carried out in Rome in order to insure his survival.

Rome.

Refusing to remember that sin, Harrison Beckett reached the steps leading to the Lincoln Memorial.

Beckett scanned his surroundings, searching for spotters, covert operatives sent ahead of the actual party to verify the safety of the meeting. Beckett saw tourists snapping pictures, and men and women in business suits walking hastily. Any one of those characters could be working for Brasfield, probably verifying the safety of the area before sending a ton of cash to pay off a contract.

Walking halfway up the memorial steps as directed by Brasfield before they parted company at the restaurant, Beckett grew more concerned. He was too exposed, too vulnerable. Was this what Brasfield wanted? Did the deputy director for intelligence of the DIA simply want to draw Beckett out into the open?

A dark sedan drove up to the curb, and a man in a gray suit got out of the rear seat and began to walk up the steps. Beckett shoved his right hand inside the suit, clasping a Beretta 92F secured to his chest holster as he stared at the narrow pinkish head, ash blond hair and mustache, and blue eyes of the young covert operative sent to pay him . . . or kill him.

Regarding Beckett with vague amusement, the DIA man glanced at a group of Japanese tourists posing for a group picture before saying, "The general sends his regards."

Beckett kept the hand inside the suit, fingers curled around the alloy handle. The contact could not have been a day older than thirty, and was just as tall as Beckett.

"Let's see what you have," Beckett said, releasing the grip on the Beretta.

The contact handed him two manila envelopes. Beckett opened the fat one first. It was packed with one-hundred-dollar bills. Closing it and shoving it under his right arm, Beckett opened the second envelope and stared at the face of Pamela Sasser, the woman the DIA claimed was an associate professor of computer engineering at Louisiana State University, and partner in crime with the late Dr. Eugene LaBlanche. *A beautiful woman, this Pamela Sasser.* The woman's lively blue-green eyes, long dark hair falling gently over her feminine shoulders, light olive skin, and high cheekbones, stared back at Beckett. Noticing the small brown freckle above her lips, the former DIA officer felt a slight chill up his spine.

Harrison . . . Harrison, my love . . .
Stop it! Concentrate!

Harrison Beckett handed the photo back to the DIA contact and studied the dossier, which showed a street address, place of work at the university, make and color of her car— all the information Beckett needed to fulfill his contract.

Under the watchful eye of the DIA officer, Beckett memorized the dossier in silence before handing it back to the young officer, who raised a hand holding up four fingers.

"Starting right now. The clock is ticking," the blond contact said before walking away.

One hour later, Beckett boarded a chartered Learjet, which flew him directly to Baton Rouge for the nominal fee of seven thousand dollars, pocket change for what Brasfield was paying him. Cautious by nature, Beckett always wanted to reach his targeted victim as soon as possible to give himself plenty of time for a clean hit. Not only were chartered flights the best way to minimize lost time traveling and have the privacy to change clothes and sleep undisturbed, but they also allowed him to fly across the country while carrying his nine-millimeter automatic and his "field bag," a waterproof nylon bag containing extra nine-millimeter rounds, a collection of double-edged hunting knives, a pair of field binoculars, and the pack of Marlboro Golds he purchased before getting on the plane.

At exactly 4:45 P.M., Beckett parked his rental car a block from the apartment complex where the DIA claimed Pamela Sasser lived. It had taken him just over four hours to reach his target. He seriously doubted any other assassin-for-hire could top that.

It took Beckett a few minutes to spot a party stalking Pamela Sasser's apartment complex from the pool across the parking lot, a woman and two men. He suspected the DIA. Perhaps Brasfield was either checking up on Beckett or just waiting for Beckett to finish this job before ordering his execution.

Beckett headed for the apartment complex's main office, his mind working overtime to come up with a plan to extract his answers before heading back to Washington and solving the puzzle behind Brasfield's assistant.

6 Feds

The overall mission of the FBI is to uphold the law through the investigation of Federal crimes statutes, to protect the United States from hostile intelligence efforts, to provide assistance to other Federal, state and local law enforcement agencies, and to perform those responsibilities in a manner that is faithful to the Constitution and laws of the United States.

—FBI Mission Statement

BATON ROUGE, LOUISIANA
Monday, November 16

Across the parking lot from Pamela Sasser's apartment, a woman holding a half-eaten stick of beef jerky sat against the waist-high wrought-iron railing surrounding the complex's swimming pool. She wore a pair of stonewashed jeans, an extralarge black New Orleans Saints T-shirt, sneakers, and a pair of round sunglasses. Her eyes scanned the crowded lot, the kids by the pool, and the afternoon traffic in Tiger Town, finally landing on her subject's first-floor apartment. She was Esther Cruz, FBI assistant special agent in charge (ASAC) of the Washington office, located in the J. Edgar Hoover Building in downtown Washington, D.C.

A tall woman, almost six feet and slightly on the heavy side, Esther carried well the extra fifteen pounds she considered an asset when bringing down a thug. Thanks to the prominent nose of her Mexican father, Esther was not a very attractive woman, but she was quite elegant in her stance, always keeping her shoulders pulled back and her chin up. Her light brown skin, a bit weathered with age and hardened by a life of hard work and few breaks, soaked in the Louisiana sun and began to turn dark. The silver-and-turquoise bracelets she wore on both wrists rattled as she took one more bite of dehydrated beef, pulled up the plastic wrapping, and shoved it in a side pocket. Next she removed her sunglasses, breathed on them, and began to polish them with the end of the T-shirt. A pair of matching earrings plus an assortment of silver-and-turquoise necklaces, partially covering the Saints team logo, always reminded Esther of her Texan-Mexican heritage. The silver band on the ring finger of her left hand reminded Esther of a life that would never be. The powerful automatic pistol safely tucked in a chest holster under the loose T-shirt reminded her of her profession.

Esther put the sunglasses back on and scanned the area once more before giving the two junior agents accompanying her a disappointing glance. They were staring at a voluptuous young blonde walking to the pool in the tiniest bikini Esther had ever seen in her life.

"Settle down, boys," she said while turning her attention back to the subject's apartment, her salt-and-pepper hair pulled back in a bun, the large earrings swinging from her ears as she moved her head. Both agents cleared their throats. One of them mumbled an apology.

"Sightsee on your *own* time, not on the Bureau's—and especially *not* during this assignment," Esther added, somewhat disappointed with the emerging generation of FBI agents, who at times seemed to lack the concentration vital for a successful surveillance job. Just a few hours into this mission and the junior agents were already falling into the classic rookie trap of slacking off, a mistake that had cost the lives of many agents since the early days of the Bureau. And to think that these two were actually among the best junior agents in the Washington office!

Esther Cruz slowly shook her head. Nothing could go wrong on this job. Just this morning she'd gotten word from a naval intelligence officer working for the FBI under direct orders from the director of the Office of Naval Intelligence that Pamela Sasser was the next link in the chain that Esther hoped would lead the FBI and the ONI to a criminal ring operating deep inside the Pentagon. Ten years ago, word reached the ONI about the existence of this corrupt network. Almost immediately, the director of the Office of Naval Intelligence met with the director of the FBI to create a joint task force to go after it. Unfortunately, the criminal ring was quite adept at breaking links in the investigative chain. Esther believed this ring was responsible for the deaths of many civilians and military officers, all of whom had probably gotten too close to the network and had either died of "natural causes," or committed suicide. In the meantime the ring of corruption apparently continued to grow. From time to time, a politician, a reporter, or even a military officer would put the spotlight on a case of bribery and fraud, like the 1991 investigation carried out by the ONI and the FBI. In that particular case, which involved over one hundred FBI agents—Esther Cruz included—fifty-four Defense Department officials were arrested. But like many times before and after that case, only the expendables got arrested. The main players remained in power by breaking the links in the investigation. Key people related to the case died. A few committed suicide, others perished in car accidents, some died of natural causes.

Others . . .

Esther glanced at the silver ring and took a deep breath. She believed this military Mafia was behind all the deaths, which broke the links that would have brought the Bureau closer to the perpetrators. Esther also feared that this network had been operating on some military or political agenda for probably even longer than ten years. The pattern of deaths associated with Pentagon scandals went back to the Vietnam era.

So when navy lieutenant Eduardo López, working undercover as a clerk, contacted Esther with news of a possible link into the Web—as Esther called this complex criminal ring—she had convinced the FBI director to let her catch the first available flight to Baton Rouge, along with three of her agents. Esther and her team had arrived shortly after lunch and rented two cars. She had sent her seasoned agent, Jessica White, in one of the vehicles to find and tail Pamela Sasser at LSU. Esther and the two rookies remained at the apartment waiting for her to show, or ready to rush off should Jessica White call after spotting Pamela.

Checking that the tiny cellular phone clipped to the belt of her jeans still had a charge, the seasoned agent stretched and yawned. Exhausted and hungry as she was, Esther Cruz couldn't help the adrenaline boosting her system into high gear. Working on a lead that might result in bringing down a criminal network—particularly this one—was what she did best.

She had joined the Bureau in 1975, at the age of twenty-one, at a time when the FBI wasn't taking in that many skirts, female agents, particularly those seeking the kind of high-risk undercover work that Esther Cruz desired. But she was adamant, smart, and a great shot. The only child of a rancher in south Texas, Esther learned how to fire handguns after school while her friends played with dolls. Her father took her on his hunting trips, where she learned the art of stalking her prey, of following her instincts, of being strong enough to kill when she *had* to kill. After graduating from the FBI Academy in Quantico, Virginia, she got assigned to the Miami office, where Esther distinguished herself by volunteering for the hardest and most dangerous undercover work. The highlight of her career in the southern state was her instrumental role in the arrest of cartel lord Mario Calderón in Miami Beach. Esther had posed as the owner of WhiteComm, an FBI-founded cellular-phone company in Miami. Drug dealers' lives depended on solid communications, and when word got around that WhiteComm would sell telephone equipment and provide airtime without requiring the drug dealers to provide Social Security numbers and driver's licenses, Esther Cruz's little business bloomed with requests. Immediately liked by Mario Calderón, Esther allowed him to conduct some of his business deals at WhiteComm. For nine months, the FBI monitored hundreds of phones calls and videotaped dozens of meetings at WhiteComm, and in the end the Bureau not only arrested Calderón and dozens of his local contacts, but also stopped $600 million worth of shipments from entering the country. WhiteComm even made a $380,000 profit—which wound up in the Bureau's coffers.

Considering herself a "brick agent," a Bureau term used to describe agents who enjoyed working the field, also called "street agents," Esther Cruz loved field operations and had a high degree of respect for anyone who pounded the bricks. She had the reputation of being an agent's agent, always willing to confront the HBOs—high Bureau officials—to support her agents.

Transferred to Washington in 1990, Esther met Arturo Cruz, a navy lieutenant commander working for the Office of Naval Intelligence. Up to that point in her life, Esther had dated little, mostly short-lived romances with a few Cubans in Miami. But with Arturo it was different. She sensed the chemistry between them an hour after they were introduced during the 1991 FBI-ONI joint investigation. Three months later they were married at her father's ranch in Texas, under the same oaks where she'd learned how to fire a pistol and throw a lasso, next to the same fields where she killed her first deer.

Esther looked at the silver band on her finger and frowned. *I will catch those bastards, mi amor.*

Esther knew her break would come sooner or later, and it did, when General Jackson T. Brasfield, the deputy director for intelligence of the Defense Intelligence Agency, informed his immediate staff that Dr. Eugene LaBlanche had information that might be damaging to his friends in the corporate world. Brasfield had been one of the few officers that the FBI-ONI task force chose not to arrest during the 1991 case. Instead, they decided to run surveillance on him in the hope that he would lead them deeper into the Web.

Esther Cruz had sent two of her top agents to Louisiana to tail Dr. Eugene LaBlanche. But this effort proved fruitless after the college professor died of a heart attack a few days later.

She sighed. *Heart attack my ass.* But Esther Cruz had declined the opportunity to perform a full autopsy for the same reason she simply didn't arrest the corrupt general: fear of tipping the Web. Esther Cruz had no idea how deep this network went. Arresting Brasfield could set back her operation for months if not more. Brasfield had gotten ahead of her and taken out Dr. LaBlanche, thus eliminating a link in the chain that could have exposed a new aspect of the criminal ring.

Esther had seen this problem happening too many times before. The professor was dead, and that was that. Now this Pamela Sasser surfaced out of nowhere, and Esther had requested to be sent to this godforsaken state without even contacting the local FBI office. Esther had argued with the HBOs that this case was too sensitive, and only the people assigned to it, who were Esther and her two dozen agents, should know about it. The director had agreed, and here she was now; in the thick of a case she considered the most important of her life.

Checking her watch before pressing her forehead against her right shoulder, Esther dried up the film of sweat that had accumulated on her tanned forehead. She felt a bit jealous of the kids swimming in that pool.

What kind of weather is this anyway? We're in November, for crying out loud! After living in the North for the past six years, Esther had forgotten about the heat of the southern states. But not even in south Texas did it get this hot and humid this time of the year. Esther couldn't wait to head home—but not before she found what she came looking for: leads.

"Hey, Calv," she said to one of her assistants, a twenty-five-year-old African American from Harlem, New York, standing by the gate leading to the pool area.

"Yes, Mother?"

"Pretty hot, isn't it?" said Esther, who got the nickname for risking her life four years ago, during a hostage crisis in a Washington high school. Two fifteen-year-old kids, armed with revolvers, held the school hostage for twenty-four hours in protest of the drug-related arrest of several classmates the week before. Posing as a social worker to mediate between the armed kids and the police, Esther had disarmed the teenagers, handcuffed them, and taken them outside while pulling them by the ears. This all happened the Friday before Mother's Day. In gratitude for her heroic act, the school gave Esther the title of "Mother of the Year."

Calvin Johnson extended the thumb of his right hand to the agent next to him, a second-generation Vietnamese immigrant who graduated from the FBI Academy just two years ago. "It's the chink's turn to get drinks."

Liem Ngo, a five-foot-two, 150-pound man capable of leveling guys twice his size in thirty seconds, said, "Bullshit, dude: *I* got the last round and I'm out of change."

Chink? Bullshit, dude? Esther Cruz shook her head, wondering when exactly the English language had gone to hell. Her eyes trained on Pamela's apartment, Esther said, "Very, *very* hot around here, isn't it, *Calv*?"

Liem grinned, his straight black hair reaching the top of his long and narrow eyes. "That's what I love about this country, dude. Justice's always served. Ain't that right, Calv?"

"Motherfucker," Calvin Johnson muttered as he began to walk away. "Always pin it on th' fuckin' nigger to do the fuckin' errand."

"We're in the South, dude," added Liem, his eyes wetting with laughter. "When in Rome . . ."

"Fuck you, man," Calvin hissed as he slowly walked away.

Esther ignored the comment while smiling inwardly. It was, after all, Calvin's turn to get sodas from the vending machine.

Just then she saw a blue Honda Accord drive up to the

open parking space in front of Pamela Sasser's unit. The vehicle matched the information in the computerized dossier she had obtained before leaving Washington.

"Calv, get your sorry ass back here. Subject's here. Everyone in the car." She tossed the cellular phone to Liem Ngo. "Call Jessica. Tell her to head on back here."

Pamela Sasser pulled up to her reserved spot in front of her first-floor apartment. She felt drained, both physically and emotionally. Aside from her sadness about LaBlanche's death and her concern regarding Microtel's probable involvement in the robbery, this was the end of the semester. Term papers and exams needed grading, and her semester project was due in a week.

She locked her car, walked up to the long porch in front of the row of apartments, and reached for the doorknob.

She froze. It was not locked.

Clearly remembering locking it this morning, Pamela's mind went immediately into high alarm.

A break-in!

Someone had broken into her apartment! She had heard of the rising wave of crime in the area and of a few of her neighbors' apartments getting broken into, but she never actually expected it would happen to her.

A hand covering her mouth, Pamela remained motionless, lips pursed in suspicion. Was the thief still inside? What if he was about to come out? What would he do if he saw her just standing there? Push her aside and run away with the loot, or kill her, or perhaps drag her inside and rape her?

Pamela took a couple of steps back and to the side, figuring that her chances of living were far better if she remained outside and waited a little longer. But how long was long enough? Five, ten minutes? She didn't know, and she grew too frightened to care.

Running back into her car, she locked the doors, cranked the engine, and let it idle. Then she laid on the horn for ten seconds, and waited.

Nothing.

Ten more seconds, and she watched two neighbors stick their heads outside their second-and third-story windows and scream obscenities. A few people by the pool were looking in her direction. But Pamela saw nothing from her own apartment.

After ten minutes of feeling growingly stupid just sitting there burning gas, Pamela Sasser worked up the nerve to get out and walk back to her front door.

Holding her breath, she reached for the knob and pushed the door.

Oh, God!

The place was torn upside down. Books were scattered across the living-room floor, covered with the white stuffing of her slashed leather couch; table lamps and picture frames were broken; the TV was lying on its side, a dozen colorful wires projecting out of the broken rear panel; her stereo was cracked open, its electronic guts spilled next to a pair of torn speakers. In the kitchen she found more of the same: pots, pans, dishes, glasses, silverware were all thrown in a pile in the middle of the room, along with the contents from the open refrigerator. A head of lettuce sliced in half next to a crushed loaf of bread made her realize that this had not been the work of a thief or a vandal. Her electronics equipment was not missing. Someone had dragged her TV and stereo from her bedroom and into the living room, but they had not been stolen, only destroyed. Running to her bedroom, she found her PC, also torn to pieces. The whole room had an eerie but strangely peaceful look. It reminded Pamela of a town the morning after a tornado.

Pamela suddenly understood what this meant. Momentarily disconnecting her emotions, she rummaged through the mess that someone had made of her worldly possessions, looking for the only item in the apartment she knew would be missing. This she did with care, because it would finally tell her what kind of people she was dealing with, and what they were capable of doing.

After ten minutes of moving trash aside, Pamela Sasser sat on the floor in the corner of her bedroom. Her box of diskettes was indeed missing, not torn, or broken, or ripped in half like everything else in this place she had called home for nearly five years, but gone. And what was worse, Pamela knew *exactly* who had taken it. She knew at this moment someone at Microtel was going through each diskette, carefully checking its contents before putting it aside and checking the next one.

Somehow, perhaps by going through Dr. LaBlanche's files, Microtel had learned of the backup and of her involvement.

A question suddenly loomed in her mind: What would they do to her after they realized that the diskette was not in her apartment? Or in her office? She had already assumed that Microtel had the entire office searched, probably even stripped like LaBlanche's after his sudden death. . . . The realization struck her like a hammer blow:

They killed Dr. LaBlanche!

Closing her eyes and rubbing fingers against her temples, Pamela began to tremble. Her fear spiraled out of control. The notion of her own life in jeopardy because of someone else's lust for money and power appalled her. The thought of what Microtel, and Preston Sinclaire, could do to her pushed her near the edge.

But through the fear and the shock, through the tears and the anger of losing her modest but significant possessions, through the cloudiness that enveloped her mind from emotions turned to havoc, Pamela heard her logical side speak.

Now everything made sense. This whole macabre play seemed to be coming together, with Pamela as the only good character left alive on the stage: Dr. LaBlanche approached Microtel with his discovery. Preston Sinclaire, trying to avoid a scandal and a costly recall, wanted the error buried. Someone under orders from Sinclaire killed LaBlanche and made it look like a heart attack, and now Microtel had its algorithm by taking possession of Dr. LaBlanche's files. But now they realized that the old professor had help, and that help was in possession of a copy of the algorithm, which

Microtel saw as a serious threat; otherwise they wouldn't be coming after it.

A fusillade of questions pounded her. Whom could she approach with this information? The police? The FBI? The NRC? And exactly how would she do this? Through anonymous calls to keep her identity secret in case Microtel wanted to retaliate? Or should she come forward and testify in court? And what would be the implications of doing so? Would she get protection from the law enforcement establishment? A new identity? A new life? She suddenly realized that she had already done this once before, over a decade ago, when she escaped the abusive fists of her father and got herself a new life. No one had helped her then. The local police had been a joke, siding with her father. Trusting no one, not even her mother, Pamela had simply vanished, left the state, and created herself a new life in Baton Rouge.

But can you do it again?

This time around she was not dealing with a drunken cop from Beaumont, Texas. This time she would be going up against one of the most powerful men in the country, someone with resources deeper than she could even begin to imagine.

Pamela Sasser's mind began to question the idea of exposing the bug in the Perseus. It was quite obvious to her that Preston Sinclaire would use every power at his disposal to prevent her from succeeding, even if that meant . . .

Walk away from this, Pamela. This is well over your head. Just leave the diskette here and run!

But how could she simply run away? Microtel had *killed* Dr. LaBlanche. How could she turn away from that and from the evidence that linked the Perseus bug to the worst peacetime nuclear disaster in history? How many other disasters would happen if she didn't come forth and expose them?

Walk away, Pamela, the voice repeated.

But Pamela Sasser felt she had already walked away from enough conflict in her life. She had walked away and left her mother alone with her abusive father, who killed her a year later, after drinking heavily one night.

Suddenly, as she sat shaking, hugging her knees in the corner of her bedroom, tears filling her eyes, Pamela's fear turned to anger: pure, raw, primitive anger. She felt it slowly burning her insides, turning her emotions around, making her clench her jaw, tighten her fists, breathe deeply. She had not felt this kind of anger since the day her father beat her mother to death, crushing her skull with the heels of his boots. But Pamela had achieved retribution. She had sat in the witness stand and described with utter detail the beatings Pamela and her mother had sustained for years at his hand.

And just like her father now paid for his sins behind the walls of a Texas state prison, so would Preston Sinclaire pay for this. The president of Microtel would pay for LaBlanche, for Palo Verde, for thinking that he could buy the right to be above the law.

Sucking up the pain and the tears, Pamela jumped up, checked that the backup diskette was still in her purse, pulled out her keys, and went outside. Looking around the parking lot she saw no one.

She got into her Honda and drove away, not really knowing where to go or whom to ask for help, but definitely knowing where *not* to go and whom *not* to see; her priorities were clear in her mind: *Protect your evidence. Hide the diskette. Then plan your counterattack, plan your revenge.*

Harrison Beckett didn't like the way this game was playing out. How in the world was he ever supposed to get close to Pamela Sasser with the place infested with tails?

Beckett found this whole charade borderline amusing. The moment Pamela drove out, a black truck with tinted windows came to life, slowly moving out of the parking lot in obvious pursuit. Several seconds later a dark sedan carrying the suspected DIA threesome pulled out. Now Beckett ran from his second-story apartment to his car, a white Ford Escort.

Beckett had made long-distance arrangements with the

apartment complex's manager while flying to Baton Rouge this afternoon. The manager, a sweet old lady, had been waiting for him at the office in front of the large complex when he arrived right before closing time. This provided Beckett access to a layout of the place, and it also gave him immediate information on vacant apartments overlooking the parking lot. The rest had been easy. After informing the manager that he would return tomorrow, Beckett parked at the end of the parking lot, sneaked his way up to the second floor, and silently broke into a vacant unit with a great view of the parking lot below and of Pamela's apartment.

From this strategic spot, Beckett had used the field binoculars to monitor not only the activities of the tails, but also to check every car parked in the vicinity of Pamela's apartment. Seeing none that matched the description in the dossier he had memorized just hours before, Beckett had come to the conclusion that Pamela was not home.

Reaching his Escort, Beckett let the caravan get a block ahead before following. His sweaty palms slipped off the steering wheel. This concerned him greatly. He never got nervous during a job. He had executed far too many of them to show any physical signs of excitement. But as he wiped each hand on his jeans, he realized that his unusual mental state was due to the fact that his mind continued to play those brief seconds at Giovanni's, when Beckett had seen the face of Layla Shariff's assassin.

Damn it, Harrison! Concentrate!

Grimacing, Beckett forced Layla and the assassin out of his mind for now. He had to focus, had to be fully aware of the current situation, which grew in complexity with every passing moment.

Pamela parked her car in front of a large grocery store in Tiger Town. Pulling out a plastic card, she went inside the store, walked up to an automatic teller, and withdrew four hundred dollars, the maximum amount she could take out in one twenty-four-hour period from the machine.

Before leaving, she cruised through the supermarket's aisles and grabbed the items she considered basic to her survival: a pair of scissors, a bottle of hair coloring, shampoo, a brush, styling gel, a pair of tweezers, and some makeup. She also got an extralarge LSU T-shirt, a small box of airtight freezer bags, and a small roll of double-sided sticky tape.

The late afternoon was humid and clear. The setting sun's wan light cast a reddish hue over the parking lot, which Pamela scanned for any tails. But in reality she didn't know what to look for. She estimated over a hundred cars filled the parking lot. Most students and faculty shopped at this time. In a single minute she saw dozens of people going into the store and dozens more coming out hauling grocery bags. Any one of them could be tailing her and she'd never know it.

Realizing she would never know if someone was following her while standing in the middle of this crowded parking lot, and also aware that Microtel no doubt knew the kind of car she drove, Pamela chose to leave her Honda behind and walk to the other side of the campus, where Nicholson Drive led straight to a Residence Inn. If she hurried, she might even make it there before nightfall.

As Pamela walked away from her car, Esther Cruz and her two assistants drove up to the side of Jessica White's sedan in the middle of the grocery store's parking lot. The two same-year-and-model rented vehicles differed only in color. Esther's was black, Jessica's white.

Esther rolled down the window. Jessica did the same. Before getting here, Esther had filled her in on the situation through cellular phones and two-way radios.

"She's leaving her vehicle behind," said Jessica, her shoulder-length blond hair outlining a pale face, a fine nose, and small lips over a pointy chin.

Esther shook her head as Pamela Sasser made her way across the parking lot, leaving her car behind. "We'll leave our car here and follow her on foot," Esther said to Liem. "Jessica, take Calvin with you and follow us in your car."

She nodded.

Esther gave the parking lot a brief scan, and an alarm went off in her head. She wasn't sure at first what it was that had triggered it, but something just didn't feel right. Then she realized that somewhere in the dozen people entering and exiting the store her seasoned eyes had briefly locked with those of a man holding a newspaper near the handicapped parking spaces by the store's entrance. The eye contact had only lasted a fraction of a second as Esther inspected the area, but it had been long enough to alert her to a possible tail. However, when Esther's eyes instinctively returned to the same spot a few seconds later to get a better look, the man had vanished.

"Careful," Esther said, her brown eyes surveying the parking lot. "I think somebody might be watching us."

"Who are the two in the truck?" asked Jessica as the pair of rough-looking characters left the truck and began to follow Pamela.

Esther shrugged. "Don't know. They were already at the apartment complex when we got there."

Jessica nodded again and rolled up the window as Calvin went inside the vehicle.

Waiting for the two from the truck to move out first, Esther began to attack her fingernails, in spite of the tiny blood blisters she had already caused on half her fingertips.

"Easy, Mother," said Liem.

Ignoring her subordinate, Esther chewed on her pinkie and watched the two brutes walk behind Pamela.

"Let's go, Liem."

Running a hand over the holstered Colt .45 under her black T-shirt, Esther Cruz stepped out and gave the parked cars around her a suspicious glance. Something didn't feel right. Was that man for real, or was she getting paranoid? She wasn't worried about Pamela Sasser or the two following the college professor. Those characters Esther felt she could handle. What bothered her was the feeling of being stalked by another party that she couldn't see.

With one final glimpse of her surroundings, Esther Cruz closed the door to her car and began to walk toward the LSU campus.

After almost getting caught looking while going through the motions of purchasing a newspaper from one of the machines at the front of the store, Harrison Beckett had quickly returned to his vehicle and remained inside, hidden from view. The tall, slightly plump woman with the faded jeans and black T-shirt in the party of three that had pulled up next to the woman in the white sedan seemed to know her business. She appeared quite weary of being followed. One of the men went inside the white sedan, while the other remained with the Hispanic-looking woman.

Now he could see the couple at the far end of the parking lot, about to disappear behind a number of buildings across from a hamburger joint. The other two officers in the white sedan drove fifty feet behind them.

With a truckload of questions, Harrison Beckett headed after the caravan of people tailing his target. What kind of sick game was Jackson Brasfield playing here? It was obvious that Beckett wouldn't be able to get close to Pamela without being spotted. Is that what the Defense Intelligence Agency had in mind? Force Beckett to come out and expose himself so that the DIA could pin a tail on him—a tail that would eliminate Beckett after Pamela's automobile accident?

This is insane, Harrison.

And insanity seemed the only logical explanation for the events developing in front of Beckett's eyes. Compounding the madness of the impossible vision from his past, the reality of a mission he felt unable to complete loomed over him like a vulture circling over a carcass. His paradox seemed unavoidable. The DIA had paid him handsomely to kill Pamela Sasser within four days, and she had to die in an auto accident. Brasfield had been quite specific about that during their meeting. Even if he wanted to accomplish his mission, how could he? How would he get a chance to get close with half of the secret agents in the world following her every move? If he failed, Beckett knew the full force of the DIA would descend on him. The military spooks didn't tolerate failure, particularly from its contract assassins. But what if the opportunity opened itself for the hit? Could Beckett execute Pamela Sasser under such bizarre circumstances? Was Pamela guilty as charged, or had the DIA fabricated the evidence to pull Beckett into the open after figuring out Beckett's real identity?

But another question came back, pounding the inner workings of his logic: Could Brasfield's assistant realistically be Layla's assassin? Beckett had seen the assassin's insides spill out on the concrete ramp. How could he have survived such fatal wounds?

These were all questions in Beckett's confused mind. However, in spite of the madness, the visions from the past, the multiple tails, and the menacing cloud of the DIA darkening his future for the second time in his life, Harrison Beckett saw only one option: Use every skill, every ounce of strength, and every resource to his name to get close to that woman and extract the truth about her involvement with Dr. Eugene LaBlanche. Only then would Beckett start untangling the web of conspiracy covering this strange mission he should have never accepted.

Hauling her small grocery bag and her purse, Pamela Sasser left the parking lot, her heart throbbing, her mouth dried, her limbs tingling. As she walked, she let the bag and purse hang from her wrists while she placed the diskette inside one of the plastic bags. Pamela put that into another freezer bag, attached two strips of the sticky tape to one side of the bag and began to look for a place to hide her evidence.

Holding her breath, she gazed across the grounds, mostly shadowed by opulent oak and magnolia trees. But her mind did not register the beautiful landscape under a crimson sunset. Pamela felt stared at. Somewhere in the corner of her mind a voice told her she was being followed. Yet, a glance around her showed tranquil grounds, empty benches lining well-trimmed lawns, a half dozen kids throwing Frisbees, others playing tag football. Nothing out of the ordinary. Yet, someone was out there. Someone who had broken into her apartment to get what she now held in her hands, what she only now realized she could not afford to lose.

Letting go of the breath she had been holding and filling her lungs with the smell of moist leaves, Pamela turned the corner behind the Department of Anthropology, across the street from the small Greek amphitheater, and spotted an old concrete bench, almost hidden from view by overgrown bushes and two large magnolias.

With a swiftness that even surprised herself, Pamela Sasser, one hand holding the purse and grocery bag and the other the protected diskette, checked around her once more, walked to the bench, and, leaning over, pressed the sticky side of the plastic bag against the underside of the bench seat. It stuck in place firmly. Even if it did fall off, the bushes and the magnolias would keep it hidden from the sidewalk.

She continued walking toward Nicholson Drive without looking back once, reaching the Residence Inn almost an hour later, after moving through the LSU campus in the hope of shaking anyone that might be following her.

An orange moon in its first quarter glowed over the skies of Baton Rouge. The sound of merchant ships sailing the Mississippi mixed with the noise coming from the Good Times Bar a block down Nicholson Drive, an undergraduate hangout and a favorite of Pamela's more than six years ago. The drumming bass of rock music traveling through the cool and humid night brought back brief memories of simpler times.

But those visions from the past quickly vanished as she walked inside the hotel's lobby and approached the counter. A medium height, dark-haired man with brows as thick and bushy as his mustache dressed in an all-brown uniform gave Pamela a welcoming smile.

"May I help you?" The voice seemed a bit high and nasal for his strong masculine appearance.

"I need a room for the night, please." She rested both elbows on the white-laminate countertop of the hotel's front desk.

"Do you have a reservation?"

"Ah, no. I sure don't, but if you can spare a room, I'd really appreciate it." Her own voice sounded distant, almost as if being spoken by someone else. Her eyelids grew heavy, her mind became less focused. She needed to get some sleep. The night before she had been unable to sleep much, worrying about getting involved and how that decision might affect her career. Now that concern had fallen low in her priority list, surpassed by her desire to remain alive.

After thirty seconds working the keyboard of a computer terminal behind the counter, the clerk lifted his gaze to Pamela. "Smoking or nonsmoking?"

"I prefer non, but I'll take anything."

A few more keystrokes and he said, "How would you like to pay?"

"Cash."

The clerk handed her a card and a pen. Pamela filled out the hotel's registry with false information. After she paid for the room, the clerk provided her with a second-floor room number and a key.

Five minutes later Pamela Sasser dropped the grocery bag and the purse on the nightstand and crashed on the double bed, wondering if she had been successful in losing the people that Preston Sinclaire might have sent after her.

Her logical side taking control of her thoughts with amazing speed, Pamela began to go through her options. With an associate professor's salary, she had managed to save about twenty thousand dollars over the past five years. She figured she could use that money to get herself a new life far away from Louisiana. First thing tomorrow morning, she would make a full withdrawal of her funds, grab the diskette, and go catch a plane to another state.

As soon as she felt safe and far away from the tentacles

of Preston Sinclaire, Pamela would strike, exposing the flaw in the Perseus and its possible link to the Palo Verde incident. She would not walk away and forget, like she did in Beaumont, Texas.

Those bastards will pay.

With the prospects of a new life dancing in her mind, Pamela got up, grabbed the grocery bag, and walked into the bathroom, spilling its contents on the counter next to the sink.

She took one last look at her long hair before reaching for the scissors, grabbing a clump of hair, and cutting. Hair began to gather by her feet as her eyes watered. She was leaving her current life behind and the falling hair seemed to symbolize that somehow. But she didn't stop. She kept on cutting, kept on crying, kept on telling herself that she would be all right, that she would survive this, that those bastards at Microtel would not prevail. She was smart, and she would use her wits to save herself and expose them.

Soon hair covered her feet, soon she saw the reflection of a twenty-year-old Pamela Sasser—the last time her hair had been that short, during her sophomore year. The short, borderline punkish hair reminded her of wilder years, before she took academics seriously. Putting the scissors down and running her hands through the inch-long hair, Pamela filled her lungs with hope. Her looks had definitely changed with just the cut. But she wanted a bigger change—enough to fool anyone who might be following her.

She reached for the bottle of hair coloring and spent the next thirty minutes turning herself into a blonde. Next came the tweezers, which she used to selectively pluck her eyebrows until she thinned them enough to get the punkish effect she desired. As a blonde, her chocolate freckle, right above the corner of her mouth, suddenly came to life, contrasting sharply with the lighter hair. She moved her lips in and out, watching the freckle dance above her upper lip.

Her confidence grew after she applied gel to her short hair and brushed it straight back, exposing a forehead that, like her neck, had been hidden by her black hair for nearly a decade.

For the first time that day, Pamela Sasser smiled. She actually liked her new self. She suddenly felt young, alive, willing to take on the challenge of letting the whole world know what kind of a man Preston Sinclaire was.

Inspecting the makeup she had bought, she decided she had chosen wisely. The dark lipstick, eye shadow, and blush would do wonders for her, helping accentuate the freckle and giving her face just the right contrast. But she would not apply it until tomorrow morning. Right now she was exhausted. Her bloodshot eyes told her she'd better get some rest. She had a full day ahead of her.

Lying down and hugging a pillow, Pamela fell asleep in minutes.

After paying the night clerk, Microtel security chief Nick DeGeaux got a key to the room adjacent to Pamela Sasser's. His brother Tom waited by the elevators, leaning against the wood paneling, one hand resting on the thick leather belt looped around the tight pair of Wranglers.

Nick approached him. "Go get the truck and then come back. I got us a room."

"You mean, we're staying here?"

"She's in two forty-one. We're in two forty-three, a single room. I get the bed and you get the couch."

"All right," Tom responded before turning around and mumbling, "Man, this is so cool."

After his brother left, Nick briefly closed his eyes, shook his head, and walked toward the elevator.

Harrison Beckett let the tails take up their spots across the street. It now became obvious to Beckett that the two rough-looking characters that went inside were not aware of the two that had followed them on foot, or of the other pair in the white sedan parked a block down the street. And nobody knew Beckett was there, up on the roof of the Chinese restaurant next door to the hotel. The spot gave Beckett an excellent view of the two tails across the street, and also of the parking lot.

All cars had been left behind, parked in front of the grocery store, except for the suspected female CIA officer's white sedan. After seeing where Pamela and her tails had landed, Beckett had returned to the parking lot and driven his own car to the rear of the closed-down Chinese restaurant, where he climbed to his current spot and realized that the black truck with the tinted windows was also parked in front of the hotel. One of its owners had apparently gone back and retrieved it.

Beckett now began to fight a new enemy: extralarge, bloodthirsty Louisiana mosquitoes. His right hand reached for the pack of Marlboro Golds in his back pocket. In the last eight hours, Beckett had gone through half a pack. *So much for kicking this fucking habit.*

He was about to reach for the lighter but decided against it. The glow of the cigarette might give his position away to the surveillance team on the street.

Damn, I need a smoke!

As he went to place the pack of cigarettes back into his pocket, Beckett noticed a mosquito sucking away at the top of his hand.

The silver-and-turquoise jewelry around Esther Cruz's wrists and neck rattled when she slapped the back of her neck, silently cursing the damned mosquitoes that infested this state. Her fingers felt a number of lumps on the back of her neck. Several lumps already grew on her forearms. Her back pressed against a brick wall and a Dumpster shielding her position from the hotel, Esther heard the flying invertebrates zooming by her ears. As tired and aggravated as she was, Esther would have gladly traded in her piece for a can of insect repellent.

"That's a bitch only for the first few days," commented Agent Liem Ngo, sitting next to Esther, a row of glistening white teeth widening in his oval-shaped face as he grinned.

Agent Calvin Johnson sat with Agent Jessica White in the white sedan a block away.

Esther Cruz turned to her subordinate. "What?"

"The bugs, Mother. After a while they don't bite you anymore."

"What kind of crap's that, Liem?"

"Something to do with your body odor, I think," the native of Los Angeles said, still smiling. "My father once told me that after so many bites your body automatically starts releasing a scent that keeps the bugs away. Dad told me these mosquitoes are tiny compared to the ones back in Vietnam, and no one used repellent over there. Your body simply learned to get rid of them. See, none of them're biting me."

Esther Cruz inspected her subordinate's face, neck, and arms, and she realized that Liem didn't have a single mosquito bite on him. *I'll be damned.* She shrugged it off before turning her attention back to the hotel across the street.

She reached for her two-way radio. "Watcher One to Watcher Two," she whispered into the small hand-held unit.

Static preceded Jessica's voice. "Watcher Two has nothing to report."

Esther looked at Liem and said, "Is Calv sleeping?"

A moment of static followed by "Yes."

"Wake him up in two hours and switch."

"Got it."

Turning off the unit, Esther looked at the Vietnamese's face in the wan moonlight. "You get the first watch," she said. "Wake me up in a couple of hours."

"Sure, Mother."

Esther lay sideways on the street and crossed her arms. The place stunk, but she had slept in worse shitholes than this one. At least she was dry and warm.

In the darkness of the alley, Mother Cruz, staring into the corroded bottom of the huge Dumpster, slowly closed her eyes and fell asleep.

*   *   *

Sitting up in bed, Nick DeGeaux stared out the window and down at the pool behind the hotel. His brother sat on the couch and watched TV.

Ten thousand bucks. On the table next to the bed was an envelope with ten big ones. *Just like that.* And ten more if he did this thing right. But to *do* it right he had to find the famous diskette, which had not been in the box of diskettes he'd found in the woman's apartment. Sinclaire had sent them back to the apartment to follow her and wait for instructions.

Nick looked at the cellular phone next to the envelope. Sinclaire had given it to Nick a few hours ago. At any moment the president of Microtel could call and order Nick to kidnap Pamela Sasser. If it came to that, Sinclaire promised Nick an additional fifteen thousand for a clean job with no witnesses.

A loud laugh broke his train of thought. His brother held his belly in laughter while watching cartoons.

Fucking Looney Tunes!

Nick reached for the remote and turned the TV off.

"Hey, man! I was—"

"We got a long day tomorrow, little brother. Get some sleep."

"Shit, man." Tom DeGeaux leaned back on the sofa while picking his nose. "That was a good 'toon, man."

Nick turned off the light. "Shut the fuck up and go to sleep. And if you start snoring I'll throw your ass out of the room."

Esther Cruz saw the rain pounding against the sidewalk as she clutched an umbrella close to her body. She waved at the man sitting in the rear seat of the yellow taxicab, and he waved back. Through the rain, Esther saw his face. She wasn't sure if the drops rolling down his cheeks were actual tears, or just rainwater from his soaked hair, but the sadness in his eyes could not be disguised. For a moment, she wanted to rush toward the car and pull him out before it was too late, but she had tried and failed many times before.

She could never seem to catch up with that departing taxi carrying her husband, Arturo.

The taxi's wheels turned, splashing water onto the sidewalk. Esther looked into the rear window as the cab sped down the street, and she saw Arturo pounding on the glass. She saw his lips move but could hear no sound through the rain, yet she could have sworn that the thunder accompanying forks of lightning streaking across the sky cried out for her.

Esther couldn't take it anymore and she broke into a run. Her husband screamed his love for her, yet she couldn't go any faster. Somehow her legs felt heavy.

Esther screamed at the driver to stop, but he just kept going, and as the car turned the corner, she saw her husband one final time before the vehicle went up in flames.

Mother Cruz jerked in her sleep and opened her eyes. The rusted Dumpster filled her field of view. Her eyes stared in curiosity and surprise at a rat standing on its hind legs checking her out. A pair of tiny red eyes glared at the FBI agent from the safety of the narrow space between the Dumpster and the brick wall.

Slowly, quietly, Esther reached into her side pocket and pulled out the last of her beef jerky. She removed the plastic wrapping and tossed it at the rat.

The rodent dropped to all fours, stuck out its head, took a whiff of the dehydrated beef, snatched it with its sharp little front teeth, and took off.

Inhaling deeply and closing her eyes brought images of Arturo, of a new house in Bethesda, Maryland, of a life that had come to an end by the metal-ripping blast of a car bomb. She remembered witnessing the powerful explosion, remembered the closed-casket memorial service, the funeral, the grieving turning to uncontrollable fury; the fury turning to cold, calculated anger.

I will catch those bastards, Arturo, mi amor. I will catch them for you!

Images of a life that would never be again filling her mind, Esther Cruz slowly went back to sleep.

Up on the roof of the Chinese restaurant across the street, another person was having a nightmare. Harrison Beckett also saw a taxicab, but it was not raining. He saw the small red Fiat cruising by the Roman Colosseum as several groups of tourists left the safety of their coaches and ventured inside the ancient structure. A potpourri of languages mixed with the gusts of winds sweeping through the large openings in the stone structure and across the street, swirling Beckett's brown hair as his eyes inspected every male tourist in the area.

The memory of Layla Shariff's dying eyes as fresh in his mind as the glossy paint of the first-class coaches parked across the street, the haunted DIA operative remained well hidden from view, standing in a recess between two narrow souvenir shops, his face shadowed by a green-and-red awning running the entire length of the block opposite the Colosseum.

Arms crossed, a pair of dark sunglasses and a three-day stubble hiding the features broadcast to every American embassy around the globe, Harrison Beckett slowly studied the crowd, carefully looking at each man, some of whom his mind quickly discarded. Too tall. Too short. Too old. Too fat. Until his eyes coolly focused on a strong possibility, on a male tourist with the right height and weight, with a similar build, within his age group.

And Beckett would follow that man for hours, through streets and sights, while browsing at a souvenir shop, while stopping at a sidewalk cafe, while pausing for a picture at the Fountain of Trevi or at the Vatican.

Beckett followed him, his mind measuring the angles, considering the possibilities, deciding on the right time to strike.

Then night came. Darkness surrounded him, engulfed the alley as he approached the stranger from behind, hands reaching for the throat. His victim turned around, eyes frozen in horror.

Please . . . no . . . no . . . stop . . .

Beckett heard the cry, saw the face of his victim, heard his plea, felt the pressure against his neck, the choking pressure, fingers digging into soft flesh, crushing the larynx.

Please . . . no . . . no . . . stop . . .

Beckett shuddered and woke up, sweating, tensed, hands on his neck, breathing heavily, the stars filling him as his wide-open eyes gazed around him almost in a trance, confused, a knot in his stomach, a lump in his throat.

Rome.

It was always Rome, the city where he found a new life, but not without a price, not without a curse.

Sitting up, Beckett rubbed the cool sweat off his cheeks before eyeing his watch. Nine o'clock in the evening. He had been sleeping for just over forty-five minutes, and he doubted he would be able to fall asleep again for some time, not while adrenaline seared his veins, while a vision of his past scourged his restless soul.

Slowly, he checked the street below to make sure nothing had changed. Harrison Beckett wiped the perspiration off his neck and leaned back down, his hand automatically going for the Marlboros he couldn't smoke, his mind wishing he had refused this contract, had turned down the DIA's proposal.

Too late for that, Harrison. You have to carry it through, have to perform.

Crossing his arms, the former DIA officer took a deep breath and simply looked at the stars.

7 Professionals and Amateurs

Knowledge itself is power.

—*Francis Bacon*

BATON ROUGE, LOUISIANA
Tuesday, November 17

Wearing the same pair of jeans and the new LSU shirt, Pamela Sasser left her room and headed for the elevators. Her short blond hair and dark makeup giving her a new radical look, Pamela stopped halfway down the hallway and turned around, opting for the stairs instead. She reached the lobby thirty seconds later, turned in her key at the front desk, and walked outside.

Fine brows now crowned her blue-green eyes as she began to walk across the parking lot. She had woken up several times during the night pondering her situation, and every time her mind told her to leave Louisiana immediately, put as much distance as she could between herself and Microtel, and only then expose them.

But first things first.

She had to reach her bank, close out the account, and take

a taxi to the airport, where she would buy a ticket for the next plane leaving Baton Rouge.

Scattered clouds moved lazily across a blue sky, slightly stained with hues of orange and yellow from the slowly rising sun. Early-morning student traffic clogged Nicholson Drive as the former LSU associate professor warily scanned the parking lot ahead. A crimson ball loomed over the magnolias and oaks lining the four-lane street.

In spite of her dilemma, Pamela actually was enjoying her physical change, especially her short hair. It was definitely easier to keep up than when it fell a few inches below her shoulders. She also liked the color, which reminded her of her early LSU days, when she had been in the habit of changing hair color every few months. One of her boyfriends had told her she looked her best as a blonde. He'd claimed that it gave her a radical, somewhat immoral air, which he'd found absolutely irresist—

An arm grabbed her across the neck from behind and lifted her off the ground. Choking from the pressure against her larynx, Pamela tried to scream, to kick, to do anything. But before she could react, another hand entered the scene, this one holding a white handkerchief.

The sun, the skies, the heavy traffic on Nicholson Drive vanished as the white cloth swallowed her face.

She inhaled once, instantly regretting it. Her throat and lungs felt on fire. Pamela lifted her hands and grabbed the arm deadlocked around her neck, long red fingernails digging into the assailant's flesh.

"Fucking bitch!"

The pressure around her neck intensified, her larynx about to give. She began to feel weak, light-headed. The shouts and curses from the man behind her slowly faded away. Her hands began to tremble. Her legs tingled. Another deep breath, and Pamela stopped kicking, her body quickly going limp, but not her mind. It struggled for a few more seconds, fighting to remain focused, thinking of a way out. Slowly, she passed out.

*   *   *

"Damn it!" screamed Nick DeGeaux as Pamela's hands finally let go of him, leaving ten half-moon-shaped cuts down the length of his tanned forearm. He cursed not only Pamela Sasser, but also Preston Sinclaire, who had ordered her kidnapping just fifteen minutes ago.

Placing an arm under her shoulders and another one under her knees, he lifted her light frame while his brother Tom got their truck.

Hearing a noise behind him, Nick turned, only to be welcomed by an elbow driven hard into his nose. Tears rushed to his eyes from the stinging pain. The bastard had broken his nose. Blood spewed out his nostrils and over his closely trimmed beard.

Shit!

Dropping Pamela and bringing both hands to his eyes and bleeding nose, the forty-five-year-old ex-marine watched the blurry image of a stranger pivot on one leg, before falling to his knees from the powerful blow to the right side of his head. Nick's knees had not even made contact with the cool asphalt when another knee came crashing against his bleeding face, before everything turned dark.

Harrison Beckett picked up Pamela. Besides the strong chloroform smell, the first thing that Beckett noticed was how little she weighed for her height. Her long black hair, now cut almost as short as his, smelled of shampoo and hair dye, and, yech! Chloroform! Her dark makeup was heavily overdone, but Beckett gave her credit for attempting to change her appearance. It showed that there were some brains behind that pretty face.

His thoughts went to the second tail, the one he had seen racing for the dark truck with the tinted windows. Scanning the parking lot, Beckett saw him behind the wheel and heard him gunning the engine.

The truck leaped forward, burning ten-foot-long tracks of rubber, accelerating directly toward him. Beckett threw Pamela over his right shoulder, turned around, and raced in between a row of cars, reaching the side of the hotel, where many oaks, cypresses, and magnolias cluttered a large field along the side of the four-story building, partially blocking the pool behind the hotel.

The screeching sound of tires followed by the clicking of cowboy boots racing over asphalt behind him, Beckett raced deeper into the woods, struggling to increase the gap between him and the second tail. Pamela restricted his freedom of action, and he had no idea how good this guy was. Although the first one had been just a muscle-head with the reflexes of a snail, his experience told Beckett to treat his current pursuer as a highly trained professional.

The unmistakable sound of a gunshot ripped through the morning air like a whip, the round exploding in a cloud of bark just inches to his left. The impact of disintegrating bark, like soft shrapnel, stung his side. A second shot rang in his ears long after the ground exploded by his feet.

Cutting left, he hid behind a wide magnolia, Pamela still hanging limp over his right shoulder, his left hand reaching for the Beretta tucked in his blue jeans.

Beckett waited. No more shots, only distant screams and shouts. No sirens . . . yet.

"I'm gonna kill you, motherfucker!"

Beckett shook his head at the comment. *An amateur. Never give out your position.*

Although common sense told him he should feel relieved that his assailant was not a professional, the seasoned operative in Beckett knew better. Professionals always abided by certain rules, and Beckett knew how to counter them. But not amateurs. There was nothing a professional operative hated more than dealing with unpredictable rookies, who at times could turn out to be more dangerous than a trained assassin.

"You fucked with the wrong guys, asshole!" the rookie screamed as he approached the wide tree behind which Beckett and Pamela hid.

Did he see Beckett actually reach this tree, or was he just walking and shouting without a target? Beckett couldn't tell.

Damned rookie!

A professional would never give out his position and simply come charging blindly through the woods. Didn't he realize that Beckett could also be armed and hiding behind one of a dozen trees surrounding him? That was one of the problems with amateurs, they made suicidal moves, but in the process of getting themselves killed they could get lucky and take out their enemy as well.

Steadily inching his body to the left, Beckett kept the wide magnolia between the rookie and him, holding the Beretta over his left shoulder, fingers tightly curled around the alloy handle, index finger fixed around the trigger.

"Come out and play, motherfucker!"

Beckett saw him now, a thin, medium-height blond slowly walking past the magnolia and clutching a large revolver. The ex–DIA officer scooted the opposite way just enough to have a clear shot with his free hand.

"This is it, asshole. No more——"

With his legs spread for balance, and with Pamela's weight now burning a hole in his right shoulder, Beckett lined him up and fired once, the explosive round taking off the rookie's shooting arm at the elbow. Blood jetted from his crippled arm like a fountain. Harrowing screams preceded the rookie turning around, staring at his own forearm rolling by his feet, the hand still clutching the dark weapon, cartilage and shattered bones protruding where the elbow had been.

Screaming at the top of his lungs, his face contorted in pain, eyes bulging in anger and shock, the blond amateur dropped to the ground, left hand grabbing for the bloody weapon.

Beckett fired again. The round hit the rookie between the eyes. He fell back without another sound. And without another thought, Beckett switched Pamela to his other shoulder and raced for the fence around the pool, reaching it in thirty seconds. The rented Escort was parked across the street, behind the Chinese restaurant.

*   *   *

Mother Cruz reached the large man with the broken face a few seconds before Agent Liem Ngo. In all her years with the Bureau she'd never seen someone as fast and efficient as the stranger who'd carried Pamela Sasser away after taking out this guy.

His friend in the truck had run after the stranger and Pamela in the woods next to the hotel. Esther turned to her subordinate, whose face showed the surprise and excitement of his first real assignment.

"Stay here and cover the parking lot."

Liem pointed to the woods to the side of the hotel. "But what about—"

"I'll handle it! You stay right here and wait for Jessica and Calv! Also, call an ambulance. This guy's pretty banged up."

Breathing heavily and already sweating, Esther stood and started running for the woods when the first shot went off, the silver-and-turquoise jewelry rattling with every step, her salt-and-pepper hair flapping loose in the wind. Reaching for the Colt .45 automatic tucked under her loose T-shirt, the veteran FBI agent flipped the safety, holding the weapon with both hands over her right shoulder, muzzle pointed at the sky.

She heard shouts, curses, and another shot. As she reached the line of trees, she could see the silhouette of a man holding a gun roughly a hundred feet away. Then another shot thundered, and the man's arm split off at the elbow. Screams of pain followed. As the gunman fell and tried to grab his weapon with his remaining hand, another shot whipped across the woods. Then there was silence.

Mother Cruz moved cautiously. She had not seen the second shooter but assumed it was the stranger who'd taken Pamela Sasser. Esther walked sideways from tree to tree, pressing her back against the bark and glancing at the terrain ahead over her left shoulder while holding the Colt over her right.

Nothing.

She continued, slowly advancing, selecting trees close

enough to minimize exposure, yet far enough to maximize terrain coverage. All senses now worked in unison. Vigilant eyes scanned the grounds, looking for a shape that didn't belong; ears listened intently for the sounds of footsteps over the ocean of leaves covering her sneakers; limbs moved together with the harmony of a ballet dancer's.

Reaching the fallen man, Esther glanced at him not out of curiosity, but to see where the shots had come from. This she quickly figured out by looking at the hole in between the eyes and remembering which way the man had faced before being gunned down.

Cutting right, Esther Cruz took pursuit. The stranger had to be close. The footprints over the blanket of leaves showed her the way to the back of the pool and into the parking lot of a Chinese restau—

She heard a car, a white Ford Escort, fishtailing as it accelerated. She could fire but could not risk hurting Pamela Sasser. Besides, her role here was limited to following Pamela in the hope that she would lead the FBI closer to the Web.

The vehicle went around the restaurant and reached Nicholson Drive heading north, toward Interstate 10. Esther reached for her two-way radio shoved in the back pocket of her blue jeans.

"Ford Escort, white. Don't lose it!"

"Got it!" said Jessica White in the backup car.

Tucking the weapon in her chest holster, Mother Cruz ran back through the woods, gave another glance at the poor bastard bleeding over the leaves, reached the hotel parking lot, and grabbed Agent Liem Ngo away from the crowd gathering around the bearded man. A woman was leaning over, checking his pulse.

"Let's go," said Esther, tugging at Liem's arm.

"What about him?" Liem asked, giving Esther a puzzled look.

"Did you call an ambulance?"

"The hotel clerk did."

Wiping the film of sweat off her forehead and brows with

the shoulder of her T-shirt, Esther began to walk away just as sirens became discernible in the distance.

"Let's go get the car."

"Wait," said Liem, trying to catch up with Esther. "Don't we want to find out what he knows?"

"Not now," Esther responded in between breaths while picking up her pace to a light jog, her heart pounding, her mouth dry and pasty, her mind cursing her luck and her extra fifteen pounds. "We gotta stay close to this Sasser woman . . . and this mysterious superman. Besides, we don't want anyone to know that the FBI was . . . was anywhere near this place. With luck nobody . . . will realize that this woman was Pamela Sasser. Now, I'm almost fucking out of breath, so don't make me talk while I'm running!"

Special Agent Jessica White eased herself into the morning traffic on I-10 heading toward New Orleans, purposely keeping her speed below fifty to let the Escort get about a half mile ahead. Her blue eyes scanned the road, looking for cars to use as a temporary shield, but without ever letting her subject out of her sight.

"You're getting too far away from them," said Agent Calvin Johnson as he buckled up and put on a pair of sunglasses.

Jessica eyed the rookie agent and gave him a condescending shake of the head. "Get too close at the beginning of a tail and risk getting burned. Didn't they teach you that at Quantico?"

The beginning of a tail, particularly when the subject was probably expecting to be followed, was the most critical phase of a surveillance job. She had to follow the Escort close enough to keep an eye on it, but far away enough not be noticed in the sparse traffic flowing toward New Orleans.

But such tasks came naturally to Jessica White. After spending several years tailing drug dealers in Los Angeles, the tough agent knew exactly where to place her vehicle to remain exactly on that fine line between losing her subject and getting burned. Instincts, honed to near·perfection by years of fieldwork, surfaced automatically for Jessica White, telling her when to accelerate, slow down, or change lanes. Her body became one with the machine, a mere extension of her senses. Jessica blended herself with traffic so that never in the same minute was she in the same relative position from her subject, but she did it without bringing any attention to herself.

"I still say he's getting too far away," insisted Calvin Johnson.

Jessica was beginning to agree with the junior agent. The man driving the Escort was making her job a lot more difficult by accelerating way beyond the flow of traffic, rapidly getting too far ahead for Jessica to feel comfortable.

Pressing her right foot over the gas, the seasoned Fed inched her way to seventy in a fifty-five zone, and she still was losing ground to the Escort.

"Slow down, damn it!" she hissed under her breath, cursing her subject for forcing her to stick out from the dozen cars separating them. Jessica White prayed that her subject would come to his senses and slow down. Otherwise, she estimated a minute, perhaps two before getting burned.

After catching himself going almost twenty miles above the posted limit, Harrison Beckett slowed down and set the cruise control to fifty-five. He didn't want to get pulled over by a state police cruiser with an unconscious woman in the backseat. The smell of chloroform made his eyes water, forcing him to lower the electric windows.

Amateurs! Nobody used chloroform anymore. Those idiots were operating in the dark ages. Chloroform was not only too obvious because of its strong smell, sometimes making the intended victim aware of its presence before an attack, but it also could cause serious damage to the lining of the lungs. And besides, Beckett had no way to jump-start Pamela back into consciousness. Unlike the passive chemicals Beckett used to incapacitate his targets, the active ingredients in chloroform temporarily deadened the section of the brain responsible for all sensory functions. Now

Beckett would have to wait at least twelve hours before Pamela would come back around.

That's just as well, he reflected while considering his options. Last night, while he'd scanned the parking lot and the hotel, Beckett had decided to take out all the tails before moving on Pamela. The sudden attack by two of the tails had forced the ex–DIA officer to come out in the open and rescue her.

He sighed at the irony. *Rescue her! Heck, I'm supposed to be killing her!*

Now, as he wondered what to do with her, Beckett decided that the one thing he could not do was kill her—at least not right away. He decided this not only because an autopsy would reveal a high accumulation of chloroform in her system—not that it really mattered anymore how Pamela Sasser died—but also because of his growing curiosity regarding her involvement in all this. What was the connection between Layla's assassin at the restaurant and this woman?

Swamplands sporadically broken up by extensive fields of sugarcane rushed past his side window. Harrison Beckett's thoughts returned to Jackson Brasfield and the mysterious assistant. His instincts told him there was a connection, but he couldn't see it. *Why does he want this woman dead?* Was Pamela Sasser really a traitor, just another seller of top-secret computer algorithms to the other side? And what about Dr. Eugene LaBlanche? Beckett recalled the proof Brasfield had shown him, and he had believed them. Otherwise, why would the Defense Intelligence Agency want an apparently harmless old man terminated? On the other hand, could this all be part of a larger game, one he couldn't even begin to piece together yet? Since he couldn't think of a single thing to refute that theory, his professional mind had to consider it as a plausible scenario: Dr. Eugene LaBlanche and Pamela Sasser had to die because of something they either knew or had created, and Beckett had been the DIA's scalpel, quietly removing the tumors without disturbing the rest of the system.

Of course, there was also the possibility that General

Jackson Brasfield knew about Beckett's past, or at least suspected him, and had one of his own men made up to look
like the Cairo assassin to test Beckett. But the question came
back again: If that was the case, why didn't Brasfield simply
kill Beckett when he had the chance? Unless Brasfield
wanted Beckett to carry out this mission first. Perhaps the
DIA wanted a good, expendable assassin to do this job but
never live to tell the story. The multiple tails on Pamela
Sasser certainly tended to support that theory.

Shaking the thought, Beckett concentrated on the road,
periodically checking the rearview mirror. He had a half
tank of gas, plenty to make it to New Orleans, eighty miles
away. One thing about driving on this road connecting New
Orleans to Baton Rouge was the visibility. The place was
as flat as a lake on a calm day, and the road shooting straight
for miles provided him with an excellent view of the traffic
ahead and behind. This morning he had seen just a few
dozen automobiles and a dozen or so trucks loaded with
sugarcane. This was the month of November, the height of
the sugarcane season, which started in late September and
ended at Christmas. Plantation owners cut the cane and
trucked it to sugar mills all over the southern section of the
state, where it was processed into brown sugar, and then
taken to a refinery to produce the fine sugar that went in the
coffee Beckett had not had in twenty-four hours. And missing his daily dose of caffeine was slowly driving him to the
edge. At least now it was safe to smoke again without the
fear of giving out his position. Reaching for the Marlboro
Golds and the lighter, Beckett lit one and took a long draw.
The nicotine relaxed him, helping him focus.

A sign on the road informed him of an upcoming exit,
where he could get something to eat and drink. But another
sign flashed in his mind: *Keep going*.

His disciplined side kept the Escort on the interstate. Until
he reached New Orleans, where he could find a million
places to hide, Harrison Beckett would feel too exposed.
Nothing but swamps, fields of sugarcane, and concrete highway. No place to hide if spotted.

His eyes constantly scanning the rearview mirror, Harrison Beckett cruised toward New Orleans.

Liem Ngo put their dark sedan in gear and zoomed toward the interstate. Esther Cruz sighed. They had lost exactly twelve minutes racing through the northern portion of the campus until reaching the parking lot, where they had left their vehicle the night before. After catching her breath and wiping off the sweat from her face and neck, Esther grabbed the cellular phone and dialed Jessica White's mobile number.

"Yes?" Calvin Johnson answered.

"Where are you?"

"About ten miles east of Baton Rouge. Subject's headin' for New Orleans at the speed limit, which just went up to sixty-five."

Ten miles away. If Jessica was doing sixty-five, then there was a good chance Esther could catch up with them before reaching New Orleans.

"All right. Stay with them, but be careful. That guy with Pamela's a professional. Don't let him spot you."

"Got it."

Esther hung up the phone and glanced at Liem Ngo as they reached the service ramp leading for the eastbound side of I-10.

"Step on it, Liem. We gotta catch up with them."

Harrison Beckett got off at the first exit in New Orleans, Veterans Boulevard, and steered into a Texaco. He propped up Pamela on the passenger seat to give the impression that she was just sleeping. Getting out and locking the car, he paid cash for a large cup of black coffee, three chocolate doughnuts, a map of the city, and two packs of Marlboro Golds. He had nearly chain-smoked his last pack in the past hour and his throat felt on fire. But Beckett didn't give a damn. The nicotine filling every inch of his system kept him calm but frosty.

He drove back to the highway five minutes later. The

coffee brought him back to life, and after not eating a thing since lunch yesterday, the mediocre Texaco doughnuts tasted like heaven. By the time he reached Causeway Boulevard five miles later, his stomach was content and his mind worked at full speed from the dose of caffeine. He tore open one of the packs of cigarettes, pulled one out with his lips, grabbed the silver lighter from his side pocket, and lit up. *Fucking habit!*

The car filling with cigarette smoke, Beckett got off at Causeway and headed north, driving under the posted limit on the right side of the four-lane boulevard until he found what he sought: a Wal-Mart with a parking lot filled with early-morning shoppers.

He drove slowly between the rows of cars, looking for the right kind of vehicle. He had to switch transportation. In fact, he should have done it before leaving Baton Rouge, but he had been too concerned about being followed by more unpredictable rookies.

Now, after having checked his rearview mirror all the way down to the Crescent City, the professional in him felt a bit more confident that he might not have been followed. Still, the rental car posed a liability he needed to shed as soon as possible before arriving at his final destination: the French Quarter and its hundreds of hotels, clubs, and restaurants packed inside a two-square-mile area. The perfect place to hide.

He found the car he needed: an old, beat-up Chevrolet Caprice, easy to steal and probably without an alarm system.

He parked two rows down from the Caprice, locked the door, and walked slowly to his target, cautiously scanning the large, sunlit parking lot.

All clear.

Pulling his hunting knife from a leg strap under his jeans, Beckett slid the stainless-steel blade in between the glass panel and the door lock on the driver's side. The lock snapped and he opened the door. No alarm.

Five minutes later, after hot-wiring the Chevy, driving by the Escort, and switching Pamela to the larger rear seat,

Beckett cruised back onto the interstate. The unfolded map on his lap showed him the way to City Park, a vast wooded area and golf course in the middle of the city. In there Harrison Beckett planned to ditch the Chevy and spend the rest of the day smoking and waiting for nightfall.

Mother Cruz smiled. The seasoned FBI agent had been waiting for the stranger to switch cars, and Esther had actually been quite surprised that he had waited this long to do it. Normally a fugitive would want to abandon the getaway car very close to the scene of the crime before escaping. That way he would leave his tails wondering which way he had gone. But this stranger, as professional as he had seemed back in Baton Rouge, had not abided by this cardinal rule.

Is he just a rookie with good hand-to-hand combat training? Esther Cruz couldn't buy that. That guy had been good enough to remain out of sight during the entire night, forced out in the open only after those two bozos had attempted that amateurish kidnapping of Pamela Sasser. And who exactly were those two clowns anyway? The question had popped in and out of her mind while she sat next to Liem on the drive from Baton Rouge. Had she made the right call by staying with Pamela and the stranger? Somehow her gut had told her that the bearded man with the broken face wouldn't lead her anywhere. And her gut feeling had guided her through perilous waters before and never let her down. Still, she couldn't help wondering who they were, and what they were doing tailing Pamela Sasser. They had been too slow and just plain stupid to belong to an intelligence or terrorist organization.

Superman also had Esther quite intrigued. Who was he? How did he fit in the picture? If he was Brasfield's latest assassin, sent to take care of Pamela Sasser and protect the ring of corruption, then why did Superman *rescue* Pamela Sasser? Why protect her? To make sure she died? Was he planning an "accident" of some sort? Could this be the same assassin who took out Dr. LaBlanche while making it look like a heart attack?

Esther Cruz shook her head as she began to attack what was left of her fingernails. Too many questions, and she had a hard time thinking on an empty stomach, whose constant rumbling had already drawn a few smiles from Liem Ngo at the wheel.

Esther Cruz briefly glanced at her subordinate while nibbling the end of her thumb. "One more laugh and you get the shit watch tonight," she said while turning her eyes to the morning traffic on the interstate.

MICROTEL HEADQUARTERS.
BATON ROUGE, LOUISIANA

Tuesday, November 17

Preston Sinclaire pounded closed fists against the mahogany table in his large conference room, his black-and-gray tie swinging like a pendulum from his neck. He had come a very, *very,* long way to get where he was, and quite frankly felt too old to be putting up with these problems.

"Fucking DeGeaux! Damn!"

Maria Torres stood rigid, her olive coloring looking a few shades lighter, her gaze on the dark gray carpet.

Sitting down and exhaling heavily, the CEO of Microtel brought a hand to his chin while he regarded his secretary, who had not said a word since delivering the news of a shoot-out outside the Residence Inn, the place where Nick Degeaux had followed Pamela Sasser. Apparently it was all over the radio and TV this morning. One man was dead, and another had been critically wounded. There was an eye-witness account of a possible kidnapping by an unidentified man, who'd also been charged with first-degree murder and one count of aggravated assault with intent to kill.

According to Maria, who'd heard the news on the way to work and had casually mentioned it while serving his morning coffee, no names had been released by the police. Preston Sinclaire feared this could only mean one thing: Pamela Sasser was on the run with his algorithm. He had to move quickly.

"Maria?" Sinclaire said in a hoarse voice.

"Yes, sir?" A pair of wet brown eyes met his cold stare.

Sinclaire stood, his tanned face arranging itself into a mask of compassion. "I'm sorry for the language. Between running this company and the campaign, this has been a very stressful week for me. Just get back to work. I'll buzz you if I need you."

"Yes, sir." She turned to leave.

"Ah, Maria. Could you get Sheriff Laroux on the line for me, please?"

"Right away, sir." She left the office.

Sinclaire stared in the distance. East Baton Rouge Parish sheriff Jason Laroux had been recently reelected thanks to the significant campaign contributions and corporate endorsement of Microtel.

After a brief conversation, Sinclaire got the rest of the story from the sheriff, confirming Sinclaire's suspicions. Nick DeGeaux had been taken to Our Lady of the Lake Hospital with a broken nose and multiple skull fractures. His brother Tom had been pronounced dead on the scene. According to eyewitnesses, which included the hotel clerk at the Residence Inn, where Nick and Tom had spent the night, an unidentified man had come and attacked Nick, rendering him unconscious, before kidnapping a still-unidentified woman. Tom DeGeaux had gone after the stranger and gotten killed in the process. The stranger was now wanted for first-degree murder, assault with intent to kill, and kidnapping.

Sheriff Jason Laroux had agreed to come straight to Microtel's headquarters after Preston Sinclaire had mentioned that he might know the identity of the woman kidnapped. Sinclaire had asked Sheriff Laroux to come alone. The sheriff had agreed.

Now, as the strapping native of Shreveport proudly walked into his office wearing a light brown uniform, Preston Sinclaire remembered a time when the sheriff had not walked so tall. It had happened almost eight years before, at a party Sinclaire had held at his plantation north of Baton

Rouge, during the first year of Laroux's term as sheriff. The
celebration commemorating the tenth anniversary of Microtel had been a twenty-four-hour private party for almost one
thousand people. Sinclaire had spared no expense, bringing
in the best Cajun bands in the state to perform for his guests.
Food flowed across six huge tents set up in a circle on the
vast lawn in front of Sinclaire's weekend country estate. The
celebration, which had started early in the morning with
horseback riding, fishing, canoeing, a dozen carnival rides,
barbecues, and crawfish cookouts, among other activities,
had turned wilder early in the evening, when most of the
families with kids left, and the all-adult party began con-
suming gallons of beer and hard liquor, and the music got
louder. Sheriff Jason Laroux was one of the special guests
at the party, and he had been drinking heavily. It turned out
that the sheriff had bumped into an old girlfriend and had
tried to make a pass. The girlfriend, now engaged to another
man, had turned him down flat. An hour later, a very drunk
and nervous Sheriff Laroux had approached Preston Sinclaire with a personal problem. According to the sheriff, the
girlfriend had changed her mind, and they had gone together
inside a bedroom in the plantation home, where, in the middle of the act, she had changed her mind again and begun
screaming rape. The sheriff never meant to hurt her, he'd
just wanted her to be quiet. When Sinclaire arrived at the
room with the sheriff, he'd found her stripped naked, bleeding from the vagina, and with her neck broken, her head
twisted to a repulsive angle.

Preston Sinclaire could have called his security staff and
the local police. An autopsy and lab analysis would have
sent the well-respected Sheriff Jason Laroux to the Louisiana electric chair. Instead, Sinclaire turned a tragedy into a
business opportunity. Sinclaire now owned Sheriff Laroux,
and he saw to it that the sheriff got reelected every term.

Sheriff Laroux removed his chocolate brown, broad-
brimmed hat. An enormous man of forty-three years of age,
with a commanding nose, short black hair, and brown eyes
narrow and attentive, the sheriff moved with an air of self-

importance, which Sinclaire found quite amusing.

Casually pointing to a chair next to him at the head of the conference table, Preston Sinclaire turned his cold stare to the sheriff, saying matter-of-factly, "Listen carefully, Jason. The woman's name is Pamela Sasser. She has something that belongs to me, a computer program stored on a diskette. Are you with me so far?"

The large head, supported by a neck that could have been the envy of any football player, nodded once. Sheriff Laroux's eyes never left Sinclaire's as he said, "Yes, Mr. Sinclaire. Please continue."

"I sent two of my boys to search her apartment yesterday afternoon. They found nothing. I made them follow her with the hope that she would lead them to the diskette, but apparently she has found herself a boyfriend, who not only killed one of my boys and wounded the other, but is now protecting her."

Preston Sinclaire stood, his armor-piercing stare burning a hole in the middle of Sheriff Laroux's face. "She has my computer program, Jason. I want you to put her picture everywhere in this fucking state. I want to turn on the news today and see her face on the screen. I want to open the newspaper tomorrow morning and see her photo on the front page. She is a thief on the run with a first-degree murderer. You get that woman for me, Jason. You bring Pamela Sasser right here, understand?"

"Yes, sir."

"And above all, don't let her talk to the fucking press. You *kill* her and her fucking boyfriend before that happens. You follow me, Jason?"

Sheriff Jason Laroux nodded once and left.

The moment the door closed, Preston Sinclaire made another phone call, this one to Washington, D.C.

NEW ORLEANS, LOUISIANA
Tuesday, November 17
At nine o'clock in the evening, a taxicab pulled up next to the Cornstalk Hotel in the French Quarter. Earlier in the day,

while he drove and smoked around City Park, Harrison Beckett had stopped by a pay phone and had made a one-night reservation using a Visa charge card registered under a fake name. Being mid-November, the historic Cornstalk had a few rooms available for the off-season rate of just five hundred dollars per night.

Getting out, the ex–DIA officer inspected the beautiful hotel. A black, shoulder-high wrought-iron fence, topped with cornstalks painted in yellow, ornamented the front of the hotel. Behind it a rectangular courtyard led to the small hotel. Twenty-five Rooms, had read the advertisement in the Yellow Pages chained to the phone booth. Four fluted columns rose from the wooden front porch and supported a second-story balcony fenced in by a waist-high wrought-iron railing. Soft yellow light behind a dozen floor-to-ceiling windows, each flanked by a pair of black shutters, gave the wood-and-brick structure an air of elegance and warmth.

Beckett paid the taxi driver and opened the rear door. Pamela Sasser half slept in the rear seat. Although her eyes opened from time to time, she was still out of it.

"Sure hope your lady feels better," said the driver.

"Thanks," said Beckett, running an arm under Pamela's shoulders. Although she had no idea what was going on, her legs were strong enough to half walk with help. The drunk-looking couple staggered across the courtyard and into the small lobby.

Massive crystal chandeliers hung from eighteen-foot ceilings framed with heavy wooden molding. Glossy, dark hardwood floors covered the length of the long and narrow lobby, ending by the empty front desk at the other side. The air smelled old, heavy, stale. To his left a pair of burgundy antique sofas with gold throw pillows flanked a small table supporting a crystal lamp. Beckett gently placed Pamela on one of them, careful to set her against the arm of the sofa to keep her from falling on her side. To his left a round staircase curved up to the second floor.

Walking to the front desk, Beckett rang a small bell on

the counter, and a few moments later a young man appeared.

"I called earlier today," Beckett said. "Justin Fergusson."

The clerk behind the counter, a skinny kid of roughly twenty-five, perhaps younger, with blond hair and a long face, smiled. "We have you all set up for room two oh three, with access to the balcony upstairs."

"Great," Beckett said. "We had a long evening in the Quarter and are ready to sign off."

Longface checked his watch. "The night's only beginning around here, sir."

Beckett tilted his head, displaying faked surprise. "Really? But it's after nine o'clock. Over in Bristow, Oklahoma, things are pretty much dead after ten. You learn to do all your drinking early in the evening."

"Well, sir, in this town the party's just warming up."

After Beckett signed the registry, Longface gave him a key. "Up the stairs, third room on your left."

Beckett went back to Pamela and nearly carried her up the steps, which, like the rest of the floors, were also made of oak and creaked on every other step. The stairs led to a long and wide hall of burgundy wall-to-wall carpet. The rooms were to the left. Beckett counted six tall doors with smoked-glass transoms and large gold numbers at eye level. To the right he noticed three unnumbered doors. Staggering, Beckett and Pamela made it to their room halfway down the hall. He pulled out the key and unlocked the heavy wooden door.

Moonlight diffused inside the room through two floor-to-ceiling windows on the opposite wall from where he stood holding Pamela. Two double beds shared a nightstand, where a crystal lamp projected yellowish light over the hardwood floors. Beckett laid her on one of the beds before closing and dead-bolting the solid oak door.

God, he was tired. A bed had never looked so good, but his operative mind kicked back in gear. He had not eaten anything of substance for some time. His body demanded

rest, but it also needed nourishment to keep up with the
events rapidly unfolding before him.

Sitting on the empty bed, Beckett turned off the lamp. He
didn't want anyone from the street looking up into his room,
and he didn't want to close the burgundy curtains because
that would show the room was occupied.

It took a minute for his eyes to adjust to the wan moonlight glazing the room. Snatching the phone on the nightstand, he dialed the front desk.

After getting the number of a twenty-four-hour deli two
blocks away, Beckett offered Longface a fifty if he would
go and fetch him a bag of sandwiches and chips. After set-
tling on seventy-five, Longface arrived at his room thirty
minutes later, took his bribe money, and went back to work.
Beckett consumed two roast beef sandwiches, three small
bags of spicy potato chips, and one large soda before checking on Pamela, who had stopped moving after curling up in
a fetal position, hands together under her chin, as if she were
praying. The sound of her steady breathing combined with
the faint moonlight glow over her slim body brought back
memories of his nights with Layla Shariff. He still mourned
her violent death after all these years.

Who are you, Pamela Sasser? What's the connection?

He needed to get all the information he could from this
beautiful stranger he had been ordered to execute, but whom
Harrison Beckett already knew he would be unable to harm,
and not just because Brasfield might be using him. Looking
down at Pamela Sasser peacefully sleeping awakened the
emotional demons of his mind, long asleep since that night
in Cairo, when a part of him died on the concrete ramp.

The situation had taken an added layer of complexity after
Beckett listened to the radio while driving around City Park
early in the evening. The word was out about the shooting.
Pamela Sasser—the newsman had actually spoken her
name—was on the run with the unidentified murderer of one
innocent civilian. A recent photo of Pamela had been dis-
tributed to every law enforcement agency in Louisiana.

Obviously somebody with the right connections wants Pa-

mela Sasser quite badly. But who? Was Jackson Brasfield now playing a different tune? Did he change his mind about staging Pamela's death after the incident at the Residence Inn? Was he now using the long arm of the law to do his dirty work, and in the process take out Harrison Beckett to eliminate all loose ends?

Beckett found he could not think clearly anymore. His operative mind needed information as much as his body demanded rest.

But first he had to have a smoke.

Pulling out the silver lighter and a pack of Marlboros, Beckett was about to light one up when his eyes noticed the smoke detector up on the ceiling. This was a nonsmoking room.

Standing on the bed, he removed the smoke detector's cover, disconnected the nine-volt battery, and leaned back on the bed. Thirty seconds later he took a long draw while closing his eyes, crossing his legs, and letting his mind relax.

Rest first, then analyze.

His years with the DIA had taught him that food and rest were formidable weapons, never to be underestimated, and just as powerful as the Beretta 92F Beckett removed from the small of his back and set on the nightstand. Without them his mind would grow cloudy, overly paranoid, uncertain. During DIA training exercises at Fort Bragg, Beckett had participated in a surveillance exercise for four days without sleep. Everyone but Beckett had lasted two days. Beckett had managed to stick it out a third day, but after that he remembered little. His performance report showed he had become highly paranoid and incapable of making the simplest decisions at around the seventy-fifth hour of the exercise. And that was after only three days. Beckett had not slept in forty-eight hours. He was only twenty-four hours away from that point.

Without further thought, the ex–DIA officer took his final draw, crushed the butt against the hardwood floor, propped his head with a pillow, and fell asleep.

                    *   *   *

Outside the Cornstalk a bearded man dressed in ragged clothes and sandals limped his way down the dark slate sidewalk, the upper portion of a bottle protruding from the paper bag he held in his right hand, his left pushing a small grocery cart stuffed with dirty sheets, tin cans, and a couple of shoe boxes. The wrinkled black hat and sores on his exposed forearms went perfectly with his knotty long hair and beard, and a body odor that could qualify as a weapon.

But this man needed only one weapon to take another man's life: the stiletto beneath his soiled black shirt. He had killed many times in his years working for the Department of Defense, and many more times before that as an officer of the Egyptian army. Known at the DIA as Hamed Tuani, he was never noticed and seldom heard until he struck, which he did with the swiftness and deadliness of a rattlesnake, quickly retreating after driving the dagger's pointed blade through the heart of his victim.

Hamed was also a superb field observer, always carefully disguised in ways that made people ignore him. And on this breezy night in the French Quarter, with the sounds of jazz bands, the screams and laughter of drunk tourists, and the smell of urine from his shredded pants, Hamed watched the hotel where he had seen a taxicab drop Harrison Beckett and Pamela Sasser two hours ago.

But his emerald green eyes had seen more than that. Hamed had also seen an Asian man and a middle-aged woman go into the hotel. Normally he would have thought of them simply as guests of the hotel, but those two had stalked the Residence Inn in Baton Rouge the night before, and had also come out into the open in the morning, when the two rookies attempted to kidnap Pamela Sasser.

Jackson Brasfield, who'd ordered Hamed to follow Beckett in order to confirm the kill, had told Hamed that the two in the black truck had been from Microtel, a pair of local thugs sent by Preston Sinclaire to bring Pamela in. *Why did Sinclaire make such a stupid move when Brasfield had already contracted a professional?* Hamed had not asked the question and Brasfield had offered no explanation for their

superior's conflicting behavior. Hamed had learned a long
time ago that no one questioned Preston Sinclaire's decisions. A man of his power and influence did no wrong.

Now it rested in Brasfield's—and Hamed's—hands to
limit the damage before it got out of control. They could
not allow anything to damage the reputation of Preston Sinclaire.

Leaving the hotel behind, Hamed quickly reached a van,
which drove him to a leased apartment off Canal Street. It
was time to e-mail his report to Brasfield.

In room 203 of the Cornstalk, Harrison Beckett bolted out
of bed drenched in sweat, holding his neck and gasping for
air. Glancing around the room, terror painted across his face,
right hand groping over the nightstand and clutching the
Beretta, he took a deep breath.

"Jesus Christ!" he whispered as he exhaled, setting the
Beretta back on the nightstand and rubbing moist, shivering
hands over his face.

The room was quiet. The sound of his own heart mixed
with the steady breathing of Pamela Sasser in the dark room.
His hands still trembling, Beckett took a cigarette and the
lighter from his side pocket and struggled to light up.

Giving up on the smoke, he shoved the lighter and the
Marlboros back in his pocket, and sat back in bed wiping
the cool sweat from his cheeks and forehead. Over fifteen
years had passed and the nightmares still haunted him.

Rome, 1981. Three weeks after Cairo.

The marked DIA operative searched for his victim among
the American visitors crowding the streets of Rome. Like a
cornered dog, he had shoved all emotions aside and acted
purely on instinct; his survival depended on his selection.
His eyes saw many tourists, all Americans, all of whom had
the right height, weight, and hair color. Soon, the desperate
officer made his selection, a visiting New Yorker traveling
alone. No one would miss him for some time. The following
night he killed the stranger with his own hands, strangling

him while the New Yorker begged for mercy. The preparation of the body came next. Alone, in the rear of a rented Fiat, the hunter prepared his prey. Fingertips needed sanding, birthmarks and scars required careful removal, teeth needed extraction. Then the officer called the military attaché at the American embassy, requesting cauterization, immediate rescue from the field. Pretending that he didn't know that it was the DIA who was after him, the desperate man led the cauterization team—which Beckett knew would be a termination team—to the rented Fiat. Then came the powerful explosion. The body disintegrated. The desperate officer had set up the charge such that the upper body would vanish beyond trace. As far as the DIA was concerned, the marked officer had ceased to exist. The DIA officer approached a plastic surgeon in Rome, who altered Beckett's face, giving the officer his freedom, his new life. Harrison Beckett then eliminated the surgeon, forever removing all possible links to his previous life. And it had all started in Rome.

Rome.

Over the years Beckett had thought of altering his face back, but he feared he would be recognized and another team sent to finish him off. Now it all seemed a wasted effort since Jackson Brasfield might have figured it all out anyway.

As he slowly rubbed his neck, Harrison Beckett leaned back down on the bed and closed his eyes, his mind slowly replaying the events that took place on that night in Rome, long ago.

8   Good and Evil

*Whoever fights monsters should see to it that in the
process he does not become a monster. And when
you look long into an abyss, the abyss also looks into
you.*

—*Friedrich Nietzsche*

THE PENTAGON. WASHINGTON, D.C.
Tuesday, November 17

XXXXXXXHB AND SUBJECT AT CORNSTALK HOTEL IN
NEW ORLEANS. NO ATTEMPT OF TERMINATION
MADE YETXXXHB'S ACTIONS SINCE SCENE IN BATON
ROUGE SHOWED HIS EXTRAORDINARY CONCERN
ABOUT BEING FOLLOWEDXXXXXPERHAPS HE SUS-
PECTS DIA SURVEILLANCEXXXXXPERHAPS HE HAS
HEARD THE NEWS ON SUBJECT AND FEARS A LOCAL
POLICE TAIL XXXAN ASIAN AND A MIDDLE-AGED HIS-
PANIC WOMAN WHO STALKED THE RESIDENCE INN
FROM ACROSS THE STREET LAST NIGHT HAVE FOL-
LOWED HB AND SUBJECT AND HAVE GONE INSIDE
THE CORNSTALKXXXXTWO MORE STALKERS A WHITE
WOMAN AND A BLACK MAN WERE SEEN IN A CAR
A BLOCK FROM THE HOTELXXXXREQUESTING IN-
STRUCTIONSXXXXXXXX END OF REPORTXXXX

For General Jackson T. Brasfield the situation worsened by the minute. Harrison Beckett had failed miserably in his mission. Although Brasfield blamed Preston Sinclaire's impulsiveness as part of the reason why the contract assassin had reacted the way he did, the director of the DIA was not about to question his superior's judgment.

This had turned into a damage-control situation. Brasfield went through the worst possible scenario: Beckett and Pamela get together. Beckett learns that Brasfield lied to him about Dr. LaBlanche, and the crafty Harrison Beckett makes some bold move, like going to the press or to the Feds with his story in exchange for their freedom. Another possible scenario: Beckett and Pamela are apprehended by the police or the FBI and confess to bargain a deal. Any way Brasfield saw it, the outcome could be quite damaging to Preston Sinclaire and their clandestine operation. He had explained the situation to a very irritable Sinclaire, who'd told Brasfield to call in as soon as the DIA tail following the assassin called in to report.

Another issue also bothered Brasfield: the team tailing Pamela Sasser and Harrison Beckett. Who were they? Who sent them there? How did they know to tail Pamela Sasser?

Brasfield felt he already knew the answer to those questions: There was a leak in the organization. He had to find it and plug it permanently.

Sitting behind his desk, his eyes on the nineteen-inch computer display, General Brasfield reached for the phone and dialed Sinclaire's mobile number.

"Any news?" came the voice of Sinclaire after the third ring.

"Hamed has called in to report. We know where they're hiding. We'll have a team in place within the hour."

"Good. Do it right this time, Jackson. Don't make me get involved and do your job for you."

Brasfield slowly shook his head and closed his eyes. Sinclaire would make a fine politician.

"There's another problem," said Brasfield.

"What is it?"

"There's another team tailing Pamela Sasser and the assassin."

"Another team? Who?"

"We don't know. Could be the Feds."

A few moments of silence were followed by a heavy sigh.

"I think there's a leak in one of our organizations," added Brasfield.

"Do what you have to do," said Sinclaire. "Just make sure Sasser and Beckett are eliminated."

"It will be handled."

"Call me when it's done. And remember, Jackson. No links. If I go down, we all go down."

The line went dead. Brasfield calmly hung up the phone before standing and walking to the windows next to his desk. Loosening the tie of his uniform, the general reached for his pack of Camels and lit one up, drawing heavily while staring at the huge parking lot below, at the few hundred cars under the yellowish bath of mercury lights. Guards with trained dogs at their sides patrolled this section of the secured complex.

Sinclaire has forced us into this situation. There is no turning back now.

Sitting down, the cigarette tucked in between the index and middle fingers of his right hand, Brasfield reached out for the keyboard and typed: TWEP. Terminate with extreme prejudice.

"Before sunrise," Brasfield muttered to himself. "Before sunrise we settle all our problems."

NEW ORLEANS, LOUISIANA

Wednesday, November 18

Sitting in the driver's seat of the sedan parked a block from the Cornstalk, FBI special agent Jessica White sensed movement down the street. Adjusting the rearview mirror, she looked at the dark street without really trying to focus on a particular object. She relaxed her eyes, allowing her peripheral vision, which was more acute at seeing in the night, to discern two dark figures moving across the murky background of the poorly lit street.

A few more seconds and Jessica recognized the black extensions at the end of their arms: automatic weapons. Pulling out her little Smith & Wesson .38 Special, a peashooter compared to an automatic rifle, Jessica suddenly felt hopelessly outgunned. She needed more firepower to survive this one, but her sawed-off shotgun was locked in the trunk. She frowned. Agent Calvin Johnson was supposed to be at that end of the street, covering the Cornstalk.

Weighing her options, she decided to go around the block, get to her weapon, and come back around. But before doing that she had to warn Esther and Liem of the nearing threat.

She reached for the two-way radio on the passenger seat and froze when she saw, through the passenger window, the shape of a hooded man dressed in black, a dark weapon leveled at her.

"Get out," the man said. "Slowly. And don't even think about touching that radio. Your friend down the street tried and never made it."

Jessica knew she had been tricked. Anger filled her. The figures moving behind her had been just a distraction.

Unlocking the door, the FBI agent stepped away from the car, hands behind her neck, her fingers now holding a three-inch throwing blade, which she usually kept strapped to her forearm and covered by a long-sleeve shirt.

"Who are you?" the hooded man asked while motioning her to move away from the street and into the shadow of the sidewalk. Jessica recognized the weapon, a suppressed Heckler & Koch MP5 submachine gun. It didn't matter. She could throw that blade with deadly accuracy in less time that it would take the hooded man to react and pull the trigger.

A look of surprise and shock painted over her face, Jessica remained quiet, hands still over her head. She moved as requested, but before she reached the sidewalk the hooded man spoke again. "I asked you a question. Who are you?"

Jessica simply moved closer, the hooded man only five

feet away now. In a few more seconds she felt she could
take him out easily.

Before she could take another step, a searing pain on her
abdomen, right below the rib cage, made her bend over and
drop the blade. It was at that moment that Jessica White
realized her imminent death.

A hand reached from behind her and clamped her mouth
shut, so that not a single word escaped her lips. The pain
quickly propagated to her upper chest and into her heart.

A van drove up the street, the side door already open by
the time it stopped next to her. A number of hands lifted
her light frame off the wet pavement and threw her into the
van, where she landed next to Calvin Johnson, whose slit
throat was the last thing Jessica White saw before dying.

FBI special agent Liem Ngo stood behind a large potted
plant, next to the stairs on the second floor of the Cornstalk
Hotel. He had been there for nearly five hours now, and
he'd hated every minute of it. His legs were cramping and
he began to feel light-headed from lack of sleep. The adrenaline rush of being right in the middle of his first major case
had long faded away in the predawn hours.

His boss was hiding in one of the empty rooms down the
hall and, unlike Liem Ngo, whose only weapon of defense
was the snub-nosed Smith & Wesson .38 Special tucked in
the small of his back, Esther Cruz carried heavier artillery:
an Uzi submachine gun. The two of them had gone inside
the hotel, flashed their FBI badges to the tall, skinny hotel
clerk, obtained Pamela Sasser's room number, and gotten
information on the second-floor layout. Esther had opted to
split up their surveillance. Wearing miniature earpieces and
small lapel microphones connected to the tiny two-way radios strapped to their chests, the two agents could maintain
constant communication and cover each other if the situation
got nasty. Liem covered the stairs, and Esther, hiding in one
of the unlocked and nearly empty rooms on the right side
of the hall, covered Pamela Sasser's suite, registered under
the name of Justin Fergusson.

Probably fake.

He turned to his right, where the stairs curved as they came up from the first floor. The four-foot-high ornamental iron pot and the six-inch-wide trunk of the palm tree rising up to touch the eighteen-foot ceiling partially blocked his field of view, forcing him to expose part of his body while craning his neck to see the outer section of the winding staircase.

Liem Ngo heard a noise. His body tensed. His breathing stopped, heart pounding in his chest, mouth suddenly turning dry. He wasn't sure what it was—the sound of a person exhaling? Licking his lips, he was about to look toward the stairs again when he saw a dark shape rising from behind the large pot.

His right hand instinctively dove behind his back, and his feet took a step toward the middle of the hallway and away from the looming dark shape on the other side of the pot. But instead of feeling the cold alloy handle of his six-shooter, Liem Ngo felt someone grab his wrist, twisting it in a deadlock just as a stinging pain from his abdomen made his legs buckle and his body shiver in pain.

He tried to scream for help, but the dark figure in front of him reached for his face, clamping his mouth shut. The pain from his abdomen streaked up to his upper chest. Gasping for air, chest being torn apart from the inside, eyes cloudy with tears, Special Agent Liem Ngo managed to use his free hand to tap on his lapel microphone three times before passing out.

Hamed Tuani had shoved the stiletto into his victim's abdomen, right below the rib cage, before driving it upward, behind the ribs and into the heart. He had killed many times this way, his victims dying in seconds with minimal external bleeding, the only mark left on their bodies being the tiny puncture made by the dagger.

The diversion created by one of the members of the termination team had given Hamed the precious seconds he had needed to close the ten-foot gap separating him from his fourth prey of the evening.

Before eliminating the skinny clerk downstairs, Hamed had extracted the information he needed to know, including the FBI team covering room 203, where Harrison Beckett held Pamela Sasser. There was a fourth FBI agent he needed to eliminate before bursting into room 203, and Hamed expected this next termination to go as smoothly as the first four.

He checked his watch. It was 4:04 in the morning. The operation had started four minutes ago, and it would be completed in another six. In ten minutes they would be in a van headed for the airport. Their flight back to Washington left at five. By sunrise the situation would be secured.

The five members of the DIA termination team slipped on gas masks and lined up single file behind Hamed, who also wore the black spandex one-piece suit and mask standard for this type of operation. Slowly, silenced Heckler & Koch MP5 submachine guns in their hands, the group moved down the hall toward the room where the last FBI agent hid.

Twenty-five years with the Bureau had given Mother Cruz a sixth sense when it came to smelling trouble. While on surveillance everything was important, including the light but sudden taps Liem Ngo had made on his lapel microphone. There had been three taps, indicating trouble of some sort, and since the taps didn't follow any of the other standard FBI radio codes or a brief verbal explanation, Esther suspected the worst. Liem had been compromised and she faced extreme danger. Still hopeful, Esther tapped her microphone five times, trying to get a response from Calvin, Liem, or Jessica. She got no answer.

Her room was roughly eighteen feet square, with two windows overlooking a beautiful courtyard with a fountain in the middle and benches and chairs scattered over the cobblestone floor. Furniture in the room was sparse: an old armoire in between the windows, the chair where she sat, a broken mirror leaning against a wall, and a yellowish mattress in the corner.

Clutching the Uzi with her right hand, Esther Cruz moved toward the windows.

Hamed Tuani approached the door first, his hands holding a small sleeping-gas canister with a thin plastic hose attached to the end. Kneeling down, he slipped the free end of the clear tube under the door and turned the knob on the canister. Gas began to flow into the room.

Flanked by the termination team, Hamed waited one full minute before getting up, putting the empty canister aside, and counting down with the fingers of his left hand from five to one. He quietly inserted the master key he had taken from the clerk, unlocked the door, and pushed it open, keeping his body out of the line of fire.

Like shadows cruising in the dark with the grace of a well-choreographed play, his team silently rolled inside, positioning itself on either side of the door, weapons aimed at chest level, index fingers caressing the triggers.

Hamed followed, closing the door as the DIA team scanned the empty room with their suppressed weapons. The white curtains on the two windows danced in the cool breeze.

Where is she? Did we hit the wrong room? Hamed didn't think so. The other agent had been exactly where the clerk had said. *Did she hear us?* Possibly, but where did she go? There was no way to leave the room without alerting Hamed, unless . . .

Hamed's eyes focused on the wooden armoire in between the windows. Too obvious.

But where else could the female agent be? These were second-story windows. He stepped across the unfinished floor and, as two of the DIA men leveled their MP5s at the center of the dark wood armoire, Hamed pulled the doors open.

Empty.

* * *

Mother Cruz hung on to a fire ladder built on the side of the two-story building, just to the right of the window. She had leaped out when she noticed the plastic tube appearing under the door. Her knees bent halfway, right hand firmly grasping the side of the ladder and her left clutching the Uzi, the veteran FBI agent listened intently and watched the edge of the window.

She was in a serious predicament. The easy way out would have been to go down the ladder and split, but she had a feeling that doing so would result in the death of Pamela Sasser and her companion. If she stayed, she might be able to warn them, but perhaps at the price of losing her life.

Think, damn it!

Quickly going through her limited options, Esther chose one which broke a basic FBI rule—firing without warning— but which maximized her chances of surviving, especially since she didn't know just how badly she was outnumbered.

The last time she'd fired a weapon outside of a training exercise was over two years ago, during a raid outside of Washington, when the FBI had assisted the Drug Enforcement Administration in destroying the largest crack house in the District of Columbia. She had killed one man that night.

As she was about to bring the Uzi's muzzle up, Esther Cruz watched a black, bulky silencer move the white curtains aside. A gloved hand cupped the round sound-suppresser attachment. A man wearing a gas mask loomed across her field of view.

Esther Cruz was out of options, and with the Uzi at the right angle, she pressed her body against the ladder and fired.

Hamed watched the head of one of the DIA operatives explode. A round had split the cranium in half. He rolled away from the window just as two more DIA officers fell victims to the sizzling-hot muzzle moving back and forth over the windowsill, sweeping the entire room at waist level. The last two crawled out of the room behind Hamed.

The former Egyptian officer heard a woman screaming inside the target's room. Choosing to ignore the FBI agent still firing into the room, he turned to his two surviving men while pointing at Pamela Sasser's room. "Storm it! Now!"

"Move away from the door!" shouted Harrison Beckett, half-asleep, as Pamela Sasser, her contorted eyes moving from his face to his gun, kept both hands cupping her face while screaming for help at the top of her lungs.

Grabbing the side of the large New Orleans Saints black-and-gold T-shirt he had bought for her, Beckett pulled her down just as gunfire rattled the heavy wooden door, which refused to give.

Dragging the stunned woman toward the windows facing the balcony, Beckett forced her facedown on the floor before dropping to one knee and cocking his weapon.

"Stay down!"

Screams now could be heard from other rooms as the firing subsided. The first burst of gunfire had awakened him and Pamela at the same time. With his mind now quite clear, Beckett realized that the DIA had followed him here. The fact that the DIA wanted to terminate him while he still had two and a half more days to carry out his mission told Beckett plenty about Jackson Brasfield's intentions. Now he would have to depend on his skills to get him—and Pamela Sasser—out of danger.

"You bastard! You animal!" Pamela Sasser pounded against his shoulders as he threw her against the corner of the room to get her out of the way. Her catlike eyes, blue-green in color, filled with hatred as she stared at him, the chocolate freckle twitching over her trembling lips.

"Stay down!"

"Fuck you!" She lunged like a crazed animal, long red fingernails, like claws, aimed at his face.

Beckett moved sideways, grabbed a clump of blond hair with his left hand, and forced her down, pressing her face against the carpet. She kicked him in the back. Beckett let go of her. She got up and ran for the door.

"Stay down, damn it!"

The door burst open, and two men dressed in black came in holding weapons, which they immediately leveled at Pamela. She screamed and braced herself.

Beckett fired four times. Both men arched back while pressing the triggers, cutting multiple tracks on the ceiling as they fell back into the hall. A cloud of white dust fell on Beckett and Pamela from the exploding plasterboard. Beckett reached for Pamela, pulling her by the wrist while keeping the Beretta trained on the entrance.

"Stay with me if you want to live!"

Barely nodding, she moved behind him, her lips quivering, her hands trembling, her eyes displaying the fear and shock that engulfed her.

Silence.

Beckett waited, the center point in the doorway lined up in the Beretta's sights. The smell of gunpowder filled his lungs.

"Open the window and get out!" he said.

Pamela just stood there, trembling, shaking, hugging herself, mumbling something Beckett could not make out.

"C'mon!" He shook her with his free hand. "The window, Pamela. Get the window!"

She jerked at the sound of her name being spoken out loud by this stranger. Who was he? Where were they?

Beckett dropped to one knee, keeping the weapon leveled at the door.

"Now, damn it!"

Pamela Sasser breathed deeply and, while Beckett clutched the Beretta, she slid the tall window up. A breeze swirled the lace curtains. Beckett felt the air cooling the back of his neck.

Suddenly a pear-shaped object shot through the doorway, skittering across the carpeted floor.

Grenade!

Harrison Beckett pivoted on his knee and lunged upward,

embracing Pamela, and propelling them through the open window. Twisting his body in midair, Beckett landed on his back, Pamela on top of him. He knew immediately that he had at least bruised a rib or two, as the breath exploded from his lungs and a sharp pain arced through his chest. But the pain did not overshadow the reality of a grenade about to go off inside the room. Without letting go of Pamela, he forced them into a roll, ignoring Pamela's cries as her back crashed against the wooden surface of the balcony's floor. He had to move away, increase the gap, get out of the blast zone.

Both windows exploded outward in an ear-shattering blast, broken glass stabbing the night in an expanding radial pattern of razor-sharp shrapnel.

Stunned, but fully aware of his situation, the ex–DIA officer pulled Pamela to her feet, the effort sending waves of crippling pain through his rib cage. Together, they jumped over the side railing and onto the flat roof. They had only a few more seconds before whoever threw the grenade inside the room realized that they had escaped.

Glancing backward, Beckett saw his Beretta on the balcony, near the blackened windows, from which gray smoke snaked up to the sky. No time to get it.

"Come on!" Beckett shouted, dragging Pamela over a white-painted roof and to the right side of the hotel, where a tall magnolia hugged the two-story structure.

"Hold on to me!" he screamed, his eyes darting back toward the balcony, smoke still coming out of both windows, his professional side cursing the loss of his weapon.

Pamela hesitated.

"Hurry! There's no time!"

As Pamela wrapped both arms and legs around him, Beckett grabbed a thick branch and used it to swing themselves toward the trunk, nearly losing his grip as his ribs screamed in protest at the effort. His arms burning from the strain, Pamela's warm breath caressing his neck, her heartbeat drumming against his back, Beckett climbed down and landed on the slate floor covering the front courtyard.

Pamela jumped off him. Beckett gave her a short glance. She was still trembling, but her eyes were clear, calmer. They even showed a hint of anger.

They hid on the side of the hotel just as a man dressed in black raced out the front, holding a weapon in his hands. "Shh," Beckett said, his face only inches from hers. "Don't say a word."

She nodded, her chest heaving as she fought to control her breathing, to get ahold of herself.

Standing in the middle of the courtyard in front of the small hotel, the gunman checked the front of the building before walking toward the other side of the hotel, the muzzle of his weapon leading the way.

Beckett waited until he had disappeared from sight before saying, "Come. Follow me."

They raced away from the hotel just as a small crowd began to gather around the entrance. Pamela kept up with him as they turned the corner and slowed down, sirens blaring in the distance.

Breathing heavily, sweat pouring down the sides of his face, his ribs aching, Beckett glanced at Pamela Sasser, her blond hair layered with white dust. Running a hand over it, he dusted it off, and did the same to his, before moving through the empty streets in silence, his hand holding hers. This close to daybreak, the crowd in the Quarter was almost nonexistent.

Pamela Sasser had never been more confused in her entire life than at this very moment, as she ran through dark streets and narrow alleys while holding this stranger's hand. Who was he? Why was he protecting her? How did she get to New Orleans? Who was trying to kill her? Microtel? Preston Sinclaire?

A fusillade of questions pounded her mind as she struggled to keep up with him. It had been over five years since she'd last run like this, since leaving her LSU track-team days behind to concentrate on her engineering career.

Her calves burned as she held on to this stranger, who looked everywhere, past her, behind her, around her, but never directly at her. Only the firm grip as they dashed over wet sidewalks acknowledged her existence.

She noticed the way he moved his body, the way he anticipated a turn, a sideways step, a full stop before suddenly cutting left, or right, or turning around. She felt the way he conveyed his intentions to her through the pressure on her hand. The stranger was talking to her, telling her how to follow him, how to remain by his side, how to remain alive! The commanding clasp, skin against skin, palms rubbing, transmitted intentions in a language far more powerful than any words could ever convey.

Pamela sensed his energy, his will, his desire to remain alive. She had felt his powerful shoulders, chest, and arm muscles while wrapped around him as he climbed down the tree. She could imagine those muscles now, flexing under the black T-shirt. She could feel his strength. He was real, far more real than any man she'd ever known.

Dashing through the night, escaping the guns of faceless men sent to kill her, Pamela Sasser ran even faster, trusting this stranger more than she had ever trusted anyone in her life.

Dressed in a pair of jeans and a loose T-shirt, Hamed Tuani had dumped his black spandex jumpsuit and the suppressed machine gun in a nearby garbage bin and had watched a couple run away from the hotel. The woman, although her hair differed from the picture in the dossier Brasfield had shown him, did fit the description of Pamela Sasser. He recognized her companion as the same man he had seen at Giovanni's. Harrison Beckett, the contract assassin.

Hamed now raced after them, his right hand reaching for the Sig Sauer nine-millimeter automatic shoved in his jeans.

Tennis shoes stomping the dark slate sidewalk, and under the dim yellow glow cast by the ornamental streetlights, Hamed concentrated on finishing off this job. The woman could not get away. In her hands she had the power to sink the entire operation.

He followed them through a dozen streets and half as many alleys, closing the gap, reaching his prey.

"Oh my God. Look!" Pamela pointed to a man racing toward them. Although he was not dressed in black like the others, the dark extension on his right hand telegraphed his intentions.

Increasing the pressure on Pamela's hand, Beckett took off, turning left on the next corner, and then right into a dark alley in the middle of the block. The stench of rotten food and urine struck him like a moist breeze. Overfilled garbage bins lined one side of the murky alley. Rats fed on decomposing food.

"Wait," he said, pressing his back against a brick wall while looking over his right shoulder.

"Who—who are these people foll—"

"Shh. Here he comes."

Beckett heard footsteps approaching. "Move back," he told her.

Dropping to a deep crouch, Harrison Beckett listened as the steps echoed in the night. He waited. The shadow of a running man grew in size. Beckett guessed he was on his side of the street.

The man suddenly ran across his field of view.

Beckett lunged, the heels of his hands aimed at the man's left temple, where a large nerve and an artery ran close to the skin. The bearded man surprised Beckett with his quick reaction, stepping sideways, dodging Beckett's initial strike. As Beckett moved past him, the man pivoted ninety degrees while raising his left knee, striking Beckett in the solar plexus, a large network of nerves located at the bottom of the rib cage.

Bent over, Beckett staggered with pain, nearly falling. He turned his head and saw the man bringing the weapon around. It was Layla Shariff's assassin!

Disciplined instincts forced him to ignore the crippling blow and, turning on his right leg, the ex–DIA officer brought his left leg up and around, striking the hand holding the weapon with a low turning heel kick.

His opponent cried out as the weapon skittered on the sidewalk. In the same move, Beckett threw a chop to the neck, but the man blocked it with a forearm and countered it with a back fist to the face.

Tears came to Beckett's eyes as the man's knuckles pounded his nose. He saw the man's cupped hands about to strike his ears in a clapping motion. The vibrations from the blow would burst his eardrums and cause internal bleeding in the brain. Beckett dropped to the ground, relieved to hear his enemy's hands collide against each other a foot above his head with a loud clap as he landed on his side. Recoiling his left leg and rapidly extending it against his opponent's stomach, heel up, toes pointing down, Beckett returned the initial blow to the solar plexus.

Blood dripped from the bearded man's mouth. Breathing heavily, he looked at Beckett while pulling out a ten-inch blade.

"I should have killed you . . . when I had the chance," Beckett muttered in between gasps, quickly getting up and positioning his body sideways to Layla's assassin.

The bearded man gave him a puzzled look as he began to circle Beckett, fingers curled around the wooden handle of the knife.

"Cairo . . . 1981 . . . Layla Shariff," Beckett hissed in between short gasps of air.

The bearded man's eyes grew large, his face showing obvious surprise, confirming Beckett's suspicions.

"You!" Hamed shouted. "*You* are the one!"

"That's right, asshole. And I'm gonna finish what I started in that train station!"

Beckett stepped back when the bearded man slashed his knife at him. Another slash, another step back. On the third time, Beckett stepped forward right after the bearded man completed the semicircular slash, one hand grabbing the man's wrist and twisting it to keep the stainless-steel blade away from him, the other hand pressing against the elbow while Beckett's left foot swept the bearded man's feet from under him. Dropping the knife, the man fell to his side while Beckett kept his right arm in a deadlock.

Placing a foot against his attacker's neck while twisting the arm and shoving the wrist forward, Beckett said, "Who are you? What do you want with me?"

The man looked up, past Beckett, at the stars fading away in the indigo sky. Dawn was just around the corner. The man's eyes turned to Beckett, burning him with the same stare of hatred that he had seen so many years before.

"Tell me who you are and what is your connection with Brasfield or I'll rip your arm off at the shoul—"

"*Hey, you!*"

Beckett turned to face the shouting down the street, and saw the dark blue uniforms of two police officers running his way, weapons already drawn.

"*You!* Step away from him with your hands above your head!" one of the officers shouted from the other end of the block.

Beckett let go of the arm and ran to Pamela, who was frozen in horror. Staggering to her side, he clasped her hand and said, "Come. We must find a place to hide."

Almost in a trance, perplexed by the lightning-fast fight she had just witnessed, Pamela Sasser obeyed and began running again, reaching the end of the alley and turning at the corner.

Her whole world had taken a surreal look, as if she were watching a movie, or living through a dream from which she wasn't sure she wanted to awaken. *Cairo. Layla Shariff. Nineteen eighty-one.* The words echoed in her mind as she ran, as she felt his body heat radiating around him, enveloping her. *What does that mean? What happened in Cairo in 1981? Who is Layla Shariff? What does that have to do with me? With Microtel? With Preston Sinclaire? With the algorithm? Where is the connection? Where?*

More questions drilled Pamela Sasser, overwhelming her. Pamela took in lungfuls of air through her nose, slowly exhaling through her mouth, just as she had done so many times years before. But now she ran to live, not just to win a race.

A few minutes later, the stranger suddenly stopped and let go of her hand as they turned a corner.

Chest heaving, perspiration flowing freely down his forehead, his back against the redbrick wall of a two-story building, the stranger brought a finger to his lips and said, "Shh . . . Hold on."

He peeked around the corner to see if they had lost the police. Apparently they had. "C'mon," he said. "We have to find a place to hide."

She tilted her head while regarding him with dubious blue-green eyes. "You just saved my life, yet you ran from the police," Pamela said, her tone of voice amazingly calm. "Who *are* you? Why are you helping me?"

Pamela noticed the stranger didn't look her directly in the eye. Instead, he kept his gaze shifting in every direction as he stood a few feet in front of her, his back still pressed against the bricks.

"Come," he said, turning around and beginning to walk down the murky street in the direction of the river. "Let's get out of harm's way first. Then I'll tell you what I know."

Mother Cruz put her weapon down and kneeled next to the limp body of Liem Ngo, which she picked up with both hands and cradled like a mother does an infant.

Bastards!

In her years with the Bureau, Esther had lost three partners, and the experience never got any easier. The overwhelming guilt consumed her. As senior agent she was responsible for all the junior agents, like Liem Ngo. This twenty-six-year-old kid had been *her* responsibility, and Esther felt she might have made the wrong call. She had left Liem too exposed in the hall, the large palm tree only offering partial cover with no back door. Esther had also tried communicating with Jessica White and Calvin Johnson but had gotten no response. She'd assumed the worst. *Three agents down!*

Esther Cruz had already examined the bodies of the five dead men, all dressed in black, carrying suppressed weapons, sanded fingertips, and no identification.

Professionals.

She strongly suspected the DIA but had no way to be certain. The military intelligence agency wasn't the only network that employed professional assassins. Brasfield had labeled Pamela Sasser as damaging to the Web, but Esther Cruz had nothing concrete, nothing solid to go on. Pamela and her companion had disappeared, probably escaping through the balcony after hearing Esther open fire on the termination team. Otherwise, Esther felt certain she would have found their bodies somewhere in the destroyed room.

"Freeze!"

Still holding the body of Liem Ngo, Esther gave the young deputy pointing a revolver in her direction a condescending glance. Realizing that the police would arrive any moment, Esther already had her badge out.

"FBI, son. Put your gun down before you hurt someone."

Still holding the gun leveled at her head, the young deputy took a few steps up the staircase and inspected the badge. Soon, three more police officers joined him.

The young officer approached Esther, who shoved her badge in a side pocket of her jeans, picked up the Uzi, clicked on the safety, and shouldered it under the surprised look of the New Orleans Police Department officers, dressed in dark blue pants and short-sleeve shirts.

"What in the hell happened here?" he asked.

Esther Cruz just closed her eyes.

Hamed Tuani stood over the two NOPD officers he had just attacked with his bare hands. They never knew what hit them. One bled from both ears from a clapping strike, his dead eyes staring at the sapphire sky. The other continued to convulse as a result of a knife hand strike to the weakest point of his spinal cord, about two inches above the waistline. Hamed had crippled the officer but had not killed him.

The job required a final blow, which Hamed delivered with icy efficiency: a single kick with the toe of his sneaker against the officer's left temple. The convulsion stopped.

Hamed looked at them and shook his head.

Amateurs.

They had holstered their weapons thinking that Hamed was just the victim of a local thug. Hamed would have let them live, but he couldn't. Not after one of the officers had insisted on taking him downtown to get the full story and file a report. In making such a request the NOPD officers had signed their own death warrants.

With many questions now filling his mind about the bizarre encounter with the DIA officer that had worked with Layla Shariff back in Egypt, and who supposedly had died in Italy, Hamed picked up his nine-millimeter weapon near the sidewalk, shoved it in the small of his back, and walked away slowly. He headed for the New Orleans International Airport, where a private jet would fly him back to Washington, D.C.

Just before sunrise, Harrison Beckett opened the door of their twelfth-floor room at the Marriott by Canal Street. Although he had managed a few hours' sleep at the Cornstalk, he still felt exhausted. A huge headache drilled his temples with the same intensity as the piercing pain at the base of his neck, his nose, and his ribs from the short hand-to-hand combat with Layla's assassin. Now more than ever Beckett needed to reach Brasfield and get his answers, but first he needed to rest, clear his mind, and come up with a plan of attack.

Pamela walked right behind him, bolting the door. She had remained quiet during most of the walk here, and he had not encouraged conversation. They had cruised through empty streets, from Canal to Esplanade, from Bourbon to Claiborne, always scanning the murky streets, peeking into dark alleys, avoiding police patrols, studying the faces of a dozen homeless or drunks sprawled on what seemed like countless sidewalks for signs of recognition. They had reached the French Market at five o'clock, where an array of street vendors filling a large plaza and a covered walkway between the river and the French Quarter prepared an assortment of goods for the morning crowd. After convincing himself that they were clean, Beckett and Pamela had headed for the nearest hotel.

Huge windowpanes gave him an excellent view of the Mississippi, stained red and orange by the rising sun's wan light. Several barges cruised the river in both directions. The wide river turned almost 180 degrees as it flowed through the middle of the city, giving New Orleans the nickname "Crescent City."

He sat on the edge of one of two double beds, observing Pamela Sasser with a curious glance. He knew this would be a long discussion and right now he didn't have the energy to go into it. He needed to catch up on his sleep or risk making the wrong call by operating on a cloudy, tired mind.

Glad that he'd remembered to ask for a smoking room, Beckett pulled out the silver lighter and a half-bent cigarette from the twisted pack of Marlboros in his back pocket. Lighting up and taking a few long draws, he leaned down, rested his head on the pillow, and closed his eyes, the cigarette tucked in between the index and middle fingers of the hand he rested on his chest, the burning end pointing straight at the ceiling.

"What do you think you're doing?" she asked, standing over him, small hands on her waist. "You can't go to sleep. We gotta talk. You promised me we'd talk as soon as we reached safety. Who are you? Who were those people at the hotel? Why are you protecting me? Why did you run away from the cops? Who was that bearded man? What happened since I was drugged in Baton Rouge?"

Christ!

Beckett knew they were clean. They had all day to discuss this, and all he wanted was to smoke in peace and rest a little, but it was obvious that this woman would not let up until he gave her some answers.

"I was hired to *kill* you," he said matter-of-factly, taking a draw and exhaling through his nostrils before getting up, grabbing the remote, and turning on the TV. Hotel walls were typically thin. He didn't want anyone listening in, realizing who they were, and calling the cops.

She didn't move, lips parted, eyes wide open, fine eyebrows rising just as much as her brown freckle. "Excuse me?"

"The DIA, the Defense Intelligence Agency," Beckett continued, sitting back on the bed, the bent cigarette, tucked in between his lips, moving up and down as he talked. Dropping his gaze to the dark blue carpet, he used his hands to massage the kinks off his sore neck and shoulders. "They hired me to assassinate you. The military spooks in the Pentagon want you dead."

She sat on the bed opposite Beckett, her catlike eyes wide open. "Me?" she said, slowly shaking her head while pointing to herself. "But—but why?"

"You—and before you, LaBlanche—were labeled for termination by the DIA. The charge was high treason against the United States of America."

She stood up, hands on her waist, head cocked to the right. "Treason? That's *ridiculous*!"

Beckett shrugged. "That's what I was told. Please, sit." He waved a hand, motioning for her to sit down. His neck was sore and it hurt to stare up at her. Pamela complied, sitting back on the bed, interlacing the fingers of her hands and placing them on her lap, knees touching, shoulders raised a dash, eyes growing impatient. She was obviously starved for information. Beckett understood perfectly. She needed to know why someone had tried to kill her so that she could justify in her own mind this bizarre situation— running away from the police and staying with a total stranger at this hotel—as motivated by self-preservation. The longer she went without knowing the reasons behind her predicament, the testier and edgier she would become. Beckett had seen that happen to many field agents. In fact, military interrogation teams used this basic human weakness as a weapon to extract information from captured soldiers by isolating them for days, until they broke down from lack of knowledge, their minds succumbing to despair because they no longer controlled their destinies. Beckett was actually impressed she'd lasted this long without breaking down.

"Look," Beckett continued, finishing the cigarette and crushing the burning butt on the tin ashtray on the nightstand next to the bed. "After all these incidents I personally don't believe that you are or that LaBlanche was a traitor."

"Well, *that's* a relief!"

Beckett closed his eyes. "Please, save the sarcasm. Neither one of us needs it right now."

They stared into each other's eyes for a few moments. "Sorry," she finally said with a slight frown, which pulled the small chocolate freckle down to her upper lip.

"Anyway," he continued, glancing at the familiar beauty mark before quickly looking away, "according to the DIA, LaBlanche sold computer software technology to hostile countries. The DIA believes you were in on it."

"That's absurd," she complained. "I have done nothing of the sort."

Beckett stood and walked to the large windows. A huge merchant ship lazily made its way up the river. "And you probably didn't, Pamela. But that's beside the point. Somehow you've jumped right into the middle of something very big—big enough to require your execution, and I was hired to do it."

"Why didn't you?"

Beckett turned around. "We'll get to that lat—"

"No. Answer the question. Why didn't you kill me, and how do I know you won't kill me soon? And who killed Dr. LaBlanche?"

Beckett didn't feel like answering those questions. He turned around, but noticed Pamela was no longer looking at him. Her eyes were glued to the image on the TV. She looked at her own face on the nineteen-inch screen. Pamela Sasser had been promoted to one of the most wanted fugitives in Louisiana, with charges ranging from stealing technology from Microtel, to accomplice in the murders of Tom

DeGeaux and his brother Nick, who died hours later in the hospital from a severe brain hemorrhage.

"But—but I don't even *know* those people." Pamela dropped onto the bed, sobbing, refusing to believe the news telecast. After a minute she stood, glaring at Beckett with a pair of wet eyes. In her stare, he saw horror, but also anger. Pamela raised her chin, her lips parted, and she breathed deeply, breasts pressing against the T-shirt, the freckle glossy from the tears that reached the corner of her mouth.

"All right," he said, turning around and gazing out the windows once again. The Louisiana Superdome's golden roof glared in the distance. "I'll tell you what I know."

Beckett spoke for a few minutes, measuring his words carefully. He told her about the multiple tails, and also that the men breaking into her apartment, who Beckett had just learned were named Nick and Tom DeGeaux, were the same guys who'd tried to abduct her in Baton Rouge. He told her about their trip to New Orleans and about her name being mentioned on the radio. Apparently someone had decided to claim that Pamela Sasser was on the run with a male companion in connection with stealing technology that belonged to Microtel. Now that same someone had piled up a few more charges on her. Beckett confessed that he was responsible for the DeGeaux brothers. He specifically left out his involvement in the assassination of Dr. LaBlanche and anything on his own background.

"Now," Beckett said, facing Pamela again. "Would you mind elaborating on this technology-theft claim? And what Microtel wants with you?"

It was Pamela's turn to speak, and she did, telling Beckett everything she knew, from the algorithm she had written with Dr. LaBlanche to her abduction in Baton Rouge. When she finished twenty minutes later, Beckett had smoked three cigarettes, his mind racing through the new information. Now he had a parallel story to which he could compare his own. From the time Dr. LaBlanche contacted Microtel to the time the DIA summoned him to assassinate the professor was only two days. A coincidence? From the time the professor died and the files were transferred to Microtel to the time Beckett was summoned a second time by Brasfield was less than a day. Another coincidence?

Beckett sighed, realizing the magnitude of the problem they faced. Only now, after Pamela had mentioned Microtel and Preston Sinclaire, did he finally understand the chilling reality of the alliance. Sinclaire was well on his way to setting up the political stage for his run for the White House, and General Jackson Brasfield was his silent partner. The connection between the DIA and Microtel explained perfectly why the military spooks cared about the bug in the Perseus computer chip. Brasfield was trying to protect Preston Sinclaire. The DIA and Microtel wanted this computer-chip flaw buried because exposure might link the Palo Verde accident to Microtel, ruining not just their chances for control of the White House, but also their lives, particularly Sinclaire's, whose company might never recover from such a blow. What Beckett still didn't know was who had fired the first burst of rounds outside his room at the Cornstalk, warning Beckett of the approaching threat and giving him enough time to get ready. Was there another party that had intercepted the termination team? Did he have an ally who had chosen not to expose himself?

Standing up, the ex–DIA officer went to the bathroom and splashed cold water on his face. "We can't stay here long," he said, coming back in the room with a hand towel, which he used to dry his face before tossing it on the bed.

"Why is that?"

"Because we're sitting ducks. There are a lot of people out there trying to kill us, all of them probably sent by Sinclaire and Brasfield, who are obviously working together on this. Going to the police is also useless. That's why I ran away. The cops will just put us in jail, where we would become even easier targets. Besides, I get the feeling that this Preston Sinclaire owns his share of local police officers and politicians, and even the local press."

Pamela raised her palms in front of her. "You mean we can't simply call the newspapers or the police with this information? We can't just expose Microtel? Wouldn't we be safer with the police? We would at least be able to tell our side of the story. We would get lawyers. With what I know and the diskette we'll have a strong case against—''

"Sinclaire and Brasfield would never let it get that far, Pam. It would ruin them. Preston Sinclaire is one of the most powerful and influential men in America, obviously powerful enough to get the DIA to do the dirty work for him. Christ, he might be our next president! If we go to jail, we would be executed within hours. The only way to get a chance to eventually tell our story is to keep moving until we figure this mess out. These people after us are professionals, Pamela. Sooner or later they'll catch up with us unless we stay on our toes. Believe me, I've been in this spot before. You can't play by the book with them.''

Pamela slowly nodded. Beckett noticed that the tears were gone when her eyes, a bit swollen from the crying, locked with his. "In that case, let's get going. I want to nail those bastards.''

Beckett almost smiled. "Let's not be too impulsive either. That would also get us killed.''

"So, what do we do next?''

"We rest awhile and then we figure a way to leave the state, probably head up to Washington.''

"Why Washington? Why not just go after Sinclaire?''

This time Beckett couldn't hold back a smile. "Because, Pam. Preston Sinclaire basically *owns* the state of Louisiana. We need to reach neutral ground, where we might have better luck approaching the press. I'm thinking maybe the *Washington Post*. Heck, we might even approach the Nuclear Regulatory Commission with this. I'm sure the NRC would love to get to the bottom of the Palo Verde disaster. I'd also like to get my hands on Jackson Brasfield and interrogate him.'' Beckett didn't mention the fact that he wanted to reach Brasfield to get another shot at Layla's assassin.

"Fine. Let me ask you another question then. Who was that bearded man?''

Beckett looked away. "Someone I knew long ago."

"Why is he after us?"

"Good question. I have no earthly idea."

"Who is Layla Shariff?"

Beckett frowned, his eyes quickly dropping from her eyes to the chocolate freckle. "Someone I knew long ago. Nobody relevant to our situation." He turned away from her and reached for the Marlboros, lighting one, and taking a drag while walking back toward the windows.

"Where are we going?"

"Nowhere this moment. The situation is too hot on the streets. It'll cool down in a few hours."

Pamela sat in the center of the bed, hugging her knees and slowly nodding, obviously frustrated and angry at her predicament, but willing to take the challenge head-on.

"Who *are* you?" she asked.

He turned around, brought the cigarette to his lips, and drew heavily, filling his lungs with smoke. "You don't really want to know that. Call me Harrison. I'm a friend." He exhaled through his nostrils.

"You said this . . . defense agency hired you to kill me?"

"The DIA. Yes," Beckett responded, taking a final drag, walking back to the nightstand, pulling another Marlboro from the pack, and using the one he had just finished smoking to light the new one before crushing the butt against the wooden surface of the nightstand. "I said that."

"Then you are a . . ."

"A professional assassin, Pamela," Beckett said, filling the silence trailing her words. "That's what I do. And this line of questioning is of no consequence to our current predicament, so let's drop it, all right?"

She looked away for a moment, and when her eyes found his again, Beckett saw them filling with tears once more, saw the lips beginning to tremble and the brown freckle dancing. Inhaling deeply, he lowered his gaze. But Beckett noticed she did this not out of fear but anger. Pamela Sasser was very angry. The emotion confused Beckett.

"Harrison, just answer one more question."

He nodded. "All right. What is it?"

"Did you kill Dr. Eugene LaBlanche?"

Looking at her straight in the face, Beckett answered the only way he could answer under the circumstances. He shrugged and casually said, "No, Pamela. I did not kill Dr. LaBlanche," before walking over to the TV and switching it off.

He checked his watch. Six o'clock in the morning. He figured he could still catch a few hours of sleep before he started looking for a car to get out of the state. He had already decided that the airport, the bus station, and the train station were out of the question. He set the alarm on his Seiko to go off in three hours.

"Let's get some rest, Pamela. We have a long day ahead of us."

Without further delay, Beckett closed the curtains, turned off the overheads, and lay down on his bed, his mind wishing he had turned down Brasfield when he had the chance, when he still could have walked away.

But could he still do it? Could he still leave, vanish? How far was the DIA willing to go to find him? Out of the state? Out of the country? Off the continent? And for how long? A week? A month? A year? Would Beckett need the services of another plastic surgeon?

Pamela's muffled weeping interrupted his thoughts.

Beckett turned his head and saw her slim figure resting on the other bed in the twilight of the room, arms hugging a pillow that also covered her face.

He closed his eyes and rolled over, his back to the soft laments of this stranger who reminded him so much of—

No, Harrison. Don't do it. Don't get involved. She means nothing. Nothing at all.

He clenched his jaw and took a deep, long breath, wondering if he should just leave, disappear.

This is the DIA you're dealing with, Harrison! They'll hunt you down just as they did fifteen years ago!

He opened his eyes and stared at the blue-and-green floral pattern on the curtains. The only way to escape the DIA was to repeat Rome, relive the nightmare. Or was there another way out? Would the DIA go to the extreme it did back in 1981? Or would they let him go after the first few weeks?

Beckett closed his eyes, his mind shutting out the sobs of Pamela Sasser.

Let it go, Harrison. Disappear. She means nothing. She's as good as dead. Everyone knows her face. Staying close to her will also make you a target. The police don't know what you look like yet. You can make a clean escape, head south, far away from Brasfield's grasp. Reach Central America, cross into Colombia. Find that army general whom you helped keep in power by assassinating his enemies in the cartel, the general with the mountaintop villa overlooking Medellín, the one with the beautiful daughters. Or go farther south, seek refuge with your friends in Rio, the ones who almost lost their oceanfront resorts to that corrupt general you killed in an airplane crash over the Amazon jungle three years ago. Find that tall Brazilian dancer who taught you a thing or two about making love, listen to her screams while the two of you roll on the sand under a tropical moon. Maybe even leave the hemisphere, hide in Hong Kong and look up the lonely wife of that business executive whose corporation you saved by drowning that corrupt government official. Surrender yourself to her uninhibited desires, help her release the steam building up underneath her silky skin after so many years of marital neglect. But you let go of this. You walk away before it outruns you.

But what about Layla's assassin? What about achieving retribution?

Layla is gone! There is nothing that can bring her back. Walk away!

No. Stay, Harrison. Stay and make those responsible pay dearly for what they did to her, to you, for what they forced you to do in Rome!

For Rome, Harrison. For Rome and for Layla Shariff. You must stay.

But it's outrunning you, Harrison. You can't keep up the

*pace! This isn't Cairo. This isn't 1981. You're not that
young. Let it go! Just let it go!*

But Harrison Beckett knew he couldn't walk away from
this. Not after having confirmed the identity of Layla's assassin. The inner workings of his mind had already begun
to formulate a plan of attack, a method to exact revenge for
Cairo, for Rome, for Brasfield's treachery. It was the only
way to survive without having to relive Rome.

*You can't let it go, Harrison. You can't let it go. You
must face it and destroy it before it destroys you!*

Pamela Sasser's crying slowly subsided, replaced by her
steady breathing. Slowly, he too fell asleep.

WASHINGTON, D.C.

Wednesday, November 18

Hamed Tuani jerked in his sleep and woke up the moment
the private jet landed at Dulles International Airport. Moist
with sweat, hands trembling, heart beating against his chest,
the former Egyptian colonel sat up on the leather sofa in the
rear of the jet. His mind still replaying a dream of the encounter at the train station in Cairo, as well as the recent
fight in New Orleans, Hamed shivered away the nightmare
and struggled to bring his mind into focus.

Sitting on the edge of the couch, he rubbed his face with
both hands before reaching for his shirt. The faded jeans he
wore bordered a thick scar that traversed his abdomen. A
second scar ran the width of his chest. A muscular man with
emerald green eyes wide and shiny, a well-kept beard, and
a fine nose, Hamed Tuani was a handsome man. The pink
scar across his reconstructed right ear, although quite no-
ticeable, added a dimension of strength to his persona.

Getting up and walking across the carpeted cabin to the
small bathroom, the former Egyptian colonel shivered when
his feet came in contact with the ice-cold vinyl-layered
floors of the lavatory. He reached the sink and splashed
water on his face.

Turning off the faucet, Hamed Tuani dried off and stared

at his reflection in the round mirror above the metallic sink. Although the beard on his face, without a trace of gray thanks to hair coloring, made him look younger than his years, his eyes gave him away. Deep lines of age surrounded a pair of intelligent, emerald green eyes, which tended to widen when he grimaced.

Thinking of the fight in New Orleans made Hamed grimace. He had faced his old adversary once again, the one Hamed thought the DIA had terminated in Rome. But it was now obvious to him that the man who now called himself Harrison Beckett somehow had survived and had come back to haunt him.

As the private jet came to a stop inside a spacious hangar, the pilot opened the side door, which swung downward and also served as steps leading down to the concrete floor. The noise of the decelerating turbines echoing inside the metallic structure and the smell of oil and jet fuel reaching his nostrils, Hamed saw General Jackson Brasfield in the rear of the hangar, next to the door leading to the small office area.

The former Egyptian colonel began to walk in the direction of his superior, who stood ramrod straight, hands behind his back, strong chin up, glinting eyes staring at the jet.

"What in the hell happened?" asked Brasfield as Hamed neared. The general kept his hands behind his back and his gaze on the craft.

"It's *him*," said Hamed. "Harrison Beckett is *Daniel Webster*!"

Jackson Brasfield's head snapped in Hamed's direction at the mention of a name he had not heard in many years. *"What?"*

"Cairo. Nineteen eighty-one. Layla Shariff. The train station. *Remember?*" Hamed brought a hand to his reconstructed ear.

"Yes . . . yes, of course I remember. How could I forget the—but how did you—"

Hamed told him, taking less than a minute to bring his superior up to speed.

"This is insane! It's impossible! The DIA . . . Rome . . . the explosion. It *can't* be! Webster died in that explosion!"

"He must have staged it, swapped bodies, *done something*. I'm telling you it's *him*. I know. He almost *killed* me."

"All right, all right. I believe you," said Brasfield. "But the fact still remains that they're on the loose. What do we do now?"

"We have an extreme situation here, and we're rapidly losing control. We must go to extreme measures, even if they add risk. Webster and Pamela are hiding somewhere in New Orleans. My guess is that they will try to leave the state as soon as they can. I doubt they'll try to contact the press or the police while in Louisiana. Sinclaire has too much clout in that state. But the fact they're wanted by the police works to our advantage. We need to set up teams monitoring police channels, and have helicopters ready to storm into action the moment they're spotted."

"All right," said Brasfield. "All right. I'll call Sinclaire from my car and set it up."

BATON ROUGE, LOUISIANA

Wednesday, November 18

The Louisiana sun had already burned through the light fog lifting off the banks of the Mississippi, where colossal barges made their way up and down the wide river with the assistance of tugboats. Preston Sinclaire could see the wakes left by their powerful screws as he rode a claybank mare, the most recent addition to his private stable.

Dressed in a pair of Wranglers, a cotton shirt, matching eel-skin hat and boots, and shiny spurs, the president of Microtel silently enjoyed the wind in his face. The dawn ride through his two-hundred-acre plantation along the Mississippi north of Baton Rouge a few times a week was a ritual Sinclaire had started almost ten years ago, after co-sponsoring a rodeo in south Texas and discovering an affinity for horses he never knew he had.

He looked behind him and saw two other men on horses, roughly three hundred feet away. His bodyguards.

This morning Sinclaire rode to purge his mind of microprocessor bugs and computer algorithms. Microtel's stock had just jumped up three points thanks to recent contract awards for the electronic brains of a new navy missile system. Sinclaire had also just approved a two-week campaign trip through thirteen states, and he had also received invitations to appear on three nationwide talk shows. Things could not be going better for the powerful CEO, who hoped his clandestine network in Washington would handle their end of the—

His cellular phone rang once, twice. He pulled on the reins and the mare stopped. On the fourth ring he reached for the unit strapped to his belt.

"Yes?"

"We have a problem," said General Brasfield, whose tone of voice told Preston Sinclaire that Pamela Sasser was still at large.

Closing his eyes while bringing a finger to his right temple, Sinclaire said, "Go on."

After a few minutes, Sinclaire slowly shook his head.

Fucking Pamela Sasser and Harrison Beckett!

"It gets worse," said Brasfield.

Almost laughing at the insane turn of events, Sinclaire simply said, "What?"

"Remember the military contract deal with the Egyptian government back in eighty-one?"

"Ah . . . yeah . . . yes, I remember," Sinclaire responded, maintaining the pressure on the reins to keep the mare from moving. The CEO recalled the large military contracts between the Pentagon and the Egyptian government that almost vaporized because of Anwar Sadat's attempt to make peace with Israel. It had been shortly after Microtel's first year in business. But the deal did go through after Sadat's assassination. Sinclaire had taken in a healthy dose of cash from the black-market transactions that Brasfield and he negotiated with the Egyptians. Sinclaire had then used the money to help expand Microtel.

"Remember the problem at the train station in Cairo?"

Sinclaire nodded and slowly took in a breath of morning air. A DIA officer had almost blown the whistle on the plan to help the Muslim Brotherhood assassinate Sadat. Hamed Tuani, Brasfield's contact in the Egyptian military, had led the hit team to kill the DIA informer.

"Hamed almost died that day," responded Sinclaire. "But we saved him and . . . what's your point, Jackson?"

"Remember the informer?"

"How can I forget?"

"He's alive, Preston. The informer is Harrison Beckett."

"That's . . . that's *impossible*!" Sinclaire screamed into the small unit shoved against his left ear. "He died in Rome! You yourself told me so!"

"That's what I thought. But he recognized Hamed in New Orleans. He knew everything that happened in Cairo."

"But—but the face! Didn't you *meet* with him? Couldn't you *tell*?"

"He must have altered his face, gotten plastic surgery."

"And he didn't recognize you?"

"We never met in person back then. He did recognize Hamed. In fact, Webster might have even caught a glimpse of Hamed during our last meeting," Brasfield said, spending another minute explaining Hamed's bizarre encounter in New Orleans the night before. Brasfield also described his current plan.

Enraged, Preston Sinclaire threw the phone into the Mississippi and raked the mare fiercely with the spurs. The horse broke into a gallop toward the stables.

Harrison Beckett is Daniel Webster! He's alive!

Preston Sinclaire dug the spurs into the claybank's sides again, riding it at full speed. The wind whipped his hat, knocking it off, but the CEO of Microtel didn't care.

Webster is Beckett! Beckett is Webster!

The words thundered in his mind, carried him back in time. Nineteen eighty-one. Five years after his departure from the army. Sinclaire controlled the underground black market then as he did today. He controlled the network's purse while Brasfield handled operations. For two years Sinclaire and Brasfield had been working the deal with the Egyptians. *Two years!* It included everything from tanks to shoulder-launched missiles, small weapons, ammunition, and a long list of expensive spare parts. The deal also included training. At the time it was by far the most ambitious and profitable deal Sinclaire's clandestine organization had ever negotiated. And Daniel Webster almost jeopardized it.

But he failed. And he was supposed to have died in Rome, damn it!

And no one knew where he currently hid. Brasfield had guessed New Orleans, but by now the traitor Webster and the woman could be anywhere.

Anywhere!

If Webster had been crafty enough to survive Cairo and Rome—and last night's assassination attempt—Preston Sinclaire doubted he'd have any problems leaving the state. Pamela and Webster held enough pieces of the puzzle between the two of them to expose his operation.

Reaching the stables, dismounting, and leaving the mare in the care of a hired hand, Sinclaire walked right up to his mansion next door and went straight for the minibar in the living room, where he grabbed a glass and dropped a pair of ice cubes in it before filling it with Chivas Regal.

He downed the scotch and poured himself another one.

Brasfield's plan better work, he thought. *It must work or . . .*

Throwing the glass against the wall, Sinclaire reached for the phone and began to make calls. It was time to pull every possible string he knew in the state of Louisiana. The flaw in the Perseus could not be exposed, regardless of the consequences.

While Preston Sinclaire made phone call after phone call to the people he owned in Baton Rouge and New Orleans, less than a mile away, Theresa Hays slowly walked up the steps of the Louisiana Cancer Center. A forty-five-year-old executive secretary at a local law firm, Theresa had developed a tumor in her left breast. Fortunately, her doctor had caught it in time, and it did not require a mastectomy. After she had undergone surgery three weeks ago to remove it, her physician had scheduled her for five doses of radiation to treat remnants of the breast cancer. This was her first session.

After filling out a number of forms and patiently waiting her turn in the crowded waiting room, Theresa was finally called in by a petite nurse, who guided her to a treatment room, four gleamingly white walls enclosing a massive stainless-steel machine towering fifteen feet. One of the walls had a long tinted window.

"That's our new X-ray system," said the young nurse, her blond hair tied up in a bun. She pointed to the Rythenon-30, the most sophisticated X-ray system on the market. "Fully automated. Your doctor sent you to the best facility in the state."

As the nurse directed Theresa onto a white table, a male technician appeared behind the glass window and sat at the controls of the Rythenon. A huge armlike protrusion at the top of the machine slowly turned and descended over Theresa as the nurse helped her lie back on the table, propping her head with a small pillow.

"Don't move, please," the petite nurse said. "It'll only take a few seconds and you won't feel a thing."

The nurse left her and walked into the control room, where the technician, following the directions on the patient's chart, programmed the machine in the low-power mode designed to destroy skin tumors.

The nurse caught the technician's mistake. He had the wrong chart on his lap, the one for the *next* patient, *not* Theresa Hays, whose chart required the use of the high-power electron-beam mode, designed to generate the searing X rays capable of penetrating the patient's breast and destroying the remnants of the tumor without damaging the skin or surrounding tissue.

Instead of resetting the system and then changing modes, the technician decided to save time by simply using the up arrow and backspace keys to erase the previous mode before entering the new sequence, setting the correct beam power, penetration level, and duration of event. His keystrokes were converted into electrical pulses, which fed the input channels of the Perseus microprocessor driving the entire system. The microprocessor read the inputs fed by the keyboard and transmitted them to the floating-point unit. Before receiving the new set of commands, the FPU had been right in the middle of calculating the low-power setting for the beam. This high-accuracy computation took hundreds of thousands of iterations, using the outputs from the previous calculation as the inputs for the current calculation while increasing the accuracy of the beam current with every pass. Right in the middle of this computation, without a system reset, a new set of commands reached the Perseus, forcing its FPU to execute a new loop with different parameters. Again, the Perseus obediently went into another high-accuracy computational loop. The new result exited the Perseus chip through its output channels, and ordered the Rythenon-30 to switch to the high-power electron-beam mode. However, due to the small flaw in the FPU, the output from the Perseus failed to convey the technician's command of inserting a tungsten target into the path of the beam. The target, normally not used during low-power treatments, was vital in the high-power mode. It filtered all harmful elements from the powerful beam, converting it into therapeutic X rays.

The system fired.

The unrestricted beam, carrying an energy level of thirty thousand volts, hammered Theresa Hays's upper chest for the fraction of a second it took the Rythenon's safety mechanism to realize the error in the setting and shut the system down. But not before she was exposed to a massive dose of radiation, equivalent to three million chest X rays.

A blinking Malfunction sign flashed on the control panel. Theresa Hays saw a flash of blue light just as a scorching beam cooked her internal organs, almost as if she had been inside a giant microwave.

Shaking, unable to scream for help, the executive secretary managed to sit up on the table, hugging her knees, blankly staring at the white walls, shivering as millions of isotopes swept across her system.

Theresa heard voices, saw the petite nurse reaching her side, asking her what was wrong, how she felt. But not a word escaped her quivering lips as the radiation consumed her skin, her lungs, her stomach, her liver, her pancreas, her muscle tissue, her intestines. Like a predator closing its jaws over the soft flesh of its victim, so did the invisible monster inside her attack her vital organs with rapacious voracity.

As the technician and the nurse helped Theresa Hays to her feet, she suddenly jerked and vomited bile mixed with blood, a putrid mixture that she regurgitated onto the white tile floor of the treatment room, the coppery smell reaching her nostrils.

The convulsions stopped, and Theresa tried to talk again, but instead felt a sudden pain deep in her chest. She projectile-vomited onto the nurse and the technician, both of whom let go of her, and she collapsed on the tiled floor. She convulsed, twisted, cringed, froze, and tensed, and more vomit reached her throat. Her dying eyes stared into the slimy liquid she continued to cough up in bursts, the nauseating smell making her feel light-headed, dizzy.

Theresa Hays died a minute later. An autopsy revealed large internal damage to her organs due to a massive dose of radiation.

An hour later, the clinic's technician ran a series of diagnostic tests on the Rythenon system and it came back clean. The system performed flawlessly.

9   Unexpected Heroes

Then out spoke brave Horatius,
The Captain of the Gate:
"To every man upon this earth
Death cometh soon or late.
And how can man die better
Than facing fearful odds,
For the ashes of his fathers,
And the temples of his Gods?"

               —*Thomas Babington Macaulay*

SOUTHERN LOUISIANA
Wednesday, November 18

Behind the wheel of a stolen gray Nissan Maxima, Harrison Beckett cruised right below the speed limit toward Baton Rouge, still wondering if he had made the right decision by staying with this woman. Alone he could have run, disappeared from sight again. With her, his only chance was to fight, to find a way to expose those who sought him before he was caught.

They needed to get out of the state immediately, and he hoped that most of the police search would be geared to block access into Mississippi, only ninety minutes away from New Orleans. In Baton Rouge he planned to steal another car and use it to reach the next large city, Lafayette, only an hour west of Baton Rouge, but closer to the Texas border. Once in Texas, they would board a plane, taking a route that would steer them clear of the airports in the southern states.

The noon sun rose high in the autumn sky, bringing temperatures to an unseasonably high eighty-nine degrees. Humidity was also up in the eighties, and Beckett was glad he had stolen a car with air-conditioning.

Finding the right car hadn't been as difficult as Beckett had originally thought. He had selected one in the parking lot of the Marriott with Just Married painted in white across the rear window and sides, as well as toilet paper taped to the roof and trunk. He figured the owners of the car would not be getting out of bed that early, and by then he would have dumped this one in Baton Rouge.

"What's going to happen to us, Harrison?" Pamela asked. She had remained quiet the entire time, and again, Beckett had not encouraged conversation. He'd said everything he needed to say to this woman. Talking to her disturbed his train of thought, and right now he couldn't afford distractions. Since they'd left the hotel his eyes had shifted back and forth between the road ahead, the rearview mirror, and the sides of the interstate. From the folded map on his lap he knew how far ahead was the next exit, the exact locations of every secondary road nearby, and the locations along the road where he could veer off if he sensed danger around him. Many secondary roads ran near I-10, and although they didn't intersect with the four-lane highway, they came close enough for Beckett to make a run for them if it ever came to that. Now Pamela Sasser was breaking his concentration with her needless question.

Giving her an annoyed glance, Beckett, cigarette hanging off the corner of his mouth, shrugged. "I wish I knew."

She lowered her gaze and frowned. Against his better judgment, Beckett decided to talk to her a bit more. This he did not out of compassion, but out of selfishness. Beckett didn't know when he might *need* Pamela's help. A little rapport between them wouldn't hurt. Or would it?

Don't get involved, Harrison. Keep it professional. She means nothing.

The phrase flashed in his mind, reminding him how dangerous it would be to let himself get dragged into this emotionally. But on the other hand, he needed this woman to remain sane, to not break down at the worst possible moment. It was his job to keep her from reaching the edge of the abyss. He knew what she felt. He had been there before, long ago, in another land and under a different set of circumstances, but he had been there, and he understood.

Wedging the Marlboro between the index and middle fingers of his right hand, Beckett took a final draw before crushing the butt in the small ashtray below the radio. "Welcome to the world of uncertainties, Pamela," he said, cautiously measuring his words.

"In here you never know who's your friend or your enemy," he continued. "Take our situation, for example. Two days ago I was hired to *kill* you. Today I'm *protecting* you." Beckett slowly exhaled the smoke through his nostrils.

"And tomorrow? Are you going put a bullet in between my eyes? Are you going to kill me when this is over, Harrison?"

Beckett considered her question for several seconds. Beams of sunshine shafting through the Maxima's sunroof accentuated the blondness of her hair, making it look borderline white, but giving her an appealing look. The dark lipstick and eyeliner that she had found in the pockets of her jeans created a contrast that the ex-DIA officer found quite exquisite. And of course, there was that chocolate freckle that slowly drove him insa—

Damn it, no! Don't do it, Harrison! Think about Brazil, Colombia, Hong Kong. Think of anything, but don't let her in. It will outrun you! Leave right now! Drop her off at the next exit, let her have the car and steal another. Head for the nearest airport. Leave the continent, go to Spain. Look up the wife of the guitar maker in Segovia, the one you freed from the claws of that corrupt army colonel. Make her help you forget Baton Rouge, Cairo, Rome, the DIA, New Orleans. But leave! Leave now!

But his eyes couldn't avoid hers, for beneath the makeup, the punkish hairstyle, the high cheekbones, and her blue-green gaze, Beckett saw fear, sobering fear, raw fear. The visceral terror flashing in her wet stare. He saw a single tear slowly conforming to the soft features of her face, reaching her brown freckle, wetting it, making it shine in ways that reminded him of Cairo, of windy Egyptian nights, of pyramids under the stars.

But the fear overshadowed any other feeling, any other image. Pamela Sasser was afraid, terrified, and not just of their pursuers, but also of Beckett. *She is afraid of you, Harrison! Of you! You must make her believe in you, make her trust you.*

Make her trust me?

The question inexorably entered his mind. It was logical, it made sense, it explained the fear shimmering in her eyes: *Would you trust your own assassin, Harrison?*

Pulling over, Beckett sat sideways, and she did the same.

"Look, Pamela. I'm not sure what to say to you that would put your mind at ease about me, but you should know that although I *do* kill people for a living, I only kill trash, dirt, the scum of the world. I'm quite selective in my clients, and I don't terminate someone unless I'm absolutely certain that the world would be a better place without him—or her."

The fear quickly vaporizing from her gaze, Pamela shook her head in disbelief. "And who gave you the right to play God?"

Taken aback by her comment, Beckett looked away, breathing deeply as he put a hand to his forehead. "Look. I won't kill you, all right. So don't worry about—"

Beckett saw the flashing blue-and-red lights of a police cruiser in his rearview mirror.

"We're in trouble."

Pamela looked back, and then at Beckett, fear returning to her eyes. "What are we going to do?"

The cruiser stopped right behind them, lights flashing. Beckett saw only one officer, who opened the door. He also saw only one way to handle this. Only one. His mind screamed at him not to do it, for it would violate every one of his self-imposed rules.

"We're newlyweds, remember?" he said.

"Excuse me?"

"He never put on the siren, so pretend you never saw him come." Beckett pulled her close, pressing his chest against her Saints T-shirt.

"Wait a minu—"

"Keep your eyes closed until he taps on my window. Play the role. Quick." Beckett cupped her face and kissed her. Surprised by this sudden violation of her privacy, Pamela resisted, but he kept her face touching his, lips pressed together, a taste of the Marriott's complimentary mints that she'd eaten caressing his palate. The moment turned on the images of soft breezes, of sandy beaches, of cobblestone streets, of—

A knock on the driver-side window made Beckett jump, pushing a stunned Pamela Sasser back on her seat, dark lipstick smeared around her lips, over her freckle, and no doubt on him.

His heart pounding in his chest, Beckett watched his own embarrassed smile reflecting on the black officer's sunglasses. A chest, arms, and neck that could belong to a professional wrestler blocked Beckett's view out of the side window. He rolled it down.

"Car trouble?" he asked, a half smile flickering across the black face.

"Sorry, Officer," said Beckett. "We're just getting over our first fight. Right, honey?"

Pamela, her mouth still looking a bit like a clown's, didn't utter a word, but at least she got her neck muscles to nod.

"Your lipstick smeared, ma'am," observed the officer, now kneeling by the door and placing both arms on the door.

Blushing, Pamela pulled out a tissue from the center console and wiped herself.

"Look, Officer. We shouldn't have stopped, but we had our first fight and—"

"Be on your way, and please refrain from stopping unless you have an emergency—a *real* emergency that is."

"Thank you, Officer."

Beckett cranked the car and took off.

"Well, that didn't go so bad," he said, turning to her and then to the rearview mirror before snagging another cigarette from the pack in his side pocket and bringing it to his lips.

Pamela slapped him hard across the face, crushing the Marlboro against his lips and right cheek. A small explosion of paper and tobacco preceded her shouting, "You fucking bastard! You disgusting animal! Don't you ever—*ever* touch me again! Got that, mister? *Never!*"

His cheek burning, Beckett spat out the torn cigarette and shot her a cold glance. He'd never been slapped by a woman before. "Damn it!" he said, rubbing his red cheek and wiping off the tobacco from the broken cigarette. "Can't you see what I was trying to—"

"You're the crafty one, remember? Next time think of something else. But don't ever touch me again! Understand? Never! Or I will be the one who'll kill you, Mr. Fucking Assassin!"

There was a moment of silence when they stared into each other's eyes with dark amusement before bursting into a loud laugh that forever broke the ice between them.

Tears filled her eyes from the half-hysterical laugh. Beckett laughed hard too, his stomach muscles tightening. Pamela used another tissue to dry her eyes as the moment passed, and the futility of their situation and the near disaster of getting caught by the police sank in.

No more mistakes.

Beckett breathed deeply a few times while holding the wheel with both hands.

Pamela handed him a tissue, pointing to his lips.

"Thanks," he said, taking it and rubbing it against his lips. "That was close. Too close."

Pamela exhaled heavily, but as she did, she pushed out her lower lip, forcing all the air up, ruffling the blond bangs over her forehead. "No kidding."

They remained silent for a few minutes, each immersed in private thought.

"Thank you for saving my life," Pamela said, giving his shoulder a soft lingering pressure with her left hand, fingers digging in his sore muscles.

Beckett smiled. "Don't mention it. I hope—oh, shit. It was a trap!"

"What?"

"That!" Beckett pointed to a dozen police cars blocking the interstate around the next turn. Looking behind him, he suddenly watched several patrols closing in, their flashing lights on, their sirens resonating across the vast fields of sugarcane and bordering swamps on both sides of the highway.

Momentarily lacking any secondary roads to veer away from the interstate, Beckett slammed on the brakes, crossed the median, and rushed back toward New Orleans in what he knew would be a hopeless effort to escape. The sewing-machine engine inside the Maxima was no match for the powerful V-8s in those cruisers.

The cars that were following him did likewise, and charged after him, joined by the cruisers that had been blocking the road.

Floored, the Maxima would only do 120 miles per hour, just child's play for his pursuers, who caught up with him in no time, under the curious eyes of dozens of workers in bulldozers loading trucks and trailers with sugarcane.

Three cruisers got in front of him while the rest flanked him. The large white vehicles with the pelican emblem on the doors forced him to slow down and stop in the middle of the interstate.

Enough guns to start a small army were suddenly pointed at Beckett and Pamela by two dozen officers dressed in light brown uniforms with chocolate-colored hats and sunglasses.

Beckett looked at Pamela.

"The end of the road, Pam."

He actually felt worse for her than he did for himself, but it didn't matter. He knew for certain that despite the best police protection, they would be executed by the DIA once in captivity. There was no escape from his old agency's claws unless he could convince the DIA that they were already dead. Somehow Beckett didn't think the corpulent officer with the prominent nose, short black hair, and narrowed brown eyes who approached their vehicle would vouch for their false death to the newspapers.

Signaling Beckett to roll down the window, the officer tipped his hat. Pamela was visibly shaken by the sight of so many muzzles pointed at them. Beckett didn't flinch, and the officer could see that in his eyes.

"Mornin'," the officer said in a deep voice, his alert brown eyes never leaving Beckett's, a huge gloved hand resting on his sidearm. "I'm Sheriff Jason Laroux, East Baton Rouge Parish. You picked the wrong car to steal, pal. Its owners watched you drive away and called the police immediately. We've been following you for twenty miles, and just to be sure we decided to play a little game with Deputy Nelson over there."

Beckett glanced at the large black officer holding a sawed-off shotgun leveled at the Maxima.

"We've been looking for you two all over the state," continued Sheriff Laroux. "Now, this can go down one of two ways. You either come out nicely, we'll handcuff you and take you to New Orleans." He paused, giving Beckett a broad grin. "*Or*, you can resist arrest, in which case I'll be more than happy to beat the shit out of you, and *then* handcuff you and take you to New Orleans. Now, which way's it gonna be?"

Twenty minutes later, handcuffed behind his back and sitting next to Pamela in the rear of a cruiser escorted by two other police cars with flashing lights, Harrison Beckett headed for his certain death in New Orleans. A strange peaceful feeling descended over him, a feeling of resignation. He had fought a good fight, and it was now time to die. In a way he should be grateful he had lived as long as he had after being labeled beyond salvage back in 1981. Since then he had lived on borrowed time. Beckett knew this, and destiny had finally caught up with him. All that remained was his curiosity about the method of assassination the DIA would use. A staged suicide? Perhaps the same binary poisons he himself had used on Dr. LaBlanche?

The list could go on forever. Beckett had used many of those methods over the years, and any of them was as effective as a bullet in the head, but without the messy aftermath. He thought the suicide tack would work best in this situation. The prisoner somehow got hold of a shoestring, which he used in the middle of the night to hang himself. Or perhaps the prisoner found a razor blade and slashed his wrists, or simply bit into his own flesh, cutting the arteries and bleeding to death. He had actually seen one instance when that was used many years ago in South America. A corrupt politician sentenced to life in prison had been eliminated by biting into his wrists and letting him bleed dry.

Beckett shook his head as swamps rushed by under a sky darkened by approaching rain clouds. Too many deaths. He had killed so many people since leaving the DIA he felt somewhat ashamed he could not remember some of their names. But the faces . . . God, did he remember the faces, starting with Rome! Aside from that sin, however, Beckett had only killed to make the world a better place.

"But who gave you the right to play God?"

Beckett glanced at Pamela, her head low, chin almost pressed against her bosom, eyes closed, tears rolling down her cheeks. An innocent victim, caught at the wrong place at the wrong time and in the wrong profession.

Destiny.

But could destiny be altered? Could he change his own fate? Was he a master of his own future? Should he have run away while he'd had the chance? Beckett was considering these questions when he noticed three tiny black spots appearing on the horizon. Soon they grew in size, their sound reaching his ears.

Helicopters! Of course! Sinclaire and Brasfield can't afford to wait. They don't want us talking to the media.

The DIA had obviously monitored the police channels and sent another team, which Beckett expected to pack far more firepower than the last one.

He looked at Pamela. "Psst."

Pamela turned her head, giving Beckett a wet stare of blue-green eyes, the wet freckle shivering over her trembling lips.

"On my mark, duck," he whispered.

She shook her head, the tracks of her tears lining her light olive face. "What . . . what do you mean?"

"Those choppers," Beckett muttered between closed teeth. "Another hit team."

He had not even finished saying that when the first helicopter made its pass, two underfuselage cannons vomiting rounds at the lead car, which exploded in a ball of flames.

"Now, Pamela!" Beckett screamed. She threw herself in the space between the rear and front seat, and Beckett jumped over her. "Don't move! You'll be fine!"

"Holy shit!" screamed Sheriff Laroux as he swerved the cruiser around the flaming wreckage while reaching for the radio. "This is a code red, repeat a code red. Three helicop—shit!"

The second chopper followed, the river of bullets ricocheting off the concrete, slicing through the hood of Laroux's cruiser.

Spinning out of control, the cruiser ran off the road and into the field of sugarcane, which drummed against the sides of the car, breaking the windows and showering Pamela and Beckett with glass. The car flipped once, twice, coming to a stop right side up just as the field met the tall trees and muddy waters of a swamp.

Silence.

An explosion in the distance. The third cruiser was in

flames. Beckett sat up, the door on his side wide open from the impact. Forcing his cuffed hands down the back of his legs and under his feet, Beckett dragged a dazed Pamela out of the vehicle, his bruised ribs protesting the effort.

"Get down or I'll blow your fucking head off!" screamed Laroux, already outside, cocked revolver in his right hand. Beckett stood next to the car. Pamela Sasser leaned against the trunk.

"We gotta get out of here!" shouted Beckett as he ducked for cover behind the car, dragging Pamela down with him. Laroux remained standing, his upper body fully exposed to the incoming DIA team. "That's a termination team! They'll kill us all!"

"Shut up, asshole! Or I'll be the one terminating—"

A bullet snapped Sheriff Laroux's head back, turning his face into a mass of cartilage and flesh. The huge officer fell to his knees, arms trembling before he landed on his side and went limp.

Pamela's screams pierced his ears as Beckett's trained instincts took over. Every second now counted.

Every second.

He leaped forward, quickly searched Laroux, took out his keys, and removed his handcuffs. He did the same to Pamela before grabbing both the dead sheriff's revolver and the sawed-off shotgun in the front seat. He also retrieved the hunting knife Laroux had taken, and strapped it to his calf, below the jeans.

While two helicopters hovered above the huge swamp at roughly one hundred feet, the third one briefly touched down at the edge of the interstate. Men dressed in black and carrying automatic weapons leaped out and raced in his direction. The helicopter then joined the other two.

"C'mon, let's move!"

"Where?" she asked, the initial shock of the explosions and of Laroux's violent death beginning to wear off.

Beckett left the cruiser and walked right into the swamp, with Pamela Sasser behind him. The water reached their waists as they lost themselves behind clusters of trees, the buzzing of mosquitoes and the stench of the putrid waters masked by the adrenaline knotting their stomachs.

Beckett could hear the termination team also jumping into the water. He could also hear the helicopters hovering overhead, but he could not see them through the thick canopy of branches.

Beckett and Pamela moved deeper into the swamp, darkness quickly engulfing them as they surrounded themselves with the strangest-looking trees Beckett had ever seen. But the woods protected them, provided a shield between them and their pursuers. Ahead, Beckett saw nothing but dark jungle and swamps.

"Come," he said, suddenly cutting left just as three beams of light began to diffuse through the dark woods. Three flashlights. Three assassins.

The helicopter noise faded away as the craft, unable to contribute to the search, were probably ordered to move out.

Beckett and Pamela moved perpendicular to the incoming team, a tactic the former DIA operative knew would force the termination team to split up.

Divide and conquer. In order to survive, Beckett had to take the initiative, had to force his pursuers to play his game, to react to his moves.

"Hey, which way did they go?" Beckett heard someone say, but he couldn't really judge distance in the swamp. Sound travels too well over calm waters. He guessed they were about a hundred feet to their left. Beckett decided to hold and wait, Pamela standing by his side clutching his hand, her heavy breathing matching her heaving chest, mouth wide open, nostrils flaring, eyes wildly gazing at him. She was hyperventilating.

Beckett set the weapons on a thick branch next to him and lowered himself into the swamp, forcing Pamela down until only their heads remained above the surface.

"Breathe with me," he whispered. "Breathe in through your nose, then out slowly through your mouth."

Eyes locked, her face only inches from his in the darkness of the bayou, Pamela Sasser began to slow her breathing.

Beckett felt her breath caress his face every time she exhaled through her mouth.

"That's it, Pam. Slow, slow, make every breath deep, make it count," he whispered as her catlike eyes, laced with a mix of terror and trust, remained trained on his, making the eye contact an intimate one, threatening to trigger emotions and images Beckett couldn't afford at this moment.

He placed a hand on her left shoulder, giving it a soft squeeze. "Hang in there. You're doing fine. Relax. Breathe."

Pamela did just that. She breathed deeply, slowly, her eyes absorbing his face, her ears listening to the jungle around them, to the distant noises of helicopters, to his soothing words, softly whispered in the dark.

"You're doing fine, Pamela. That's it. Breathe slowly. Stay with me. Don't fall apart. I'll take care of you."

Beckett stood and grabbed the firearms: a revolver and a large sawed-off shotgun, weapons which would give away his position to the rest of the termination team. He handed them to Pamela.

"Take these and wait here," he whispered while finding her eyes in the dark, a trickle of sunlight filtering through the thick canopy providing the only illumination. "Don't move. Don't do anything. I'll be right back."

"I'm coming with you," she said.

It took Beckett by surprise, her determination to come with him. For a moment he thought it was fear of being left alone, but then he realized it was more than that. They'd been forced into a partnership but, just as he had become her protector, she had become his. Untrained and unskilled, of course, but he knew that her wanting to come with him was about much more than fear of being left alone. And it made whatever last bit of emotional discipline he had fall away.

Beckett slowly shook his head and put a hand to her face, his index finger running over the freckle. "You'll get us both killed. Now, trust me on this one. I'll come back to get you as soon as we're clear."

Putting a hand over his, Pamela simply nodded.

Leaving her behind, in the safety of the dark and the trees, Beckett reached for his hunting knife and slowly immersed himself in the swamp, feeling the warm black water reach his neck, his chin. Beckett briefly closed his eyes and listened to the jungle, listened to the sounds of birds, of insects, of the rustling of leaves as a light breeze swept through the swamplands of southern Louisiana. He felt mud bugs crawling over his sneakers as they sank in the bottom. Slowly, Beckett used his free hand to reach for some of that mud and smeared it over his face and neck, blending himself with the surroundings, with the black waters, with the murky jungle. He slowly became just another creature of the dark, part of the local wildlife. Beckett became a predator, his eyes turning to his prey, a man wearing a dark jumpsuit holding a suppressed MP5 submachine gun twenty feet away.

Water reaching his waistline, the dark figure slowly scanned the woods around him with the weapon's muzzle, listening, anticipating, behaving just as Beckett would have expected him to behave. The man in dark had been trained by a U.S. intelligence agency. No doubt about that. The tactics were all the same. Beckett had seen them too many times in too many places.

Slowly, only part of his blackened face breaking the water's surface, Beckett moved slowly, quietly, with purpose. His legs kicked against the muddy bottom, his right hand clutched the blade's handle, his left arm propelled him through the water, closing the gap, bringing himself to within five feet of the unsuspecting operative.

Without warning, Beckett lunged, blade extended in front, aimed at the base of the neck. The sound of broken bones and ripped cartilage filled the dead silence of the swamp for just a few seconds, as predator and prey collided in the wild, as Beckett's blade found its target, cutting clean through the throat.

The operative was dead by the time he hit the water, the MP5 falling into the swamp without being fired once, the waterproof flashlight lighting the bottom of the bayou. Beckett moved quickly, pushing the bleeding body away from him while reaching below the surface and turning off the flashlight.

He groped around the muddy bottom, where he had seen the weapon go into the water, and found it. A quick look at the silenced barrel, and Beckett threw it back into the bayou. He wished he could have gotten his hands on the suppressed weapon before it had fallen into the swamp. The wet MP5 was now not only useless, but actually quite dangerous. The amateur operative had failed to protect the end of the barrel with an airtight plastic cap, or maybe a kid's deflated balloon—or even a condom—to keep water from seeping through the bulky silencer and entering the barrel, where it would create an acoustic wall. Anyone firing the submachine gun ran the risk of it exploding in his face as the igniting powder of a nine-millimeter round, unable to expand down the length of the barrel due to the accumulated water, concentrated all of its detonating pressure in the weapon's chamber, stressing the metal alloy casing beyond its rating.

The still figure floated away in the darkness. *One down. Two to go.*

Beckett distanced himself from the floating body. He didn't want to be around it when the other two operatives arrived. And he certainly didn't want to be near it when the local wildlife, most notably the large southern Louisiana alligators, smelled the spilled blood.

Beckett heard voices and lowered himself into the putrid waters once more, taking a deep breath and leaving only his eyes above the surface.

Two beams of light, crisscrossing each other in the dark, moved directly toward him, their yellowish glare cutting through light patches of fog lifting off the water surface. He immersed himself completely, eyes closed.

Beckett felt vibrations in the water. He sensed movement. The owners of those flashlights were near, very near, probably too close for Beckett to come back up for air. His lungs beginning to burn, Beckett turned around in the water and moved toward a cluster of trees behind him. Just then, he hit a trunk, but the trunk moved. It wasn't a trunk. It was a human leg!

Instinctively, Beckett slashed his knife up, toward the groin area, while propelling his body out of the water.

"Aghh!"

The ear-piercing scream whipped across the bayou, but Beckett barely heard it. The adrenaline boost kept him focused on his target. The man had already dropped the automatic weapon and was holding on to his bleeding testicles. Beckett surfaced in front of him, keeping the blade buried in the man's groin before swiftly moving it up, disemboweling him.

The second operative, merely six feet away, momentarily froze in horror and surprise at seeing a muddy figure suddenly emerging from below the swamp's surface. He turned his weapon in Beckett's direction and let go a single shot just as Beckett threw the blade at him with all his might.

The bloody knife dashed through the darkness and embedded itself in the operative's chest, right below the left shoulder, a full inch of the stainless-steel blade cutting into the victim's heart. In the same instance, Beckett fell into the swamp, a crippling pain from his right leg making him lose his balance. He had been shot.

As the inert bodies of both operatives floated a few feet from him, Harrison Beckett struggled to swim away from them, his mind exploding in colors as his fingers came in contact with the bleeding wound, the warm liquid streaming through his fingers telling him he needed help immediately.

The intense pain made him tremble, but his mind relaxed somewhat. His fingers had felt the gauge of missing flesh right above the knee, but the bone had not been touched.

Slowly applying pressure to swim away from the dead operatives and toward Pamela Sasser, Beckett verified his femur was intact. Although the searing pain sent chills across his body, he could still use the leg. Lifting it to raise the wound above his heart, Beckett breathed deeply, silently taking the pain while he removed his T-shirt and began to tie it above the wound to control the blood flow. As he finished securing the knot, he sensed movement behind him. He turned around and a bright light blinded him.

A fourth operative!

"Hello, asshole," said the operative, a tall, well-built man with short orange hair and a face full of freckles, training the MP5 on Beckett while using the flashlight to sweep the bayou. Two bodies floated facedown twenty feet away. "You're gonna pay for this."

Beckett didn't answer. He remained in a crouch, only his head breaking the water's surface. His eyes locked with the operative's harsh stare.

"Up, man! On your feet!"

Slowly, leaning most of his weight on his left leg, Beckett stood, black water dripping from his chest and arms, the throbbing in his leg multiplying the moment the wound dropped below heart level.

"Where's the woman?" the operative asked.

Beckett didn't respond.

The operative smiled when he noticed that Beckett was wounded on the right leg. "Hands above your head," he said, taking a step toward Beckett.

As Beckett lifted his hands, the operative swung the MP5 barrel in a semicircle, striking Beckett across the face.

The blow stung. His knees gave and he fell back in the swamp, blood dripping down his face from the track the metallic silencer had cut across his left cheek.

"Who told you to get down?" The operative asked, kicking Beckett flat in the face with a boot, an instant reminder of the back fist he'd received the night before.

Tears filled his eyes and everything began to spin as he absorbed the blow. Blood now flowed freely not just from his lacerated cheek but also from his nose.

"On your feet!" the operative screamed.

Feeling dizzy, light-headed, Beckett blinked rapidly, trying to bring his attacker into focus while struggling to regain his footing. But everything stung. His leg, his cheek, his nose, his bruised ribs from last night's fight.

Slowly, he managed to set his left leg firmly on the bottom and testily began to get up.

"I asked you, where's the woman?"

"Go to hell," Beckett responded in between his teeth.

Another muddy boot came out of nowhere and struck him flat in the solar plexus, adding injury to injury, pumping the air out of his body. Bending over, Beckett went back down again, this time struggling to keep his head above the water while gasping for air.

"I'm through playing games," the operative said. "Brasfield wants the woman. Where is she?"

Beckett couldn't answer even if he had wanted to. His body demanded the air he could barely deliver in short sobbing gasps. While using his arms and legs to steady himself to keep his head above water, he felt a pair of hands reaching for his right leg, pulling it out of the water and forcing his upper body into the swamp.

Flapping both hands to remain afloat, Beckett tensed as he watched the operative reach for a knife while tucking Beckett's ankle under his armpit.

"Where is she?" he asked again. "Tell me and I'll kill you quickly."

His face just breaking the surface, his arms moving up and down underwater, Beckett said, "Go to hell, asshole."

The operative tore off the tourniquet, pressed the blade against the exposed wound, and began to wiggle the edge against the raw flesh.

Beckett's back arched like a bent bow, his lids twitching convulsively, the agonizing pain reaching every square inch of his body, taking possession of his soul. The pain devoured him, like a ruthless predator, invading him, possessing him, scourging him. Painmaddened, eyes rolling to the back of his head, Harrison Beckett prayed for death.

He went under, below the boiling surface, where he could no longer hear himself scream, where he felt surrounded by a dark hell of mud and fetid waters that closed in on him

in the same manner as the DIA was finally making him pay
for his sins . . . for Rome.

From a distance of just a couple dozen feet, hiding behind
a cluster of trees while the waters of the swamp reached her
slim waist, Pamela Sasser had heard the questions. She had
also heard the responses.

Pamela looked at the weapons in her hands. A black revolver and a sawed-off shotgun with a dark-stained wooden
butt.

She felt a demon coming alive inside of her, sweeping
over her senses, rolling around her, taking total possession
of her. She wasn't sure if it was the adrenaline searing her
veins, or a primal survival instinct that had spiraled out of
her core, but she dropped the shotgun in the water and
clasped the revolver in both hands, a thumb pulling back
the hammer.

But could she really do it? Could she really pull the trigger while aiming the weapon at another human? But was
that a human being? Or was she killing a beast, a trained
assassin, the trash of society? An animal just like her father?
Is this what Harrison meant?

The questions drilled the inner workings of her logical
and emotional sides as she took one step toward the struggling men, toward the figure in black standing over Beckett,
her guardian, her protector, the man who would rather die
than disclose her location, the man Pamela felt an overwhelming desire to save, to protect, to keep *alive*.

But Pamela sensed something deeper, almost untamed,
savage, wild, kept buried deep in her heart for the past decade. Was the guilt of her mother's death and the anger
against her father shaping the wave of boiling rage that now
consumed her?

The figure in black stood just a dozen feet in front of her,
his back to her. In the twilight of the swamp, her eyes
shrouded by a veil of hate she could no longer control, Pamela saw him holding one of Beckett's legs. And for a moment Pamela was back in Beaumont, back in her house. Her

father was beating her mother, kicking her as she crawled away from him on the living-room floor, into the kitchen, across the dining room. Pamela heard her mother's cry, her father's laugh.

Bastard! You fucking bastard!

Instincts she didn't know she had surfaced with unequivocal clarity of purpose, making her thin arms lift the weapon, level it at the figure in black.

"Enough!" she screamed. "No more! No more!"

The figure, hands busy holding Beckett's leg, turned to her in surprise.

And Pamela Sasser, former associate professor of computer engineering at Louisiana State University, pulled the trigger once.

Beckett didn't hear Pamela's scream, but he did hear the muffled crack of a gun. The operative had finally done it. He had fired into Beckett, but Beckett felt no sting, no pain, no burning wound. His leg was free, his body was free, his mind liberated from the inconceivable pain that had pushed him to the brink of hell's abyss.

Momentarily confused, Beckett tried to reach the surface, but his arms would not obey him. His body failed to respond to his commands, his tired self longing for the peace offered by the dark, warm waters enveloping him. His body grew weak from the blood loss, his mind hoping to hold on to the calm silence of his surroundings.

There Beckett floated, between the surface and the muddy bottom. In the dark he heard Pamela's voice call his name. He saw her in the distance, by the shores of a jungle pool, under the tropical stars, calling his name, pulling him under, closer to her, below the surface, below the violent world he wished to depart, if only temporarily, while she absorbed his stress, his anger, his guilt. Harrison Beckett was falling, uncontrollably falling, reaching a place he had never seen before, a level of reality that was suddenly shattered when a pair of hands pulled his head above the water's surface.

Air.

The smell of gunpowder and decomposed trees reached his nostrils. His lungs filled once, twice. He coughed, eyes closed, mind wandering. He breathed deeply again, and again, surrendering himself to the mercy of his attacker, no longer caring for his life. Visions from the past came and went in multicolored flashes. He saw the lands, the faces, heard the screams of anger and the screams of passion, felt his victims' hands reaching for his own as Harrison Beckett carried out his missions with icy efficiency.

Through the pained howls of his victims, Beckett sensed something else. A pair of hands held his shoulders, shaking him, trying to pull him away from a surreal world he wasn't sure he wanted to leave. He also heard his name being spoken. Not in shouts, like his victims' screams, but in whispers—the soft whispers of Pamela Sasser's lips pressed against his ear.

"Harrison. Please, Harrison. You must tell me what to do. Where to go."

The words caressing the side of his face carried with them a hope Harrison Beckett didn't think existed. Pamela had shot the last operative!

"Please, Harrison. You can't leave me here. I don't want to die. I don't want to go to jail. Please, don't leave me alone. I *need* you!"

Her breath caressed the side of his face with the pleading whispers he could not ignore. He had already ignored enough pleas to last him a hundred lifetimes.

But not this one.

He inhaled deeply, letting her warm breath graze his face, touching him in places not even the sands of Rio or the slow tango on the streets of Segovia could ever reach. Only Cairo. Only the sands of the Great Pyramid, the smell of caravans traveling through the desert, her perfect smile . . . only Layla Shariff had ever reached—

"Please, Harrison. Please come back to me."

He heard the words again. Her words. Pamela's words.

Slowly, the reality of their situation throwing a blanket over the past, Harrison found the strength to say, "Blood

. . . I'm losing blood . . . my leg . . . tourniquet.''

He heard no answer to his words, but felt her hands reaching for his thigh, felt the pressure of a bandage wrapped above the wound, felt her arms helping him to his feet.

"No . . . don't. Get down here,'' he said, his mind partially coming back, realizing that they were still in grave danger.

"What?''

"Don't stand . . . vulnerable. Hide with me . . . in the waters.''

Pamela, her face barely visible in the gloomy swamp, lowered herself next to Harrison, who kept his right leg off the bottom, using his left one to support his body while immersed up to his neck in black water.

"That way,'' Harrison mumbled, using his face to point in the direction that would lead them directly to the small town of LaPlace, on the outskirts of New Orleans. "LaPlace,'' he added. "Reach LaPlace . . . motel . . . money belt.''

"I understand,'' Pamela said, moving next to him in the murky waters, the sounds of police sirens echoing inside the swamp.

Dropping the revolver in the swamp, hoping that the thick waters would not only absorb the metal and powder, but also the guilt of taking a man's life, Pamela Sasser moved in the direction Harrison had pointed, her thin arms helping her muscular, yet exhausted and wounded, guardian.

She pressed the side of her body against his while wrapping an arm around his wide shoulders, every nerve on her skin tuned to the muscles flexing under his wet skin. She felt them pump against the soft flesh of her arms, of her side. His arm wrapped around her neck, his hand occasionally brushing against her breasts as they struggled to keep their balance while moving in a crouch through the bayou. She welcomed his head slowly leaning against her shoulder, tucking itself between her collarbone and her cheek, greeted the gentle squeeze of his strong arm around her neck as he pulled her closer to him, and him to her.

For an hour they moved parallel to the interstate while police cruisers and ambulances rushed to the site of three burning police patrols. Harrison grew weaker. Even with the tourniquet, which had clamped any further blood loss, enough of the precious liquid had left his system to send chills through him.

"Cold . . . ," he murmured between rattling teeth. "So cold."

"Hang on," came the reply from the figure next to him, nearly invisible in the darkness, one of her arms wrapped around his back, keeping his bruised body pressed next to hers as they cruised through the black waters. "You can do it, Harrison. You can do it."

The mud on his face hardened, pulling on the deep cut he'd gotten from the operative's silencer, broadcasting a new wave of pain, which Harrison found somewhat invigorating. The pain kept him from fading away, kept his mind from getting cloudy. He realized he could use the pain as a weapon to help him and Pamela survive. And so he did, intentionally pressing his wounded leg against the swamp's bottom every time he began to feel light-headed. The pain was his ally, his own shot of adrenaline, his weapon, one he never knew he had, but one which Harrison continued to use as they advanced through the thickening waters, minute after minute, foot after agonizing foot, leaving the madness of their near-death encounter behind.

Twenty minutes later, his body almost drained, Harrison began to discern new noises from the buzzing of mosquitoes, the rustling of branches, the sounds of the swamp.

A town . . . a city. LaPlace.

Harrison felt light-headed again, and again he pressed his wounded leg against the bottom of the bayou. But he did not feel any pain. He was fading, fading away as the entire murky world around him began to spin, to close in on him. His vision tunneling, Harrison looked for Pamela in the darkness, and he found her, distant, remote, at the end of a tunnel that continued to narrow.

"Motel . . . money belt . . . motel . . . ," Harrison managed to whisper before the darkness fell.

10 Adversity

Fire is the test of gold, adversity of strong men.

—*Seneca*

MARYLAND
Wednesday, November 18

General Jackson T. Brasfield stared out the side window in the rear seat of his black limousine. Snowflakes danced by the Armorlite glass pane, covering a wilderness of bare trees with a layer of white. A stiff wind blew a cold front through the Maryland countryside, dropping the temperature into the teens, and bringing with it the light gray clouds that had darkened the blue skies of just an hour ago.

But the DIA's deputy director of intelligence did not grimace at the chilling weather, he frowned at another dark cloud shadowing his life. A cloud in the shape of Daniel Webster.

The situation in Louisiana worsened every minute. A phone call he had received five hours ago had frozen any hopes both Sinclaire and Brasfield had of putting a lid on this problem before it got out of hand.

The limo turned off the Georgetown Pike and off to a secondary road, where it cruised east for another ten minutes before turning into an unpaved access road that led to an iron gate.

A security guard left the comfort of his booth by the side of the gate and ran up to the limo as Brasfield lowered the rear window.

"Afternoon, General," said the guard, reaching for a remote-control unit strapped to his belt and punching a code in the small keypad.

The gate slowly slid to the right as the guard returned to the booth.

The limo driver drove through the entrance and up a snow-covered driveway that ended at the doorsteps of a large Victorian mansion hidden among towering pines caked with snow.

His driver let him out. The DDI took in a whiff of frigid air as snowflakes pelted his dark gray trench coat. His leather shoes leaving a neat set of soft prints on the thin layer of snow covering the cobblestone walkway, General Brasfield approached the entrance, where another guard opened the door for him.

"Good afternoon, General. The others are already waiting for you in the library. Mr. Sinclaire will join you shortly."

"Thank you," he responded, going inside, where the warm air fogged his glasses. Removing them and polishing them with a handkerchief, Brasfield eyed the antique furniture scattered over the waxed hardwood floors, overlooked by massive artworks hanging off walls that reached thirty-foot-high cathedral ceilings. The mansion was one of several Preston Sinclaire owned across the country.

The general knew his way around, and he walked toward the back, where the library faced the snow-covered forest behind the house.

The library, a room about twenty feet in depth and almost fifty in width, had one long table in the middle and was surrounded by three walls of floor-to-ceiling bookcases. Two dozen men paced the room, some smoking, others drinking. Silk business suits mixed with uniforms from all four branches of the U.S. armed forces.

Many eyes converged on the organization's second-in-command.

Through a false bookcase at the other end of the room, followed by two bodyguards, Preston Sinclaire made his entrance into the dimly lit room, already filling with cigarette smoke. Sinclaire knew each one of the attendees quite well. Perhaps *too* well. But none of them was his friend. Sinclaire had no friends, no wife, no kids. He had not seen his brothers and sisters in over two decades.

He had no weaknesses.

He had *nothing* that anyone in that room might use as a weapon against him. But the head of America's most powerful criminal network had *plenty* on each of the men chatting and smoking while waiting for his arrival. He had enough dirt on each one to fill a filing cabinet, and each of them knew it. That's why they were here this afternoon, that's why they had dropped everything they had been doing and rushed to meet with him at his request.

That was power.

His mere presence quieted everyone in the room. Cigarettes were put out, backs were straightened, seats were taken, except by Jackson Brasfield, who walked over to the bar on the side of the room and poured himself a glass of water.

While Brasfield calmly drank, the remaining sets of eyes converged on Preston Sinclaire, flanked by his bodyguards and wearing a dark gray Armani. He held a leather attaché, which he put down at the head of the table before slowly looking at each face, making sure everyone was here.

"The woman is still alive," he said while sitting down, setting his hands on the white tablecloth and interlocking his fingers. Sinclaire kept his gaze on his hands. A West Point graduation ring, class of '65, adorned the ring finger of his right hand. A gold Rolex hugged his left wrist. "The woman is still alive. Jackson, could you explain to us *how* can that be?''

Brasfield didn't answer right away but calmly put down the empty glass and removed his overcoat, exposing a chest full of ribbons and medals. The proud army officer folded the coat over the back of a chair before taking a seat on the next one, at the other end of the table from the CEO.

Placing both hands on the polished surface, fingers interlaced, Brasfield inspected the quiet group before turning to Sinclaire. ''Preston, I told you many times that assassination missions using a termination team on very short notice have a historical fifty-fifty chance of being successful. That's why we minimize our use of them. There are other methods to remove problems, but they take more time to set up.''

Sinclaire raised his gaze to Brasfield. ''Jackson, you sent half of our men after those two. They blasted a dozen Louisiana cops into hell, but Sasser and the assassin still got away.'' Sinclaire chose to refer to Harrison Beckett as the assassin in front of this group.

''I have my people on the lookout. They're still monitoring all the police channels in the state. If they show up anywhere, I'll have another team standing by to take them out. This time there'll be no mistakes.''

Sinclaire opened his briefcase, pulled out a half-inch-thick document, and leafed through it without really reading it. ''What makes you think they're still in Louisiana? Couldn't they have crossed into Texas or Mississippi already?''

Jackson Brasfield contemplated his former army buddy for a few moments before saying, ''An unlikely possibility. It's been only six hours since the shoot-out outside New Orleans. No, they're still in Louisiana, possibly still in New Orleans, looking for a way out of the state. I have people covering every airport and bus station. Also, the fact that they're the most wanted people in the state puts the entire law enforcement organization of Louisiana on our side, even if they don't know it. We're monitoring everything, Preston. If Pamela and the assassin just breathe the wrong way we'll find them. Our people are checking every hotel and rental-car agency, and six-hour-old records of stolen cars. We'll find them.''

Putting a finger to his chin, Preston Sinclaire looked away in the distance for a few moments before glancing around the room. ''Our records are pristine, gentlemen. We've worked very, *very* long and hard to get to where we are today. The polls say I'm in the lead for the White House race. The fucking press can't seem to find anything wrong with us, but believe me, those pit bulls are still looking. This kind of crap attracts reporters like vultures to carcasses. I called you here today to emphasize, face-to-face, the magnitude of the problem. You must do whatever it takes to put a stop to this before those scavengers from the press dig any deeper into this technology-theft claim and somehow someone links this shit to us.''

Just then there was a knock on the door. Brasfield checked his watch. ''It's Hamed,'' he said to Sinclaire.

''Come in!'' Sinclaire said.

The door inched open and Hamed Tuani, dressed in a two-piece suit, entered the room. He took a seat next to Brasfield.

''Hamed,'' Sinclaire began. ''You have been down in New Orleans and know this assassin better than any of us. How do you think we should proceed? Do you have any theories about the best way to eliminate this problem?''

The former Egyptian officer planted his elbows on the table, a pensive look painted over his bearded face. ''I believe we need to take the initiative, sir. We need to force them to play by our rules. We need to draw them in and then eliminate them.''

''Do you have something in mind?''

Hamed gave him a slight nod before saying, ''I believe I know where the assassin and the woman are headed.''

Brasfield turned to Hamed. ''You do?''

''Where?'' asked Sinclaire.

For the next five minutes, Hamed explained his plan to the group.

"Do it," Sinclaire said the moment Hamed finished speaking. "Set it up immediately."

"There's another issue," said Hamed, crossing his legs and resting his hands over his lap.

"What's that?" asked Sinclaire, keeping his eyes on the former Egyptian officer.

"It has to do with the leak. I think we've found him."

Brasfield and Sinclaire exchanged glances. "You did?"

"I ran checks on everyone here and came out empty-handed. I then ran a background check on every person with access to your executive suite," Hamed said, looking at Jackson Brasfield. "And I mean *everybody,* down to the secretaries, janitors, and clerks, which included one Eduardo López. A little investigating on the activities of Mr. López showed that he always delivers the department's mail and supplies while you hold your daily staff meetings in your office, General. According to your secretaries, López always has a tendency to hang around the reception area for a little longer than he should, either slowly going through the supplies, or picking up a magazine and browsing through it, or engaging in small talk while slowly cleaning the area. A little checking on López's personal items in his office, while he was on his lunch break, turned up a cellular phone, which held fifteen preprogrammed phone numbers. One of the numbers turned out to be the main exchange for the Federal Bureau of Investigation. We also found a laser eavesdropping device disguised as an alpha pager. Your secretaries stated that López always wears it while delivering supplies to your area, General."

"That son of a bitch!" barked Brasfield.

"Bring him to me," said Sinclaire.

"I've already sent a team to pick him up," continued Hamed. "He'll pay for what he's done, but first I'll personally see that he tells us everything he knows, including the name of the agent running this investigation. We're about to turn the tables, gentlemen."

NEW ORLEANS INTERNATIONAL AIRPORT
NEW ORLEANS, LOUISIANA

Wednesday, November 18

Mother Cruz left the NOPD escort behind as she reached her gate and checked in. She was mentally and physically exhausted. She felt nauseated from lack of sleep and was in a terrible mood. She had been ordered by the director of the FBI to get her ass back to Washington. Another team of Feds was on its way to Louisiana to continue the investigation. The most recent shooting, resulting in the deaths of a half dozen Louisiana police officers, had apparently caught the president's eye. The FBI director wanted a full briefing from the agent running the investigation before heading for the White House.

She walked down the concourse and reached the plane that would take her back to Washington, where she would have to explain to the director what had gone wrong.

Fuck.

As she stared out the window and watched a jetliner take off into the night sky, her mind replayed the events of the past twenty-four hours. The faces of Liem Ngo, Calvin Johnson, and Jessica White had joined the other agents that had perished while on assignment with her. At least their deaths had been sudden, clean, without much pain, unlike some of the murders Esther had witnessed during her years in Miami. Drug dealers were quite imaginative when it came to killing a Fed.

She shoved the painful thought aside and leaned her head back to gather her thoughts and hopefully come up with a theory that seemed sane enough to present to her superiors.

MARYLAND

Thursday, November 19

An hour before dawn, Preston Sinclaire and General Jackson Brasfield watched Hamed Tuani and three other men arrive at the mansion and go inside through a side entrance.

Sinclaire led the way as the two of them left the library
and headed down to the basement, where Hamed already
waited for them. Four white walls made of cinder blocks, a
concrete floor, a fifteen-foot ceiling sporting two surveillance cameras, and two armed guards assured Sinclaire that
Eddie López, who currently sat tied to a chair in the middle
of the room, would not attempt to escape.

The young Hispanic's eyes opened wide when he recognized Sinclaire, who walked into the middle of the square
room flanked by Hamed and General Brasfield. The two
guards walked next to Eddie López and pointed their weapons at him.

"Hijo de puta," the Latino said, slowly shaking his head.
"This country's really fucked now. So you're the cabrón
who's behind this mess."

Sinclaire grinned at Eddie López. "I'll take it you know
who I am."

"Fuckin' A, man," responded Eddie. "Caramba. And I
thought the chinga'o Mexican politicians were corrupt!"

"Do you know where you are?" asked Hamed Tuani.

"Nope. You bunch of pendejos blindfolded me, man. But
it doesn't really matter, right? I already know I'm screwed."

"Tell us the names of the lead FBI agents working this
case, and we'll kill you quickly," said Brasfield.

"Mierda," Eddie responded. "I ain't tellin' you shit. You
and the rest of your putos can go'n fuck yourselves."

Brasfield smiled, and he looked at Hamed, who in turn
looked at the guards and said, "Go get the stuff out of the
trunk of my car."

"You'll talk, Eddie," Preston Sinclaire said, leveling his
stare with Eddie López's defiant glare. "In less than an hour
you'll tell me everything I want to know."

11 Retaliation

Vengeance is mine; I will repay, saith the Lord.

—*Rom. 12:19*

DULLES INTERNATIONAL AIRPORT
WASHINGTON, D.C.

Thursday, November 19

At nine o'clock in the morning, Mother Cruz left the crowded concourse hauling her single carry-on garment bag. Feeling a bit tired after spending the night at O'Hare International in Chicago while waiting to catch a shuttle to Dulles, the brick agent rubbed her face in disappointment. She had not been able to get a room in the crowded airport hotel, forcing Esther to half sleep on a bench near her gate. It had been four days now since she'd last slept a full night in a bed, and her body was beginning to rebel.

But she could not lessen her drive now. The situation seemed to be worsening by the minute. Although her people in Louisiana and the local and state police were conducting a formal investigation, Esther Cruz didn't need a fifty-page report to figure out that Pamela Sasser and her protector had either been kidnapped by the same people that tried to assassinate them at the Cornstalk, or they simply had defeated the overwhelming odds against them and survived another hit. The oral report she had gotten almost seven hours earlier from the team of three agents sent to work with the New Orleans office indicated that the cops had been the first to die in the shooting. Then there had been some cat-and-mouse chase in a nearby swamp. The bodies of four men in black who had died from a variety of wounds were fished out of the swamp, three of them half-eaten by alligators. But no sign of Pamela Sasser and her crafty companion.

Now there's a handy son of a bitch, Esther Cruz thought as she spotted the elevators that would take her to the parking garage. She wouldn't mind meeting this character one day. Somehow she had the feeling that the four deaths in the swamp had been by his hand.

Checking her watch, Esther Cruz yawned again. This damned job was really getting to her. She had not taken a vacation in two years and the stress was beginning to take a toll. On the other hand, she felt unable to quit the rapid pace at which she went after the Web. She couldn't. She owed it to her husband.

Arturo.

The thumb of her left hand toying with the silver band on the ring finger, Esther cruised through the crowded terminal and toward the elevators, but in her mind she saw a woman in white holding hands with a tall Hispanic man in a black tuxedo. Esther saw her own smile, her own eyes looking at the man she'd sworn to love for a lifetime, however short.

I think one of them is Brasfield, Esther. He's one of the bastards on my list. I'll call you from the office.

Those had been Arturo Cruz's words as he'd walked out of their Bethesda, Maryland, home that rainy morning seven years ago. After months of running the ONI's portion of the joint investigation, Arturo Cruz was apparently ready to approach the secretary of the navy with irrefutable proof of corruption in the Pentagon. The ONI-FBI task force had enough evidence to terminate a dozen military careers. And indeed, the two intelligence agencies did end many careers that week in 1991, fifty-four stellar military careers in all. But the Web promptly assassinated the key ones, bringing the domino effect to a halt before it gained momentum. And the criminal ring also killed the lieutenant commander, ensuring that the investigation would end with his life.

A tear slowly rolling down her cheek, Esther continued to fiddle with the silver band. The Web had been optimistic. Esther's inner fire still burned strong. She would not rest until she nailed them.

Esther would need all her concentration and wit later today, when confronting her superiors, who would question her handling of the operation, every judgment call, and every decision made, including the one that resulted in the deaths of Special Agents Liem Ngo, Calvin Johnson, and Jessica White.

But before going to the Bureau, Esther Cruz wanted to stop at her home to freshen up. She owned a small apartment complex on the other side of town. Arturo and Esther had purchased the old three-story building shortly after their marriage, as an investment. After pouring their life savings into renovating it, they leased twenty of the twenty-five units in the first two floors and also hired a company to manage the apartment complex for them. After Arturo's death, unable to live at their home in Bethesda, Esther had sold the house and moved into a large unit in the unoccupied top floor of her building. Esther planned to manage the complex herself after her retirement from the Bureau.

But not before I catch those bastards, Arturo. Not before I make them pay for what they did to you, to us!

Esther ran a hand over the Smith & Wesson Model 659 in a chest holster under her jacket, feeling safe when her fingers felt the extralong, high-capacity magazine that stuck an inch out of the butt of the pistol. She had switched to this weapon after her close encounter at the Cornstalk in New Orleans. She now possessed a lethal twenty-one-round nine-millimeter automatic monster with more firepower than an M16 assault rifle. Carrying it wasn't a problem. Her extralarge jacket was large enough to hide a bazooka.

Esther reached the elevators. Following professional habits, she pressed the button for the floor below the one where she had parked her five-year-old Renault earlier in the week, before leaving for New Orleans. Although the New Orleans Police Department had agreed with the Bureau to keep Esther's identity a secret, it didn't mean Esther was safe from retaliation. Just as the FBI and the Office of Naval Intelligence had a mole in the DIA, Brasfield could very well have his own people planted inside the Bureau. If word got out that Esther had been responsible for stopping the execution of a termination order, then her ass would definitely be on the line.

She got out of the elevator and began to walk up the concrete ramp, close to the inner edge to peek up to the next level, where she spotted her light gray Renault exactly as she had left it a few days ago.

She heard another car approaching, and instinctively hid behind a dark sedan, leaving her carry-on under the front bumper. A black Mercedes-Benz slowly drove up the ramp, turned the corner, and went up to the next level. Esther Cruz stood and ran up the incline until the concrete ramps met at waist level. She crawled onto the next level and, on her belly, inched forward under a truck.

A few seconds later, the wheels of the Mercedes drove by. The car stopped and backed up, the wheels coming to a halt in front of the Renault. Two people got out and ran toward it, leaving the car's engine running.

Walking in a crouch by the side of the Mercedes, Esther pulled out her Model 659 and glanced at the other side, where two well-dressed and well-built men circled the French compact car. One carried a silenced Heckler & Koch MP5 submachine gun.

Again, she debated between following FBI procedures and identifying herself to the people Esther Cruz felt certain had been sent to kill her . . . or simply starting to fire. She opted for a compromise.

She leveled the weapon at the MP5 and fired twice. The loud rounds ricocheted off the weapon and the man let go of it. Both turned their heads in surprise as the MP5 fell on the ground with a loud clank.

"FBI! One move and you're dead!"

Neither of them responded. Esther heard the distant scream of a woman and the clicking of heels against the concrete floor.

"Put your hands over your head and lie flat on the floor facing down! Move it!" Esther commanded.

The taller of the two, wearing a blue pin-striped suit, complied immediately. The second one looked back at Esther arrogantly. He was shorter but stockier than the first. Esther knew she was being tested.

Hardening her gaze, Esther continued. "You have three seconds, asshole. You'll be on the floor by then, one way or another. It's your choice. One."

Esther noticed the defiant expression on the man's face fading away.

"Two."

The man dropped to the floor.

"You made the right choice," Esther said as she walked around the Mercedes and reached the Renault.

With her free hand she opened the trunk of her car. Someone would no doubt have called the police by now. All Esther had to do was hold these two characters until the cavalry arrived.

"I hope neither of you's claustrophobic. Now, you, get up."

The man with the blue suit looked at Esther, puzzled.

"I said get up, *now!*"

He complied.

"Get your butt in the trunk."

"Wait a second . . ."

"You got three seconds."

"Okay, okay," he said as he crawled into the relatively small trunk.

"You too, Shorty. Get in."

"We'll get even for this, bitch. I swear—"

"Oh, blow it out your ass and get in the car before I kill you. I'm getting tired of—"

Esther saw a red spot on the man's coat. It moved around the man's chest for a second and then onto Esther. It took her another second to realize what it was, and she instinctively dropped to a crouch. A fraction of a second later a bullet hit the trunk of the Renault. It had been targeted at Esther's heart. The short man briskly spun around and raced for the cover of nearby vehicles to the left while reaching into his coat.

With her ears ringing from the powerful blast of the initial gunshot amplified by the enclosed concrete structure, Esther Cruz leveled the Model 659 and fired twice. Both bullets impacted the middle back of the short man, propelling him forward. The hollow-point rounds expanded after they pierced through the short man's back, changed trajectories inside his body, and exploded through his chest with an outburst of blood and tissue. More screams followed the gunfire. Esther could hear people running in the parking garage.

She brought the Smith & Wesson around and aimed it at the man in the trunk, who was about to jump out. The FBI agent fired once, the round striking the man between the eyes, shoving him back into the trunk.

Esther Cruz dove and crawled to the side of the Mercedes. Not exactly sure where the shots had originated, she slowly raised her head over the passenger-side door and was about to peek at the other side through the tinted-glass window of the Mercedes when a red flash momentarily blinded her. A loud blast followed.

Esther jerked her head back as the bullet impacted the glass panel on the driver's side, but it did not go through. The round merely left a small scratch as it ricocheted off of the Armorlite glass.

Bulletproof!

Instinctively, she crawled into the Mercedes from the passenger side, jumped into the driver's seat, and heard three more impacts on the glass.

Fully aware that even the best armored glass had its limitations, Esther quickly put the car in reverse and sped down the ramp. The tires screeched as the German car zigzagged down the incline. Esther floored it and struggled to keep the wheel straight.

Suddenly, the FBI agent saw two men jumping in front of the car holding MP5 submachine guns as they opened fire in unison. Esther blinked in disbelief as nine-millimeter bullets peppered the armored windshield before deflecting upward. Rapid flashes from an FBI background in guns raced through Esther's mind as she recalled that the MP5 was quickly becoming the weapon of choice for police and criminals alike because of its rapid rate of fire without loss of accuracy, the reason much of the gunfire concentrated on her side of the strong windshield.

She kept her foot on the gas, struggling to put more distance between herself and the two guns. Suddenly, the back of her head rammed against the headrest when the Mercedes crashed into a small car at the corner. Quickly, she put the car in forward gear, turned left, and floored it again, accelerating down the concrete ramp until she reached the first level, where she parked the vehicle in the first spot she could find, jumped out, and lay against the cool, oil-stained concrete surface.

Esther Cruz heard the screeching tires of a car darting by at full speed, and exhaled as she watched a gray sedan speeding down toward the exit. The two gunmen were in it.

LAPLACE, LOUISIANA

Thursday, November 19

For Harrison Beckett the nightmare returned with formidable force. The smell of diesel fuel and engine smoke mixed with the stench of small animals exiting third-class cars led

by their Arab masters. Men and women carrying or hauling
cages with rabbits, chickens, ducks, monkeys, and goats
headed for the Cairo bazaar. The chatter of the people
around him and the quacks and squeals of the animals
drowned the noise of the black-and-gray diesel engine towering three stories high next to him. The wheels alone were
twice his size. But his senses were not as much aware of
the noise around him as of the four men clutching automatic
weapons who had shoved travelers aside while making their
way toward Harrison and Layla. Gunfire erupted. The explosions, amplified by the enclosed concrete-and-brick station, pounded his ears, mixing with the screams from the
crowd and those from Layla Shariff as she fell to her side,
taking with her the promise of a life that would never be
for Harrison Beckett.

"No ... please ... don't ..."
    Pamela Sasser bolted up from the couch next to the single
bed in the small motel room outside of LaPlace. She was
exhausted. She had helped Harrison reach the edge of the
swamp by the outskirts of town, just outside New Orleans.
The swamp waters bordered a small cemetery, where Pamela had dragged Harrison and left him hiding behind a
large mausoleum, before following his instructions to use
the cash in his money belt to find a motel room. Inside the
thick nylon belt, Pamela had also found fake driver's licenses and passports. By that time, a storm had moved into
the area, and that had served Pamela well, cleaning off the
mud from her body. The former LSU associate professor
had then walked a few blocks in the rain and found a motel,
where, pretending simply to have gotten caught in the storm,
she paid the night clerk with wet twenty-dollar bills for a
one-night stay. By the time she returned to the cemetery,
Harrison was stirring in his sleep. Pamela helped him walk
to the motel, where she stripped him to his undershorts,
wiped his face, arms, and legs, and carefully cleaned the
wound using wet towels. After leaving him snoring in bed,
Pamela had taken a long, hot shower, washed her clothes,

and let them dry under the bathroom's heat lamp for nearly an hour, before dressing and walking to a nearby shop, where she bought several large T-shirts, a pair of denim shorts, some peroxide, and several two-packs of Extra Strength Tylenol. She had also stopped at a fast-food joint and gotten a bagful of junk food. She had used the peroxide to clean the leg wound before tearing one of the white T-shirts to wrap his upper thigh.

Pamela approached Harrison, messy brown hair over his forehead, full lips murmuring something. She looked at his body resting on the queen-size bed, a white sheet reaching his waist. He wasn't as big as she had first thought. In fact, now that she'd had a good chance to inspect him without running through an alley or hiding in a swamp, she decided that he was actually on the thin side. But he was solid. The muscles on his stomach and chest tightened as he mumbled words that still made no sense to her.

She placed a hand on his forehead. No fever.

"Please . . . no . . . Layla . . . Layla . . ."

Pamela walked to the bathroom, wet a clean towel, returned to his bedside, and lightly pressed it against his forehead and cheeks.

Who are you, Harrison? In the past twenty-four hours this stranger had saved her life over and over. *But why? Why are you doing this?*

Pamela Sasser wasn't really sure of anything anymore. Her thought process could not go beyond today, her mind blocking the uncertainties of tomorrow. The newspaper she had bought at the souvenir shop, now sprawled between the couch and the bed, told a bizarre story of technological robbery, of violent assassinations, of explosive encounters between law enforcement officials and unidentified terrorists. For a good portion of the evening CNN had shown the scene by the interstate and the swamp, where the dead kept piling up. Four unidentified men in black, wearing state-of-the-art weaponry and communications gear, had been found dead from a variety of wounds—including alligator bites—in the middle of the swamp. The number of dead deputies, including Sheriff Jason Laroux, had the entire police force of Louisiana in rage at the perpetrators.

Pamela pushed back the thought of one of those deaths being at her hand. Right now she didn't feel like dealing with the guilt, which she knew would eventually catch up with her. But not now.

Dressed in a clean T-shirt and her new shorts, Pamela Sasser lowered the rag to Harrison's neck and upper chest, her mind wondering about the life of such man. Who was he? Where did he come from? What makes an assassin? What forces compelled him to chose this way of life? And who was this Layla? A wife?

She stiffened at the thought of Harrison being married, of belonging to another woman. Pamela Sasser suddenly realized she didn't want to part company from this man.

But why? Why those sudden feelings? Was it because she longed for the protection he provided, or was there something else? Would she have the same feelings if her life was not at risk? *Would you have wanted this man a week ago, Pam? Before the madness began? Before the deaths?*

She couldn't answer that. Too many things had changed since last week. Her entire *life* had been turned upside down many times over since last week, and she couldn't even guess how many more times it would change before she was either killed or somehow—with Harrison's help—managed to pull through and survive.

And what about that man in New Orleans? The one Harrison had wrestled the knife from and was about to interrogate when the police appeared? Who was he? What was their past connection? Harrison had refused to talk about him, claiming it was not important to their current situation.

She didn't buy that. She smelled a connection somewhere, and Harrison was piecemealing this whole situation to Pamela, telling her only what she needed to know and nothing more.

"Layla . . . no . . . Pam . . . Pamel . . ."

Pamela Sasser stared at Harrison. He was slowly coming around.

"Pamela . . ."

Harrison's eyes flickered open before closing again. He did that for another minute before murmuring her name again.

"Yes, Harrison. I'm here," she responded, rubbing the rag over his forehead again.

"Where?"

"At a motel in LaPlace."

"How long?"

"It's nine o'clock in the morning. You've been out for almost eighteen hours."

Eighteen hours? He bolted up, startling Pamela. "We can't stay here. They're looking for us. We have to move out imme . . ."

He felt light-headed. He had gotten up too fast and collapsed back in bed, still weak from the blood loss and the stress.

"Easy," Pamela said. "You've gone through a lot. You need to rest now."

Breathing heavily, Harrison Beckett looked at the punkish blond hair, the light olive skin, the blue-green eyes staring back with a condescending look.

Briefly inspecting his half-naked body, he said, "Did you . . ."

"You were nothing but mud from head to toe, but don't worry. You have nothing I haven't seen before."

Harrison laughed briefly, his eyes looking at the shotgun wound, before he pointed a finger at the bandage job.

"Yes, I did that as well."

"How did we get here?"

Pamela smiled and spoke uninterrupted for a few minutes. By the time she finished, Harrison's inquisitive gaze had changed to one of admiration for this beautiful stranger, who only a day and a half ago had panicked at the sight of his weapon.

"You've done well, Pamela. Thank you for saving my life."

Her eyes brightened at the compliment. "I'm the one

who's grateful, Harrison. You saved my life again in the swamp.''

His face sobered at the thought of the termination team. "Heard anything on the news?''

Pamela told him of the CNN broadcast. "Looks like we're the two most famous people in the state.''

His eyes staring into the distance, Harrison said, "We won't stay here long enough to receive any awards.'' Slowly sitting up, he rubbed a hand over a two-day stubble, his rested mind slowly coming together again. They had to move and fast, first out of this state and then up to Washington, D.C. He had to reach Brasfield and get his answers. He also needed to know who had fired first on the termination team at the Cornstalk, giving Harrison the few seconds' warning he had used to grab his weapon and prepare their escape. He felt stuck in the middle of three different factions: the DIA and Microtel, Louisiana cops, and the group that had saved his life at the Cornstalk.

"Who is Layla, Harrison?''

"Who?''

Pamela crossed her arms and cocked her head at him. When she spoke her voice was cold, her tone of voice strong. "Don't *fuck* with me, Harrison. I believe I've earned the right to get my questions answered. You kept mentioning her name in your sleep. Who is she?''

"Where are my clothes?''

Pamela tilted her head toward the bathroom.

Harrison stood, keeping most of his weight on his left leg while testing the strength of his bandaged leg. Slowly, he began to walk to the bathroom, the motel's blue sheets falling to his feet.

"Damn it, Harrison! I've got the entire state of Louisiana after me! This Layla is connected somehow to that bearded man who tried to kill us the other night. Just the mention of her name made him quite angry and surprised. Now who in the *hell* is she? And what's the *damned* connection?''

Harrison glanced back at Pamela, her blue-green eyes filled, lips twisted into a frown, the chocolate freckle reminding him of Layla Shariff. Standing next to the couch while peeking at the clouds through a crack in the curtains, Harrison began to speak, his words slow as he told her the story of Layla's death.

"Oh, dear God!" Pamela said, bringing a hand to her face. "How horrible it must have been. I'm so sorry."

"Like I said. It happened a long time ago."

"But—but how did you escape the DIA?"

Harrison lost himself in her blue-green eyes, in her brown freckle. He replayed the events after Cairo out loud. "I made it to Rome in one piece, but then the military began to corner me again. All of my DIA-issued passports were useless. In fact, they were *worse* than useless. Had I used any of them, the DIA would have tracked me down in minutes. At the time, I was labeled 'beyond salvage.' The DIA had people all over Italy looking for me. They really left me no other option but to . . ."

Harrison closed his eyes and turned away from her, his hands clasping the doorframe next to the windows.

"Harrison?"

He shook his head. "I didn't have a choice, Pam. Bastards had me cornered. I was out of options. The only way they would leave me alone was to make them think that I was already dead . . . and so I did."

"How?"

"It . . . it doesn't matter. I just did."

"It *does* matter, and you know it. How, Harrison? How did you manage to fool the DIA?"

"I faked my death in a car explosion." He turned back to face her.

Pamela remained silent for a few seconds as she considered her next question while absorbing the incredible revelation. "But . . . if you weren't in that car when it exploded . . . who was?"

Again, Harrison turned to the windows. "You don't want to know that."

"Who was in that car, Harrison? You obviously escaped

the DIA. That means you succeeded in fooling them. Who was in that car?''

Harrison stared at his own hands as he finally responded. His words echoed inside the small motel room. It was with his bare hands that he had killed that innocent man, whose only fault was to have been born with physical characteristics similar to Harrison's. That innocent man had to die to save Harrison Beckett.

Harrison told her about the assassination contracts, told her about the jobs in Brazil, Honduras, Hong Kong, Spain, Colombia. He told her about the missions, about the payments, about the results, about the injustices he had ended, about the good his work brought to people.

Harrison then stopped talking. He couldn't go on. He had said enough, more than he'd ever thought possible. He was trembling, his mind wondering how things ever got so complicated.

"Christ, I'm not sure who am I anymore," he said, walking into the bathroom without looking at Pamela. He wasn't sure if he could stare her in the eye after opening up to her this way. He wasn't sure why he had done it in the first place. He only knew that it was important to him that she understood how it was that he had become the person who had been hired to kill her, and who now had been unable to do that when he learned the truth.

"So," she said, leaning against the doorway. "What is the connection between the algorithm and Layla's assassin?"

Harrison shook his head, grabbed his pants and one of the large T-shirts hanging from the shower curtain rod, and dressed quickly. "I wish I knew. All I know is that the bastard's Layla's assassin. I proved that the other night. He's also associated with Brasfield and Sinclaire somehow. Those three are up to something big."

"That much is obvious."

"How powerful is this algorithm?"

Pamela rolled her eyes. "*Very* powerful. It points out a flaw in the design of a very popular computer chip manufactured by Microtel, which I believe is at the heart of the accident in Palo Verde. The algorithm exposes a flaw in the design that otherwise goes on undetected, until it surfaces totally unexpectedly to cause a disaster before hiding again. It's a pretty nasty and bizarre problem, and my algorithm just happens to force the chip into the state that exposes the problem fairly consistently.''

His brows lowered in curiosity, Harrison said, ''And where is this backup diskette?''

Pamela told him, explaining in detail exactly where on campus she had hidden it. Harrison knew the place. Still unknown to Pamela was the fact that he had spent a few days at LSU planning and executing the assassination of Dr. LaBlanche, a secret Harrison intended to keep to himself for some time, if not forever.

Pamela walked back to the room, sitting on the couch, and crossing shapely, tanned legs. The denim shorts, cut off to her midthighs, pulled up a bit when she sat. ''So, what now?''

Reaching for his money belt on the nightstand, Harrison removed several hundreds and one of his driver's licenses and Visa cards registered under a fake name, put them in his pocket, and smiled. ''Trust me.'' He headed for the door. Pamela went to follow him, but he turned, bringing his left hand up, palm extended toward Pamela.

''I shouldn't be gone for more than a few hours. Be ready to leave by the time I get back.''

''A few hours? Wait a minute. *Where* are you going?''

Again, Harrison smiled. ''Just be ready to leave. We've got a long trip ahead of us.''

''Trip? Where?''

''You're a size seven, right?''

''Excuse me?''

''Your size. It's seven, right?''

''Well, yes, but—''

''Shoes?''

''What kind of—''

''We're running out of time here. Shoe size?''

"Six."

"Be back soon. Bolt the door and don't let anyone in. If something goes wrong, go out the back window in the bathroom and hide in those woods behind the hotel until I get back. Got it?"

"Where are we going after you come back?"

"Washington, D.C."

FBI HEADQUARTERS. WASHINGTON, D.C.

Thursday, November 19

After spending an hour with the police and declining to go to her apartment or to police headquarters, Mother Cruz reached the lobby of the J. Edgar Hoover Building. There was no place safer than the headquarters of the Federal Bureau of Investigation. Only an idiot would try to send a hit team after her in here.

"Damn, I feel like shit," Esther said, flashing her badge as she cruised through the security checkpoint and headed toward the elevators, dressed in the same pair of blue jeans and T-shirt from two days ago.

Esther stepped inside an empty elevator and pressed the button for the fifth floor, catching her reflection on the polished metallic surface of the elevator's control panel. She looked terrible. She wore no makeup. The turquoise-and-silver jewelry hanging off her neck and ears rattled as she shook her head and ran a hand through her hair. Purple circles surrounded her bloodshot eyes.

Esther looked away. She wasn't headed for a beauty pageant but to meet the director of the FBI to discuss the most important case of her career.

The elevator's door opened and she stepped out, instantly catching the attention of a dozen agents and secretaries, who stopped what they were doing and stared at Mother Cruz as she headed for the rest rooms.

"Yes, yes. I know how I look. Now, get busy!" she told the puzzled group as she reached the ladies' room, where she relieved herself, splattered water on her face to wake up, and took another look at her reflection under the bright overheads. The puffy bags below a pair of bloodshot eyes in sunken purple sockets told Esther that she'd better get some real rest soon or risk passing out from exhaustion. Even a person of her endurance couldn't keep this up much longer. But where could she go to sleep? Certainly not to her apartment. Everyplace she went, she not only risked being killed, but she also compromised the people around her.

Leaving the rest room, Esther Cruz went straight to the office of the director of the FBI, the Honorable Frederick Vanatter. Aside from the receptionist in the waiting area, Esther saw two of the director's bodyguards, both of whom gave her a curious glance.

"Don't even say it, boys." She knocked on the door and went inside.

Smoking a cigar, Director Vanatter sat behind his desk wearing a starched white shirt and a gray tie that matched his slacks and suspenders. Esther knew Vanatter from the old Bureau days, when Vanatter had been special agent in charge of the Miami field office. Vanatter was a no-nonsense type who'd always shown respect for brick agents.

"Damn, you look like shit, Mother," barked Vanatter at the sight of his subordinate.

"Feel like shit too, sir," responded Esther.

"Hang in there. We'll bag the assholes that tried to kill you," Vanatter said, tucking his thumbs under the suspenders as he stood and walked around his office, the cigar hanging off the corner of his mouth. He was just as tall as Esther. With a bald head, pale and wrinkled skin, and broad shoulders, Vanatter had been director of the FBI long enough to know the way the Bureau moved internally. Vanatter could find anyone at any time. He knew where the red tape was and how to cut through it to get a particular job done, or how to pile up enough of it to stall a job for months, or even years. Vanatter was a blessing to have on your side and a curse to have as an enemy. He knew enough people in Congress, at the Departments of Justice, State, and Defense, and at the White House to get his way most of the time.

"Okay, Mother. Let's hear what you have."

"Not much, I'm afraid. But it's pretty damned obvious that I'm getting closer than we've ever been before, otherwise those bastards wouldn't be trying to take me out."

Esther proceeded to tell him everything she knew on the case, from the surveillance of Brasfield, which led her team to LaBlanche, to the most recent attack outside New Orleans. Esther also mentioned the mysterious man protecting Pamela Sasser.

"You're right," Vanatter said after listening for a few minutes. "There's lots going on, but we don't have anything concrete. The fact that you're marked for termination can only mean that you're getting your nose deeper than ever into this mess."

"That's right, sir."

"What's the connection with Pamela Sasser?"

"Another big question mark, sir. But obviously she's also very key to this whole thing, otherwise Brasfield wouldn't be trying to eliminate her."

Vanatter shook his head and said, "What now?"

"For starters, I would like your permission to monitor all police radios in Louisiana. I would also like to step up the surveillance of Jackson Brasfield, even if we increase the risk of getting burned. I want to keep the general on a short leash, particularly since I'm quite certain he's the one who's trying to get me killed."

The FBI director nodded. "All right. I also need to get you some more backup."

"I'd rather not, sir. No more backup for now, please. I want to go solo for a little while."

Vanatter drew on the cigar while pulling on the suspenders with his thumbs. Looking away, he said, "I read your report on the incident, Mother. I also read the official NOPD report. There's nothing I'd have done differently in your position. You deployed your forces in the best way you could. This kind of shit happens. I know it hurts to lose partners, but they all knew the risks when they signed up to work here. This ain't a country club. People *die* in this business."

"I know, sir. I'd still like to work alone for a while, at least for the next week. The fact that I'm now marked for termination puts everyone around me at risk. But that also works to my advantage, because my being alive will force those bastards to surface again, and when they do, I'll be ready to catch one alive."

"All right," Vanatter said. "You go solo for now."

SOUTHERN LOUISIANA

Thursday, November 19

Harrison Beckett gazed out of the passenger window of the semi truck pulling a refrigerated trailer filled with Texas beef, headed for New Orleans. Catching a ride at the outskirts of LaPlace had been a breeze for Harrison, who selected this truck because it was headed back east, and the closest city, New Orleans, was to the east.

He kept his gaze on the bayou flanking the road, not because he was enjoying the southern scenery, but because he wanted to limit the driver's view of his face. The human brain has a tendency to forget or distort the faces the eyes see for a short period of time. By keeping the back of his head and a partial profile exposed to the driver, Harrison tricked the driver's brain into painting an incomplete picture of himself. The driver would not realize this until later, if he ever tried to remember what his passenger had looked like.

"Where do you wanna get off?" asked the driver, a huge man dressed in blue overalls and a pleated cotton shirt with the sleeves rolled up to the elbows, exposing massive bronzed forearms covered with tattoos. A black beard and thick hair dropping to his brow line hid his features. The inquisitive blue eyes glanced at Harrison before going back to the road.

"Ah, it doesn't really matter. Somewhere within the city

limits should do. I'm looking to buy a used car," Harrison
responded, forcing a monotone midwestern accent. This
voice-control technique, combined with a passive manner,
minimized the attention that Harrison brought upon himself.
These techniques were actual weapons of disguise, at times
more powerful and less obvious than makeup or clothing.
Human memory relies heavily on physical peculiarities to
remember an individual after a short meeting. By forcing
the truck's driver to think he was seeing an average, unin-
teresting person, Harrison was in essence erasing this short
encounter while he was experiencing it.

The driver nodded, his eyes on the road as he negotiated
a turn. "In that case, let me drop you off by Williams Boulevard. Plenty of used-car dealerships there."

Still looking out the window, Harrison said, "Sounds
good."

An hour later, Harrison Beckett drove out of a used-car lot
behind the wheel of an '89 Camaro he'd purchased using
his fake driver's license and nine hundred dollars in cash.
Although the metallic blue paint job had a number of door
dings and scratches, and he'd seen a few rust spots below
the driver-side door, the engine and transmission were in
good enough shape for the job Harrison had in mind.

Driving the speed limit, he followed the directions the
dealer had given him to a nearby Wal-Mart, where Harrison
got Pamela and himself new Levi's, long-sleeve cotton
shirts, Reeboks, a small can of cigarette lighter fluid, three
packs of Marlboro Golds, and a few other essentials to trans-
form their appearances even more. With that he'd headed
back to the motel, smoking four cigarettes by the time he
pulled up to their room.

Pamela was shocked when she opened the door. Harrison
had already changed into his new outfit, and he now wore
a pair of black-rimmed glasses, which by themselves gave
him a studious look.

"Hi," he said, walking past her and unloading the contents of a paper bag on the bed. "Put these on and let's go."

Pamela held the jeans to her waist and smiled. "Hmm, didn't know men could actually pick up women's clothing."

Harrison closed and locked the door and checked his stainless-steel Seiko. "There's a bottle of hair coloring on the bed. Hurry up."

She went into the bathroom and came back an hour later as a redhead, dressed in a pair of tight jeans and a white long-sleeve cotton shirt. "There," she said, grabbing the hairbrush, the small can of gel, and the handful of makeup Harrison had bought for her. "How do I look?"

Harrison smiled, before the professional in him took over. "Good. Apply the makeup heavily, particularly around the eyes and lips. Also use the blush to tone down your cheekbones and nose. They're a bit too pronoun—"

"Hey!" she snapped, her eyes full of dark amusement. "Watch it, mister. I'll take your advice on the makeup, but you leave my nose and cheeks out of this."

"I was just—"

"I've been putting on makeup for fifteen years. I think I *know* how to make myself look different." She disappeared behind the bathroom door in a whirl of short cinnamon hair and white cotton.

The uneventful drive to Houston took six hours, time Pamela Sasser used to interrogate Harrison Beckett on his past. Her outgoing personality, combined with her witty, and at times snappy, disposition, made Harrison feel more and more at ease with her, and he eventually loosened up enough to tell her bits and pieces of his past.

"Do you find pleasure in killing someone, Harrison?" Pamela asked after a long silence. The question felt like a kick in the stomach.

"Christ, not *that* line of questioning again." Harrison rubbed a temple.

"I'll take that as a no. Why do it, then?"

Harrison couldn't believe this woman. In such a short period of time she had learned to see things about Harrison he thought were invisible. The irony of it was that he was supposed to be the secret agent, the master of deception. Yet, here was this Pamela Sasser, ex–associate professor at Louisiana State University, reading him like a book.

"Because they deserved it. The world's a better place without them." The reply left Harrison's flanks wide open for a side punch, and he knew Pamela would take it.

"A better place according to whom?"

Harrison briefly closed his eyes. "Have you ever seen a crack baby, Pamela?"

She blinked in surprise. "What's that got to do—"

"Have you ever seen a twelve-year-old girl selling herself for a gram of coke? When the State Department asks me to do a job on a cartel figure and make it look like an accident, so that there will be no reprisals against Colombian political figures, I do it *regardless* of the price they're willing to pay. When a military tyrant overthrows an elected president and starts his own reign of terror, I do him for *free*. When women and children starve because some corrupt strongman has an entire nation scared to death, I stage an accidental death with a smile on my face."

Pamela was silent.

"This world is full of corruption. The lust for political power knows no boundaries, geographical, social, or moral. I lost Layla Shariff to that corruption. My *life* was turned upside down because I tried to fight that corruption, but I was naive to think I could do it going by the book."

"You know," Pamela said, "my father was a corrupt cop who used to beat my mother and me. I tried to expose him, but his cop friends stood up for him and all I got was another beating. So I ran away from home after high school and settled in Baton Rouge. A year later I received a call from home. My father had beaten my mother to death. Believe me, Harrison, I wanted to grab a gun and kill the bastard, but instead I agreed to testify for the prosecution. I resisted taking the law into my own hands and went by the book. The jury sent my father to prison for life. You, on the other hand, have apparently nominated yourself jury, judge, and executioner." Arms crossed and head cocked, Pamela focused her eyes on him like a light beam. Her moussed auburn hair reflected the sunlight. The dark eye shadow, deep burgundy lips, and brown freckle stole the attention from her nose and high cheekbones, giving her a radically different look.

"I'm just doing what everyone else out there wished they could do with this world's trash but won't."

"That's right. They won't because they believe in the system."

"Wrong, Pam. They won't because they don't have the guts to do it."

"Don't tell me about guts, Harrison. It took guts to try to expose my father—even if I didn't succeed right away. In fact, I wish I would have persisted instead of running away. Maybe my mother would still be alive today. This country's so great because people believe in the system. Without it everything goes to hell."

Harrison sighed. "Sure, Pam. I can see how good this system has been to you. You can stand in your ivory tower and dispense justice to the world, but I noticed how much you abided by all that *system* crap the moment your own life went to hell and the *system* that you love so much turned against you. Don't you see that it's all a facade? Our government officials are just the puppets in a show controlled by the forces of corruption. You got a little taste of it a decade ago. You're getting the full dose now. People like Preston Sinclaire, Jackson Brasfield, and Layla's assassin are the ones in control, and believe me, there's only one way to deal with them. I tried the other way in Cairo, and I paid the price for my innocence. I don't intend to make that mistake again."

Silence. Interrupted a moment later by Pamela.

"I killed a man, Harrison."

Harrison Beckett had been waiting for that one to pop up any moment. Pamela had not mentioned it and he wasn't about to bring it up. Again, he understood exactly what she felt. She had been running away from the guilt, hoping to escape it, but he knew that was an impossibility. It was finally catching up with her.

"I killed him, and I didn't even feel guilty as I was doing it," she added, her eyes beginning to fill. "I shot a man and I didn't feel an *ounce* of guilt. . . . In fact, I almost enjoyed it. I felt like I was killing my own father. . . . Oh, God, what is happening to me? Why do I feel so terrible all of a sudden? Why?"

Harrison was about to pull over when he remembered the last time he'd done that. His professional side kept the Camaro on the road as he reached with his right hand and pulled her closer to him, her face already buried in her hands as she cried.

"I . . . I don't know what's happening to me. I killed someone . . . I pulled the trigger . . . and at the time I wanted to do it, wanted to kill him. . . . I keep justifying it in my mind that that man wasn't human, wasn't a man but an animal, a beast, just like my corrupt father. . . ."

Harrison simply hugged her closer, her head resting on his shoulder; her hands, fingers interlaced, rested on his right thigh as the palm of his hand caressed her shoulder.

Harrison Beckett turned his head and softly kissed her forehead. "I know how you feel Pam," he finally said. "It's a hell of a thing. But you did it in self-defense. Had you not shot him, he would have finished me and then gone after you. You had to *kill* to survive. You followed the most primitive directive of any animal species, and you shouldn't feel guilty about it."

She abruptly pulled away, her lips trembling, her eyes wide and shiny. "Easy for *you* to say that. You—you who have killed so many people . . . for money! For *money*!"

Harrison scolded her with his stare. "That wasn't fair, Pamela. That just wasn't fair."

Trembling hands clutching the steering wheel, Harrison Beckett returned his eyes to the road. *That'll teach you about sharing secrets with a woman, you dumb ass!*

As he silently berated himself for having opened up to her, Harrison Beckett felt her by his side again. Pamela pressed her body against his while grabbing his right arm, lifting it over her head, and resting it on her shoulders, exactly as it had been less than a minute ago.

"Sorry," she whispered. "I didn't mean that. I really didn't. Please forgive me."

Harrison didn't answer. He simply hugged her tight and turned his head to kiss her forehead. But Pamela raised her face and brushed her lips against his. Harrison, surprised by the intimacy, quickly turned his face back to the road.

Bringing a hand to the cut on his cheek, Pamela softly ran a finger around the purplish hue under his eye, slowly lowering it to his lips, his chin, his neck, before kissing the corner of his mouth.

"Sorry," she repeated, resting her head back on his shoulder. "I'm very sorry."

They arrived at Houston Intercontinental in time to catch a flight to Chicago, where Harrison planned to spend the night at the airport hotel and hop on a morning shuttle to Dulles International. But the airport hotel was booked, costing Harrison over five hundred dollars in bribe money before the clerk behind the counter agreed to let them have a single room.

That evening, Harrison Beckett sat on the queen-size bed in their hotel room, the empty steel cart of their room-service meal blocking the door, just in case. An empty wine bottle lay amid empty dishes and half-drunk glasses. Pamela was in the shower, where she had disappeared after giving him a long, passionate kiss.

The distant whine of jetliners departing to places all around the globe mixed with the sound of running water.

Harrison Beckett felt awkward, his mind struggling to do the right thing. He could still walk away, could still leave before this went so far and so deep that he feared he would never be able to return.

But the bathroom door was already opening, the lights were already dimming, the lithe figure underneath an extralarge Chicago Cubs T-shirt was already moving in his direction.

Harrison Beckett knew he would not be able to stop now, did not want to stop. He wished he could stay by her side forever, however long or short their forever would be. Harrison closed his eyes as he embraced her, and he and Pamela found themselves slow dancing to the soft music of the radio, barely moving as they held each other close, her breasts under her T-shirt pressed against his chest.

"This is crazy," he whispered. "This is wrong."

Pamela didn't respond, letting his strong arms take her to faraway places, where fires burned in the night, where ships sailed across endless oceans, where the wind and the sky became one in their universe of uncertainty. She let herself go, surrendered all fears and anxieties to his tender touch as the music played, softly, slowly, to the rhythm of his hands caressing the sides of her thighs, inching up the T-shirt. Open palms conformed to the curves of her back, moved in the space between her flesh and the cloth, between heaven and earth, carrying her across rain forests, through virgin beaches, high above the mountain peaks of South America and deep below the serene surface of the China Sea. Until slowly, carefully, setting her down gently on the bed, naked, her eyes half-closed, his hands moving over her breasts, against her belly, exploring her thighs, her torso, her neck.

Unity.

That's what Harrison Beckett felt as he held himself above her. Complete, dreamlike unity, far beyond the rapture of a beach in Brazil or a straw hut in Honduras; mightier than a slow street tango in Segovia or a mountaintop villa in Colombia.

Unity.

He felt dominating and dominated all at once as they slowly moved in unison, her eyes on him as he swept over her again and again, time after time, her fingers running the length of his back, her face lost in his neck, her tongue licking him, tasting him.

In the half-light of their world, Harrison saw her eyes in

the distant stars, saw her face in a crimson sunset on a deserted beach, heard her voice whisper his name at dawn in the jungle, felt her shivering body gliding under him as they traveled through their new universe of certainty on the wings of mythical birds.

Unity.

Lost in a rapture neither of them wished would ever end, Harrison and Pamela left the guns of termination teams behind and circled long-forgotten lands, contemplated a blood-red sun sinking below the scarlet horizon, watched campfires light up the night, listened to the locust and the cricket sing in the forest.

Images, sounds, smells, tastes. The two of them moved slowly, their wet bellies gliding back and forth, back and forth. His chest pressed against her breasts, his hands on her waist, on her back, on her torso. Her ankles caressed the back of his thighs as he entered her, hard, yet gently; deeper, yet with care, until they felt the end coming, until their bodies shivered, tensed, relaxed.

Time.

"This is nice," she whispered, placing her arms over his. "This is very nice."

A minute later, he heard her breathing steadily. She had fallen asleep. Harrison kissed the back of her head, listening to the jets, as he too faded off to sleep.

One of those jets was American Airlines flight 563 with service to Orlando, Florida. One hundred sixty passengers were aboard the advanced Boeing 767. Three dozen business travelers shared the cabin with twenty different families headed for Walt Disney World and six elderly couples seeking refuge from the cold winter months. The captain, a former navy F-14 pilot and fifteen-year airline veteran, had flown this route countless times before. He had been one of the first American pilots trained in the new-generation plane, which featured a glass cockpit composed of six CRT screens. The CRTs constantly displayed the information traditionally monitored through the maze of gauges and dials that had crowded the cockpit of every jetliner prior to the 767. Thousands of systems, from cabin-pressure control to navigation, fuel management, and even in-flight movies, were controlled by a number of independent computers, their status displayed on the CRTs.

The captain read their current cruising altitude and heading from one of the monitors and, satisfied, he engaged the autopilot, Boeing's most advanced automatic flight-control system.

"Copilot's plane," the captain said to his relatively inexperienced right seat, who simply nodded and kept an eye on the information displayed on the screens.

The silver-haired captain unstrapped himself, stood, and headed for the lavatory. He actually felt sorry for this new generation of pilots, who didn't get to do as much actual flying as the pilots of his generation. In trying to eliminate pilot error by inserting many layers of software and hardware between the pilot and the machine, Boeing was inadvertently creating a whole new crop of fliers who might not be able to react quickly enough in case of an emergency. Sure, all new pilots had to put in the hours in emergency training, but in his opinion, it was the *actual* flying, the day-in, day-out piloting of an aircraft *without* the help of a million lines of computer code, that truly familiarized the pilot with the machine.

Leaving the cockpit in the hands of Boeing's programmers, the captain went into the lavatory of the first-class section.

The sophisticated flight-control system consisted of a computer program so complex that it almost challenged the space shuttle's. It read parameters such as wind direction, wind speed, air density, outside temperature, magnetic north, true heading, altitude, airspeed, ground speed, vertical speed, fuel pressure, fuel temperature, fuel consumption, external air pressure, cabin pressure, attitude, and programmed navigation route. It constantly tracked signals from a dozen different airports and used them to pinpoint its location in time and space. It then used that data to correlate with the information updated ten times each second by the plane's global-positioning system. Finally, the autopilot transmitted its commands to the fly-by-wire system, where another computer read the commands, enhanced them to compensate for the 767's aerodynamic design and several other factors, and then translated them into the electrical pulses that drove the actuator motors controlling the twin turbines and the control surfaces: the elevators and rudder in the tail section, and the ailerons in the wings. The system would even guide the jetliner down to the runway in zero visibility.

It was a marvel of engineering.

The control of the cabin air pressure, one of the most vital systems in the airplane, particularly when flying at thirty-two thousand feet, rested in the millions of transistors inside a Perseus microprocessor. The sophisticated system handled the constant adjustments in pressure and temperature as the plane cruised through the lower stratosphere at 540 knots. The control-systems program performed the same monitoring functions over and over, at the rate of ten thousand times each second, taking as inputs the current atmospheric conditions inside and outside the plane, and adjusting them to correspond with preset values. The system kept the pressure inside the cabin at exactly 14.7 pounds per square inch, the same as sea level.

The control box was located right below the cabin's floor, where most avionics and computer systems worked in an environment also controlled by the Perseus.

The extreme cold weather, combined with the mild change in air pressure as the jetliner left a low-pressure zone over central Illinois, resulted in a combination of data inputs that exercised the flawed circuitry in the chip's floating-point unit. This occurred right in the middle of a calculation to determine the proper adjustment to the cabin pressure. Instead of adjusting the air pressure by the intended—0.07 pounds per square inch—a normal change during flight—it shifted the decimal point two positions to the right and dropped the cabin pressure by a dangerous 7 psi. The air-pressure control system slaved to the Perseus automatically bled off the programmed pressure in five seconds.

Inside the cabin, passengers screamed as their eardrums ruptured. Many passed out. The ones that remained conscious bent in pain as bubbles of nitrogen formed and expanded in their bloodstream. Some managed to reach for the dropping oxygen masks above each seat and braced in pain and terror.

The flight-control system, sensing the sudden loss of cabin pressure, operated as designed, automatically dropping the 767's nose by almost forty-five degrees to reach a safe altitude in the shortest amount of time. The sudden change in attitude, however, caused the captain to crash his head against a lavatory wall, rendering him unconscious. In the cabin, flight attendants were run over by the food carts they had been pushing. Havoc set in as food and beverages flew across the compartment, where an emergency video came on. Its protagonists, eerily detached from the reality of the situation, almost comically lectured terrified passengers on the proper use of oxygen masks and how to prepare for a crash landing.

In the cockpit, the copilot nervously stared at the CRTs, wondering if he should let the flight software handle the emergency until the captain got back. But the captain never returned, and the single unharmed flight attendant had her hands busy handling maddened passengers.

Afraid of disengaging the autopilot, which the copilot knew had been programmed to handle this and many other types of emergencies, the rookie flier simply monitored the controls as the plane dropped below fifteen thousand feet.

At ten thousand feet, the copilot expected the nose to level off, but the autopilot program had reached an impossible situation. Its altimeter reading conflicted with the monitored cabin pressure. At ten thousand feet the autopilot had expected a higher cabin pressure than the Perseus's flawed view of the cabin pressure. The software locked, keeping the flight controls in the last programmed position.

Eight thousand feet. Speed 580 knots.

The copilot began to tremble. The 767 was not leveling

off, and the autopilot showed a major malfunction in its control software.

At five thousand feet, he held his breath and disengaged it, for the first time taking command of the vessel.

He cut back engines and began to pull back, but the jetliner's reaction time to his commands, as relayed by the fly-by-wire system to the turbines and the airplane's control surfaces, was almost eight seconds, time in which the 767 dropped another two thousand feet.

At three thousand feet, the 767 slowly began to respond, but it was too late. The elevators struggling to bring the nose up could not offset the downward momentum before the jetliner struck the ground, just three hundred miles south of Chicago.

Nose first.

The fully fueled 767 disintegrated on impact. A massive sheet of flame lit up the skies of southern Illinois, followed by a thundering explosion that shook towns as far as twenty miles away.

12 Deception Games

Open not thine heart to every man, lest he requite thee with a shrewd turn.

—*Eccles. 8:19*

WASHINGTON, D.C.
Friday, November 20

The air by the bar was heavy and the smell of smoke and pasta filled Pamela Sasser's lungs as she tried to squeeze her way out of the crowded place. The fifty-year-old bartender, a chain-smoker with a wrinkled face and a bad cough, smiled and waved, a cigarette hanging off the corner of his mouth.

Pamela forced a smile and waved back. Her hair was moussed and parted on the side, changing her punkish look of just an hour ago into the mature, distinguished reflection cruising across the wall-to-wall mirrors behind the bar. Her exposed forehead gave her an air of elegance she didn't know she could have. Harrison had suggested the change in hairstyle, and Pamela had been surprised at the results. It seemed that every time she looked in the mirror lately she saw a different person.

A chameleon, Harrison had said last night, after they had awoken an hour after making love and had talked for a long time before loving again. *In order to survive in this business you must change constantly.*

And to that end, she had highlighted her catlike eyes and accentuated her full lips, but not with the cheap makeup Harrison had picked up at Wal-Mart. Pamela had used the high-dollar cosmetics she'd purchased a few hours before at the same department store where she'd bought the coat, evening dress, and matching suede high-heel boots that had caught the eye of several men at the restaurant. In the fifteen minutes she had been in the club, she had learned from the bartender that Generale Brasfield always arrived at the restaurant at 8:30 P.M. This he had disclosed to her after she insinuated to him that she was looking for good male companionship and had heard that Jackson Brasfield was very generous when it came to pleasing attractive, friendly women like herself.

Pamela grinned, thinking back on Harrison's initial concerns of her going into the restaurant alone. But unlike Louisiana, where she had been a wanted woman, at Giovanni's Harrison was the one who ran the risk of being recognized. Besides, she knew that bartenders would be more willing to talk to an attractive woman than to a man. She had been right.

Pamela inhaled deeply as she stepped outside the restaurant, welcoming the night's cold air. Her heart drummed inside her chest, and she felt the adrenaline pumping through her. The entire deception episode in the restaurant had been like a drug. The realization of seeing people believe she was who she claimed to be had calmed her nerves after the first minute inside, making her feel more and more at ease with her new personality. She began to understand why so many people just couldn't leave this type of work. This was a truly stimulating experience. But she also realized why some went crazy after a lifetime of pretending to be someone they were not.

Buttoning up the full-length coat, Pamela Sasser glanced

up and down the snow-covered street. A yellow hue from
the mercury streetlights reflected off the recently fallen
snow.

"Leaving already, miss?" asked the doorman.

"Yes," she responded, rubbing a finger on her left temple, "I'm feeling a little sick."

"Would you like me to get you a cab?"

"Ah, no, thanks."

"Well, come back and see us someday."

"I will. Bye."

As she walked away from the front door, Pamela noticed
a man dressed in several layers of ragged clothes sitting on
the sidewalk under a covered porch drinking from a bottle
inside a paper bag.

"Hey, baby, wanna join me?" asked the homeless man.

"I don't think so," she responded.

"Hey, I thought I told you to get the hell out of here a
few minutes ago!" screamed the doorman.

"Sidewalks are public property, man!" the homeless man
snapped back, taking another sip. "Whadaya say, baby?"
He grinned broadly at Pamela, showing her two rows of
blackened teeth and gums.

"That's it, I'm calling the cops!" screamed the doorman.

"All right, man, I'll go somewhere else!"

Pamela just kept on walking to the end of the street and
disappeared around the corner, where Harrison sat behind
the wheel of a rented Mustang smoking a cigarette.

"Back so fast?" Harrison wore a black leather jacket.

"Yep. Learned all that I needed to learn." She unbuttoned her coat and leaned over to give him a kiss on the
cheek.

"Well?"

"According to the bartender, Brasfield's due in here at
eight-thirty," she said, sitting sideways to him, exposing a
tan thigh while running her hand through her cinnamon hair.
"He always drives up in an unmarked sedan, and has a
driver and two bodyguards with him."

"Not bad for your first undercover mission," Harrison

said, taking a final draw, rolling down the window, and tossing the butt outside. He started the car and drove around the
block, stopping fifty feet from the restaurant on the opposite
side of the four-lane street. He checked his watch. It was
8:14 P.M.

"Who's the bum sitting on the sidewalk by the entrance?" he asked, punching the Mustang's cigarette lighter
before releasing the magazine from the handle of the Colt
.45 he'd purchased from a black-market arms dealer an hour
after landing. The high rate of crime in Washington, D.C.,
made it easy to purchase firearms. After checking the magazine, Harrison shoved the Colt in the small of his back,
grabbed another Marlboro from the pack, and snatched the
car's lighter the moment it popped back out.

"Some drunk. The doorman's been trying to run him
off."

Lighting up and taking a long draw, Harrison cracked the
side window and stared at the large sign over the entrance,
still trying to figure out a way to get close enough to Brasfield. Although he didn't show it externally, he felt relieved
that Pamela had made it out of there in one piece. Many
scenarios had floated through his mind during the long
minutes after she had gone inside. What would he have done
if she hadn't come out as planned? Would he have gone
inside? And what if she wasn't anywhere to be found? Then
what? A sudden feeling of loneliness had flooded Harrison
Beckett at the thought of losing her just as he had lost Layla
Shariff.

Glancing at Pamela Sasser, he saw the ex-associate professor inspecting her sharp fingernails, which had not broken
in spite of the commotion of the past two days. He remembered last night, remembered her touch, her feel, her smell,
the look in her eyes as they made love.

"You did good out there, Pam," he said, his right hand
reaching her face, fingers caressing her cheek. "I'm proud
of you."

Shapely blue-green eyes sparkled at the comment in the
murky interior of the rented Mustang. The low-cut burgundy

dress she wore below the unbuttoned coat showed the smooth curves of her honey-colored breasts.

"What's going to happen to us, Harrison?" she asked.

This time around he didn't mind the question at all.

"We'll work it out, Pam. I'll take care of you. I'll make sure nothing happens to you."

The flash in her eyes leaped the void between them. "Somehow I know you will."

Harrison stared at the chocolate freckle, then pulled her over and kissed it.

Suddenly, he heard a car coming down the street from his left. A pair of headlights approached the restaurant's entrance, snow shoved aside by the dark limousine's front tires coming to a full stop by the heavily illuminated front.

"That might be it," said Pamela, pointing toward the limo with the tinted windows.

At the same time, the drunk got up and began walking in the direction of the unmarked sedan just as a gray van came in from the opposite direction. The engine sounded powerful. Harrison turned his head and spotted the second set of headlights going straight toward the drunk, who was slowly getting closer to the limo.

"Harrison. That man's gonna get run over," said Pamela, letting go of his hand and cupping her face.

Harrison didn't respond, brown eyes analyzing the situation, the cigarette held up in between his index and middle fingers. Why would a homeless drunk be out here on such a cold night instead of at a warm shelter? And why would he get up and walk toward the limo as the van approached? Several bells went off in his head as a sign flashed in his mind with the same intensity as the neon sign flickering over the restaurant's entrance: *A setup!*

The van came to a screeching stop right in front of the drunk, who screamed some obscenities to the driver while pounding on the short hood. The driver got out and started shouting back for the drunk to get out of the way. The two bodyguards approached the drunk as the limo's chauffeur got out and opened the back door.

Suddenly, the driver of the van pivoted on his left leg, bringing his right leg up and around, smashing it against the head of one of the bodyguards.

Damn! Harrison thought as the powerful kick pushed the man back against the sedan's chauffeur. Simultaneously, the drunk punched the second guard behind the right ear, making him collapse facedown on the asphalt. The chauffeur reached inside his coat but didn't get a chance to pull out a weapon. The van's driver spun furiously toward him. This time, instead of elevating his right foot, he remained in a crouch and palm-struck the guard in the middle of the chest.

Harrison saw the chauffeur take a few steps back holding his chest. His mouth was open, as if he wanted to scream, but nothing came out. The driver then drove his right knee into the man's groin.

Both the van's driver and the drunk dragged Jackson Brasfield out of the backseat of his sedan and into the van. Within seconds the old vehicle accelerated down the street. The entire incident had taken less than thirty seconds, leaving hardly enough time for the doorman or anyone inside the club to react.

Harrison floored the Mustang and turned the wheel. The sports car leaped forward and around, its rear wheels leaving a wide track on the snow.

"Hurry, Harrison, they're getting away!" Pamela screamed as the car completed the turn. She was pushed back against her seat as the Mustang accelerated after the departing van. Harrison swiftly worked the gears, closing the gap to about two blocks. His headlights were off.

"Good job, gentlemen," said Brasfield as he sat in the middle seat of the van, flanked by two bodyguards packing side arms.

"That went pretty smooth, Jackson," said Preston Sinclaire, sitting sideways in the rear seat and checking the back window.

"They're following us?" Brasfield asked Hamed, who sat next to Sinclaire in the rear of the van.

The Egyptian nodded. "Right behind us." He pointed to an automobile without headlights following them two blocks behind.

Brasfield squinted, and saw the dark shape as it came under a corner streetlight. "Good. Now let's lead our friends to a place where they won't be able to escape."

Brasfield turned and faced the front again. They had taken Highway 270 out of Washington, which would lead them straight into the snow-covered Maryland countryside, where a blizzard was nearing.

Jackson Brasfield felt this was his lucky night.

Drawing heavily and nervously on his last cigarette, Harrison Beckett didn't like the way this was going down. He was driving straight through the beginning of the blizzard forecast on the radio an hour ago, and it didn't look like the van was anywhere near stopping.

Pamela also grew nervous. Harrison could see her fingers fidgeting, and the crossing and uncrossing of her legs. She hadn't said a word for the past thirty minutes. After leaving the city, she had changed back into blue jeans and a long-sleeve shirt. They were definitely heading the wrong way here, and if something went wrong and they were forced out of their cars, he didn't think they would last long with their thin blue jeans, sneakers, and leather jackets.

Visibility decreased steadily, forcing Harrison to close the gap to a mere five hundred feet, which increased the chances of being spotted. But he didn't have a choice. Since leaving the city, Harrison had been forced to turn on the headlights to see the road, but at least he had been on an interstate and could afford to increase the gap to almost a half mile. But on the winding mountain road they now traveled he didn't have that luxury. He turned off the headlights, leaving only the parking lights on.

With visibility reduced to a dozen feet, his concentration skyrocketed. He almost had to anticipate a turn to make it smoothly enough to avoid skidding into the snow-covered, towering pines hugging the road.

The van disappeared behind the next turn. Harrison kept the wheel centered as he squinted to make out the curving road. As he entered the turn, a bright light blinded him.

A trap!

"Harrison!"

Polished instincts took over, quickly shifting down while stopping and turning the wheel. The Mustang skidded sideways, but Harrison kept his foot on the gas as he finished the one-eighty turn and headed back the other way, tires spinning furiously, their deep tread biting into the icy road. A sheet of snow sprayed over the van and a sedan blocking the road behind him.

Pamela glanced back. "They're not following!"

Something was wrong, Harrison decided, heading back to the same turn he had just negotiated in the opposite direction.

More lights.

"Damn it!"

They had sandwiched them. Harrison Beckett saw an opening in the woods and pointed the Mustang in that direction.

They bounced as the sports car left the road and cruised over the uneven terrain hidden in six inches of snow.

"Aghh!"

Pamela grabbed the dashboard with both hands as the Mustang came to a stop inside a deep trench on the side of the road.

He got out, and the wind chilled him to the bone in the first second outside the Mustang. Pamela also hurried out, and they began to race toward the dark woods. Pamela fell and Harrison ran almost thirty feet before he realized she wasn't by his side. He turned, brown eyes searching for her.

"Pamela!"

Two shots cracked the night in half, the sound waves dislodging the snow shrouding the towering pine above him.

"Harrison!"

The falling snow blinded him, just as the sound of a near miss buzzed in his ears.

Squinting through snow gusts obscuring the field, Harrison moved to the left. Someone was hunting him, but not Pamela. He could barely see her through the squall, on her knees in the snow, near the Mustang in the roadside ditch.

A pine exploded to his right, another to his left. The multiple blasts cracked through the frigid air. Harrison realized he would not be able to reach Pamela. Dark figures now loomed over her, but in a way he felt relieved. She would not have survived out here. He doubted if he would be able to prevail in this cold for long.

Another shot, and Harrison took cover behind the trunk of a pine. Back pressed against the frozen bark, he looked behind him over his right shoulder as more figures appeared on the road.

"Harrison! Help! Get your fucking hands off me! Harrison! Harrison!"

Harrison Beckett closed his eyes. It could not be happening to him again! His gut told him Layla's assassin was out there. He was taking away from him the woman Harrison now realized he loved.

Three shots came in rapid succession, all impacting the pine. The noise mixed with his anger for having fallen in the trap, for having lost her.

No, Harrison! Pamela is safe. Pamela is safe. The phrase repeated in his head. He had to believe it, had to get it straight in his mind in order to survive his hunters. A voice inside him told Harrison they wouldn't touch Pamela until they got the algorithm.

The diskette!

Harrison now had the answer. He had to get to the diskette, had to reach it before they extracted the location from Pamela, who would resist at first, but not against chemicals. With the diskette he would have bargaining power for a trade. It was his only chance. It was Pamela's only chance.

No time to analyze! Move out! Escape!

Snow clinging to the sides of his face, the wind stinging his eyes, Harrison raced deep inside the storm-obscured forest, increasing the gap between himself and his pursuers. He reached for the Colt and flipped the safety, the cold metal burning his skin.

Two more shots. Two more explosions of bark and snow. Harrison zigzagged deeper into the woods, the cold weather slowly weakening him, reducing his limberness, decreasing the elasticity his fingers would need to fire the automatic now frozen in his hand.

Breathing rapidly, small white clouds rising above him as he exhaled, Harrison Beckett stopped and hid behind a tree. The figures ran in his direction, halogen spotters crisscrossing in the night, their yellow lights diffusing through the woods.

Arms and legs shockingly cold, Harrison Beckett lined up one of the incoming lights with the sights of his weapon and fired three times in rapid succession. The light fell to the ground, momentarily forcing the other two lights to stop. *One down, two to go,* he thought as he moved out. Multiple shots followed the moment of silence as the two remaining guns resumed their pursuit.

The cold continued to bite him, stripping him of life-supporting heat, his body temperature dropping even as he ran, snow striking his eyes. His arms numb, his fingers swollen, the ex–DIA officer slipped on a snow-slick slab and fell headfirst in the snow, striking the frozen slab with his side. He quickly sat up, disoriented by a combination of the cold, which began to cloud his judgment, and the blow to his right shoulder and arm. But his hand still held the Colt.

Three shots brought him back to the reality of the moment, to the hunters converging on him, to the thin white clouds rising off their dark faces as they searched the woods fifty feet away from him.

Shivering, his back turned toward the gusts, Harrison took in the cold air once, exhaled, and breathed it again as he broke into another run. An explosion of bark to his right reached his eyes, momentarily blinding him. He collided against the trunk of a pine a second later, the blow to his bruised ribs making him tremble. He fell, bumping his body against the rocks and branches hidden beneath the layer of white, finally crashing his right shoulder against another pine.

Pawing through the snow and dirt on his belly, Harrison struggled to get up but failed. His legs would not respond. The wind slapped his face, stung his eyes. He noticed his empty hand. The Colt had fallen in the snow.

Mustering strength, feeling the urge to vomit, Harrison held on to a low branch and managed to pull himself up, regaining his footing. Feeling the wind puncturing holes in his skin, chilling his core, Harrison kicked the snow and propelled himself forward, away from his—

Another shot cracked, the round nipping the collar of his jacket. He cut left but lost his balance and fell again. Caked with ice and snow, appalled by the pain in his joints, Harrison Beckett tried to get up but his body would not obey him. He found it harder and harder to breathe. His vision grew foggy, cloudy. The shadowy figures loomed in front of him, the muzzles of their weapons pointing in his direction.

Harrison clenched his teeth in dread. His ears picked up several shots and he tried to brace himself, but his arms only moved part of the way. His body was too rigid. Harrison didn't feel any impact. He couldn't feel most of his body. He could be bleeding to death at that moment and wouldn't even know it. He tried to find the shadows of his executioners, but they were gone. They had shot him and left him to die.

A figure suddenly came up over him and began to lift him to his feet. Were the assassins dragging him away? Why not just let him die in the freezing woods?

Harrison tried to open his mouth to say that he didn't care anymore, but his body was past the brink of exhaustion and would not respond to his commands. A sense of desolation took over him as he felt life slowly escaping him.

Esther Cruz holstered the Smith & Wesson Model 659 and ran an arm over the stranger's shoulders, pulling him out of what would have been his snow grave in a few more

minutes. Esther had lived in the northern states long enough
to know how to dress to survive in the woods.

Her instincts were paying off. After checking out a Bureau sedan and spending most of the afternoon tailing Jackson Brasfield, she had witnessed the kidnapping of the
general outside the restaurant. After a perilous drive through
a snowstorm, she discovered that the kidnapping had been
a setup to draw Pamela Sasser and her companion in.

She continued to drag the unconscious man toward her
car, which she had left hidden behind the frozen overgrowth
at the edge of the road, five hundred feet away. With a small
flashlight to guide her through the pitch-black woods, Esther
followed her own tracks—already half-filled with fresh
snow—back to the vehicle, and laid Harrison across the rear
seat.

Pamela Sasser's protector was in bad shape. He was still
breathing, but his face and hands were almost frozen.

Taking out the bottle of Wild Turkey that Esther had half
drained before venturing into the woods, she brought it to
the stranger's mouth, letting a few drops fall in between the
purplish lips, which quickly parted.

The body reacted to the hard liquor, sensing its life-giving
energy, and instantly demanded more. Esther let him have
a few sips before replacing the cap and driving off. She
didn't know who this frozen stranger was, but the professional in Esther Cruz felt certain that in the rear seat of the
sedan were some of the answers she sought.

Esther Cruz knew that the moment the termination team
failed to report, Brasfield would know that Harrison had
escaped alive. Esther also suspected that her apartment complex would be under surveillance by Brasfield's men. As the
headlights of her vehicle cut through the blizzard, the seasoned brick agent began thinking of a way to use that surveillance team to her advantage.

The plan coming together in her mind carried high risk,
but it was the only way Esther saw of cracking this case. If
she could not get closer to the Web, perhaps she could get
the Web to get closer to her.

*   *   *

Jackson Brasfield rode in the rear of a black sedan with Preston Sinclaire. Pamela Sasser and three of Brasfield's guns followed them in the van.

"Pamela Sasser and Harrison Beckett are severe liabilities," said Brasfield. "I have Sasser, but I can't eliminate her until after I make sure there isn't a copy of this algorithm floating about."

"Well, Beckett should be done for by now," Sinclaire said, checking his watch. "Any news from the men you sent after him?"

Brasfield shook his head. "Radio silence until we reach the estate."

Sinclaire nodded. "Now, let's talk about Esther Cruz."

The DDI lowered his gaze while he said, "I have a dozen of my best men staking out her apartment complex and all of her usual hangouts. She's due to show up sooner or later, and when she does—"

"You will kill her, just like you did at the parking garage," said Preston Sinclaire, eyes staring at the dark countryside.

"This time there will be no mistakes."

Sinclaire slowly shook his head. "I've heard *that* before."

"I'm leading the termination team this time," said the DDI.

Sinclaire turned to him, a slight grin flashing across his tanned face. "*Are* you? Well, well, well. So you're going to get your hands dirty. I'm so relieved to hear that. What about her?"

"The basement," Brasfield responded, ignoring Sinclaire's sarcasm. "She *will* tell us everything we want to know, just like that informer we caught." The general checked his watch. "I need to get to the Pentagon."

"How are you going to explain the kidnapping?"

"I'm a professional operative, remember? I escaped. I'll state that I outsmarted a small group of terrorists sent after me in retaliation for the neutralization of one of their overseas training camps. It'll look great on the news and will boost my popularity. Just drop me off at the nearest gas station. I'll manage after that. Hamed will make sure the woman talks.''

Five minutes later, as the limousine pulled up by a Texaco, Sinclaire grinned while staring directly into Jackson Brasfield's dark eyes. "Do it right, Jackson. Esther Cruz must be killed.''

"She will be," responded the DDI, leaving the vehicle, which sped away the moment he shut the door.

As Brasfield walked to the pay phone, his beeper went off. He checked the number and walked even faster, depositing a quarter into the machine and dialing the number flashing on the small display.

"We've found her," a voice said at the other end. "We've found Esther Cruz.''

13 Improvise and Overcome

In every sort of danger there are various ways of winning through, if one is ready to do and say anything whatever.

—Socrates

Saturday, November 21

The hooded men left the van the moment it came to a stop in the dark and quiet alley behind the small apartment complex. The leader of the four-man team had not done this in ten years, but he felt confident it would come back to him.

As he cruised over the sidewalk with the ease of a street cat he realized he had been right. The leader pushed the rear door and ran swiftly over the worn-out carpet of the hall leading to the stairs. It was one in the morning and the place was silent, the tenants no doubt sleeping.

But tenants of the three-story building just outside of the nation's capital were of no interest to the team's leader. He was after the owner, Esther Cruz, the FBI agent who had become a nuisance to Preston Sinclaire and his network.

A spotter had seen Esther drive up to the building an hour ago. The brick structure housed a single-car garage with a door connecting to the interior hall. Esther Cruz had pulled into the garage and closed the door behind her. The spotter had immediately called his superior, the leader, who ordered him to remain in place and stay with Esther if she left the building. The Fed never did.

The leader, closely followed by three armed men, went up the stairs first. Esther Cruz lived on the third floor.

The slow-turning black ceiling fan went in and out of focus as Harrison Beckett blinked. The sweet aroma of freshly brewed coffee reached his nostrils and he inhaled deeply, taking in the warmth that came with it.

Warmth, heat, life . . . Pamela.

He stretched on the sofa and his sore joints quickly reminded him of his near encounter with death. Now he began to remember as his vision slowly cleared. He had been running in the snow, trying to escape from the bullets of his hunters, the ones who had taken Pamela away from him. The ones who had shot him . . . *Why am I alive? Where am I?*

Harrison tried to sit up but failed. He was too weak, his body demanded more rest, but not his mind. He knew Pamela had been captured. He had little time before she disclosed the location of the diskette containing the algorithm.

Harrison had to get to Louisiana, had to reach the LSU campus. He remembered what she had told him, remembered her exact words, pinpointing the location of the diskette. But first he had to figure out where he was.

Had he been captured? Somehow he had survived the frozen episode, but he had no idea how or why. *What in the hell happened out there?*

Sitting up, Harrison scanned the room.

He saw the blurry image of a woman sitting in a chair across the room. Blinking rapidly, he forced the image into focus: a middle-aged woman with salt-and-pepper shoulder-length hair and a protuberant nose on a light brown face lined with age. The full lips crowning a delicate yet strong chin flashed an easy-knowing grin at the ex–DIA officer.

Harrison remembered her. She was the same woman that had almost caught him staring at her in the grocery store parking lot outside LSU.

Harrison tried to stand but the woman brought a handgun up, leveling it at Harrison.

"Stay where you are."

Quickly sobering up, Harrison Beckett raised both hands, palms facing the armed stranger, and slowly leaned back on the blue sofa, his eyes panning away from the gun to scan the room. Old furniture, mostly cheap, was scattered around the brown-carpeted room. Steam rose from a cup of coffee on the cocktail table separating him from the stranger. He could see a refrigerator through the doorway to his right, and a narrow hall to his left. The drumming rock beat coming from the floor below told Harrison this was an apartment or condo, and he was at least on the second floor. He crossed his legs and rested his hands on his lap.

"You should be dead," the woman said, the deep, authoritative female voice matching her harsh appearance.

Harrison didn't respond, analyzing eyes sizing up the stranger.

"And you might just as well die," she continued. "Unless you give me a reason why I should let you live."

Harrison looked down to the cup of steaming coffee before lifting his gaze back to the woman's powerful stare, waiting for a reaction.

"Go right ahead," she said, waving the weapon, which Harrison now recognized as a Smith & Wesson Model 659. "But if you try to throw the coffee at me, I'll blow a hole in your chest larger than the Grand Canyon."

A possible professional. Harrison slowly leaned forward, picked up the brown mug by the handle, and brought it to his lips. The liquid burned his palate but it felt good, slowly warming his core as he swallowed and took a few more sips before setting it back on the table.

"Now," the stranger continued. "Why don't you tell me who you are and what's your involvement with Pamela Sasser."

Although externally he didn't flinch, Harrison was taken aback by the unexpected questions. If the tough woman worked for Brasfield then she surely wouldn't be asking Harrison something she should already know. After all, it was Brasfield himself who had sent Harrison on this mission. On the other hand, this could be a trick. Perhaps this was one of Brasfield's soldiers, with instructions to make Harrison think that she wasn't DIA.

Harrison's initial reaction was to play along. If this was indeed one of Brasfield's soldiers, then Harrison would at least be buying himself some time to figure a way to escape and get the diskette. On the other hand, if this woman was *not* DIA, then Harrison stood the chance of learning something he didn't already know, and perhaps he could even get help to get Pamela back. But who could she be, if not the DIA? The FBI? Not likely. The Feds would have identified themselves already before taking him into custody. Or would they? What if this woman was undercover? What if the Feds were videotaping this conversation? How many people were listening in on this? What if the woman was from the CIA? Or perhaps naval or army intelligence? Maybe Harrison was thinking too hard. This woman could just be a local detective or cop.

Possibilities. Harrison needed to narrow down the woman's professional background before choosing to share any information. The life of Pamela Sasser hinged on his next few words.

"What is your interest in Pamela Sasser?" Harrison asked, reaching for the mug and taking another sip. This time he held it over his lap.

The woman smiled a crooked smile. "I asked first."

"If you're with the ones that hunted me in the forest then you should know the answers to those questions."

"I am *not* one of them," she responded, her face becoming stern.

Harrison concentrated not on the words but on the brown eyes, which sparkled not only with annoyance at Harrison's answer but also with honesty. The woman had responded

and acted as someone not associated with the DIA but somehow involved in the case. Then again, anyone with the right
training, like Harrison, could paint any type of expression
on his face for just about any circumstance. Harrison narrowed down the woman to one of three categories: an honest
amateur, an honest professional, or a deceitful professional.
The honest brown eyes that accompanied her words had
eliminated the possibility of her being a dishonest amateur.

"Prove it," Harrison responded.

Her lined face stiffened as she stood, deep creases of ex-
asperation forming across her wide forehead, rippling over
a pair of eyes reduced to mere slits of glinting anger.

"Listen, *asshole*," she said, pointing at Harrison with the
Model 659's muzzle. "I'm the one who fired on the bastards
who tried to kill you and Pamela at the Cornstalk in New
Orleans, and I'm the one who pumped a half dozen rounds
into the hooded motherfuckers that were about to turn you
into frozen sushi in the middle of the woods. Had it not
been for me your sorry ass would have remained frozen until
the spring! Now, *asshole,* are we damned clear about which
side I'm *not* on, or do you intend to keep up this bullshit
little game to check me out?"

Drinking the last of the coffee and setting the mug on the
table, Harrison laid a thumb against his lower lip, coldly
studying the woman, who took a deep breath before perch-
ing herself back on the armchair.

This could still be a trick. Although someone did fire on
the termination team at the Cornstalk, warning Harrison, the
ex–DIA officer clearly remembered seeing at least one
hooded gun looking for them while Pamela and he hid by
the side of the hotel. Everything the woman had said so far
was information Brasfield already had. Harrison decided to
take a different angle on this woman simply because the fact
that the woman had kept Harrison alive meant she desper-
ately wanted information Harrison possessed. Also, the fact
that they were having this conversation meant the woman
didn't have immediate access to chemicals, otherwise why
bother with the chitchat? Harrison pressed on.

"What do you know about Dr. Eugene LaBlanche?" Harrison asked.

Wrinkling her whole face in suspicion, the woman considered the question for a moment before saying, "LSU professor. Died of a heart attack, according to the newspaper article I read."

"Do you always believe the papers?"

The woman grunted. "They're as good as the information they are fed. . . . Look, pal, I just nearly got my ass shot by the same people who are after you. It happened earlier today. Now, I warned you about playing this little game." The woman cocked the Model 659 and aimed it at Harrison's groin. "What's your involvement with Pamela Sasser? And I would be *very* careful how I answer that, or today could turn out to be the first day of the rest of your miserable, cockless life." The woman pulled out a thin black vinyl billfold and threw it at Harrison, who opened it. On one side of the laminated ID holder was a badge, on the other an ID card with her photo.

Esther Cruz. FBI.

Harrison tossed the ID over the table and contemptuously looked at the Fed. Although the ID could be a fake, Harrison decided to assume it was real for the time being, just to see where things might lead. "Are you recording this?"

The Fed shook her head.

Harrison sighed, deciding that releasing selected information would not hurt at this point. If this gal worked for Brasfield, then she would already know the information Harrison was about to disclose. If she was authentic, then he had nothing to lose by sharing some of the information he knew. Perhaps the Feds could even be of help.

Quickly deciding on how much to disclose and how much to retain for future bargaining power, Harrison said with abrupt sharpness, "I was hired by the DIA to assassinate Pamela Sasser."

Glaring brown eyes opened wide, her lined face cocked to one side, Esther shook her head. "That you do undercover work is obvious." She pointed at the table next to her. Harrison recognized his own brown wallet lying on the glass tabletop next to his thick nylon belt. "Driver's licenses and U.S. passports under three different names, but all showing your photo. Credit cards to match each of the names, and a money belt with tens of thousands in cash. Yes, I'll *definitely* say you do undercover work. But we'll get to that later. Now tell me why the military spooks hired you to kill Pamela Sasser."

"The DIA claimed she was assisting Dr. Eugene La-Blanche in the sale of top-secret computer technology to hostile nations."

"Did you assassinate Dr. LaBlanche?"

"No."

"Why didn't you assassinate Pamela Sasser?"

Harrison considered the question for a few seconds and decided that an honest answer wouldn't hurt regardless of who she was. "The multiple tails made me suspicious."

Esther smiled. "I was one of the tails. I saw you in action at the Residence Inn."

Harrison met the comment with a stone face.

"And afterward? After you abducted her? Why didn't you kill her then?"

"I sensed something much larger at stake in all this."

Esther gave him a grin as she relaxed a bit, the gun now pointing at the floor. "So? Why should you care? You're just a hired assassin."

"That's besides the point and of no consequence here. I felt something big and decided to check it out. I stay alive by being cautious," Harrison said, screwing his features into a mask of pure honesty.

"Well," Esther Cruz said. "There's certainly something bigger going on here, but I can't see how Pamela Sasser fits into it."

Harrison checked his Seiko. It had been over five hours since the attack in the forest. Time was running out for Pamela Sasser. He had to get to the diskette before her captors did, otherwise he would lose her forever.

"Look," Harrison said, leaning forward, a motion which

immediately caused Esther Cruz to train the Model 659 back on him. "Pamela Sasser is in great danger, and only I know how to get her back alive."

"How?"

"There is something I must retrieve in Louisiana. Something her captors want badly."

Over Esther's face came the look of suspicion, lips tightly pursed, eyelids half-down, head tilted to the side. She no longer cared to control her external features. "And what might that be?"

This was Harrison's paradox. Tell this stranger, who could still turn out to be one of Brasfield's guns, and risk losing everything. Hold out until the right time to escape, and risk being too late to save Pamela. Based on the way Esther Cruz had handled herself so far, Harrison felt escaping would not be easy.

Harrison wasn't a gambler, but he decided it was time to play. He had to get to the diskette immediately. "I will tell the story to your director, and only after the FBI guarantees my freedom and safety, and that of Pamela Sasser."

Esther shook her head. "Nope. The FBI doesn't make deals with criminals."

"That's not up to you to decide, is it? All I know is that I have information that could save Pamela Sasser and perhaps assist you in whatever it is you're trying to solve here, but I will not release it without a full agreement with the director of—"

Harrison stopped talking when Esther abruptly got up. "Shh," the female federal agent said, bringing a finger to her lips. "Don't move."

"What is it?" Harrison whispered.

"I heard someone in the hall." Keeping the gun leveled at Harrison, Esther slowly walked to the door, placing an ear against the white wooden surface.

The leader of the termination team stood in front of the door, silenced MP5 trained on the dead bolt. It had taken his team an extra five minutes to reach the top floor because they had

had to make an unscheduled stop on the floor below. An old man had walked outside his apartment hauling a garbage bag. The leader had had no choice but to kill him with a silenced round to the face. The team had then spent the next minute dragging the body back inside the apartment.

Flipping the fire-selection lever to full automatic fire, the leader looked both ways and nodded once. His team nodded in response.

Standing in front of his target's front door, he pressed the trigger. The rounds pounded on the wooden surface, their sound similar to that of multiple hammers working a plank of wood.

Esther Cruz jerked away from the door the moment she heard the hammering down the hall.

"What in the hell's going on?" Harrison asked, getting up.

Esther cocked the weapon and pointed it at Harrison's head. "Stay down, damn it!"

Harrison didn't sit but didn't move forward either. "What's going on out there? Who else lives on this floor?"

Keeping the gun on Harrison, Esther shifted her gaze back and forth between the closed door and the ex–DIA officer, who stood ten feet away from her. "Just me. I own this place. The other apartments on this floor aren't rented. Now, don't *fucking* move!"

Esther unbolted the door and opened it just enough to inch her head out and peek down the hall. She quickly closed and bolted it before looking at Harrison.

"Shit. They *were* staking out my place," Esther said, more to herself than to Harrison. "I was right. The bastards have come after me."

Harrison took a few steps in Esther's direction. "They're here? How many did you see?"

"I think four. They're down by my place."

"Your place? I thought that this was—"

"One of my vacant units. I told you the bastards were after me too."

Harrison nodded. "Let's get them."

"What?"

"Let's take them. You and me."

Esther gave him an incredulous glance. "You're nuts."

"I'm damned serious. Do you have another gun?"

Esther Cruz regarded Harrison wryly.

"C'mon, Esther. How else are we—"

Harrison stopped as they heard footsteps nearing, followed by more hammering noises. Esther and Harrison locked eyes. The team was moving in their direction. They were not going to leave until they had searched the place.

"Damn! You better not cross me, whoever you are."

"Harrison."

"Well, *Harrison*," Esther said, walking past him and opening a closet door. "Here you go."

Harrison Beckett grabbed the Beretta 92F that Esther passed on to him. Trained fingers moved almost on automatic, releasing the magazine, checking that it had all fifteen rounds, slamming it back in place, flipping the safety, and chambering a round.

More footsteps.

Her weapon pointed at the ceiling while she clutched it with her right hand and held it over her right shoulder, Esther turned off the lights and moved to one side of the door, Harrison to the other. The glow from the streetlight just outside the living-room windows diffused through the thin curtains, bathing Harrison and Esther with wan yellow light.

The footsteps stopped. Harrison and Esther dropped to the ground, weapons trained up, toward the intruders that had not yet crashed through the door. The silence stretched out for another ten seconds, but for Harrison Beckett it felt like an eternity before the deafening hammering, accompanied by a cloud of exploding wood, rang in his ears as the dead bolt and a section of the door rocketed past them.

Two men followed, both wearing black pants, sweaters, and hoods. Their gloves hands clutched the suppressed submachine guns that unleashed a spray of bullets across the living room.

Harrison and Esther fired in unison, the report of their weapons drowning the silent rounds pulverizing furniture, drywall, and glass.

The dark figures arched back, their limp bodies crashing over the carpet, their weapons landing by Harrison's feet. He snatched one, threw the second to Esther, and shoved the Beretta in his jeans.

Running footsteps followed a few seconds of silence. The rest of the team was moving out. By the time Harrison rolled out to the hallway, the team had already reached the first floor. He heard a car accelerating, then suddenly screeching to a halt, and accelerating once again. They were gone.

Harrison returned to the room. "They're gone. Professionals."

Esther nodded, kneeling by the closest man in black and removing the hood.

"Recognize him?" she asked Harrison, who eyed the stranger, a man in his late twenties with ash blond hair and mustache, and a pair of dead blue eyes staring at the ceiling. It was the same operative who'd met Harrison by the steps to the Lincoln Memorial following his lunch meeting with Jackson Brasfield.

"One of Brasfield's guns."

Esther approached the second man, who had landed almost five feet away from the first. This one had taken four rounds in the chest. The FBI agent pulled off the mask and froze.

"What is it?" Harrison asked Esther, whose body blocked the dead man's upper body.

"Come and take a look."

Harrison Beckett walked around Esther Cruz before lowering his gaze at the second member of the termination team.

Then Harrison saw the dead face of General Jackson T. Brasfield.

Two hours later FBI director Frederick Vanatter crossed the barricade the police had set up along the entrance to the small apartment complex. Although it was just past five in the morning, the director felt quite awake. In fact he had been fully awake after his short but incredible phone call from Esther Cruz. Before leaving his house, however, the director had called Dulles International Airport to arrange emergency transportation to Baton Rouge.

Flanked by his bodyguards and two of his deputy assistants, Vanatter led the caravan across the small lobby, up the two flights of stairs, and to the room where the officers guarding the entrance had told him Esther would be.

Walking past a half dozen police officers in the hall, the director went inside the apartment, where the smell of gunpowder still hung heavily in the air. Another half dozen cops were scattered around the room. Vanatter spotted Esther sitting with her back against the wall. A single body, covered with a blue police blanket, lay by her feet.

Esther Cruz turned and recognized her superior. Standing, she said, "Morning. Gentlemen care for some coffee?"

"Jesus Christ, Mother," said Vanatter. "Look at this place."

"Cleaning day," she said.

"Get everyone out of here," Vanatter ordered one of his agents. "I want to talk to Mother alone for a few minutes."

The agent nodded and began to motion the cops out of the room. The director knelt next to the body and lifted the blanket, staring at Brasfield's face for a few seconds.

"So," Vanatter said, standing up, a taut, downcurved mouth matching the ire shimmering in his black eyes. "What's next?"

Mother Cruz put her fingers over her eyes and rubbed. Little sleep, two attempts on her life, plus the near miss at the Cornstalk and the trek through the frozen woods were pushing her to the brink of exhaustion.

Turning a bloodshot gaze to her director, Esther Cruz said, "First thing's getting our team positioned in Louisiana. Harrison should get to LSU in three hours and get things rolling."

"Who does he have down there assisting him?"

"We got him plenty of help."

Vanatter ran a hand over his bald head: "What about the woman?"

"They've got Pamela Sasser, but Harrison feels they won't touch her if we have the diskette. He's thinking about setting up a trade."

Vanatter stared into the distance with an air of profundity. "But if this algorithm is as important as this Harrison person claims it to be, we can't possibly just turn it over to them."

Esther looked Vanatter straight in the eye. "I gave him my word that we'd help him get Pamela Sasser back, sir. I intend to keep that word. Harrison didn't have to tell me his story. Brasfield hired Harrison to do the job on Pamela Sasser. And it was during that meeting that Harrison saw a man he claims belonged to the radical Muslim Brotherhood. Harrison fought this same person in New Orleans, just minutes after the Cornstalk shoot-out. We also know from my source inside the DIA that Brasfield wanted Eugene LaBlanche and Pamela Sasser dead because this algorithm of theirs was a threat to the Web."

"How?"

"First we help Harrison get Pamela back, sir. Then he'll tell us that and much more."

"I don't like this, Mother. This guy could be bluffing us just to get us to help him get this woman back."

"Maybe. But we don't have much more to go on, sir. Our prime lead, General Jackson Brasfield, is dead. The link to the Web, once again, has been severed. This thing obviously goes much further than the deputy director of intelligence of DIA, sir. Harrison and Pamela are our only chance."

"Crap. If someone as high as Brasfield was expendable, I dread the thought of *who* might be at the helm," commented Vanatter. "Now, who's this Harrison person? Where does he come from?"

"Part of my agreement with him was that I wouldn't ask questions that weren't pertinent to the case, and that the Bureau would provide for his safety and freedom, and that of Pamela Sasser."

"If she makes it."

"Of course."

Vanatter nodded again. "I would like to run Harrison through the computer, just to be on the safe side."

Esther frowned at the comment. "Sir, I gave him my word."

"And the FBI will back it up, Mother. However, that doesn't prevent us from finding out who this fellow really is. Now, let's call the analysis lab and get them over here on the double. I want this place dusted."

"That won't be necessary, sir." Esther pulled out a clear plastic bag holding the empty coffee mug Harrison had used. "I've got his prints right here."

Vanatter flashed Esther a grin.

"Just remember, sir. Whoever he is, we made a deal. We help him get Pamela back. He then helps us crack the Web, and then we take care of him and of Pamela Sasser, including transferring the cash I promised him if his information resulted in the destruction of this ring of corruption."

"I'm still pissed at the amount, but we'll keep the deal. Either way, I still want to know who we're dealing with."

While Esther and Vanatter held that conversation, Harrison Beckett and four FBI agents boarded the Bureau's Sabreliner jet at Dulles. The direct flight to Baton Rouge would take just under three hours.

MARYLAND

Saturday, November 21

Pamela Sasser walked down the wooden steps ending in a door that probably led to some basement room. Two men walked behind her. One was the same bearded man who'd fought with Harrison in New Orleans. He called himself Hamed.

Pamela didn't know what to expect, and Hamed had already taught her not to speak until spoken to. The bump on her head, the purplish bruise on her left cheek, and the busted lip reminded her of the slap Hamed had given her for asking questions. The blow had sent her crashing against a table, knocking her out. She had awakened, with a massive headache, tied to a bed in a room upstairs. Now her captors took her to another room.

What drove her to the edge was the fact that no one had asked for the location of the diskette yet. No one. In fact no one had asked her *any* questions. After she had lost sight of Harrison in the frozen woods, two gunmen had shoved her in the rear seat of a van, blindfolded her, and taken her here—wherever here was, a mansion in the middle of nowhere. She had not traveled by car long, perhaps two hours, maybe less. She guessed she was in either Virginia or Maryland.

She reached the bottom of the steps. Hamed walked down and opened the door, pushing her inside.

"Move!"

Pamela landed on her side on the concrete floor. Her shoulder and knees stung, her headache flared, but she didn't utter a word. In her mind she saw her father pushing her into the bedroom, kicking her when she'd refused him.

Pamela slowly got up, her skinned knees and left elbow burning, her eyes slowly focusing on the lone figure strapped to a chair in the middle of the large room, under the flickering overheads.

She saw a short, wiry man wearing nothing but a pair of underpants and a shirt. He slowly turned to look at his visitors, and it was at that moment that Pamela Sasser saw his eyes. They were white and glossy, with streaks of red. Blood, mucus, and white foam hung off his nose, resting on his upper lip. Blood stained his chin, neck, shirt, and underpants. But not just blood. Pamela saw black clots in the blood accumulated next to the chair.

The man didn't breathe normally. He heaved, taking gulps of air with his mouth before suddenly leaning forward on the chair and vomiting. Pamela took a step back, but Hamed pushed her forward, toward the convulsing man. A half minute went by and the man would not stop regurgitating onto

the concrete floor large amounts of a slippery black liquid—
long after his stomach should have emptied.

The man stopped throwing up but remained in the same
position, sitting up, head hanging forward, dead eyes staring
at the black vomit.

"Meet Eddie López," said Hamed. "He dared challenge
me. He lost."

Pamela stood in a trance, frozen, her catlike eyes staring
at a man who seemed to be in terrible pain.

"That's how we used to deal with traitors back home,"
said Hamed. "First we burned his eyes, one at a time. Then
I forced him to drink a few teaspoons of bleach diluted in
a gallon of soapy water. The stomach pains as the detergent
and bleach eat away the lining of the stomach and intestines
are about the worst there is, and they can last for a couple
of days before causing death. I let the maddening pain soften
him up for just one hour before offering to fire a bullet in
his head in exchange for information. He told me *everything*."

Hamed turned to Pamela. "Like I said, that's how we
dealt with traitors in Egypt. With male traitors, that is.
Women got a more civilized treatment."

Pamela defiantly glared at the bearded man, Harrison's
arch-enemy. She hated everything he stood for. He was Sinclaire's pit bull, responsible for so many deaths, probably
even the ones at Palo Verde. "Is that why you're still alive
then?" she asked, her eyes filled with female contempt.
"Did you get the more *civilized* treatment?"

The slap came before she even had a chance to blink. In
less than a second she was back on the floor, her cheek
burning, her head about to explode. Then she felt Hamed's
hands on her.

"Where is the diskette?" he asked, kneeling in front of
her as she lay on her back, dazed, light-headed.

Pamela barely heard the words as the pain brought back
old memories.

"The diskette!" Hamed persisted, grabbing her by the
thighs and pulling her against his groin. "Tell me!"

Pamela felt her father's hands on her. She smelled him, heard him, saw his contorted face as he tried to spread her thighs. It was happening again! The pig was trying to rape her! He had already beaten her mother and now wanted Pamela. But she would not give in. She would fight!

Pamela felt the hands on her jeans, heard a zipper being lowered.

"No!"

Ten sharp fingernails reached for his face and slashed it with a fury she'd contained for ten years.

"Aghh!"

She heard the scream and the man was gone, his bleeding face buried in his hands. Then she heard other voices as she began to come around.

"What's going on?" screamed another man.

Pamela quickly stood and zipped up her jeans. As Hamed dropped to his knees in pain, she saw a face she had only seen before on television. It was Preston Sinclaire in the company of several armed men. The CEO of Microtel was dressed in plain blue jeans and a red denim shirt.

"Damn it, Hamed! I told you to get me when she woke up!"

The Egyptian slowly got to his feet and turned around, right hand reaching for his side arm. Pamela saw the deep cuts on his face, and only now she realized she had broken most of her nails. Her fingers stung as much as her head, her face, her side, but she had pushed him away.

Hamed freed his side arm from the leather holster, cocked it, and aimed at her face.

"Stop!" Sinclaire shouted, jumping in between them. "Put that gun down! I need the diskette!"

Hamed remained frozen, his eyes trained on Pamela Sasser, who stood a few feet behind Sinclaire, hands on her slim waist.

"Put it down! Now!" Sinclaire repeated.

Slowly, Hamed Tuani lowered the weapon and said to Sinclaire, "After we get the diskette, *she's mine*!"

The president of Microtel turned to face her as the Egyptian stormed out of the room screaming words Pamela did not understand.

"So, Ms. Sasser. We finally meet. I'm Preston Sinclaire," he said casually, as though he were meeting her at a country club.

"I *know* who you are," she responded, using the sleeve of her shirt to wipe off the blood running down her chin. "And I know what you want."

Sinclaire tilted his tanned face. "Come, let's get you cleaned up first. Then we'll talk."

"I'm just fine, thank you," she said, not moving. "Why don't you take care of *him* instead?" She tilted her head at Eddie López.

Sinclaire grinned at the slim woman before slowly looking at one of the guards, who clutched a machine gun. "You heard the lady. Take care of him."

The guard swiftly aimed the weapon at Eddie López and fired three rounds in rapid succession. The report drilled her eardrums as the rounds lifted Eddie López and the chair, sending him rolling down the floor, blood gushing from his face and chest.

The smell of gunpowder filled the room as Sinclaire turned back to Pamela, who was frozen in horror. "Anyone else you want us to take care of, Ms. Sasser?"

"Butchers! You're all a bunch of butchers!" she heard herself scream.

"He was as good as dead anyway," Sinclaire said, eyeing the body and shrugging. "We just put him out of his misery."

Pamela filled her chest and clenched her jaws. "You killed him in cold blood, Sinclaire, just like you killed the people of Palo Verde."

Preston Sinclaire smiled. "*Now* we're getting somewhere. I want the diskette, Pamela. Where is it?"

"Forget it," she said, hitching a shoulder.

"Oh, you'll tell me all right. One way or another, you *will* tell me."

"What if I don't?"

Sinclaire slowly shook his head. "You don't *really* want to know. And if you're thinking that Harrison Beckett will come to your rescue, you better think again. My men killed him shortly after we took you in."

Pamela Sasser locked eyes with Sinclaire. She had seen Harrison in action, had seen the way he fought, the way he ran, the way he had defended her against the men in black. Somehow she didn't feel his death. Somehow.

"You lie," she said, so matter-of-factly that she even surprised herself. She wasn't sure why she acted so bravely in the face of death. Perhaps it was the pain from her teenage years, or maybe it was the turn life had taken in the past few days. Maybe the fact that she had killed a man. In any case, Pamela found herself filled not with fear but with anger and contempt for these men.

Sinclaire smiled again. "Do I?"

"Then prove it," Pamela said. "Show me the body, and I'll reveal the location of the diskette."

Sinclaire's smile vanished. "You're in no position to bargain, and I'm tired of this little game. Guards, let's help Ms. Sasser with her recollection. Bring her upstairs."

As Sinclaire turned around and left the room, two guards grabbed her by the arms and dragged her after him. The guards' grip almost crushed her thin arms, but Pamela felt a wave of elation sweeping through her. Preston Sinclaire had backed down when challenged to produce a body, meaning Harrison was still alive, probably trying to find a way to rescue her.

But how?

The guards forced her up the stairs and into a bathroom, where Sinclaire was already filling a large sink with tap water. Sunlight filtered through a frosted window next to the tub. It mixed with the soft white overheads.

While one guard stood behind her and held her arms behind her back, another clamped a hairy hand on her head, fingers pressing against her cranium, amplifying the headache. And she still refused to admit the pain to her captors.

"Where is the diskette, Pam?"

The diskette! Of course! Harrison is getting the diskette! He knows where it is and he's trying to get it to get me back!

As the guard forced her face toward the sink, Pamela Sasser took a deep breath. She had to hold on. She had to buy Harrison time to get to Louisiana and retrieve it.

Underwater, her eyes closed, Pamela tried to remember how long it had been since the ambush. How long was she unconscious? She had seen light outside, meaning it had been at least ten hours, if not more . . . air. She needed air, and she tried to move up, but the hand kept her face shoved against the porcelain at the bottom of the sink. She felt her chest about to burst, fought the overwhelming desire to inhale, to fill her lungs.

Suddenly, the same hand that pressed her down now grabbed a clump of hair and pulled her up.

Air!

She breathed just in time. Her face went back down with a loud splash. Seconds went by. *How many? Ten . . . twenty . . . thirty.* The pressure began again. The tingling in her chest, her arms, her legs. Her headache hammered her temples, her eyes, her neck.

The hand pulled her back up and she coughed and breathed, and coughed some more. Her vision cleared and she saw Preston Sinclaire.

"Where, Pamela? Where is it?" he asked, checking his watch. Pamela saw it was almost ten o'clock in the morning.

Five seconds of silence and Sinclaire motioned the guard to push her head back into the water.

"Wait," she said, her mind adding the hours. Twelve, plus the time it would take her to explain, plus the time it would take one of Sinclaire's guns to get it. It'd have to do. "You win. I'll tell you where it is."

Sinclaire smiled, motioned the guards to let go of her, and handed her a towel. "I knew you would."

14 Identities

The worst of all deceptions is self-deception.

—Plato

Saturday, November 21

Frederick Vanatter was sitting behind his large mahogany desk when Esther Cruz came into the office. Dressed in a chalk-striped, double-breasted suit, Vanatter looked more like a bald Don Vito Corleone than the director of the Federal Bureau of Investigation.

"You wanted to see me, sir?" asked Esther, wearing a fresh set of jeans, a heavy woolen sweater, and running shoes. She definitely felt better after grabbing a change of clothes from her bullet-riddled apartment and taking a steamy shower in the FBI's basement, where the Bureau kept an exercise room.

Vanatter waved her in. "You know Admiral Roman Keitherland, Mother? The director of the Defense Intelligence Agency?"

Esther Cruz felt like the world's lousiest agent for having

missed the lanky and gray-haired DDIA, standing with a book in his hands near the bookcases layering the entire left wall of Vanatter's large office.

"Ah, no, sir. I don't believe we've met."

Keitherland flashed Esther a slight grin. "How do you do, Ms. Cruz?" he said, his voice a mere whisper.

"Fine, Admiral. It's a pleasure to meet you." Esther actually felt bad for the old DDIA, a decent man of sixty-seven who was due to retire in six months, and who now had to leave the DIA with his reputation stained for having had a corrupt subordinate like Jackson Brasfield under his wing. For reasons of security, only the Office of Naval Intelligence and the FBI knew about Brasfield. Vanatter himself had declined informing the DDIA about the corrupt general for fear of a leak. At least things were contained for now since his death had been kept secret to prevent the sudden vanishing of the Web.

Wrinkled, pale hands closed the book and set it back on the bookcase before the DDIA walked to a chair across from Vanatter. Esther sat next to him and crossed her legs.

"Mother, I think there's something you should know about Harrison," Vanatter said.

Esther leaned forward when she sensed the gravity in her superior's voice. "Yes?"

"While you remained at the apartment wrapping things up, I had Harrison's fingerprints run through the computer, and guess what? They came back C-thirteen," Vanatter said, referring to the code given to U.S. intelligence officers killed in the line of duty.

"Wh-what?"

"You heard me."

Esther glanced at the pale old man sitting next to her in a white navy uniform that seemed two sizes too big for his lanky frame. The DDIA's emaciated face turned to Vanatter's desk, and he reached for a manila folder. The name Captain Daniel Webster was written in black across the bottom.

Keitherland opened the dossier and leafed through the

half-inch-thick stack of documents, newspaper clips, and photos. "He's one of ours," he said, pulling out a five-by-seven photo of a man who bore little resemblance to Harrison Beckett.

"You've got the wrong guy. That's not Harrison," said Esther.

"Prints don't lie," Vanatter said.

"Plastic surgery," added Keitherland in his low voice.

Esther's gaze migrated between the heads of two of the most powerful intelligence agencies in the world. "Who *is* he?"

"What you're about to hear is highly classified," said Keitherland. "Captain Daniel Webster was a DIA officer in Cairo, who tried to prevent the assassination of Anwar Sadat in 1981. Unfortunately, he became the target of extreme factions within the Egyptian military, who wanted Sadat out for making peace with Israel. Several corrupt DIA officers in Operations and Intelligence, including several members of the military attaché at the American embassy, were assisting the Egyptian military, and when they discovered what Webster was up to, they labeled him beyond salvage."

"Why—why would the DIA want Sadat dead?"

"Military contracts," responded the aging DDIA. "The Pentagon was quite involved in this. It appears that certain military officers, like Brasfield, got together with some officers from the DIA in Cairo to keep Sadat from making peace with Israel, which would then ruin ongoing military contracts worth several billions of dollars."

Esther shook her head while looking at the silver band on her finger. "It's those bastards, isn't it?" she finally asked Vanatter, whose burning stare was all the answer the seasoned agent needed.

"Damn it! How many more lives will those assholes ruin before we can catch them?"

"We'll get them," Vanatter said. "This is the closest we've ever been, thanks to you and Harri . . . Captain Webster."

Esther fiddled with her wedding band as she asked, "What happened to Harrison after that?"

"A termination team was sent after him," said Keitherland. "But he managed to escape. Another team finally caught up with him in Italy and Webster died in an auto explosion—at least that's what we thought until several hours ago, when your director requested more information on this C-thirteen file."

"But how did he—"

"He must have faked his own death, Ms. Cruz. The irony of this whole mess is that a few months later we got evidence of the great injustice done to Captain Webster. One of the DIA officers broke down and confessed, also fingering four other DIA officials. But before we could arrest them, they were all executed. Two died in a car explosion. The other two were gunned down in the streets of Cairo. The one who confessed also ended up dead, suicide. To protect the reputation of the DIA, we kept the incidents out of the newspapers."

"What happened to the Pentagon officials involved?"

"Nothing. The deaths broke the link. We were never able to find them. After another year of useless investigations, we closed the case. We had no leads, only a pile of deaths. We opened up the case five years ago, when . . ."

Esther simply nodded while fidgeting with her wedding band. "I know."

"Now this Daniel Webster suddenly comes out of nowhere," added the DDIA.

"Jesus," Esther said, sinking in her chair for a few moments. "So all these years . . ."

"He had no way of knowing," said Keitherland. "The link was broken. We thought he was dead, and he apparently created a new identity for himself."

"And a new way to make a living," added Vanatter. "Let's not forget that the guy is now an assassin."

"That's right," said Esther. "But we created him. We left Daniel Webster with no choice but to become Harrison

Beckett, the international assassin. We're as much responsible for what happened to him as he is.''

The room went silent for a few moments. Then Esther turned to Keitherland. ''With Brasfield dead . . . can we go through his files? Maybe there's some evidence that might lead us to—''

''Remember that Brasfield's supposed to be alive,'' said Vanatter.

''True,'' said Keitherland. ''But I've already ordered two of my most trusted men in the Office of Security to go through Brasfield's office. Nothing's come up yet, except for . . . you're not going to like this one, Ms. Cruz.''

Esther wasn't sure what else to expect here. This entire conversation had been insane from the start, and it seemed to be getting even madder. ''What?''

''Does the name Eduardo López ring a bell?''

A terrible shrinking feeling descended on Mother Cruz at the mention of her contact in the Pentagon and at the words that flowed out of Keitherland's mouth. Her contact had vanished, most likely taken out by Brasfield.

More silence.

''Mother, have you heard from Harri—what in the hell do we call this guy anyway?'' asked Vanatter.

''His name is Harrison,'' responded Esther. ''They're at LSU.''

Vanatter stood up, unbuttoned his suit jacket, took it off, folded it, and laid it gently on the side of his desk. Wearing a maroon tie and a starched white shirt with gray suspenders, he shoved his hands in his pockets, turned around, and faced the windows and the Washington skyline. ''Damn it. There's too much at stake here.''

''We have our players in place, gentlemen,'' said Esther. ''Now we need to sit tight and wait for things to develop.''

BATON ROUGE, LOUISIANA

Saturday, November 21
The DIA officer moved through the crowd gathered in front of the LSU Union building. Most of the kids there listened

intently to a man with long hair standing on a bench speaking about student-council politics. The Free Speech Alley, it was called. A place where every afternoon students gathered to discuss the hot topic of the day, taking turns at the improvised podium.

But such insignificant problems were of no concern to the tall man with the dark brown skin sneaking his way through the crowd. Dressed in a pair of faded jeans, a white Phi Delta Theta fraternity T-shirt, white sneakers, an LSU baseball cap, and shades, and with a purple-and-gold backpack hanging off his right shoulder, the operative blended perfectly with the crowd. Keeping his head low and his eyes gazing about the strangers around him, he crossed the street, walked in front of the Memorial Tower, and turned left by the Department of Anthropology.

The officer immediately spotted the overgrown bushes across the street from the Greek amphitheater, where a dozen drama majors rehearsed for a play while twice as many watched them. Casually scanning the grounds, he approached the bushes, also noticing the concrete bench hidden behind the unkempt shrubbery.

Leaning down, he ran thick fingers under the seat until they came in contact with something, which he pulled free. A couple of layers of airtight bags protected a 3.5-inch diskette; CSA-BU46 was written on a blue label. He shoved it in a rear pocket, picked up his backpack, and pulled out a small radio.

"All set. Come and get me."

"On our way," came the reply on the radio.

The DIA officer headed back to the west side of campus. Preston Sinclaire would be most pleased with his performance.

"He's got the object," said Harrison Beckett into his hidden lapel microphone. He sat with a book in his hands near the flagpole in the middle of the large field in front of the Union building. Wearing just jeans, a red T-shirt, and sunglasses, he blended perfectly with the few dozen kids sprawled around the well-trimmed lawn taking in the sun and studying from books, or, like the couple several feet to his right, studying each other.

"Concur. He's got the object," responded one of the FBI special agents mixed with the students watching the rehearsal.

"Let him go. Repeat. Let him go," said Harrison, controlling the urge to follow as the man disappeared around the corner. Harrison had already made his move, and the former DIA officer could only hope his plan would work. Pamela Sasser's life depended on it.

15 Enemies

If you hate a person, you hate something in him that is part of yourself.

—*Hermann Hesse*

MARYLAND
Saturday, November 21

Late in the evening, inside the library of the Victorian mansion, Hamed Tuani inserted the diskette into the side of a Microtel work-station. Behind him stood Pamela Sasser. Preston Sinclaire sat across the table, flanked by three armed guards.

Hamed waited for the screen to display the main menu of the algorithm, but the screen remained blank.

"What is wrong?" Hamed shouted while glancing over his right shoulder at the former associate professor.

Pamela, looking a bit pale, except for the purplish bruises on her right cheek and her swollen lower lip, slowly braced herself and shook her head. "I'm not sure. Perhaps . . . perhaps it got damaged."

"If you lied to us . . . ," Sinclaire said, letting his words trail off while peering into Pamela's eyes.

"I told you everything I know about that algorithm," she said. *"Everything."*

Hamed reinserted the diskette and typed a single UNIX command to look at the contents of the diskette. The following message appeared at the center of the twenty-inch screen:

UNIX VERSION 8.0.1
DRIVE A
FILES >>> CAIRO.TXT
** END OF DATA **

Cairo? Webster!

Hamed leaned back on the leather chair while staring at the screen with contempt. *It cannot be!*

Using the mouse to bring the cursor over to the only file in the diskette, Hamed clicked the left button twice. The file name turned black, and then the screen went blank for a second before a message appeared.

Slowly, Hamed read the two paragraphs. He stopped and read them again while bringing a hand to his ear, remembering that day in Cairo and the brief hand-to-hand combat with the renegade DIA officer, remembering the searing pain of his chest and abdomen sliced open like a dog, his insides pouring onto the concrete ramp.

Only by a miracle of Allah had he survived.

Yes, Hamed had fought the evil Daniel Webster once before, and he had lost, but not before taking out Layla Shariff, the whore that Daniel Webster had embraced after leaving Hamed for dead less than six feet away. But Hamed Tuani had not lost consciousness after the fight. Through the harrowing pain, his ears had listened to the cries of sorrow escaping the American's lips. Hamed had remained still, eyes closed, ears taking in the doleful whispers that filled his soul with joy, with happiness.

Hamed Tuani had inflicted pain on Daniel Webster once before, and this time around Hamed would make Daniel Webster pay even more. The words he had just read could only be written by someone who loved this woman dearly, and the former Egyptian colonel knew *exactly* how to turn those feelings into a weapon.

Getting up and looking at Preston Sinclaire, Hamed said, "We've been tricked by *him*. He wants to set up a trade."

"What?" responded Sinclaire, also standing. "A trade?"

"Yes. The diskette for the woman."

"Christ!"

"He also requested that I come along," said Hamed. "He wants me to deliver her to him personally."

"Take her to the holding room!" Sinclaire barked at one of the guards. "Get her out of my face!"

As the guards dragged Pamela out of the room, the CEO sank back into his chair, hands on his face. "What a fucking mess! We're doomed if we agree and doomed if we don't."

"There is a way out," said Hamed.

"How?"

"I'll make the delivery and bring back the diskette to you."

"You're out of your mind, Hamed. The place's probably going to be swarming with Feds. I never heard back from the team sent to kill Webster, or the one Brasfield led to terminate Esther Cruz. For all we know Brasfield's dead, and Webster and Cruz have teamed up against us. That meeting is a setup."

"Probably," agreed Hamed. "If they're together, it means the FBI already knows about the diskette. But we don't know that for certain. In fact, Webster claims to be working alone. The fact that no one intercepted our operative when he picked up the diskette at LSU certainly indicates that Webster is still on his own. Remember, Webster is an outlaw, a criminal. He will probably try to *avoid* the FBI. He is also a loner."

"I still don't like it," said Sinclaire.

"We don't have any choice. If we ignore him and kill the woman, then I can tell you for certain that the FBI and possibly the NRC will get their hands on the diskette. As it stands, meeting with him is our only alternative . . . aside from closing down accounts and heading to South America.''

''I've already got the wheels in motion to do just that. I'll be damned if I'm going to spend the rest of my life behind bars after working so hard. I have a safe backup plan in case Webster has already contacted the FBI,'' commented Sinclaire while turning around and pacing the room. ''But even if we *do* go along with his proposal, Pamela Sasser still must die.''

''And she *will* die,'' said Hamed, rubbing a hand over his beard. ''I know a way to get the diskette back, and also eliminate the traitor Webster and his new whore once and for all, even if the FBI is on his side.''

''How in the *hell* are you going to do *that?*''

Hamed smiled.

FBI HEADQUARTERS. WASHINGTON, D.C.

Saturday, November 21

A weary and nauseated Harrison Beckett, escorted by three FBI agents, went up to the fifth floor of the J. Edgar Hoover Building, where Frederick Vanatter and Esther Cruz waited for him with a third man. Harrison immediately recognized the skinny man dressed in a white navy uniform: Roman Keitherland, director of the DIA.

Wearing a wrinkled white shirt, the sleeves rolled up to his elbows, the tie loosened to the second button down from his neck, Vanatter sat behind his desk, a mug of steaming coffee in his right hand. Esther sat across the desk, next to Keitherland.

As the federal escort left the room, Esther stood and gave Harrison a pained look. ''I hate to be the first to bring this up, but we know who you really are.''

Frozen by the door to the large office, Harrison Beckett stared at all three with surprise, not certain what to say. How would the Bureau and the DIA receive the news that the man they'd been working with, the same man who might lead them to the Web, had at one point in his life been labeled beyond salvage by the DIA?

Keitherland stood, his eyes displaying a warmth Harrison Beckett had not expected to see.

"Hello, Daniel Webster."

Harrison Beckett heard the rheumy voice speak the name he had not heard since Rome. And another voice returned now. Harrison whipped his hands to his ears, the guttural plea of the stranger hammered his mind as a pair of stiff thumbs collapsed the windpipe. *Please . . . no . . . I don't want to die. . . .*

Involuntarily, Harrison closed his eyes, palms jammed against the sides of his head, struggling to shut out a world that would not stop reminding him of his sins, of . . . *Rome.*

DIA officer Captain Daniel Webster, beyond salvage, escaped termination. His agent, Layla Shariff, terminated on site. Webster must be terminated with extreme prejudice.

That had been the life of Daniel Webster then. Those had been the terms of his existence: kill or be killed, the paradox of a marked man.

Slowly opening his eyes and lowering his hands, Harrison stared at the perplexed trio. "I . . . my name *was* Daniel Webster, DIA code A45821BXZ, marked for termination on October first, 1981, terminated in Rome on November twentieth, 1981."

Esther Cruz walked up to Harrison and patted him on the shoulder. "You don't understand, do you?"

Harrison looked at the lined face of his new friend. "What is there to understand?"

"The termination order was a mistake, Mr. Webster," said Keitherland matter-of-factly.

Harrison stared at the old DDIA in silence. A *mistake*? But it was the Pentagon that issued the order. Only the Pentagon—the DDIA himself—had the power to label an operations officer beyond salvage.

"We realized the mistake six months after the car explosion in Rome," added Keitherland.

Feeling light-headed, Harrison took a step back, his knees about to give. *Six months later!* He had been on the run for *seventeen years* living not only with the constant fear that the DIA might one day figure out his deceptive plan in Rome, but also with the guilt—the *fucking* guilt—of taking out two innocent men!

"So . . . so, all these years," Harrison started, his hands trembling, his body cold. "All these years in hiding, all the nightmares . . . Christ . . ."

Esther helped Harrison to a chair and said, "This nightmare is over. Welcome home, Daniel. Welcome home."

16 Unexpected Difficulties

If at times our actions seem to make life difficult for others, it is only because history has made life difficult for us all.

—John F. Kennedy

WASHINGTON, D.C.
Sunday, November 22

Mother Cruz dropped the heavy bag on the wet concrete surface of the sewer pipe several feet under the street in front of the Lincoln Memorial. The stench of putrid water filling her nostrils, she unzipped the bag and removed a Kevlar vest, which she put over her lightweight black jersey. Her slacks were also black.

Esther fastened the bulletproof vest around her torso using the attached Velcro straps. Once secured, she moved her arms from side to side and twisted her trunk to make sure her mobility wasn't impaired by the Kevlar shield. Next she slid heavy elbow pads on both arms and followed that with knee pads.

She leaned down and grabbed a gear vest, which she slid over the armor. It contained an assortment of pockets and pouches. Esther fastened the vest with a heavy-duty zipper.

She inserted two smoke grenades in two pouches over her right hip and a flashlight on the pouch over her left hip. She extracted her Smith & Wesson Model 659 pistol and inserted it in the modular pocket located in the midchest area of the vest and secured it with a Velcro strap. Exactly underneath it, two extra fifteen-shot magazine clips were already safely tucked away.

Esther jumped up and down, feeling the added weight and listening for rattling sounds. Hearing none, she leaned down once more and lifted the already assembled Heckler & Koch PSG-1 semiautomatic sniper system, which had the fastest follow-up shot capability available for high-accuracy, long-range rifles. A necessity, reflected Esther, considering she might have multiple targets today.

She grabbed three twenty-round magazines, inserted one into the rifle, and stored the other two inside a pouch next to the 659.

Esther pulled a black hood in place, exposing only her eyes. She slung the rifle, extracted the flashlight, and moved to a location she had committed to memory.

She stood underneath the four-foot-wide hollow post supporting a large billboard down the street from the memorial, and reached up for the handle positioned directly over her.

The heavy metal door swung down, revealing a metal ladder built into the side of the vertical tunnel. Esther went up the steps and reached another door. This one had a combination lock next to the handle.

Training the flashlight on the knob, she dialed in the number sequence she had been given at the billboard company and turned the handle. This time she had to push the circular door up. After crawling through the opening, Esther closed the door and looked up. The long vertical tunnel, in reality the hollow section of the post, also had a metallic ladder built into the side. Esther started her long ascent to the top of the post.

Five minutes later she reached the top, where her hands grabbed the handle of a third and final door, which she slowly lowered.

The sun stung her. She blinked several times, trying to adjust her vision. Esther waited a few moments before lifting her head and scanning the area. She had a superb view of the memorial, the Reflecting Pool, and the Washington Monument.

The post ended almost at the top and behind the billboard, out of sight from the street and facing the Reflecting Pool. She could see Harrison Beckett pacing the lawn at the far end of the pool.

She reached for the PSG-1 and placed the short butt under her armpit, rested her head on her shoulder, and peeked into the Hendsoldt bullet-drop compensating scope, critical for long-range shooting. She estimated his range, about five hundred yards, and adjusted the scope's wheel to compensate for his distance.

With the billboard's black, glossy background and the sun shining directly on it, Esther blended in perfectly. Removing her radio from a Velcro-secured pocket, she tuned it to Main One. During the operation there would be two main frequencies of communication. The first frequency, Main One, linked all the agents and Harrison together. The second frequency, Main Two, broadcast the output of an audio-amplifier device connected to a two-foot-diameter parabolic antenna, which a two-man FBI team controlled from atop the Lincoln Memorial. One of the two agents controlling Main Two would update everyone listening on Main One when the operation got under way. Her people had swept the entire area and had found no one. No spotters, snipers, or bodyguards were anywhere near West Potomac Park. Esther saw only FBI agents through her spotting scope: couples pushing empty strollers; tourists and visitors walking around the Vietnam Veterans Memorial; joggers down the trail near the river; two dozen tourists snapping photos by the steps of the Lincoln Memorial while listening to their tour guide. Everyone was a Fed, and everyone was fully armed and ready to snap into action. But until they received the order to move in, they would play their roles. Esther

Cruz called the shots here and no one would make a move until she said so.

Satisfied, Esther carefully positioned a black poncho over herself and continued using the Hendsoldt scope to scan the park, from the Reflecting Pool, past the Vietnam Veterans Memorial, to Constitution Avenue. Then she checked the other side of the long pool until reaching the Potomac.

All clear.

Wearing a blue jumpsuit and a bulletproof vest, Harrison Beckett took another drag from a cigarette and checked his watch for the fifth time in the past three minutes. He grew impatient and he knew that was a mistake, but he couldn't help himself. The thought of seeing Pamela Sasser again sent chills through his exhausted body.

And tired he was, reflected the ex–DIA officer as he walked at the edge of the Reflecting Pool. The short nap he'd caught during the flight back from Louisiana had been the only sleep he'd gotten in two days, and after the encounter in Vanatter's office, he had been unable to sleep the rest of the night. The revelation had been downright shocking, especially when Esther suggested that the same network which had caused his downfall at the DIA could also be responsible for this mess. That certainly explained the presence of Layla's assassin.

But then Harrison had regained his composure and had reminded the Bureau of his agreement for freedom, security, and cash upon disclosure of more information on the network and delivery of the diskette. Harrison was still holding on to his one ace—the fact that Preston Sinclaire apparently was involved with Brasfield—until he could get Pamela back.

Now, after four cups of coffee and three doughnuts, Harrison Beckett readied himself for the most important mission of his life, one where he knew he could not fail.

"Subjects just past the Vietnam Memorial. Everyone stay cool. Harrison, they're heading your way."

The monotone words spoken by Esther Cruz echoed inside the flesh-colored earpiece connected to a thin wire coiling into the side of his jumpsuit.

Harrison turned toward the long granite wall a hundred yards away, and he saw two lonely figures walking in his direction. A man and a woman. The man carried a small briefcase. He took one final drag before throwing the cigarette on the lawn.

The hammering inside his chest felt like the pistons of a sports car, revving up to the red, demanding more oxygen from his lungs. Inhaling deeply, and slowly letting out his breath through his nostrils, Harrison finally got a good look at Pamela. Her olive skin looked ashen, her blue-green eyes glassy and bloodshot. With the chocolate freckle twitching over her swollen lips, the fragile figure in a gray trench coat stopped ten feet in front of Harrison Beckett. Her resolute stare, however, told Harrison that, although she'd been physically abused, her spirit was far from broken.

Controlling his anger, Harrison turned to Layla's assassin, who wore a pair of jeans and a bulky leather jacket. "I see that you're not man enough to take up your problems directly with me. I still think I should have killed you when I had the chance." Harrison's voice was as cold and remorseless as the piercing glance he had shot at the assassin.

"The diskette," the assassin said, shrugging off the remarks, eyes boring into Harrison.

Harrison reached inside his jacket and pulled out a black 3.5-inch disk. "Pamela, come by my side."

The assassin smiled and said, "Are you sure?"

After curiously contemplating the bearded man, Harrison waved her over. The assassin nodded and Pamela walked by Harrison's side near the edge of the Reflecting Pool.

"The diskette," the assassin repeated, extending his hand. "No tricks this time or she dies."

Harrison gave it to him and turned to Pamela. "Are you all right?"

She slowly shook her head, her hands unbuttoning the trench coat, letting it fall off her back. Harrison's heart sank below the soles of his shoes the moment he saw the dynamite vest wrapped around Pamela's chest.

She's booby-trapped!

The long jeans met the thick vest right below the waistline. The vest extended up to just below her neck. A mesh of wires connected brown tubular sticks together and to a small black box in the center of her chest. A three-inch-tall antenna stuck out of the top of the box. A digital readout showed 1:37:00 and decreasing. The timer was set to go off in just over an hour and a half. A green LED on the timer indicated that the detonator was inactive. Harrison had seen this type of setup before, and his professional mind began to look for weaknesses in the design.

Mother Cruz pulled away from the spotting scope and reached for her radio. "She's hot! I repeat, she's hot! Everyone hold your place. Repeat, everyone hold your place. No one fires! That's an order!"

Esther Cruz put the radio by her feet and pressed her shooting eye against the rubber end of the spotting scope. The tables had just been turned, and she cursed herself for failing to anticipate this scenario, which explained the lack of "enemy soldiers" in the area. Pamela Sasser's booby trap was the Web's insurance policy. The moment the agents deployed around the area showed themselves to arrest the courier, Pamela Sasser would be blown to bits.

"The range of the remote-control device is five miles," the assassin said as he opened the briefcase and extracted a notebook computer, already powered up. He also pulled out a pair of shiny handcuffs and threw them at Harrison. "Put these on. I wouldn't want to separate you lovebirds any longer."

Harrison caught the cuffs but did not obey.

"Do it, or she blows this minute. My people are watching. All I have to do is give the signal and you'll lose her just like you lost the whore Layla Shariff."

Harrison burned the assassin with his stare. "You'll regret this." Harrison turned to Pamela, whose eyes glowed with terror. "It's all right," he said to her. "Now we're together." He put one cuff on her left hand and the other on his own right hand. Pamela clasped his hand, giving Harrison a frightened glance.

Kneeling on the lawn, the assassin inserted the diskette and invoked the algorithm. The system turned to the set of menu options Pamela had described during the interrogation. Removing the diskette and pulling out a small plastic bag, the assassin left the computer on the lawn and stood, placing the diskette inside the bag and closing the airtight seal on the top.

"This concludes our business transaction," the assassin continued, shoving the diskette into an inside pocket. "The readout on the vest will tell you how much time you have left. I have just enough time to make it back to my people and deactivate the remote triggering radio. If you try to follow me, one of my men, who is watching nearby, will activate the detonating mechanism, and the police will be picking up pieces of you two from here to the White House."

"How do I know you'll keep your word?"

The assassin smiled. "You fool! Don't you know you're out of choices?"

Layla's assassin turned and began to walk away. Harrison used his left hand to reach out and grab him by the back of the leather jacket. "Not so fast, asshole!"

The ex–DIA officer brought his other hand, along with Pamela's, up to apply a deadlock on the terrorist and hold him until the agents could reach him. Whoever was watching surely wouldn't detonate the dynamite with his leader only a few feet away.

The assassin dropped to a crouch and pivoted on his right leg, sweeping the left at shin level, kicking Harrison's legs from under him.

"Aghh, Harrison!"

Harrison fell, dragging Pamela with him.

The assassin raced away as agents began to move in.

Stunned, but fully aware of his situation, Harrison Beckett

quickly got to his knees and helped Pamela while glancing at the departing terrorist, who had already pulled out a small rectangular box. *A radio? The remote-control trigger?*

Trained instincts told him he and Pamela had seconds to live, and without further thought he did the only thing he could do, the only thing that made any sense: Harrison jumped into the Reflecting Pool, pulling Pamela Sasser along.

The cold water stung him, making him shiver, but the alternative was less appealing. He quickly got up, the water reaching right below his waistline.

"Keep the vest underwater!" he shouted as Pamela began to get up, bracing herself, lips quivering.

"But it's freezing," she said, her voice trembling, her short wet hair stuck to her head.

"It's the only way!" he said, submerging himself in the frigid shallow waters and noticing the LED still green. The water prevented the remote-control device from detonating the charge strapped to the vest.

"I don't want to lose you!" he said, resurfacing.

Pamela's contorted eyes softened at his words. Harrison Beckett reached out and pulled her shivering body directly in front of his, her face only inches from him, water dripping down her cheeks and nose, wetting the chocolate freckle. A purplish hue appeared on her swollen lips. "I don't want to lose you," he repeated before embracing her.

Agents began to converge around Hamed Tuani, who ran as fast as he could toward the Potomac River, cold wind stinging his face, legs burning, hands reaching into his jacket for the tools of his escape.

Four agents got within twenty feet of him and dropped to the ground as silenced rounds struck their Kevlar vests. Holding on to their bruised chests, the agents tried to get up, but Hamed had already rushed past them. Five joggers raced directly for him, only to fall on their faces as a fusillade of silenced rounds impacted the ground around them, striking their vests and exposed legs.

Through all the commotion, and with his legs burning from the strain, Hamed Tuani's ears listened for the explosion that would mark the end of Daniel Webster and Pamela Sasser. But the explosion did not come.

Mother Cruz frantically searched for the sniper with the suppressed weapon who'd just downed several of her agents. Using the radio at this point was useless as a dozen agents tried to talk at once and one downed agent screamed in pain directly into his lapel microphone.

But Esther Cruz was a patient woman, and her coolness paid off the moment another pair of agents went down just as they were about to tackle the runaway assassin. This time she could trace the direction of their falls to the origin of the shooting: one of several trees lining the west side of the Lincoln Memorial. *How did we miss that guy?*

Lining up the dark figure just barely visible halfway up the tree, Esther Cruz fired twice. The figure fell from the tree and onto the sidewalk.

Hamed Tuani saw his sniper fall off the tree a second after two gunshots cracked in the morning air. As the closest agent got within fifty feet of him and six more agents ran in his direction from the Potomac, Hamed Tuani pulled the safety pin out of a smoke grenade, and threw the grenade at the incoming agents.

The loud explosion created a rapidly expanding cloud of blue smoke that swallowed everything within a fifty-foot radius.

Hamed immediately cut left, pulling out another grenade as he ran parallel to the river, roughly a hundred feet away. Agents ran toward him from several places. The moment Hamed reached a patch of grass that gave him a clear run to the shore, he cut back toward the Potomac and threw the grenade ahead of him.

A second explosion. The new cloud expanded toward the first, blocking Hamed's view of the river, which met the water at the south end of the park.

Blue smoke engulfed Hamed Tuani before any of the agents could close the gap. Hamed pulled the pin out of his third and last grenade, which he threw as hard as he could in the direction of the river.

A third explosion. More smoke, overlapping the second cloud and expanding over the water. His chest burned from taking in rapid lungfuls of frozen air, but the former Egyptian colonel would not let up the pace. He had to reach the water before the clouds dispersed in the morning breeze.

Sirens blared in the distance. Shouts and screams filled the air. He could hear the footsteps and heavy breathing of FBI agents running in every direction inside the thick smoke, but not a single one of them came within ten feet of the terrorist, who felt his feet reach the water.

He kept running as the cloud thinned, as the water reached his knees, as other agents also splashed nearby. Pulling out a pair of swimming goggles, Hamed Tuani stopped when the water reached his waist, put on the goggles, took a deep breath, and dove in. Underwater, he removed his jacket and jeans, exposing the wet suit he wore underneath to keep his body warm. Lead weights sewn in every article of clothing made them fall to the bottom of the river, out of sight of the agents on the surface. A belt of lead weights also kept him from floating back up to the surface as he kicked his legs and moved his arms, the diskette safely secured in an insulated pocket of his suit.

A light shone ahead and below him. Hamed followed the bottom of the river toward it, head throbbing from the exhaustive run, ears pounding from the mounting water pressure. His body screamed for oxygen, his mind urged him to surface. But he couldn't. He was out of the escape clouds. The FBI agents could spot him. He had to swim toward the nearing light, had to reach it before his lungs burst.

He became light-headed, weak. His eyes saw black spots in the water. His arms and legs tingled from lack of oxygen. He fought the uncontrollable desire to breathe, to fill his lungs. He had to continue, had to persist, had to reach the safety of the light.

And so he kicked; he swung his arms; he kept his body moving through cold dark waters toward a light he thought he would never reach, but he did. And the Egyptian saw a pair of hands reaching out for him, holding a rubber mouthpiece connected to a tank filled with oxygen, with life.

Stiffened fingers brought the mouthpiece to his lips, and Hamed took a deep breath, exhaled, and took another one, closing his eyes as the oxygen reached every inch of his body. He had made it. He had prevailed against an armada of agents, all of whom had underestimated him.

Hamed Tuani donned the small oxygen tank and followed his team away from the empty claws of the Federal Bureau of Investigation.

Submerged in forty-degree water up to his neck, Harrison Beckett embraced a shivering Pamela Sasser as a fully uniformed member of the police department's bomb squad approached them, a pair of heavy-duty wire cutters held in his right hand. Two dozen agents surrounded the area as an ambulance arrived for one man shot in the leg and several others with painful but nonlethal chest bruises.

By the time the bomb squad arrived, Harrison and Pamela had been submerged for nearly five minutes. However, the immediate problem was not disarming the bomb. By the time the timer triggered the explosives in another ninety minutes, Harrison and Pamela would have been long dead of hypothermia.

"We're gonna cut you loose first, and then we're gonna work on her," said the man, a hooded stranger dressed in black, wearing a helmet and visor, and sporting Kevlar shields on his chest, arms, and legs. To Harrison's displeasure, the man looked like a member of a termination team.

"Forget it," Harrison responded, his voice cracking from the cold, his eyes locked with Pamela Sasser. "I'm not leaving her!"

"Be reasonable, sir!" the man in black responded. "That bomb could go off any—"

"You're wasting time!" screamed Harrison as Esther

Cruz, also dressed in black, ran toward them. "Can't you see we're freezing to *death*?"

"What's going on here?" Esther said, short of breath. She squatted by the edge of the Reflecting Pool.

"Tell this guy to worry about the bomb later, damn it! You gotta warm us up somehow, or we'll be dead in ten minutes! And leaving the pool's not an option. The only reason we're still alive's because the receiving unit's underwater."

"You sure that unit's still working?"

"Yep, and the clock's still ticking."

Mother Cruz ran a hand through her hair, her sniper gear rattling. Harrison was right. The bomb squad could wait until after figuring out how to get those two warmed up. Taking them out of the water was out of the question. The remote triggering device could be sending a continuous activation signal at this moment. The instant Pamela Sasser raised the receiver above the surface, there was a very good chance that the explosives could go off. They were trapped.

A vision of her husband's car going up in flames flashed in front of her eyes.

No time for that! Think ... think ... there has to be a way. It's too late for Arturo, but not for them. There has to be a way! THINK!

Turning away and scanning the fiasco of another FBI operation that didn't go as planned, Esther Cruz watched the ambulance speed away, followed by two patrol cars, their tailpipes leaving a white trail of condensed exhaust.

Exhaust gas ... hot exhaust gas!

Suddenly, Esther Cruz found herself shouting orders to her subordinates, a few of whom initially thought that she had lost her mind, but quickly realized the brilliant solution to the immediate predicament of Harrison Beckett and Pamela Sasser.

"Harr-Harrison," Pamela said, her head snuggled in his shoulder as Harrison breathed warm air on her neck. "Cold. I'm so ... cold."

Harrison simply hugged her tight, not knowing what else to do. He was losing her to the same cold that slowly drained the life out of him. Barely able to control the shivering, Harrison moved his swollen fingers over her ice-cold hair. Totally oblivious to the agents moving back and forth around the Reflecting Pool, and the sounds of several cars revving up their engines nearby, Harrison Beckett grew dizzy, disoriented, unable to move, his jumpsuit shockingly cold, his legs losing sensation.

"Hang on, Pamela," he heard himself whisper in her ear as he breathed warm air over her. "Hang on."

"I . . . can't," came the weak response, barely audible over the deafening noise of the engines.

Harrison closed his eyes and breathed deeply, filling his lungs with the sweet smell of Pamela Sasser, however cold and shivering. This was his second chance, his second love. In his arms he held the promise of a future, of a normal life, but the cold continued to strip it all away. The same frigid waters that had saved them had now taken a menacing turn against Harrison and Pamela, layer by layer peeling away their life-supporting heat.

But he refused to give up, rejected the idea of surrendering so easily.

"Hang . . . on, Pam. You must . . . hang on," he repeated, Pamela mumbling something totally incoherent in response.

"I'm . . . here . . . with . . ." Harrison could not talk any longer, his jaws frozen shut, his mind once more longing for the heat of southern Louisiana, of the warm, muddy waters of a bayou. Eyes closed, Harrison felt the warmth as he swam toward his hunters, quietly, swiftly, with a layer of perspiration on his forehead, with beads of sweat rolling down the sides of his face.

Sweat. Perspiration. Heat.

He felt heat, sensed warmth around him. Although he could see or hear nothing, Harrison detected a change in his environment. But the heat did not come from within. He felt a current of warm water tickling his back, the smell of automobile exhaust suddenly reaching his nostrils, the growing heat radiating around him, around her. Pamela reacted to it by moving even closer to Harrison, squeezing herself against his chest, wedging a thigh between his legs.

Harrison felt his arms and legs warming first, then his stomach and chest. Pamela squirmed against him. Her face moved under his chin, her free hand ran the length of his back, her lips parted, and warm air caressed his neck.

Harrison wasn't sure how long they remained like this, drawing heat from their surroundings and thrusting it into each other, melting their bodies in a warming rapture neither hoped would ever end, mutually smothering their senses in total unity.

Slowly, Pamela Sasser pulled away and stared into Harrison Beckett's eyes and smiled.

Esther Cruz sat by the edge of the pool holding one of four fire hoses she and her agents had attached to the tailpipes of four vehicles, two patrol cars and two FBI sedans. Agents gunned the engines, and the hot exhaust gases rushed through the hoses and into the water, creating a spa-like effect on this corner of the Reflecting Pool, and quickly raising the water's temperature into the comfort zone. The fire hoses Esther had cut up into fifteen-foot sections belonged to one of the fire trucks that had arrived at the scene after someone had mistaken the blue smoke for a fire.

With the help of several firemen, FBI agents had carried the heavy hose to the edge of the pool while others backed up and positioned four vehicles by the end of the pool near Harrison and Pamela. Members of the bomb squad laid large shields into the water to isolate Harrison and Pamela from the rest of the pool. The rest had been easy, connecting the sections of fire hose to the tailpipes with duct tape courtesy of the Washington, D.C., Fire Department, and gunning the engines.

Fifteen minutes later, after Harrison and Pamela had been warmed up in the improvised hot tub, bomb squad members spent another thirty minutes disarming the vest. An unmarked sedan then took them to Georgetown University

Hospital, where they were both treated for mild hypothermia.

MARYLAND

Sunday, November 22

"The FBI already knew," Hamed commented while standing in front of Preston Sinclaire. "Webster had teamed up with them."

Preston Sinclaire held the diskette in his right hand as he sank into a leather sofa in his living room. The news could not be worse. And Pamela Sasser had survived. *She had survived!*

Pamela Sasser would make a star witness for the prosecution. She would link the Perseus bug to Palo Verde. She would link Preston Sinclaire to several deaths in the past week.

The damage could not be contained. His network had been exposed.

Surrounded by his closest associates, Preston Sinclaire looked at Hamed Tuani and said, "My backup plan is now our only alternative. We're leaving immediately."

Epilogue

WASHINGTON, D.C.
Monday, December 21

Wearing an extralarge white woolen sweater, a pair of faded jeans, sneakers, and her silver-and-turquoise jewelry, Esther Cruz walked inside the office of the director of the Federal Bureau of Investigation. Frederick Vanatter, his hands holding the ten-page report that Esther had finished typing that morning, looked up and gave the seasoned agent an approving nod before waving her over to a chair across the large mahogany desk.

"Give me just a minute to finish this," Vanatter said, his eyes lowering to the document, stamped For the Director of the FBI's Eyes Only in red on every page.

Taking a seat and crossing her legs, she glanced around the office while Vanatter read. Mother Cruz had time. Actually she had all the time in the world now that she had obtained a three-month leave of absence.

The day after Pamela disclosed her information, the Bureau stormed Microtel's headquarters with court orders to obtain a list of all the equipment sold that included the Perseus microprocessor. In less than twenty-four hours every single customer using the Perseus in the industrial market had been contacted. Equipment was pulled from production floors, hospitals, jetliners, and assembly lines. At four nuclear plants, control systems were switched over to analog backups until they could be replaced with other brands. An investigation carried out by the Nuclear Regulatory Commission in conjunction with the FBI and the new Microtel resulted in the confirmation of Dr. Eugene LaBlanche's claim about the flaw in the Perseus and its devastating consequences. When the connection between Microtel and Palo Verde finally made the papers a week later, Microtel's stock plunged a record sixty-eight points in a single day. Rumors of a hostile takeover by a competitive firm immediately reached Wall Street. The new board at Microtel negotiated a deal with several banks to get the funding required to prevent a takeover. The board also started a total recall of the Perseus in both commercial and industrial markets, taking a loss of nearly three hundred million dollars. Class-action lawsuits also began to flood Microtel's legal department at such a rate that the federal government had to get involved to prevent the angry citizens of the state of Arizona from sinking the conglomerate. Settlements were still being negotiated.

In addition, the FBI, the DIA, and the Office of Naval Intelligence went through the personal records of Preston Sinclaire, Jackson Brasfield, and a dozen other Pentagon officials. This led to secret bank accounts in the Cayman Islands and the Bahamas. Unfortunately, by the time the Feds reached those accounts a week after the incident at West Potomac Park, most of the funds had already been transferred out. However, by the time the dust settled, the FBI had confiscated assets in the United States worth over one hundred million dollars, and had managed to get its hands on just over half of the members of the Web, some of whom, in the process of trying to cut deals with the FBI, confessed that the missing Preston Sinclaire was the leader of the band. Sixty-seven people were arrested in all.

A frown, which Esther caught in her own reflection on the large glass windowpanes behind Vanatter, flashed across the veteran FBI agent's face at the thought of Preston Sinclaire and his inner circle escaping the FBI. Just last week, a report had arrived from the American embassy in Mexico City. Mexican authorities had received a report about a shooting at a small airfield in the Yucatán Peninsula, near the border with Belize. Apparently three clerks and two mechanics had been shot dead after a twin-engine plane stopped to refuel. Someone had jotted down the aircraft's number and it had matched a VIP transport plane owned by Microtel.

Although information on the runaway plane was passed on to authorities in all Central American countries, Esther didn't hold much hope for that. It was bad enough dealing with the slower and quite corrupt Mexican authorities. Down in Central America all bets were off. Communications were atrocious, and the governments of countries like Guatemala, El Salvador, Honduras, and Nicaragua had too many of their own internal problems to deal with to worry about Preston Sinclaire and his accomplices. In addition, those systems of government were so corrupt that Sinclaire should have no problem buying his way out of any situation. In fact, Esther even wondered if Sinclaire had not paid off local Mexican authorities to let him escape south.

"It's indeed too bad about Sinclaire," said Vanatter, tossing the report on his desk and rubbing his eyes. "We almost nailed him."

"At least we exposed the son of a bitch, sir," Esther said. "We stopped his corrupt machine dead in its tracks before it could gain more momentum, before it took control of the White House."

Vanatter smiled. "*That* we did, thanks to you."

Esther shrugged. "We all pitch in, sir."

Nodding, Vanatter asked, "So, what are you going to do with your time off?"

"I turned my apartment complex over to a rental agency. Figure I'll visit Canada and Alaska for a while. I just bought me one of those four-wheel-drive Explorers."

The FBI director raised an eyebrow. "Hmm. Sounds like fun."

"Better do it while I still can."

With a slight grunt, Vanatter picked up the report and stood, flipping through it. "I read about Microtel this morning. Looks like the company's going to survive this mess after all."

Esther nodded.

Vanatter reached the last page of the report. "Is this what Harrison Be—"

"Webster, sir. His name is Daniel Webster."

His face showing a shade of annoyance, Vanatter said, "Fine. Is this what *Daniel Webster* wants?"

Esther gave Vanatter a slight nod. "That's what he and Pamela want—in addition to the money we already transferred to their joint account in the Cayman Islands."

"Don't remind me of *that,*" he said with a slight grunt.

"A deal's a deal, sir," Esther said.

"But there's no destination specified here. Just a pilot and a fully fueled private jet."

"They'll inform the pilot where to go *after* they're in the air. They're breaking away and it's probably a smart thing to do. That's part of the reason I'm also splitting, sir. Figure I'll let this thing cool off before hitting the bricks again."

"Can't say I blame you. Can't say I blame those two for also trying to disappear." Vanatter walked over to his personal paper shredder, shoved the document inside, and pressed a square button on the side. The machine came alive, sucking all ten pages and turning them into confetti a few seconds later.

"So, that's it, then?" Esther asked as the final shred of evidence of Harrison's and Pamela's last known whereabouts fell inside a circular wastebasket.

"That's it. Enjoy your time off, Mother." Vanatter thrust an open hand across the desk. Esther stood and pumped it.

Ten minutes later, she drove out of the parking garage and into a sunny afternoon.

Esther Cruz slipped on a pair of sunglasses as she steered her fully fueled Explorer through the light downtown traffic, a smile reaching her lips, but not at the thought of going on an extended vacation. Esther Cruz would never dream of taking time off while her husband's murderers were still at large.

She smiled because she had won one battle and had forced the enemy to retreat, to hide in Central or South America. She had forced her enemy to run south.

South.

Esther Cruz got on Interstate Highway 66 and headed west until it intersected I-81, where she turned not north, a route that would have taken her straight into Canada, but *south,* through Virginia and into Tennessee, stopping at roadside motels just to sleep, grab a bite to eat, and get back behind the wheel.

Enjoying the scenery, she drummed her fingers against the leather-wrapped steering wheel to the rhythm of the *rancheras* coming out of the eight speakers of her premium stereo system, the same system which then played the Spanish tapes she had purchased at a travel shop in Maryland the week before. She remembered a lot of Spanish from her younger days, but a little refresher course wouldn't hurt.

Spanish words and phrases she had not heard in decades filled the interior of her vehicle as she crossed Arkansas and reached Texas, a smile still painted on her lined face.

She had won the first battle, forced the enemy to retreat, and it was during that hurried retreat that her prey would be most unprepared for her surprise arrival, wherever they were.

Esther smiled.

She smiled as she reached I-35 and cruised through Dallas, down to Austin, San Antonio, and finally arriving at Laredo by the Rio Grande an hour before dusk.

Mexico.

Esther Cruz smiled as she crossed the legendary river in the direction that would take her closer to her quarry, closer to the survivors of the Web.

As the United States of America disappeared behind a cloud of dust and debris kicked up by the oversize tires of her four-wheel-drive, Mother Cruz watched how the silver band on her ring finger reflected the setting sun's crimson light.

I will catch those bastards, Arturo. I will catch them for you!

The same day that Esther Cruz left the United States, Harrison Beckett became Daniel Webster thanks to the skills of a top plastic surgeon in Bethesda. He and Pamela boarded a private Learjet and were taken to JFK International, where the former DIA officer had already arranged transportation to leave the country. Aware of the possibility of the FBI or another agency tailing them, Daniel Webster and Pamela Sasser spent one unforgettable week in Rome, pretending to be tourists while Daniel hunted for a woman with physical characteristics similar to Pamela Sasser's. At the end of the week he had found her, a schoolteacher on an exchange program with a local university.

A meeting took place in a small café three blocks away from the Colosseum. Money changed hands and an agreement was reached. A week later, Daniel Webster returned to the United States in the company of a woman whose passport claimed she was Pamela Sasser. That same day, a report reached the office of Frederick Vanatter informing him that the couple had returned to the United States.

Exactly a month later, a bank executive in Zurich spent an hour one afternoon working on the transaction requests of a woman with short red hair and olive-colored skin who had presented him with the correct multiple combinations of numbers and letters to access a recently opened account. It being Switzerland, no name or identification was required to complete the multiple transactions, which included a six-

month lease of a lakefront apartment in Zurich, and a trans-
fer of a portion of the funds to a bank in Nairobi, Kenya.
Intrigued, however, the banker did ask the woman with the
blue-green eyes and the dark freckle above her upper lip
what was her country of origin. She had simply replied that
her ancestors were from the southern United States.

A month later, convinced that the DIA, the FBI, the CIA,
and whoever had survived this network no longer cared
about his whereabouts, Daniel Webster clandestinely left
the United States of America forever via Mexico. A month
later, the Kenyan government received a generous offer
from a wealthy foreigner for the purchase of three hundred
acres of land between Lake Victoria and the Serengeti National Park, in western Kenya. The land, although not part
of a government-protected game reserve, was the home of
many wildlife species, particularly the Grevy's zebra, the
Somali ostrich, many baboon troops, and numerous hippos
and crocodiles by the shores of the lake. After the foreigner
signed an agreement to preserve the land and its natural in-
habitants, the Kenyan government agreed to a one-hundred-
year lease of the acreage to the eccentric man of unknown
nationality. He had preferred to remain anonymous, and because of the amount of money he had paid, the Kenyan
government decided to respect his wish, finally granting the
lease in the month of May.

Soon after, residents of Musoma, a city of about eighty-
five thousand people by the shores of Lake Victoria, began
gossiping about the stranger building a large house in the
distant hills overlooking the plain leading to the lake. He
drove to town in a Toyota Land Cruiser once a week to
purchase lumber and other building supplies, and also to hire
temporary help to assist him in the construction, which went
on for the remainder of the summer. By September, the residents of the lakeside town could see the lights of the house
at night, high up on the hills.

One day in late October, the man came to town and purchased half of the furniture on display at the town's largest
department store, including a king-size bed, a mahogany

dining-room table, two living-room sets, a patio set, and, oddly enough, a crib and a variety of infant clothing and toys.

Then, one day in early November, a Kenya Airways twin-engine shuttle from Nairobi arrived at the Musoma Regional Airport. Some of the residents that happened to be at the airport on that lazy sunny Sunday afternoon witnessed a peculiar encounter.

The "man of the hill," as Daniel Webster was now referred to by Musoma residents, had driven his Toyota Land Cruiser into town, parking it in the gravel lot behind the one-building terminal of the small regional airport. Residents commented on how sharply dressed the "man of the hill," who carried a dozen red roses in his hands, looked on that day. Aside from the usual group of adventure-seeking American, European, and Japanese tourists on the way to a photo safari, local residents watched a tall, thin woman in her early thirties get off the plane. In her arms she cradled a bundled infant. Her hair was black and shoulder length. Her skin was tanned. She wore plain clothes, just a tight pair of jeans, a white T-shirt, and penny loafers. But many of the men present claimed they had never seen a pair of blue-green eyes like the ones that intriguing woman had. Others commented on her elegant stride as she walked across the Tarmac. The pilot had mentioned to a few locals that the woman had flown into Nairobi on a direct flight from Switzerland.

As the small crowd went about their business, the "man of the hill" took the woman and the infant to the Land Cruiser and they drove off into the hills.

That evening Daniel Webster put month-old Layla Webster to sleep in her new crib for the very first time. She was an odd mixture of Daniel and Pamela, the product of a moment of love in another continent not so long ago. Layla definitely had the blue-green eyes of her mother, but the color of her skin came from Daniel's side of the family. The Websters were always fair skinned. The Swiss doctor that had assisted

Pamela during the delivery in a hospital in Zurich had told the proud mother that little Layla would most likely be a tall and strong woman one day.

The autumn evening air felt cool, dry, refreshing. Daniel Webster stood on the front porch of the house gazing at the stars as they shed their minute light on the mirror-smooth surface of Lake Victoria. What he loved most about the place was not only how dark it got at night, but also how peacefully quiet it was. If he listened very carefully he could make out the distant sounds of baboons hunting on the vast plain leading to the game preserve. It really seemed to him as if he had traveled to another world. Perhaps he actually had.

Pamela walked out to the porch wearing a plain white cotton dress that dropped to her knees. She was barefoot. Her hair hung over her shoulders in lustrous waves that seemed to reflect the soft white light from the porch's overheads. Her blue-green eyes were on him. The chocolate freckle above her lips moved up as she smiled. She carried two cups filled with hot tea and handed one to Daniel, who took a sip before setting it on top of the wooden railing fencing the porch.

"Is she asleep?" Pamela asked.

Daniel nodded while looking into the glistening eyes of the woman he loved as dearly as he had loved Layla Shariff. He took her in with a totally greedy, selfish glance. "She looks just like you, you know. I'm gonna have a hard time keeping the boys away from her."

She regarded him with a slanted stare before also setting down the cup of tea on the railing and letting his strong arms embrace her.

"I love you, Daniel Webster," she said, her small freckle dancing over that mesmerizing face.

Daniel simply hugged her close, tightly embracing his second chance for a new life.